Weekend in Amsterdam

Roy A Higgins

Strategic Book Group

Copyright © 2011

All rights reserved – Roy A. Higgins

No part of this book may be reproduced or transmitted in any form or by any means, graphic, electronic, or mechanical, including photocopying, recording, taping, or by any information storage retrieval system, without the permission, in writing, from the publisher.

Strategic Book Group
P.O. Box 333
Durham CT 06422
www.StrategicBookClub.com

ISBN: 978-1-60911-951-5

Printed in the United States of America

Book Design: Suzanne Kelly

I would like to thank my daughter Laura for assisting me with the grammar, formatting, and layout of the manuscript, and I would like to thank all of the staff at AEG publishing group, who have been most helpful and patient with my inadaquacies.

PART ONE

CHAPTER ONE

"I can't believe that they lost again; and to Charlton Athletic at home."

Ray Evans was sitting on his ten year old BSA motorcycle while talking with his friend Ron Cook.

Rovers will go down if they keep losing home games," replied Cookie sadly.

It was late November 1968. Although they had started the season well with three wins and a draw in August, they had now lost three of their last four games.

It was especially cold for November, and Ray was wearing his World War II leather flying jacket with fur collar, motor cycle boots, jeans, and thick grey fisherman's socks folded neatly over the top of his boots. He rarely wore a crash helmet as the law didn't require it, and in any case it wasn't regarded as cool by his contemporaries. When he did choose to wear one he looked like a bee, with yellow and black stripes which began just above his flying goggles, while ending at the nape of his neck.

At the bus stop in front of Cookie's house, the number forty-nine Outer Circle bus came to a halt. A girl in her late teens or early twenties smiled at them from the top deck of the bus. Ray smiled back but Cookie sullenly ignored her. She was a pretty dark haired girl with a round slightly chubby face. Although Ray could only see her head and shoulders from his low vantage point on the street, he had a great imagination and a clear mental picture which encompassed the rest of her. She continued to smile, sticking out her tongue and giving them a cheeky wave as the bus left the bus stop.

"I've got to go."

Ray started up his motor cycle and pulled out to follow the bus as it slowly moved off.

"See you tonight?" shouted Cookie, rather more in hope than in expectation as Ray drove away.

"Maybe," Ray called back, the meaning being clear, that it would depend on the outcome of his forthcoming meeting with the girl.

"In The Legs O' Man at eight?" called Cookie hopefully.

"Okay," replied Ray half heartedly.

He followed the bus for two stops until the girl got off. She looked just as he had imagined that she would. Some might say that she was a little on the plump side, although Ray preferred to think of her as cuddly.

She was wearing a pair of very tight fitting blue jeans, a sloppy fitting grey speckled polo neck sweater, which looked too big for her, shiny black high heeled boots which finished well above her knee, and a long dark coat with a shaggy lining, which curled out to form a collar. Even though it was cold, her coat had been purposely left swinging open, to reveal her wide hips and ample bosom.

He felt apprehensive, even though he had been rehearsing his chat up line for the last two stops. His misgivings soon evaporated however as the girl confidently approached him.

"Hi, my name is Christine but everyone calls me Chrissie," she said by way of introduction.

"Raymond," he replied. "But everyone calls me Ray."

Ray had been popular with the girls since well before the age of puberty, although in those early days of innocence he had completely failed to notice. Although he wasn't short at five feet ten inches tall, some of his friends, including Cookie, were much taller, and he often wished for an extra couple of inches. He wouldn't have minded being taller either, but his fashionable high heeled boots helped.

Although his hair was light and often bleached blonde in the summertime, he had dark brown eyes, long eye lashes which could have been purchased from Boots the Chemist, and rather unruly eyebrows, which he kept in check by using the moustache trimmer on his electric razor. His mother quite regularly chased him around the house with a pair of tweezers, in order to rectify the eyebrow problem, but as she plucked her own eyebrows to destruction, before replacing them with a thin pencil line, he made sure that she never caught him. His teeth were even and white, and people often refused to believe that they were in fact his own, insisting to his annoyance that they must be dentures.

He'd had more than his fair share of experiences with the opposite sex, but because of an ingrained shyness, which wasn't apparent to the casual observer, he preferred girls to take the initiative as Chrissie had done.

"Doing anything tonight?" he asked.

"Are you asking me out?" she asked giggling.

"If you like," said Ray, sensing not for the first time that he was onto a winner.

"Okay, where are you taking me?" she asked.

"Where would you like to go, the pub, the pictures, Blackpool Tower, the Moon?"

He knew the instant that the words had left his mouth that his statement sounded corny, and he felt himself colour with the embarrassment of what he had just said.

"The pictures," she said laughing. "I think that the Moon is a little too far for a Saturday night out."

"Any idea what's on tonight?" he asked.

"Live a little, love a little at the Empire," she answered.

"Sounds good to me, but what's the film called?" he quipped.

"Cheeky," she said, smiling at his attempt at a joke.

"Who's in it?" he asked.

"Elvis," she answered.

"Elvis who?" asked Ray, as if he had no idea who Elvis was.

She reached over and slapped him playfully on the arm.

Ray had been a big Elvis fan during the late fifties, religiously buying every Elvis record the minute that it was released. He had also enjoyed the early Elvis films, "Loving You, Jailhouse Rock," and "King Creole" being his particular favourites, but in Ray's opinion he hadn't made a decent film since GI Blues, and he had no great expectations of this evenings film at all.

"Ok, I'm game, what time does it start?" he asked.

"Eight I think."

He free wheeled his bike along the gutter as she walked, pushing the curb with his foot to give it some momentum until they reached her front door.

"Is this your house?" he asked.

"Yes. Twenty-seven Shadcroft Road," she answered. "Don't forget will you?"

"Pick you up at seven-thirty."

"Not on this I hope," she said, pointing to Ray's motor bike.

"What's wrong with the bike?" said Ray, pretending to be hurt and patting it lovingly on the petrol tank.

"Well for a start it's a horrible maroon colour. Secondly, I don't want to get blown to bits on the back of a motor bike after I've just had my hair done, and thirdly, I have no intention of showing my backside when I get on or off it."

Ray had to admit that he would have preferred to own a Norton Dominator, or a Triumph Bonneville, but he couldn't afford to purchase either of them on his current salary, and was forced to admire them from afar. Anyway he'd owned the BSA for a number of years, and he had become very attached to the old girl.

■ ■ ■

He had bought the bike a number of years earlier. Initially it had been fitted with a sidecar, which was not an uncommon occurrence with nineteen-fifties motorbikes, as many families, who couldn't afford to own a car, purchased such a vehicle out of necessity.

He hadn't realised just how difficult it would be to ride this type of three wheeled vehicle, having only ever ridden a tricycle in his early childhood, and with a completely different wheel configuration. Difficulty apart, it wasn't at all cool for a red blooded young man to be seen riding a motor bike and sidecar, and so he had negotiated a purchase price to buy the bike separately.

While it was still a motor bike and sidecar the bike had started easily, but once the sidecar had been removed the bike had flatly refused to start, not because of the amputation of the sidecar, but because the battery was desperately in need of charging. Ray had attempted to bump start the newly segregated motorbike, on the steep cobbled side street on which the garage was situated. The engine had finally agreed to fire after two or three attempts, just before he had reached the bottom of the hill. Not realising the power of a 500 cc motorbike, in comparison to that of the Ariel Colt 250cc bike which he used to ride, he had given the BSA far too much throttle. Shooting across the main thoroughfare, whilst still riding side saddle, he had narrowly avoiding oncoming traffic, before hitting a pedestrian barrier, which had catapulted him onto the pavement in front of an oncoming mother and pram.

His father who had accompanied him to view the bike, had tried to persuade him to rethink the situation, worried that this could be a premonition of worse things to come, but Ray would have none of it, and the old BSA and Ray had been inseparable ever since.

■ ■ ■

"Ok, if you're absolutely sure that you wouldn't like to show your arse, I'll borrow my dad's car," he said, as if the thought had only just occurred to him, even though it had been his plan all along.

In addition to the old motor bike, Ray also owned a Triumph Spitfire sports car, which he had only driven for a matter of a few short weeks, when someone had maliciously put sand into his petrol tank, leaving him stranded on the motorway and requiring extensive engine repairs, which currently he had been unable to fund.

His father was the proud owner of his second Ford Anglia, which he was reluctant to entrust into Ray's care, as Ray was responsible for wrecking his first one, after leaving it sitting on the top of a partly demolished wall on the Lancashire / Yorkshire border. Even though he had promised Chrissie that he would pick her up in his father's car, the borrowing of it was far from a foregone conclusion and he would have to grovel, possibly even agree to do chores in order to secure the loan.

■ ■ ■

The film had already started as they entered the cinema. His father had reluctantly allowed him to borrow the family car, after much pleading on Ray's part, and assurances that he would not be drinking. They picked their way through the darkness without the aid of the usherette and her torch, as she completely ignored them, being more intent on filing her nails.

The cinema was almost empty and they found a quiet spot on the back row.

"Not many in," Ray said by way of conversation.

"You sound disappointed," she answered, unable to understand why he would be concerned.

"Not at all, it means that we've got more privacy," he reassured her.

He put his arm around her shoulders and she snuggled up to him, putting a warm hand on his chest and her head on his shoulder.

On screen Elvis was on the beach, and kissing a pretty girl in a swimming costume. Watching for any signs of a false move, was a huge Great Dane named Albert, looking for the world as though he would eat Elvis if he stepped one inch out of line.

"Who's she?" asked Ray referring to the female lead.

"Michelle Carey," Chrissie answered authoritatively.

"I've never heard of her," he complained.

"Neither have I," she admitted, "but it was on the billboard as we came in."

"Why don't they use someone that we know?" he grumbled.

"Have you come to watch the film or not?" she asked, beginning to lose patience.

"If I have to choose the answer is not," he replied.

He lifted up her chin and kissed her with mock passion full on the mouth; she coughed and spluttered, pushing him away in order to regain her composure, before smacking him playfully on the knee.

She was wearing the same coat that she had worn when they had first met in the afternoon, but the jeans that she had worn then had been replaced by a tight black leather mini-skirt. Ray smiled to himself in the darkness, as he had a vision of her getting on and off his motor bike whilst wearing it. The sloppy sweater that she had worn earlier in the day, had been replaced by a very low cut plain white tee-shirt, which showed quite lot of her cleavage, and a not inconsiderable amount of her lacy black bra.

He put his hand inside her coat as he kissed her again. He was wondering if it was a little too early to make a serious move, when he felt the zipper of his trousers being gently pulled down.

They came out of the cinema at ten-thirty. Once back at the Shadcroft Estate, she guided him to a piece of waste land behind a row of council houses, where six or seven self assembly wooden garages had been built, for the small minority of families on the estate who could afford to own a car.

Once they had parked up he wasted little time in unfastening her bra strap. He was very experienced at removing support garments, proud of the fact that he could unhook a bra using only one hand, before the wearer was even aware that he had done it.

She stopped his progress as she felt the bra strap slacken. At first he thought that he must have completely misread the situation, although the signals could hardly have been clearer if she had been wearing a neon sign, but reaching up her sleeve, she pulled her bra strap down one arm and slipped it over her wrist. Finding the strap up the other sleeve, with one quick movement like a pickpocket stealing a watch, the bra came down her sleeve and she threw it onto the back seat of the car. What a good trick thought Ray, wondering if it was a skill that he could one day perfect himself, although on reflection he deciding that it was probably a better idea to leave it up to the experts.

Once the bra had been removed, he pulled up her tee-shirt exposing her not inconsiderable breasts. He noticed a mark on her right breast, which on closer examination turned out to be a small rose tattoo.

Ray had always wanted a tattoo of his own when in his teens. Not a rose, which he felt was rather girly, but something which would give the casual observer an impression of the wearer's bravery. Perhaps a skull and crossbones motif, or alternatively a dagger with a snake coiled around it, but when he had mentioned the tattoo at home his mother had hit the roof.

"Only rough people and sailor's wear tattoos," she had snapped angrily.

This he knew was not strictly true, but was a reasonable generalisation at the time, and not being brave enough to challenge her, and therefore not fit to wear the intended insignia; he had never mentioned the subject again.

■ ■ ■

"What did your parents say when you got your tattoo?" he asked, while circling it with his finger.

"My parents don't know about it, I'm not in the habit of flashing my tits at my dad, that's why it's hidden inside my bra."

"Have you any more hidden ones?" he asked hopefully.

"No but my brother has. He has a complete hunting scene all the way from his shoulders and down his back. Horses, huntsmen in red coats, fox hounds, the works, and a fox's tail disappearing up his arse."

"Very tasteful," said Ray ironically, his mind working overtime to envisage the scene.

He put his hand upon her knee, slowly climbing her stockings until he reached her stocking tops, which were supported by suspenders, a rare treat in a world which now appeared to be dominated by pantyhose. He felt the warm flesh of her inner thigh, and was aware of a slight quiver running through her body at his touch. She halted his progress momentarily to remove a pair of blue silk French knickers, which appeared from beneath the hem of her skirt, sliding easily over her silk stockings until they reached her knees, before dropping unaided onto the floor. Stepping out of the aforementioned undergarment, she kicked it carelessly into the foot-well of the car, before making the suggestion that they should climb into the back seat of the car, where they would have more room for manoeuvre.

All was going according to plan, until the moment that a torch light shone through the passenger window of the car, while a tapping was to be heard on the steamed up window glass. Chrissie whispered that it was probably her father who had come looking for her, and they froze in the mistaken hope that the intruder would go away. When the frightened couple failed to respond to the tapping, the intruder became impatient and the passenger door, which they had carelessly failed to lock, opened to reveal a face, a face which was peering at them from beneath a policeman's helmet.

"You can't do that sort of thing here," said the face.

Ray was startled and embarrassed by the intrusion, but despite the fact that her naked breasts were in full view of the intruder and spotlighted by his torch, Chrissie made no attempt to cover them up.

"Bugger off you pervert," she shouted at the copper, obviously relieved that it was only the constabulary, and not her father who had discovered them.

"No need for that miss," said the policeman patiently. "Come on now, let's be having you, I'll return in five minutes and you had better both be gone," and then the door closed and the face was gone.

"I'd better be going anyway," said Chrissie. "I'm already on a midnight curfew, and if I don't go now my dad really will come looking for me."

She found her bra on the back seat of the car where she had thrown it, but not bothering to replace it, she pulled down her tea shirt to cover her breasts, and stuffed it into her coat pocket.

"Can you put the light on?" she asked, while searching for the French knickers that she had carelessly kicked into the foot-well.

They searched the car thoroughly both inside and out, under the seats, in the back, in the front, everywhere in fact, but the

French knickers were nowhere to be found. Ray even put on the headlights and checked around the outside of the car, but the missing undergarment could not be found.

An hour later, a policeman walking his beat on the Shadcroft Estate stopped at number Twenty-seven Shadcroft Road. The house was in total darkness, as he removed a pair of blue silk French knickers from his tunic pocket, and hung them on the gatepost of the house.

CHAPTER TWO

Ray studied the sign above the doorway before entering the shop.

GOFF EASTMAN, GENTLEMAN'S HAIRDRESSER.

Goff was a hairdresser; he thought like a hairdresser and he looked like a hairdresser. He was an inch or so smaller than Ray, with backcombed bleached blonde hair, which curled over his forehead as if he had only recently taken the rollers out.

Anyone could be excused for thinking that Goff was a homosexual, but he wasn't; far from it in fact, and many an unsuspecting female had found herself compromised in consequence of that misconception.

Goff had piercing blue eyes and a permanent tan, which like his hair colour came straight from a bottle. He always looked professional while at work, wearing a short white hairdresser's jacket with a high round collar, with scissors and a comb tucked neatly into his top pocket as a badge of his office.

Goff's real name was a mystery to everyone; Ray suspected that it was Geoffrey, although Goff never would admit to his real name, no matter how hard he was pressed on the subject. Although most people naturally assumed that he was a single man, and always would be, he was in fact estranged although still married to his wife of four years Sandy, with two beautiful daughters of four and two years of age respectively.

He had separated from his wife over two years before, while she was still pregnant with his second daughter, leaving to work as a gentlemen's hairdresser on a Caribbean cruise liner, until returning a year later with an American lady hairdresser who he had met while at sea, and they had opened up the salon together. Unfortunately the hands across the sea relationship hadn't lasted for very long, and his business come sleeping partner had returned alone to the United States.

■ ■ ■

Ray's first meeting with Goff had been an embarrassing one for Ray, as he had been sleeping with Goff's wife at the time. Their paths had crossed for the first time, when Goff had arrived at the house of his wife in order to visit his children. Ray had felt uncomfortable by the encounter, although Goff appeared to be totally unconcerned by it and they had later become friends.

Ray had first spotted Sandy, while holidaying on the North Yorkshire coast when in his early teens. Although she had red hair and freckles, which didn't usually float his boat, he had fancied her from the first moment that he had laid eyes upon her. In fairness her hair could better be described as sandy rather than red, which may have accounted for her name. In any case his taste in women was quite eclectic, tall or short, chubby or slim, dark or fair, even sandy; it was all the same to Ray.

Sandy had been holidaying with her parents when they had first met, and the relationship had never evolved beyond drinking Coca Cola, listening to the jukebox, and holding hands. Both being extremely shy at the time they had talked very little, in fact he knew so little about her, that he had failed to realise that she lived in his neighbourhood, so consequently he had been astonished to see her many years later on his home turf.

Although it had been a number of years since their first encounter, she had made such an impression on him that he had recognised her instantly, and she him. Her hair was much shorter than it had been, much shorter even than his own, and cut with a side parting rather like that of a schoolboy. The freckles had faded somewhat, and two children had taken their toll on her figure, but despite the negative changes that time had wrought, he still found her very attractive.

After driving her home she had asked him in for a coffee, which Ray with his usual mindset had interpreted as would you like to come in for sex, and which as it turned out proved to be the correct interpretation. After dispatching the baby sitter she had disappeared, promising to slip into something more comfortable, before returning a few minutes' later carrying two mugs of steaming coffee.

Something more comfortable, had not conjured up in Ray's imagination what he witnessed, when she had reappeared wearing a grubby old fashioned floral dressing gown, worn above fluffy pink slippers. The dressing gown was threadbare, and reminded him of something that his grandmother might choose to wear, although it didn't take Sherlock Holmes to tell him that she was naked beneath the robe, as it had been left swinging wide open, either deliberately or through lack of the necessary buttons; either way the message was clear, just in case he was in any doubt.

After placing the coffee mugs on the table in front of him, he had taken just one sip, but his mind was definitely not on the coffee, and when the morning came, two mugs of cold coffee were still standing on the coffee table, where they had been placed the night before.

From that day he became monogamous, and began to stay overnight at her house two or three times a week. He even began to arrive before the children had gone to bed, bringing them small presents that he had picked up at the petrol station, a bucket and spade, a beach ball, or a plastic duck for bath time.

Their relationship however came to a very abrupt end on the eve of his annual holiday in July. Beginning to itch in the trouser area, he discovered that he had unwanted guests living there. At first she had denied that she was the cause of his infestation, convinced that he must have had other lovers, and that he would therefore not be able to identify, with any certainty, the real culprit of his misfortune, but not having slept with anyone else for the past three months, there could be only one conclusion, she had.

■ ■ ■

Ray and his friends met at Goff's hairdressing salon on most Sunday afternoons, for a coffee, a chat, and a half price hair cut or blow wave. Goff's was unlike most of the other barbers shops in the East Lancashire mill towns, which by enlarge hadn't changed much in over half a century. Most sporting red and white striped wooden poles outside of their shops, resembling huge candy canes angled towards the sky.

In days gone by, barbers were not only seen as barbers, but were also surgeons, performing tooth extractions, amputations, and abortions, between haircuts and shaving, and bleeding people in a misguided attempt to cure them of their maladies. The red of the pole in those early days, had represented the inevitable blood from such occupations, while the white had depicted the necessary bandages. Not that the modern day customer expected to see much blood or bandages when they went for a haircut, except for the occasional nick of a child's ear, intentional or otherwise, when one of the little darlings failed to keep still.

Very few of the local barbers had made any concessions at all to the longer hair styles of the late nineteen-sixties. Even though long hair had been the fashion among young men for half a decade, they still persisted in offering only the short back and side's style of haircut favoured by the older generation.

Appointments at these establishments were unheard of, while young and old alike, would wait patiently for the better part of a Saturday morning, sitting for hours on mismatched and uncomfortable dining room chairs, handed down through the generations, or bought from local second hand shops for the purpose. The time was passed on this twice monthly ritual, by reading old dog eared copies of Practical Mechanics and The Model Maker, which had been read by the very same customers on previous bum numbing occasions.

Goff's establishment was completely different; it had a comfortable waiting area, with soft armchairs and settees with contrasting cushions. Coffee tables were strewn with up to date magazines depicting style and fashion in hairstyles, clothing, and the home, while motor magazines, with pictures of desirable and unaffordable cars like the Ferrari, the Porsche, and the E type Jaguar, were popular talking points amongst the young men who frequented Goff's establishment. Coffee was available in glass jugs warming on chrome coffee machines, while customers were encouraged to help themselves, while waiting for hair styling, rather than for haircuts. Appointments were the norm at Goff's, and waiting times were reduced to the minimum, unless of course you preferred to make an afternoon of it, as Ray and his friends quite often did.

When Ray entered the salon, Cookie was already sitting in the chair having a trim. It was the era of the Beatles and the Rolling Stones, with shoulder length hair being very much the fashion of the day, but Cookie had made no concession to the times, and had stuck with his traditional short back and side's hair cut, which made him look like a younger version of his father.

Unlike Cookie, Ray preferred to be at the opposite end of the follicle spectrum, and with his shoulder length hair and beard, was quite often referred to as Jesus by some of his contemporise, because of his biblical appearance.

Some of his older work colleagues found his appearance disrespectful, as for generation's young men had emulated their fathers, as Cookie still did, by dressing and grooming in exactly the same way, from the moment that they were allowed out of short trousers. They had even listened to the same music as their parents, and danced to the same ballroom-dances, while this had been accepted by the older generation as a tribute to their good example.

Ray's generation had broken that mould by adopting their own musical heroes, dances, and fashions, and this had caused considerable distaste in some of the more traditional members of the older generation, which manifested itself as bullying by older men who should have known better.

■ ■ ■

One lunch time, this intolerant faction of male society at Ray's place of work, had chosen to give Ray a hair cut as a peevish lark. Ray was not easily bullied unless being drastically outnumbered, which on this occasion he most certainly was. With one of the bullies holding each arm and another one holding each leg, they had held him writhing on the floor, while a fifth member sitting on his chest, had cut the hair from half of his head, and the beard from half of his face, using a pair of blunt scissors, which had left his hair patchy and his face sore.

Although he had pleaded to borrow the scissors in an attempt to remedy the mess that they had created, he had been refused, as it was much more amusing, to see him spend the rest of the day looking as if he were two different people joined down the middle. That was a number of years ago however, and his hair and beard were now as defiantly luxuriant as ever.

■ ■ ■

"I suppose that you went out with that slag Chrissie last night?" said Cookie peevishly.

"Do you know her?" asked Ray in surprise.

"Everyone knows her; she's the Shadcroft bike," said Cookie in a disgusted tone of voice, before continuing, "everybody has ridden her."

"Have you?" asked Ray apparently innocently, although Cookie caught the barb in the comment and instantly changed the subject.

Cookie didn't appear to like girls, but actually it was the girls who didn't like him. He was taller than Ray by a couple of inches, with dark wavy hair, and a large beer belly which hung over his trouser belt. He also had a pronounced under-bite, which gave the impression that he had a large chin, which along with his unfashionable look, didn't enhance his appearance, or endear him to members of the opposite sex.

Because he found it difficult to attract the girls, when all of his friends appeared to find it so easy, he had begun to resent girls in general, and especially the ones who showed any kind of interest in any of his friends. To ensure that he was never without a companion, he had adopted a mechanism to ruin his friend's chances of success, making remarks like how's the wife and kids, or when is your next venereal disease appointment, but while he could be a right royal pain in the arse, he was definitely the one to have around when the going got tough.

■ ■ ■

In the summer of 1967, Ray and Cookie had decided on a whim to visit Torquay, a popular holiday resort, and the jewel in the crown of the English Riviera on the Devon coast. They had tramped around the town for several hours looking for lodgings, but there was no room at the proverbial inn. Every hotel in the town appeared to be fully booked at this time of the year, until finally they had come across Madge's guest house, about a mile from the sea and on the outskirts of the town.

Madge had answered the door wearing yellow rubber gloves, and a floral apron of yellow and mauve pansies, which considering that Madge was a male and as camp as a row of tents, seemed to be very apt. Not knowing any homosexuals on a personal level, they weren't sure what kind of accommodation to expect at Madge's, or even worse how accommodating they would be expected to be. It was somewhat of a relief therefore, when Madge had told them that just like everyone else in the town, he currently had no vacancies, before escorting them across the road, while still wearing his apron and rubber gloves, to the house of an elderly couple who he suggested may be prepared to rent them a room.

The old lady had readily agreed to the arrangement once money had been discussed, while her husband, who didn't appear to hear or to see very well, kept asking in a very loud voice, "Who is it Doris. What do they want?"

They rented a double bedded room; a converted front parlour on the ground floor, which closely resembled a museum, filled to the point of restricted movement by Victorian furniture and flat back Staffordshire ornaments, with monochrome prints of nymphs and fairies in the sentimental Victorian taste, mounted in glossy black mourning frames.

Although a little creepy, it was spotlessly clean, and the old lady insisted that they accept a front door key of their own, so that they could to come and go as they pleased, explaining that as she and her husband were both hard of hearing, they would not be disturbed if the young gentlemen wanted to return after ten in the evening.

The room at the old couple's house turned out to be very satisfactory, except for the large numbers of sea gulls, which appeared to prefer the roof of the old couple's house, a mile away from the sea, rather than their more traditional cliff top haunts, and squawked incessantly from first light until dusk, ensuring that Ray and Cookie had very little sleep.

Every day they walked to the seafront, passing on the way large numbers of Swedish students, who for some inextricable reason, chose to inhabit the low walls which surrounded numerous traffic islands on their journey to the sea. Ray had hoped that they might encounter some of the extremely striking blonde girls on the seafront, but they never did.

He could accept that as students studying English at summer school, they were not on holiday, but had he been studying Spanish in Barcelona, or Portuguese in Lisbon, he would definitely not have been spending his free time sitting on a traffic island, and chattering like the bird colony over his bedroom window, rather than sitting on the beach or promenading on the seafront, and he came to the conclusion that the Swede's were an attractive but very peculiar race.

On the final evening of their holiday, they loaded their suitcases into the car ready for their return journey to Lancashire. They had planned to drive home overnight after a final evening out on the town, which was not such a brilliant idea after a night of heavy drinking, but the absurdity of the plan never even occurred to them.

On the seafront, they entered an upstairs bar room with a beautiful view overlooking the marina, where they purchased two pints of beer and two very large cigars, with colourful paper bands bearing the head of king somebody or other wrapped around them. Cookie had always been partial to an occasional cigar, smoking small cheroots regularly and more expensive cigars on special occasions. Although Ray didn't smoke, he did have an occasional cigar at Christmas time and on other special occasions, while the grand opening of Cookie's wallet, without having to twist his arm up his back, was a very special occasion indeed.

As Ray and Cookie debated whether or not to order another round, a group of young Scots entered the bar, they were wearing kilts, extremely drunk, and obviously intent on causing as much of a nuisance as was humanly possible. Within a matter of minutes of their arrival, the barman had pulled down the metal shutters which protected the bar, and had switched off the jukebox, refusing to serve anyone until the Scots had left the premises.

Ignoring the barman's pleas for good behaviour, the Scots began singing their songs of defiance.

We shall not
We shall not be moved
We shall not
We shall not be moved
Not by the English, the Welsh or the Irish
We shall not be moved.

It appeared that no one was prepared to stand up to these northern invaders, and Ray could understand why the Emperor Hadrian had chosen to build a wall in order to keep them out of England.

Ray wasn't a violent man as long as common sense prevailed, but he had always housed a demon, which took control of his words and actions when he was angry or felt threatened.

His beer glass being empty and his cigar now little more than a stub, the singing and the taunts soon became a personal, if not an issue of national importance, and although vastly outnumbered Ray approached the group of noisy Scots; carefully selecting the one who seemed to be the leader of the clan, by virtue of having the biggest mouth, he grabbed him by his tie, twisting it around a number of times until the boy's face began to turn purple, before stubbing out his cigar on Big Mouth's forehead, which left a large red burn. Not content with this act of barbarism, he then dragged the choking youth to the top of the stairs like a dog on a lead, where he announced very loudly, so that the whole bar-room could hear, that he was English and that he would move him, with which he pushed the boy 'arse over tit' down the very steep staircase.

For a few minutes Big Mouth's friends had appeared to be shocked into inactivity, but having recovered some of their composure after seeing their leader forcibly ejected, they belatedly arose in unison just as Cookie decided to enter the fray.

"Come on then, which of you Jock bastards wants some more of the same?" he had yelled angrily, his face red and his eyes popping out of his head as if he were demented.

At the sight of this madman screaming like a banshee, the clan appeared to have second thoughts about the intended retaliation, and meekly left the bar in single file, with Cookie shepherding them towards the exit, like a sheepdog with his small dejected flock.

A huge cheer had gone up in the bar and people offered their congratulations, as the shutters once again opened and the jukebox sprang back into life. Half an hour later while relieving his bladder at the urinals, Ray received a warning from a well-wisher, that the Scots were returning with national reinforcements for a counter attack. Discretion being the better part of valour, Ray and Cookie had left in a hurry and drove through the night back to Lancashire.

■ ■ ■

Goff had finished cutting Cookie's hair and so Ray replaced him in the chair.

"Where did you get to last night?" he enquired of Goff.

"Remember the two girls that we picked up last Sunday night at the Miners Club?"

"How could I forget the lovely Angela; but tell me, why is it that when we go out together, you always end up with beauty and I always end up with the beast?"

"Funny that you should mention that," replied Goff. "That's exactly what Angela's friend said to her last week when we met them at the Miners Club."

Cookie found Goff's remark hilarious as it obviously embarrassed Ray, but Ray was far from amused. "Piss off," he said, for want of a better retort.

Goff continued with his story.

"Well, I arranged to see Angela again last night."

"Any joy?" asked Ray."

"I'm coming to that," said Goff irritably, not liking to be interrupted when his story was in full flow.

"We went dancing at the Mecca ballroom, and then we went to an Indian for a curry."

"Never mind that, did you get anywhere?" Ray repeated doggedly.

Goff ignored him as if he hadn't spoken at all and continued with his recital.

"When we got close to her house, she told me to turn into the colliery yard. She said that it was always quiet on Saturday nights, as the miners last shift ended at ten, and they wouldn't be on duty again until Monday morning. I asked her how she could be so sure, and she told me that her father and brother both worked at the colliery, and that they never worked nights on a Saturday. One thing led to another, and before long we both ended up naked on the back seat of the car."

"It's bloody November, wasn't it cold?" Ray interrupted.

"We had a car rug, but it was bloody cold at about six this morning, when we were woken up because the car was rocking. There were lights shining in through all of the windows, and I had the impression of black faces, and white teeth grinning at every window, although it was impossible to be sure because of the lights."

He paused, obviously reliving the experience and Ray urged him to continue. "What on earth was it?" he asked intrigued.

"It was the miners with lamps on their helmets coming off a night shift.

Ray and Cookie were hysterical with laughter, and Goff nearly cut of Ray's ear because he was moving so much.

"Watch it you nicked me then!" complained Ray.

"Serves you right," said Goff laughing now himself. "It was bloody embarrassing don't you know."

"Did you see Archie last night?" asked Ray, turning his attention to Cookie.

"He came in The Legs O' Man about seven, and a good job that he did because I can't rely on you."

Archie was even more popular with the ladies than either Ray or Goff, and was just as likely to have made a date, but Cookie as usual had a point to make.

Archie worked with Ray at the local Vallard factory, he hadn't been christened Archie at all, but as he shared his name with the radio ventriloquist Peter Brough, naturally he had become known as Archie, named after Brough's dummy Archie Andrews.

Ray had never been able to understand the concept of a radio ventriloquist, as the whole point of ventriloquism as he understood it, was speaking while appearing not to do so. He had only once seen Peter Brough on the television in the late nineteen-fifties, after a decade of listening to the Archie Andrews' show on the radio, and it soon became apparent why Brough was a radio ventriloquist, as he moved his mouth more while communicating as the dummy than Archie Andrews did.

Archie, the namesake not the dummy, was tall, very tall at six feet four inches, and so good looking, that he was banned from entering some of the female dominated departments at the Vallard factory, as it caused a great deal of disruption to production, while some of the more excitable girls, would stand up and scream, as they would at the entrance of a film star or a pop star.

Ray himself had a similar effect on some of the girls at work, but not to anything like the same degree. Archie definitely had film star good looks, with blue eyes and fair hair which covered his ears and reached his collar, without being particularly long. Although his skin was pock marked from an earlier bought of teenage spots, he was always clean shaven, and Ray could never understand why he didn't grow a beard to cover the marks, as beards were currently the height of fashion.

■ ■ ■

Ray had his first introduction to Archie a few days before his sixteenth birthday, while on holiday in North Wales. His only sexual experiences at that particular time, had consisted of fumbling on the back seat of the cinema, or behind the bike sheds with willing girls from his school.

On this particular occasion, he had met a slightly built dark haired girl of around his own age at the holiday camp, and finally it seemed that it was time for him to say goodbye to his virginity, which had long been an ambition, although until now, he had not met with anyone willing to help him to achieve this milestone in his education.

Entering her chalet after the bars had closed for the evening, they had stripped to their underwear before slipping nervously between the sheets, excited but apprehensive about what was about to take place. Before his ambitions could be realised however, a commotion had begun to take place outside of the chalet. Peeping through a chink in the curtains, Ray had come face to face with Archie looking back at him through the same chink. It had startled Ray, especially when Archie had begun to roar with anger at the sight of the interloper, and had stood up to his full height, waving his arms around and threatening to break down the chalet door. Ray was informed by his bedfellow that the angry giant outside was in fact Pete, who she had known since her early school days. It appeared that she had loved Pete for many years, even though he didn't feel the same way about her and only used her as a convenience.

Archie was a gentle giant although he could be very loud, always singing rugby songs in the pub or on the street. Ray had later discovered that he himself was by far the more aggressive of the two, but without his current insight into Archie's passive nature, he had been pretty scared by the noisy giant, until the Blue Coats, who operated as security, had arrived in response to complaints about the noise and moved Archie on.

A few moments before the incident, losing his virginity had been the uppermost thought in Ray's mind, although now his priorities had changed somewhat, and self preservation had taken a much higher priority than his carnal desires, and so he had reluctantly made his excuses to the girl and left.

After the annual holidays the new intake of apprentices always arrived at the factory, as Ray himself had done the previous year, and he had been dismayed to discover that Archie happened to be one of them. Having spent the second week of his holiday trying to avoid this crazy person, he would now have to face him on a daily basis, but Archie didn't recognise him, and Ray never enlightened him that they had ever met before.

■ ■ ■

"Are we meeting in The Legs O' Man tonight?" asked Cookie when they were all about to leave.

"I can't," said Ray. "I have an eight o'clock flight to Amsterdam in the morning, I haven't packed my suitcase yet, and I have to be up at the crack of dawn."

CHAPTER THREE

In the late 1960's a revolution was taking place in British homes; colour television. The first colour broadcast in Britain had already taken place in July 1967, although colour television broadcasts had existed in the United States since the early 1950's, RCA having demonstrated the first electronically scanned colour television set as far back as 1940.

The trip to Holland was in the nature of a business trip. Ray worked for the British subsidiary of a large international electronics company, which was based in the Dutch city of Eindhoven, and he was on his way to Holland, to study the techniques required to repair and to maintain the new machinery, which was expected to arrive presently at the Vallard factory, and which would make the glass delay-lines for the new colour television sets.

When the taxi arrived Godfrey Hillendale was already sitting comfortably in the back seat. Although he was a little younger than Ray, he was also Ray's boss by virtue of a university degree. He was reputed to be an electronics boffin, but Ray had yet to see proof of that claim, as he had never seen him with as much as a screwdriver in his hand. He was much taller than Ray, well in excess of six feet tall, very slim and with a sharp bird like face. His hair, which grew over his collar, was wild and red, and already receding significantly at the temples.

Godfrey usually spent most of the day in his office with the door firmly closed. He drank copious amounts of coffee, and amassed a huge collection of polystyrene coffee cups, which were stacked in huge towers all around his office, making it almost impossible for anyone to enter. Ray couldn't see the fascination of collecting used coffee cups, but apparently they all carried different batch numbers Godfrey explained, which made Godfrey's hobby rather like collecting train numbers, which to Ray was equally mystifying.

"Good morning Ray," Godfrey said cheerily.

"Good morning God," said Ray a little less cheerily, as he was not really an early morning person.

At first, Ray had only resorted to calling Godfrey God behind his back, and admittedly in malice, as he himself had initially been promised the job as head of the department. After performing that duty for a six month period in an unpaid capacity, he had been rewarded for his efforts by the unannounced arrival of Godfrey to take his place, which had resulted in some unhelpful behaviour on Ray's part.

As they had become more familiar with each other, Ray had realised that Godfrey had very few management skills, and was happy to hide away in his office with his coffee cup collection, while Ray continued to run the department just as before. Realising that Godfrey relied upon him and was also probably a little bit scared of him, he had soon begun to call him God to his face, and Godfrey seemed quite happy to accept the promotion.

Ray had dressed in his best blue suite straight out of Burton's window, while wearing his brand new Crombie overcoat in an attempt to look business like for the occasion. He was what they called in the rag trade a stock size, the outfitter explaining to him that his measurements exactly matched those of the shop window dummies, so that the display suits always fitted him perfectly. As he was convinced that they were of a superior quality, and what's more fitted him much better than a made to measure suit, he would regularly ask if any of the suits in the shop window were for sale, which they quite often were, as material runs came to an end and the sample suits became redundant.

Godfrey had made no such concessions for the trip. He was wearing his usual grey flannels, blue blazer, and camel coloured duffle coat with peg buttons, finished off as always with his university scarf, which he wore with pride as a badge of his academic achievement.

Weekend in Amsterdam

Ray and Godfrey had little if anything in common, and the initial flurry of excited conversation about the trip quickly dried up. Ray tried all of the subjects on which he felt knowledgeable, music, television programs, books, history, news, and even politics, but Godfrey was not a man of the world, and had little or no knowledge on any of these subjects. His only love, other than his precious coffee cup collection, and his beloved electronics, was radio signals.

To Ray's surprise it turned out that Godfrey had a girlfriend, but it was of no surprise to find that she shared his passion for radio signals. It transpired that for a night out, they would drive onto the moor which overlooked the town in his well equipped Land Rover, so as to receive messages from like minded people as far afield as France, Norway, and Rotherham. By the time that they reached Manchester Airport they were sitting in total silence, and Ray wondered what on earth they would talk about until Wednesday, which was when Godfrey was due to return home to England.

Ray was as excited as a child about flying, even though it wasn't the first time that he had flown. As a child he had flown on family holidays, from Blackpool Squires Gate Airport to Ronaldsway Airport in the Isle of Man. On those occasions, he had flown on World War II transport planes like the Dakota and the Bristol Wayfarer, which had been converted by the addition of seats to become passenger aircraft after the war. This time he was flying for the very first time on a jet aircraft, something that he had always wanted to do since BOAC had introduced the Comet in the early 1950's.

Manchester Ringway Airport was a very different kettle of fish to the Squires Gate airport of Ray's childhood, which as memory served him, was a single story prefabricated building, akin to the ones where fighter pilots were scrambled from their battered old armchairs during World War II. In contrast, although it was still in its transition stages, Manchester's airport was of ultra modern design, in testament to the changes being witnessed in 1960's architecture throughout the country, built in concrete and of enormous proportions, with huge chandeliers of water droplet shaped glass.

Ray and Godfrey were separated on the aeroplane, as Godfrey was a member of Vallard's senior staff. This entitled him to travel business class, while Ray, who was only junior staff, had to travel economy as his reduced status dictated. On the plane he sat next to a boy of eight or nine, who although travelling with his mother, shared Ray's enthusiasm for flying and insisted on holding his hand as the plane took off.

It was not the first time that Ray had been abroad; it wasn't even the first time that he had been to Holland. Just over a year before leaving school, he had been to Belgium on a school holiday, although on that occasion they had not flown but had sailed from Dover to Ostend. During their stay they had crossed the border into Holland, in order to visit a model village in the Dutch town of Middleburg. Although Ray could not remember very much about the trip, except for a party of nuns with enormous upturned wimples, which reminded him of some of the origami projects featured in his childhood Rupert Bear annuals.

He met up with Godfrey at the baggage collection, and they caught a bus from Schiphol Airport to Amsterdam *Centraal* Station. Opened to the public in 1889, it was a beautiful twin towered building of brick and stone, with a number of Dutch gables along its frontage. The roof fabricated in cast iron spanned forty meters, while the station was situated on three man-made islands, which rested on over 8,000 wooden piles driven deep into the mud.

It was a far cry from their local Blakewater railway station, which although built in the same decade, and with an attractive grade II listed frontage of similar brick and stone construction, had been allowed to deteriorate, with it's now permanently closed buffet room, smoke stained platform, and broken glass roof. Its only concession to the modern age being electric lighting, which was by now so filthy with the smoke from the steam trains, that it was no more efficient than the gas lighting which it had only in recent years replaced.

They drank a strong coffee and enjoyed a tasty Danish pastry, in the comfortable station restaurant while awaiting the train, which arrived exactly on time, something unheard of in England. Godfrey suggested that they shared a first class carriage, although their staff status dictated otherwise. Ray was unsure if this was a good idea, but Godfrey reassured him that if the inspector challenged them, he would pay the difference in the fare out of their travel expenses.

Soon after they had settled into the carriage, two men entered and stored their luggage onto the luggage rack. Ray recognised one of the men instantly, as the foreman of the tool-room at the factory where he and Godfrey worked, although the other one he had no recollection of ever having seen before. They said good morning as they sat down, and soon realised through conversation, that they all worked at the same factory in England, although visiting different factories in Holland.

"Are you senior staff?" asked the tool-room foreman, very conscious of his own senior staff status.

"Yes," said Godfrey telling no lies.

The tool-room foreman studied Ray very closely, and although he looked the part in his new Crombie overcoat, suspicion showed on the tool-room foreman's face.

"He isn't," said the tool-room foreman, pointing his stubby finger at Ray. "He did some wiring in the tool-room a couple of years ago, he recounted, his memories flooding back. If you don't leave the carriage immediately," he said glaring at Ray spitefully, "I'm going to call for the ticket inspector."

Ray hated the class system at Vallard. There were three separate and very different restaurants, one with upholstered chairs, table clothes, waitress service, and jugs of water on the tables for all of the senior staff members. Another which was a small serve yourself cafeteria, with cheap plastic chairs and melamine table tops for the junior staff, and a huge free-for-all of a canteen, with the same cheap dining room furniture as the junior staff canteen, for the non-staff production workers.

They also had senior staff toilets which the rest of the workforce were not allowed to use, the key to this status symbol, being highly prized amongst the privileged few who had access to one, while the chief executive of Vallard, a Dutchman named

Van Dyke, had his own personal toilet that not even senior staff members were allowed to use.

■ ■ ■

As an apprentice Ray had been working with Rick Mackay, an electrician famed for his propensity for being accident prone. Queen Elizabeth II had been due to visit the Vallard factory, and it was decided that the chief executive toilets would be completely refurbished, just in case the Queen should wish to spend a penny, or to put on a bit of lippy during her visit.

The toilets had been newly tiled in the highest quality duck egg blue tiles, with brand new top of the range sanitary ware to match, and Rick had been given the job of fitting a strip light above the mirror in order to illuminate the scene. He had been using a large aluminium bodied drill, with a handle attached to the back of the drill body using screws.

While drilling holes for the wall plugs, the handle had become detached from the drill body due to the vibration, allowing it to fall from his grasp, and in the process smashing the washbasin into numerous pieces. Unable to replace such a unique piece of sanitary ware at such short notice, the whole suite had to be replaced with one of sage green, and consequently the room had to be re-tiled to match.

■ ■ ■

The mood in the carriage had become very tense, while Ray glared at the tool-room foreman. Godfrey, who knew from experience what was about to happen, tried to rescue the situation, by explaining that they intended to pay the discrepancy in fares when the ticket inspector put in an appearance, but Ray was not in an explaining kind of mood. He didn't normally swear but the demon inside of him definitely did.

"You little shit," he yelled. "Who the fucking hell do you think you are? It's only a few years since you were a rag assed fitter, and you probably still live in a two up and two down with a tin bath in the backyard. Get up you little prick and I'll knock you down faster than you can fall."

"You can't talk to him like that," said his travelling companion in disbelief. "He's senior staff."

"I don't give a flying fuck what he is, or you either for that matter," roared Ray. "But if he is not out of this carriage in two seconds flat, he goes out of the fucking window and you along with him."

The tool-room foreman had gone quite white, he was shaking and all of his bravado had left him. He quickly gathered his belongings, and along with his travelling companion, they left in a hurry, in order to look for another first class carriage with a better clientele.

The ticket inspector arrived shortly after they had left. Perhaps it was the tool-room foreman's parting shot to Ray, but the inspector had been expected anyway, and Godfrey paid the discrepancy in the fares from their travel expenses.

Ray was angry that because of internal factory politics, it wasn't possible for four men who came from the same British factory, to support one another when on foreign soil. Godfrey was concerned that the tool-room foreman would cause trouble for them on their return to the Vallard factory, although Ray wasn't worried on that score at all. The tool-room foreman was a jumped up little pipsqueak, he was scared but he wasn't silly, and he knew that Ray would track him down and punch his lights out if he caused any more problems.

Ray tried to calm himself down and forget about the tool-room foreman, by looking out of the window in search of windmills. He was amazed when he didn't see any, as he had been led to believe that Holland was the land of windmills.

■ ■ ■

As a child, Ray had always played 'spot the windmill' with his parents, every time that they had gone on a day trip to Blackpool, the most popular seaside resort in Britain, and luckily for a young lad like Ray, right on his own doorstep. His father always said that the last one to see the windmill, which surprisingly stood on a housing estate on the outskirts of the town, would have to pay for the ice-creams. He himself of course was always the last to one to see it, while Ray was always allowed to be the first.

The Fylde coast of Lancashire was abundant with windmills, some still intact, while others stood derelict, stone towers with missing sails, rising high above the villages which they had once supplied with flour for the baking of bread, or for the pumping of water from boggy farm land.

Although the one at Blackpool had resulted in many free ice-cream cones over the years, his favourite one, which was still very much intact and a popular tourist attraction, had always been the one at Lytham St. Anne's. It stood on the promenade surrounded by large expanses of grass, where he and his father had played cricket on warm summer Sundays, and football in the spring and autumn when the weather was cooler.

■ ■ ■

When he had watched the boring flat landscape for well over an hour without spotting a single windmill, he gave up the challenge and dropped off to sleep, only to awake as the train pulled into Eindhoven Central Station.

As they disembarked, Ray spotted the tool-room foreman and his travelling companion, getting off the train at the far end of the platform. Leaving his suitcase on the platform with Godfrey, he chased after them. They panicked as they saw him bearing down on them at speed; running to the exit as fast as they could, while not daring to look back as they stumbling along, half carrying and half dragging their heavy suitcases, even after Ray had stopped chasing them. Leaning forward with his hands on his knees in order to catch his breath, Ray laughed heartily at their panic stricken retreat.

As they left the railway station, they spotted the tool-room foreman and his friend once more, getting into a taxi for their journey to the Eindhoven factory. Ray and Godfrey were travelling to Valkenswaard some eleven kilometres away, and in order to save on their expenses for more important things like beer, they caught the service bus.

It was much colder in Holland than it had been when they had left England. As they travelled on the bus, Ray tried to explain to Godfrey, that the Gulf Stream keeps England milder than it would otherwise be, whilst Eindhoven, although much further south than Lancashire, has no such advantage and hence the freezing cold weather.

They passed a number of ponds, and caught fleeting glimpses of a canal, which were all frozen solid and were being used by the locals for skating. At home, skating on the canal would have been a very risky occupation, as the ice was rarely thick enough to support the weight of a child let alone an adult, and could never be totally relied upon even on the coldest of days.

The driver called out Valkenswaard at their request, and they alighted in the market square, which was quiet on their arrival, but on market days was alive with activity. Many of the stallholders would dress in national costume on market day, with painted clogs stuffed with newspaper in the winter, as insulation against the cold.

Clogs were still worn by some Lancashire people, but mainly confined to the older generation, traditionalists who had never worn anything else but clogs since childhood. Ray had never worn clogs as a child, as his parents, who both earned good money, could always afford to buy him shoes, but many of his less affluent classmates had no choice, as clogs were cheaper to buy and lasted much longer.

In Holland they made their clogs entirely from wood, while in Lancashire, although having a wooden sole which was clad with irons rather like a horse shoe, the tops were made from very stiff split leather, which rubbed the wearer's feet mercilessly, and caused horrendous blisters until they had been worn in.

Some of the market stall holders sold clogs, or *klompen* in the Dutch vernacular. Ray thought that *klompen* was an extremely good word for them, as people couldn't help but clump around while wearing them. They were quite often made from plain unvarnished wood, or painted red for local use, but stained and varnished with transfers of windmills for the tourists. Some had been converted to become table lamps, with a single clog representing a boat, while the elliptical lamp shade gave the appearance of a sail.

Ray had purchased one of these lamps for his mother, when as a child he had visited the Dutch town of Middleburg. Although she had professed to like it at its presentation, it had been put away in a cupboard, and had never seen the light of day from that day to this.

The market square was surrounded by some of the most important buildings of the town, and they found the 'Hotel Cordial' easily, as it was positioned close to the bus stop. The ground floor consisted of a long and narrow room, with a wooden bar which ran for half of its length along the left hand wall. It was filled with knick knacks, as appeared to be the Dutch tradition, with foreign coins glued to the bar top, while banknotes from all around the world, jostled for position with photographs of residents and visitors around the walls. Adjacent to the bar were a number of circular tables with a solitary glass ashtray on each one, and with copious quantities of beer mats, so that the drinkers would not leave rings on the highly polished table tops, while at the rear of the room the tables were not circular but square, laid with crisp white table cloths, nickel silver cutlery, and condiments for use by the diners.

There was no reception desk at which to check in, and except for a small group of elderly men who were playing cards and drinking Bols Genever, the room was completely empty. Amongst the card players, a man of late middle age, who was wearing a white shirt with dark trousers and a food stained apron around his waist, welcomed them.

"*Heir* Hillendale?" he enquired, looking directly at Ray, as he looked by far the more prosperous of the two, in his best blue suite and overcoat.

"I am *Heir* Hillendale," said Godfrey, a little peeved that he had been mistaken for the underling. "And this is *Heir* Evans;" he gestured towards Ray.

"*Heir Bos*," said the man, patting his chest so as to indicate that his name was *Heir Bos,* or Mr Forest in translation.

"Ah so you're the boss?" said Godfrey, mistaking his name for his title. The man failed to correct Godfrey's mistake, as being unable to speak any significant amount of English, he was unaware that any confusion existed.

They were very hungry as it was mid-afternoon, and with the exception of a Danish pastry consumed at the railway station in Amsterdam, they hadn't eaten all day. Godfrey tried to make *Heir Bos* understand, by pointing down his throat and saying food very loudly. *Heir Bos* wasn't at all deaf, but Godfrey, like most English people abroad, have a tendency to treat people as if they are, as it takes less effort to shout at them rather than to learn a foreign language.

"*Yah,*" said *Heir Bos*, proving the theory that shouting really does cross the language barrier, after which he disappeared through a door at the far end of the room, which Ray assumed quite correctly lead into the kitchen. Almost immediately, a much younger carbon copy of *Heir Bos* appeared through the same door, he was dressed exactly like the man who had just exited, as if the door led into some kind of age reversal chamber.

"*Heir Bos,*" he announced.

Now Godfrey really was confused, surely they couldn't both be the boss. Seeing his confusion Ray whispered into his ear.

"I think that this is probably *Heir Bos* junior, the son of *Heir Bos.*"

Godfrey turned a bright pink, as he always did when he was embarrassed, which was usually every time that anyone spoke to him.

"My father will prepare some food for you, if you would like to follow me, I will show you to your rooms so that you may freshen up."

He showed Ray to his room on the first floor, and Godfrey to a similar room three doors along the landing. The bedroom was old fashioned, with a large walnut veneered wardrobe, inlaid with marquetry tulips and chrysanthemums, and featuring two bow fronted drawers beneath mirrored doors, which were being used to store bedding.

The beautiful old wooden bed looked like Santa's sleigh, with a scroll shaped headboard in highly polished walnut veneer, and a footboard to match. It was decorated with the same floral patterns as was the wardrobe, which must once have been inlaid with highly coloured woods, but which had now faded to become almost indistinguishable in colour from each other. An old cast iron radiator, similar to the ones that Ray remembered from his school days, sat beneath one of the windows which overlooked the market square, while a second window on an adjacent wall overlooked the *Eindhovenseweg*, the road on which they had arrived, and on which they would return to Eindhoven when the time came for their departure.

The radiator was stone cold, as was the water in the one and only tap on a small washbasin, which was attached to the wall by metal brackets in the corner of the room. Ray discovered hot water in the only bathroom on the landing, which was situated a few doors from his own room and next to Godfrey's room. He had a quick hands and face wash, before meeting Godfrey downstairs for some very welcome sustenance.

Heir Bos had prepared coffee, with cream in a small white jug. Cubes of brown and white sugar jostled for position in a clear cut glass sugar bowl, with nickel silver sugar tongs laid on top. Ham and cheese, some sliced salami, and a very pink and rather rubbery meat, which Ray and Godfrey had failed to identify even after extensive discussions, was arranged neatly around a huge charger, like domino's which had toppled over.

Godfrey pointed to the rubbery looking meat, and asked *Heir Bos* if he could possibly make some kind of identification, only to be met with a blank stare. Changing tack, he worked his way around the plate pointing at each item in turn.

"Ham," suggested Godfrey.

"*Yah, ham.*" agreed *Heir Bos.*

"Cheese," pointed out Godfrey.

"*Kaas,*" corrected *Heir Bos,* thinking that what Godfrey wanted was a Dutch translation.

"Salami," said Godfrey, pointing at the pink circles with flecks in them.

"*Yah,*" agreed *Heir Bos,* feeling as if the lesson was going very well

"Meat," stressed Godfrey pointing at the pink rubber.

"*Paardenvlees*," said *Heir Bos*, happily translating into Dutch before leaving them to their meal.

Having failed to satisfy their curiosity but being ravenously hungry, they ate the questionable meat, before taking a constitutional walk around the market square before it went dark. Three doors down from the hotel they passed a butchers shop, and looking up Ray pointed out the sign to Godfrey.

"*Heir Van Der Gaag, De Paard Slager.*"

This meant nothing to Godfrey, until he noticed what Ray had already seen, the picture of a horse's head at each end of the sign.

■ ■ ■

Ray came down for his evening meal around seven, after first having had a long hot bath in the bathroom along the landing. Godfrey was already sitting at the bar, and talking to a pretty teenage girl who was serving him with drinks. She had shoulder length blonde hair, which she had tied with a black ribbon into a short pony tail. She wore a white blouse and a dark skirt, presumably to match the clothing worn by *Heir Bos* and *Heir Bos* junior, with a white apron and sensible shoes, which was obviously the uniform of the house.

"This is *Ellaweis, Heir Bos's* daughter," said Godfrey by way of introduction.

"I prefer to be called *Weis*," she said, looking at Ray through the prettiest blue eyes that he had ever seen in his life.

"I prefer to be called Ray," he said, holding out his hand for her to take. She held his hand for much longer than was sociably acceptable, until finally he reluctantly broke contact, unable to hold her gaze under the relentless scrutiny of those beautiful blue eyes.

She came out from behind the bar in order to show them to their table, explaining that this would be their table for the duration of their stay. Ray noticed that she filled her uniform to perfection in every department. Some may have said that she filled it a little too well but Ray was not one of them, as he was not usually attracted to skinny girls.

The evening meal consisted of *erwtsoep,* which turned out to be a pea-soup rather like his grandmother used to make, but with pieces of salami sausage instead of the pig's trotter which she always favoured. This was followed by *biefstuk, gebakken aardappelen en erwten,* which they managed to translate in advance of its arrival as beef-steak, and which was accompanied by chips and garden peas. Just like the homemade soup it was excellent. The final course on the menu was *aardbei ijs,* which after much wracking of brains and wild guesswork on their part, remained a mystery until the arrival of strawberry ice-cream. This would have been extremely welcome had it been summertime, but in these bitter winter temperatures, something hot with custard would have been far more appreciated.

After their meal they returned to the bar and to *Ellaweis*. It transpired from conversations with *Weis,* that during the winter months the hotel was very quiet, they being the only current guests, with the exception of an elderly German lady who lived in the hotel on a permanent basis. *Weis* explained that the family did not live in the hotel, but because of the old ladies residency, she stayed in the hotel most nights, in case the old lady, who was not in the best of health, needed assistance.

It soon became obvious that despite having a fiancé at home, Godfrey was extremely smitten by *Weis*. He dominated the conversation throughout the evening, boring everyone silly with his talk of radio signals, while *Weis* continuously flashed Ray rescue me glances. In fairness, Ray did, on a number of occasions, try to steer the conversation in a different direction, but Godfrey continually steered it back to the subject that he knew and loved the best.

At ten-thirty Ray admitted defeat, leaving *Weis* to her fate, he excused himself on the grounds that it had been a long day, and went to his bedroom to read. The old radiator was still not working and the room was freezing cold. He wasn't in the habit of wearing pyjamas in bed, in fact he hadn't even brought any with him, and sitting up in bed with a bare chest didn't appear to be an option under the circumstances. He stripped to his boxer shorts, put on a thick sweater from his suitcase for extra warmth, before climbing into bed and began to read.

He awoke around midnight to a tapping sound on his bedroom door; his book was still open at page one, indicating that he must have fallen asleep pretty much instantaneously. He went to the bedroom door feeling a little disorientated, while wondered who could possibly be knocking on his door at this hour. He didn't bother to dress, reasoning that it must be Godfrey on his way up to bed, and wanting to discuss work schedules for the following day. Opening the door only slightly at first, as he had no intention of letting Godfrey in at this hour, he was surprised to see that it wasn't Godfrey at all, but *Ellaweis* tapping at his door. Her hair was hanging loose around her shoulders, the apron had gone, and she had unfastened an extra button on her blouse.

CHAPTER FOUR

He awoke the following morning to the sound of his alarm clock. *Ellaweis* was gone. He quickly bathed in the old bathroom, wasting no time in dressing, as it was a freezing cold morning and the heat was still not on. When he entered the dining room, *Weis* was serving Godfrey with his breakfast of two lightly boiled eggs in a double egg cup, cheese and ham slices were set out on a plate in two neat rows, and there was plenty of bread and jam. Her hair was controlled once more with the black velvet band, her apron was back in place, and all of the buttons on her blouse were once again fastened.

"Good morning sir," she said formally. "How would you like your eggs?"

"Boiled for four minutes please miss," he answered equally formally.

When his eggs arrived the whites were runny and he sent them back, explaining that he would like them cooked until the whites were solid and only the yoke was runny. They appeared five minutes later looking exactly as before, admitting defeat he ate them anyway.

After breakfast Godfrey went upstairs for his briefcase, there was only the old German lady in the restaurant, and as she didn't understand a word of English they could talk freely.

"Why do you tease me?" she asked.

"You started it with the good morning sir," he replied.

"I do not mean this morning," she corrected him, "I mean last night."

He had no idea what on earth she was talking about. "I don't understand, I haven't teased you," he protested.

"Last night, you kissed me like my father would with the mouth closed," she complained.

■ ■ ■

To the best of Ray's knowledge French kissing hadn't reached popularity in East Lancashire by 1968. He had once experimented on the recommendation of a friend with disastrous results.

Goff was great with a chat up line, a master in fact. On this particular occasion he had chatted up two bottle blonds with skirts like belts, one of them looked very much like Nancy Sinatra, with long hair and wearing a tight sweater and knee length plastic boots, while the other one, who's dress and coiffure exactly matched that of her more attractive friend, looked like Nancy's ugly sister or her brother in drag, while both of them had reputations for being easy.

Goff, as usual, because he was good with the chat had bagged Nancy, while Ray had been left holding the short straw. When they had returned to Goff's flat above the salon, Ray had drawn the short straw once again. Goff had gone into the only bedroom with the attractive one, while Ray had been left on the settee with her much inferior friend.

She hadn't complained when he had felt her breasts, nor had she complained when he put his hand up her skirt, but when he had tried to force his tongue between her teeth, she had pushed him away and told him not to be so disgusting. Angry and embarrassed, he had informed her that she was an ugly bitch and that he had never wanted to kiss her anyway, before storming out of the flat, and leaving her to wait until dawn for her friend. Never the less he had been left feeling like a pervert by her comments. Since that time had been reluctant to try French kissing again.

■ ■ ■

"I'm sorry if I upset you," he apologised. "You will have to teach me how to do it properly tonight."

Her face changed from a frown to a broad smile, and she kissed him on the cheek just seconds, before Godfrey reappeared looking business like with his briefcase.

At the Valkenswaard factory *Heir Wiener* met with them in reception; he didn't look very Dutch to Ray, with olive skin, his dark wavy hair swept back, and a pencil thin moustache in the style of a 1930's movie star. He was also much shorter than Ray, while in comparison a lot of Dutch males appeared to be quite tall.

Heir Weiner was Godfrey's opposite number at the Dutch factory, although probably a decade older. He had a pleasant and welcoming manner, taking them back to his office for coffee, where he asked about the journey and the standard of the hotel accommodation, before moving on to give an overview of the Valkenswaard factory. Giving Godfrey the opportunity to comment on the Vallard factory in England, he showed much interest as they compared notes.

When they had drunk their coffee, which Ray found extremely bitter, they were given a guided tour of the factory. It was very small in comparison to the Vallard factory, which employed four thousand people, while the Valkenswaard factory probably employed less than four hundred.

They ended the tour at a small repair workshop, which housed three or four control panels in various states of repair or modification. A handsome young man in his late twenties was hard at work; he also had dark hair, but not the same dark complexion as *Heir Weiner,* and he was over six feet tall. He wore a brown nylon smock, similar to the one worn by Ray at the Vallard factory, except that the badge on the pocket was completely different.

Heir Wiener introduced him to Ray and Godfrey.

"This is *Heir Peeters* our electronics repair man," he said.

"*Heir Peeters,* meet *Heir* Hillendale and *Heir* Evans from England."

Heir Peeters greeted them warmly in excellent English, before *Heir Wiener* turned his attentions to Ray.

"You will be working with *Heir Peeters* for the next week repairing the delay line machines. We will meet again at lunch time, when we will all dine together at a restaurant in the square where lunch has been arranged," and with that he turned and left the workshop taking Godfrey with him.

"Have you brought tools and an overall?" asked *Heir Peeters*.

Ray had been expecting some kind of conventional training, if not in a classroom situation, he had at least expected full time one to one tuition, perhaps watching repairs taking place, and pouring over diagrams in quieter moments. He had not anticipated having to work for his bread and butter and he was taken aback.

"I wasn't told that I would need to," he protested lamely.

"I will get you an overall and you must borrow my tools, please." said *Heir Peeters* obligingly.

Returning with a brown nylon smock exactly like his own, but in approximately Ray's size, he gave Ray a circuit diagram written in Dutch, and set him to work repairing one of the machine panels. Ray was dumb struck; he hadn't a clue how to repair the panel, or even read the diagram for that matter. Had he been able to, there would have been little point in the visit to the Dutch factory at all. He wondered if he should complain to *Heir Wiener*, but decided on reflection that it might be better to speak to Godfrey first.

Lunch was booked each day at a café, which was only a few doors away from the Hotel Cordial and next door to the horse butcher. The menu of ham and cheese, salami sausage, and horse meat, was the staple diet each day, although a different soup with crusty bread began each meal. Managing to get Godfrey on his own he told him of his dilemma. Godfrey turned a bright red, as he often did when faced with a problem that he would rather not have to solve, or a person that he would rather not have to deal with.

"Don't make waves," he said, "just pick up what information you can, and we'll sort everything out when we get back."

This didn't make Ray feel any better, he had been hoping for a little more support, but on reflection he should have known not to expect anything more from Godfrey.

■ ■ ■

Godfrey met Ray in the repair workshop at five o'clock; he'd had a good day, having spent the whole of it in *Heir Wieners* office discussing technical manuals and drinking coffee, two of his favourite occupations. Ray hadn't had a good day and he wanted to discuss his work problems, but Godfrey just wanted to talk about *Weis*.

"I think that she likes me," he said. "Last night we talked until nearly midnight and we got on really well. Do you think that she likes me?" he asked.

Ray wondered if he should enlighten Godfrey as to the facts of life, especially as Godfrey had really pissed him off, but on reflection he decided against it.

"I don't know," he said disinterestedly, "I went to bed at ten remember."

When they arrived back at the Hotel Cordial, *Weis* was in the bar serving the card players with drinks. Both men said hello, and Godfrey blushed before going upstairs to wash and change for dinner.

The evening was a repeat performance of the previous day, with Godfrey talking once more about radio signals, and repeating his conversations of the day with *Heir Wiener*. Ray and *Weis* managed to snatch a moment alone when Godfrey went to the toilet.

"Is he always such a boring man?" she asked, breathing out heavily, as if she had been unable to breathe while he had been in the room.

"He thinks that you fancy him," giggled Ray.

"I don't understand fancy." She looked puzzled.

"He thinks that you are attracted to him," translated Ray.

"I could never be attracted to *Heir Hillendale*," she said and gave a shudder.

"He is boring, and not a very good looking man."

"What type of man are you attracted to?" queried Ray expectantly.

"You have a mirror in your bedroom," she said with a smile. "I suggest that you look into it."

As Godfrey reappeared Ray changed the subject and asked about the lack of heating in his bedroom.

"My father does not put on the heating until it is winter," she informed him.

"How much winter does there need to be, the ice is a foot thick on the canal and people are skating?" complained Ray.

"My father says that winter begins in December, but if you would like me to talk to him, I could tell him that the English softies would like on the heating."

It was the twenty-ninth of November, one more day, two more nights, and the heating would be on, he lent forward while Godfrey was distracted and whispered in her ear.

"I can wait until Thursday for the heating to come on if you promise to keep me warm in the meantime."

When Godfrey continued the conversation where he had previously left off, Ray decided to have another early night. It was ten-thirty and the card players were beginning to leave the hotel. The old German lady hadn't made an appearance all evening, and Ray figured that if he went to bed early Godfrey might decide that it was time to do the same. She would then be able close up the bar and join him in his room.

He sat up in bed wearing his sweater as insulation against the cold and awaited her arrival. He read for a short while until he unwittingly fell asleep, waking the following morning still sitting up in bed with the book in his hand.

Weis hadn't made an appearance, and he wondered what he had done to offend her on this occasion. He remembered how annoyed she had been with him about the French kissing, or the lack of it, was she annoyed with him this time because he had left her to cope with Godfrey alone. She wasn't at breakfast either, and Godfrey it turned out, hadn't seen her since going to bed soon after Ray, so why hadn't she come to his room?

Heir Bos appeared to be the waiter as well as the chief cook and bottle washer at breakfast. Ray wanted to ask him what had happened to *Weis*, but he didn't want to tip off the old man to their relationship, and in any case, conversations with *Heir Bos* were extremely difficult due to the language barrier, and usually ended in total confusion. He worked throughout the day, his thoughts wandering to *Weis* and what he might have done to upset her.

Tuesday was a little better at work; *Heir Peeters* was more talkative, and a little more helpful than he had been the previous day, when he had appeared to be very busy and a little under pressure. He told Ray that he was married with two small children; both of them girls, but that they were hoping for a boy next time. He rented his home, which appeared to be the norm in *Valkenswaard,* and he owned a yellow Daff 600 car, which he showed to Ray at morning break. He explained proudly that it was the world's first belt driven car with continuously variable transmission. Ray pretended to be impressed, but on appearances he couldn't help thinking that the original owner may well have been Noddy.

They lunched at the same café in the market square, while after lunch, Godfrey had to leave for Amsterdam in order to catch an evening flight back to England.

Weis was not in the bar when Ray returned to the hotel at five o'clock, and he asked her brother, who was now on duty, where she was.

"She will be down in half an hour to cycle to her English class in Eindhoven," he answered.

Ray bought a small beer and waited in the bar until she appeared. When she came down he followed her outside.

"Why didn't you come to my room last night?" he asked her apprehensively, in case he was in any trouble.

"Did you miss me?" she responded cheerily.

"Is the Pope a Catholic?" he remarked.

"Of course the Pope is a Catholic, why are you talking about the Pope?" she asked totally confused.

"Forget about the Pope, what happened to you last night?" he wanted to know.

"*Frau Muller* was taken ill in the night," she answered. "I had to send for the doctor and sit with her until morning. I have been in bed for most of the day trying to catch up with my sleep."

"I thought that I had done something to upset you again," said Ray, the relief showing in his countenance even though poor *Frau Muller* had been taken ill.

"No not this time," she laughed, as she retrieved her bicycle from a multitude of other bicycles, which were parked in racks outside of the hotel.

"Does everyone in Holland ride a push bike?" Ray asked, changing the subject.

"What is a push bike?" again she looked puzzled by his adjective.

"Sorry, I mean a bicycle."

"Why do you call it a push bike?" she asked.

He thought for a moment, never having considered the origin of the adjective before. When the concept of pushing the pedals in order to propel the vehicle failed to materialise, he made up his own explanation.

"Where I live in the north of England," he explained, "It isn't flat as it is here in Holland. Because it's very hilly and hard to peddle up the hills, you have to push your bicycle more than you can ride it."

He wasn't trying to be funny, in fact he was trying to give her the most rational explanation that he could think of, but she became hysterical with laughter and fell off her bicycle. She put her hands on his shoulders to stop herself from falling, and as he put his arm around her waist to steady her, their lips came together. He remembered to part his lips, and he felt her tongue slip between them and explore the inside of his mouth.

"That is much better," she said; "but you will still need more practice tonight."

She picked up her bicycle.

"I will return around nine-thirty," she called, as she rode off down the *Eindhovenseweg* towards Eindhoven, looking back just once she give him a cheery wave.

■ ■ ■

After a solitary evening meal, Ray decided to explore one or two of the bars in the market square before *Weis* returned. He entered the first bar and ordered himself a large beer. The barman filled a glass with one quarter beer and three quarters froth, before placing it on the bar before him. Ray waited for the froth to settle, expecting the barman to fill it up, but he just wiped the froth from the top of the glass with a wooden paddle, and pushed it forward.

"Is that it?" asked Ray.

"Good top yah?" replied the barman, looking pleased with his efforts and expecting Ray to feel the same way.

"To hell with good top," said Ray angrily. "Fill the bugger up."

"*Engels*," announced the barman loudly.

Everyone in the bar nodded and sighed knowingly, as if that explained Ray's strange behaviour.

In Amsterdam the announcement of *Engels* wouldn't have even raised an eyebrow. Here in this small market town it caused quite a stir amongst the half dozen or so male customers, who came to the bar to escape from their wives for a couple of hours after work, and to drown the sorrows of the day.

One of the men, who sat alone on a barstool at the opposite end of the bar, moved closer to Ray and in very good English asked.

"What part of England do you come from?"

"Lancashire," answered Ray, generalising so as not to cause too much confusion.

"Is that near to London?" the man queried.

He decided that it would be too complicated to explain that Lancashire was a county and not a town or city, and so he picked the name of a city some twenty miles from his home, which he expected his new companion to recognise.

"No, it's near to Manchester."

"Ah, Manchester United; Bobby Charlton; Georgie Best; Dennis Law," and then the Dutchman ran out of all of the names that he could recall.

Ray felt obligated to buy his new found friend a drink, in exchange for this scintillating piece of conversation. He pulled out a few coins, threw them onto the bar counter, and ordered a small beer for his companion. Pretty soon he had six new best friends, all firing questions about England and Manchester United, but even though their motives were blatantly mercenary, after two nights of radio signals with Godfrey, Ray was more than glad of the company.

He left the bar at ten o'clock and staggered back to the Hotel Cordial. *Weis* was behind the bar and she looked at him sternly, as a mother would when chastising a naughty boy. He ordered himself another beer but she gave him a black coffee instead.

"Drink that and then go to bed and sleep it off," she said.

"Will you come and tuck me in?" He asked, trying to wink but failing dismally.

She tried hard to be annoyed with him, but found it difficult to conceal a smile.

"If you drink your coffee and go straight to bed, I will call to see if you are asleep when I come up."

"And what if I'm still awake?" he asked hopefully.

"Then we will have to see," she replied.

■ ■ ■

Thursday was her day off, and they arranged to go to the cinema in Eindhoven, to see the Lionel Bart musical Oliver. Unfortunately, being her day off meant that he wouldn't see her at breakfast or at dinner, and worst of all she wouldn't be sleeping at the hotel, as her brother would be standing in for her.

He had arranged for an early evening meal with *Heir Bos,* and she arrived in the hotel bar at seven o' clock in order to meet him. She was wearing a long red winter coat and a red beret, which went beautifully with her blonde hair. She opened the coat and did a twirl. Under the coat, she wore a white polo neck sweater and a very short red mini skirt, with white knee length boots.

"How do I look?" she asked.

He had only ever seen her when she had been wearing her uniform, and of course when she hadn't, which he had to admit he had enjoyed immensely, but he had never seen her dressed up and in full makeup before.

"You look fantastic," he replied, and he really meant it.

She had told her father about the date, and so it went without saying, that the card school of old men had also been kept in the picture. As they were leaving for the cinema, there were lots of nudges and winks. Ray didn't know what was being said, as it was all in the Dutch vernacular, but some of the teasing made *Weis* blush, so that her face became almost indistinguishable from the colour of her coat.

Ray was expecting the film dialogue to be dubbed into Dutch, but as he didn't intend to watch it anyway, it hardly seemed to be of any importance. He was surprised therefore to find that the film was actually in English with Dutch subtitles. He was even more surprised to find that *Weis* insisted on watching the film, only allowing him to hold her hand throughout the whole evening.

Lionel Bart had made a brilliant musical from a classic story by Charles Dickens, and Ray came out of the cinema feeling proud to be British, so proud in fact, that if he had been in possession of a Union Jack he would have gladly waved it.

After the film she took him to a dance hall not very far away from the cinema, where records by British bands like the Merseybeats, the Hollies, and Procal Harem were played. The DJ, who was of Indonesian descent, with long crinkly black hair which hung down to his waist, announced all of the record titles in English. While watching the DJ, Ray had a revelation. The reason that *Heir Wiener* didn't look very Dutch was that he was in fact Indonesian, or at least Dutch-Indonesian.

"Why doesn't he speak in Dutch?" asked Ray.

"Because he thinks that it sounds much better in English," she told him.

"Do people understand him?" he enquired.

"Not everyone," she answered. "But that doesn't matter because they also think that it sounds better in English."

They danced to Gerry and the Pacemakers, Herman's Hermits, and Freddie and the Dreamers, before the Indonesian DJ played Barry Ryan singing Ellaweis. Ray had heard the song a number of times before, as it had been released in England in October, but *Weis* had never heard it before, and became very excited that someone had recorded a song using her name as a song title.

They stayed for just over an hour, until at midnight they hailed a taxi, as they both had to be up early for work the following morning. When Ray entered his bedroom the heating was finally on, but he would have exchanged the hot radiator in a second if *Weis* could have been there to share his bed.

■ ■ ■

The following morning Ray was summoned to the office of *Heir Wiener*. He had stopped coming out to lunch as soon as Godfrey had left for England, and Ray hadn't seen him at all for a couple of days. He asked Ray to sit down and arranged for two of the ubiquitous bitter coffees to be brought in.

"How is everything?" he asked, but before Ray could reply he continued, "*Heir Peeters* tells me that you are finding it difficult to learn."

Ray was embarrassed, as he was not used to being labelled a failure. At school he had been captain of his house, head of school, and the captain of the school football team, while after leaving school, he had been awarded apprentice of the year prizes from both his employer and his local tertiary college. He was also the youngest electrician to have been made responsible for the maintenance of a production area, at just twenty one years of age, a job usually reserved for the older and more experienced men. It was time to air his concerns.

"To be truthful, I haven't been happy with the training that I have received whilst I have been here," he began.

"I never expected to be asked to repair the delay-line machines the moment that I arrived, especially as I have only been given diagrams and manuals in Dutch, which I can't of course read. To be brutally frank, I may as well have stayed at home for all of the good this visit as been to me."

Heir Weiner looked a little taken aback.

"I'm so sorry to hear that you are unhappy with the training, but as you will have noticed *Heir Peeters* has been very busy this week and has possibly not had enough time to spend with you. As for the manuals, I was totally unaware that the information that you have been given was not translated into English. I will provide you with some translated material, which you can take back to England with you when you leave."

With that *Heir Weiner* quickly changed the subject, as this was not how he planned that the conversation would go.

"Now that *Heir Hillendale* has gone home and you are alone, my wife and I would like to invite you to our home this evening for a meal. Later, if you would like, we can go to play bingo at our local social club."

Obviously *Heir Weiner* was unaware that Ray did have company, and very pleasant company indeed, but Ray thought that it was a nice gesture on his behalf, and as *Weis* was at her German classes until nine o' clock, he thanked him kindly and accepted the invitation.

■ ■ ■

Heir Weiner picked him up at his hotel an hour after the work day had finished. He'd had just enough time to inform *Heir Bos* that he would be out for dinner, before he had bathed and changed. *Frau Weiner* had prepared a lovely meal for them and it was nice to be in a domestic environment once again. It was hard to believe that he had only been away from home for five days, as already it felt has though he had never lived anywhere else but in the Hotel Cordial.

The *Weiner's* had two children, the oldest of which was a girl of eight, who excited at having a foreigner to dinner, talked incessantly in a mixture of primary school English and Dutch. The youngest child, a boy of four, was shy and withdrawn until after dinner, when he suddenly became more confident and brought out a jigsaw puzzle for Ray to play with.

The picture on the box was of Hansel and Gretel eating the gingerbread house, with the wicked witch peering at them through the window. Ray had a good deal of sympathy for the witch, who when you think about it, was a lonely old lady living all alone in the woods and minding her own business, when a couple of brats suddenly appeared and started eating her house. The jigsaw puzzle consisted of twenty or so large pieces made from transfer printed wood, which Ray started to assemble. As soon as the picture began to materialise the boy took the initiative. Quickly fitting in the missing pieces, he turned towards Ray and smiled broadly, looking extremely pleased with his efforts.

Heir Weiner rescued Ray by giving him a guided tour of the house. It was a pleasant but very ordinary looking house, not unlike the house that Ray himself lived in, but as home ownership appeared to be relatively rare, *Heir Weiner* was very proud of his achievement, just as his son had been moments earlier on completion of the jigsaw puzzle.

As soon as the baby sitter arrived to relieve them, they all set out to play bingo, which was held in what appeared to be some kind of church hall. They each paid an admission fee, which entitled them to four bingo tickets and a bottle of beer. Ray had never been fond of bingo, as he considered it to be a game for old ladies, but he had to admit he did like a beer.

The hall was filling up fast, and *Heir Wiener* managed to find them seats near to some of his friends. Ray sat between *Heir Wiener* and *Heir Van Der Vaalk,* a friend of *Heir Wiener's* who spoke only broken English with a strong American accent. When Ray enquired if he had acquired his accent while living in the USA, *Heir Van Der Vaalk* explained that he had taught himself to speak American, as he put it, by watching television shows like Mr. Ed, I Married Joan, and I Love Lucy. They had barely settled into their seats when the bingo began.

"*Drie en vier, vierendertig,*" announced the caller.

"*Een en zes, zestien.*"

Because English and Dutch numbers looked exactly the same in print, Ray had expected the numbers to be called out in English, especially as other entertainments had favoured the English language to Dutch, and he looked to *Heir Wiener* for assistance.

"Thirty-four and sixteen," he said, recognising Ray's bewilderment.

Heir Wiener continued to translate until the interval, and Ray was glad that he hadn't won, as he would have hated to have had to call house and draw attention to himself.

At the interval everyone formed an orderly queue; to purchase a further four tickets and a subsequent bottle of beer for the second half. *Heir Wiener* took the opportunity to visit the toilet, and while he was away the bingo resumed, necessitating translations from *Heir Van Der Vaalk* in his absence.

Twee kleine eendjes," shouted the caller and everyone quacked.

"Two small birds, two," was *Heir Van Der Vaalk's* inaccurate translation, although Ray had recognised that the number was twenty-two, because of the quacking which was taking place around the auditorium.

"Een en Negen, negentien."

"Ninety-one," said *Heir Van Der Vaalk,* even though ninety-one did not exist on Ray's bingo card, or on anyone else's card for that matter, and the translation should in fact have been nineteen.

Some of the English speaking people sitting nearby began to giggle.

"Een en een, elf," shouted the caller.

"Two little ones," translated *Heir Van Der Vaalk,* for what should have been eleven.

Other people had started to take notice because of the giggling, and soon the giggling turned into laughter, and the laughter became louder, until the hall was in an uproar and the house had to be abandoned until everyone had calmed down.

When Ray returned to the hotel he had expected to find *Weis* behind the bar, as her German class had finished at nine o'clock and it was now well after ten. The bar-room was completely empty except for the presence of her brother, who was drinking a black coffee and waiting for Ray to return, so that he could lock up the hotel for the night.

"Where is *Weis* tonight?" asked Ray, puzzled as to why she wasn't there.

"My father is not happy for her to stay in the hotel while you are staying here," replied *Heir Bos* junior." He knows that you are attracted to each other, and so she must stay at his house until you leave tomorrow."

If it was her father's intention to keep her *"Virgo intacto,"* then he was a little too late, but because of their high profile date at the cinema, they had revealed their hand in a monumental way. *Heir Bos* had now closed the stable door even though the horse had already bolted several nights ago, and probably not for the first time, as she had required very little persuasion.

■ ■ ■

Saturday was market day in the square, and Ray spent the morning shopping for presents and soaking up the atmosphere. He bought a wooden jewellery box encrusted with shells for his mother; exactly like the one that he had purchase for his grandmother on his previous visit to Holland. His mother had always admired it, and since his grandmother's demise she had used it to destruction. The hinges had broken so that the lid balanced precariously on top of her fake pearls, and many of the shells had broken off and gone missing, leaving an imprint into what may well have been plaster of Paris.

His father had recently given up smoking cigarettes, preferring instead to smoke a pipe, which aided him in the early stages of his withdrawal symptoms. Ray purchased a rather ornate and very Dutch looking meerschaum pipe, to add to the collection of five or six other more ordinary looking pipes, which he kept in a brass-bound oak Victorian smoking cabinet on the sideboard.

When Ray returned to the hotel in order to pack his suitcase, *Weis* was serving lunch. It was obvious that she had been crying. It was also obvious that she was unhappy with her father, as there was an atmosphere between them whenever they were in the same room together.

"What time is your train?" she asked.

"Half past two," he replied.

"You will need to catch the two o'clock bus into Eindhoven; I will come with you to the bus stop," she volunteered.

■ ■ ■

Roy A. Higgins

They clung to each other while they waited at the bus stop. She had tears in eyes already red from an earlier bout of crying, and made him promise that he would write as soon as he arrived home, but deep down inside, both of them knew that he never would.

CHAPTER FIVE

The bus passed the skaters on the canal on its return journey to the railway station. Even though they were skating in huge numbers, while wearing multi-coloured bobble hats and scarves, Ray hardly noticed them as his thoughts were with the Hotel Cordial and *Weis*.

The train was on time just as it had been on the outward journey, and he settled down for the long return trip to Amsterdam. He had slept for most of the way from Amsterdam to Eindhoven, and resolved this time to take in the scenery while it was still light. Although he tried his best to become interested in what he saw, he soon bored of the flat Dutch landscape, and decided that he would read his book instead.

After an hour of reading, it became very difficult for him to concentrate on the pages. He found himself reading them over and over in an effort to follow the story, until he gave in and once again fell asleep.

When he awoke it was already dark and the train was pulling into a station. He saw the letters "AMSTE" flash past his window, and forgetting that Amsterdam was the terminus in his drowsy state, he panicked, and jumped off the train with his suitcase and overcoat over his arm, only to find that he was not at *Amsterdam Centraal Station* at all, but in Amsterdam Amstel, a station on the outskirts of Amsterdam to the south-west and named after the river Amstel, necessitating a wait of some thirty minutes in freezing cold temperatures, and with snowflakes falling, for the next train heading to Amsterdam.

He was booked in at the *Rode Leeuw* or Red Lion, which he had been told was on the *Damrak,* which as it turned out was not difficult to find, for as he came out of Amsterdam Central Station the *Damrak* stretched out directly before him.

The *Damrak* appeared to be the main road of Amsterdam, with many of the large stores and hotels along its length. Trams ran up and down the *Damrak* to and from the railway station, and with hindsight he wished that he had caught one, as it turned out to be a long walk when carrying a heavy suitcase.

The hotel was a very different proposition to the Hotel Cordial. In contrast, this hotel had a large reception desk, with a number of attractive female receptionists wearing navy business suites and red cravats. Uniformed porters wearing pork pie hats were fighting with each other for the suitcases of guests, so as to enhance their meagre salaries by way of tips.

There appeared to be no staircase in the reception area, and the porter took his suitcase straight into the lift. The lift operator, who sat on a high stool, enquired of the porter in English which floor sir would like. Ray quickly learned that he was expected to tip, not only the porter for carrying his suitcase, but also the lift operator on every single occasion that he travelled in the lift. With this realisation he resolved not to travel in the lift more often than was absolutely necessary.

His room turned out to be extremely spacious, with a king size double bed, a sitting area with two comfortable looking arm chairs, a coffee table, tea and coffee making facilities, a mini bar, and a bathroom with a separate shower. The decor was modern but impersonal in neutral creams and white, with pictures on the wall so boring that no one ever even noticed what they depicted. A single chocolate had been left on each pillow of the bed, and so he made a cup of coffee, sat down in one of the comfortable armchairs and devoured them both.

After drinking his coffee, he unpacked his suitcase and went into the shower, the water was hot, and in contrast to the washbasin at the Hotel Cordial, with its single cold tap, was quite a luxury. Having finished his shower he dressed for dinner, putting on his best blue suit and a pair of suede Chelsea boots, which although currently the height of fashion in England, had not impressed *Weis,* who had expressed her dislike, by asking him in her usual blunt way why he always wore brothel creepers. *Weis* could be honest to the point of being rude, and her criticism of his new shoes had offended him, but the recollection made him smile as he pulled them on.

He still hadn't found a staircase other than the one marked fire escape, which on further inspection failed to lead into the reception area, but instead to a door with a push bar which lead into an alleyway and out onto the street, and was obviously not intended to be used by hotel guests, except of course in the case of an emergency. As it didn't offer him an alternative to using the lift he was forced to make other plans, which included taking his overcoat with him into the restaurant, and purchasing a packet of chewing gum at a nearby newsagents shop, so as to avoid the necessity of returning to his room in order to clean his teeth after meals.

He was given an English language menu in the restaurant, choosing white bait for a starter, mainly because he had never tried it before, while for his main course he chose *Weiner schnitzel* for the very same reason. He wasn't keen on either of his choices, and so he played it safe and ordered apple pie and cream for his sweet, which turned out to be Dutch apple pie made from tiny crab-apples and damsons, but very tasty none the less.

He had heard a lot about Amsterdam's prostitutes, who he had been told sat in illuminated windows in order to ply their trade, they were quite a tourist attraction he had been told, and he wanted to see them for himself. He had no idea in which direction he would find them, and being too embarrassed to ask, he turned right outside of his hotel and walked up the *Damrak,* which proved to be the wrong direction to take entirely.

Ray felt uneasy and not for the first time. Since the moment that he had arrived in Amsterdam he had been convinced that he was being followed, although he had no reason whatsoever to think so. He had turned around suddenly on a number of occasions, expecting to spot a familiar face in the crowds, although he never spotted anyone who he recognised as ever having seen before. He told himself that he was being paranoid, but still the feeling persisted, growing stronger to the point where he was convinced that he would be mugged, if he strayed ever so slightly from the tourist route, and swore that he would be careful to stay among the crowds in the more brightly lit areas of the city.

After a long walk, he left the *Damrak* and following the crowds he found himself in *Rembrandtplein*, a square which had little connection to the great man himself, other than that his statue occupied the gardens in the very centre of the square, which was surrounded by bars, restaurants, and clubs, with enormous doormen resembling gorillas in evening suits, cajoling people to enter their establishments as they passed.

At first he resisted the carefully rehearsed sales pitches; a little scared, and rightly so, that he would be taken advantage of, but finally after a full circuit of the square, feeling cold and needing a drink, he succumbed to the pressure and accepted the very next invitation.

The doorman, who followed him into the club, insisted on helping him off with his overcoat, which he then spirited away so that Ray could not make a speedy exit. The club consisted of a single room some twenty feet square, with a curved bar in one corner which took up a quarter of the room. Bench seating surrounded the remainder of the walls, while a few tables and chairs increased the seating capacity to some forty or fifty people. It was quiet and dark, taking Ray a few seconds for his eyes to adjust to the poor lighting conditions. Five or six men sat dotted around the room in the shadows, all of them alone just as he himself was.

He went up to the bar, which was the only illuminated area in the room, and ordered a beer.

"Shorts only," grunted the barman.

"Bacardi and coke then," Ray grunted back.

After paying an extortionate price for his drink, he sat on a high stool at the bar. The barman reached under the counter and the lights in the centre of the room came on. Almost immediately a door opened, and a young girl came out and began to dance in the centre of the room. She couldn't have been more than sixteen or seventeen years of age, and was wearing a red cowboy hat, cowboy boots, a red leather waistcoat with tassels, a similarly coloured leather bikini top, and leather chaps, also with tassels, which showed her cheeky little bottom through cut outs at the rear. Around her wrists she wore red leather cuffs.

In Ray's limited experience, most of the strippers who labelled themselves exotic dancers only wiggled while removing their clothing, but this girl could dance. Twirling a lasso she jumped in and out of the loop, sending it up to the top of her head and then down again to her ankles repeatedly. At one stage she dropped the loop over Ray's head and pulled it tightly around his chest, trapping both of his arms to his sides. She danced away backwards holding the loose end of the rope, before shortening the distance between them once again using climbing hand movements along the rope. When she reached Ray she wiggled her small breasts in his face, before releasing him from his captivity.

Removing her leather cuffs, she dropped them one by one onto the floor at Ray's feet. This was followed after lengthy teasing by the removal of the waistcoat. The chaps came off with one almighty tug to reveal a red leather G-string, before she teased the onlookers by placing her thumbs inside of the G-string, inching it up and down a number of times in order to tantalise the audience. The leather bra finally came off to reveal her not yet fully formed breasts, while after removing the boots, she danced for a short while wearing only the cowboy hat and a red leather G-string.

Ray had been to strip clubs on bachelor nights with the boys from work; the strippers there had bared their breasts readily enough, but if they removed their G-strings at all, they immediately covered their genital area with a hand or a prop before anything could be witnessed. Ray was resigned to the fact that her act was as good as over, expecting the music to stop at any minute and then she would be gone.

Her hair was still hidden beneath the cowboy hat, which she removed in order to cover herself, as she dropped the G-string onto the floor after first waving it triumphantly around her head. Her hair was long and as she removed the hat, it tumbled down into the small of her back. It was chestnut brown and completely natural in colour, as Ray was able to verify by comparison from his privileged vantage point.

The music stopped, the lights went out, and everyone clapped politely. Instead of the girl disappearing through the door from which she had entered however, she crossed the room in the darkness and sat naked on the barstool next to Ray. He had watched her happily as she danced, enjoying every minute, but now he found himself embarrassed to look at her, even though he wanted to do so very badly.

"Would you like to buy me a drink?" she asked in English.

It was obvious that she had been briefed as to his whereabouts, and also that he was English. Perhaps she had been chosen to dance for him deliberately because she spoke English so well.

The doorman who had enticed Ray to come into the club in the first place, now came across to the girl carrying a silk dressing gown. As she got up from the stool, she gave Ray one last look at what was on offer as she put on the dressing gown, leaving it wide open at the front as she flicked her long hair over the collar. The doorman stood guard until Ray had ordered the drink that she had requested, before moving away. The drink, which was green and served in a wine glass, appeared to Ray to be either crème de menthe or chartreuse, which in either case should have been a green liqueur. Ray had once tried one or the other in England, were it had been served flaming like the brandy on a Christmas pudding, and he had foolishly burned his mouth on the glass, not realising that it would have been heated up by the flame.

There was no way that this drink would light, because although he had paid an extortionate price for it, this was not a spirit at all, but a green peppermint drink affectionately known by the girls as green sticky. The girls were expected to extract the cost of an expensive drink from every customer, and crème de menthe was easily assimilated.

Greta was of Eastern European origin. She had always wanted to be a dancer from the age of three, when she had begun to take her first dancing classes. When she was younger she had harboured dreams of joining the Bolshoi Ballet, but having failed to make the grade she had been forced to work in less exhorted circles. Thinking that she would be beginning her dancing career in the chorus line of a major show, she had responded to an advertisement in her home country for dancers to work in the capitals of Europe, but now found herself forced into stripping in order to pay off her exorbitant travel and boarding expenses.

"I have a room upstairs if you are looking for a good time," she announced to Ray quite out of the blue.

Ray wasn't expecting to be propositioned, he thought that the scam was charming him into buying overpriced drinks, not realising until this moment, that she had also been forced into prostitution to pay for her overpriced lodgings.

She was very beautiful; her lifestyle hadn't had time to take its toll on her youthful body and pretty face, and he was extremely tempted to take her up on her offer, but considering the extortionate price of the drinks, it made him wary of how much he might have to pay for Greta's private services, and what might happen to him if he couldn't afford to pay the bill. He hoped that he wouldn't get her into any kind of trouble, but after serious reflection, he decided that the best course of action was to reluctantly decline her offer.

Another punter had entered the club while they had been talking, and soon the lights came on again to herald the next stripper. Greta left her expensive drink untouched on the bar beside Ray, and silently slipped away.

The new stripper was twice the age of Greta, probably in her mid thirties. She was dressed as a Turkish belly dancer, and Ray waited until the last of her seven veils had fallen to the floor before finishing his drink, retrieving his overcoat, and walking out from the warm smoky atmosphere of the club and into the cold fresh air of the street.

He decided that under no circumstances was he going to be enticed into another of the seedy clubs around the square, and ignoring the calls from doormen for him to enter their premises, he walked around the square until he came to what appeared to be a regular bar and entered.

It was a huge, but very old fashioned building, which had not been modernised since Victorian times. It had a high nicotine stained ceiling, with half a dozen large and opulent, but very dusty chandeliers hanging from it. Some charitable people may have called it faded splendour, while others with a less romantic view may have called it scruffy.

Most of the occupants of the bar were also faded, or scruffy, depending on the observer's viewpoint, and were mainly of the male gender, with long unwashed hair with beards to match, and wearing ex-army greatcoats and fingerless gloves, rather like Ron Moody's Fagan, who Ray had seen only days earlier with *Weis*. They were predominantly young people, almost all of them in their teens and early twenties, and a few even wore wide brimmed hats similar to the one worn by Fagan in the film. At that moment, he wished that he had once again been watching Oliver with *Weis* rather than drinking in this tatty bar, all alone and in a strange and scary city.

When Vallard had informed him that his flight home wasn't until Monday morning, offering him the choice of staying at the Hotel Cordial over the weekend, or spending the weekend in Amsterdam, he had jumped at the chance of seeing Amsterdam. That was before he had met with *Weis,* and with hindsight he now wished that he had taken the alternative option.

Once he had accustomed himself to the atmosphere of the place, he realised that transactions were taking place on almost every table. Everyone appeared to own a small folding brass weigh scale, which was kept in an inside pocket of the greatcoat. Some of the Fagin look-alikes were in negotiations with rather better dressed individuals, as they weighed out white powder on their scales, before paying for it with dirty crumpled notes. Before Ray could reach the bar to buy a drink he was surrounded by addicts, who mistaking him for a drug dealer, pestered him relentlessly for drugs no matter how loudly he protested his non-ownership of the commodity. He finally left the bar without buying a drink, deciding that he was in the wrong part of town, he abandoned the square to the drug addicts and the dirty macintosh brigade.

He retraced his steps passing a couple of cinemas on the way, and wondered if he should go in rather than run the gauntlet of any more seedy bars and clubs. Shalaco was playing at the first one, with Sean Connery and Bridget Bardot, while Barbarella was playing at another. He had heard that Jane Fonda did a striptease in Barbarella, which he would like to have witnessed, while Bridget Bardot was as far as Ray was concerned the sexiest woman on the planet, but he decided that he had come to see Amsterdam and not a film.

On the *Damrak,* he found a bar with very loud music and the sound of people emanating from within. When he tried to peer through the window however, his view was blocked by a heavy burgundy velvet curtain, supported by a brass pole situated half way up the window frame, and although he stood on tiptoe and even jumped into the air, he failed to see over it, which should have served as a deterrent but it didn't. Taking pot luck he entered a hallway and was greeted by another huge doorman, who once again took his coat and hid it so that it was impossible for him to leave. Being directed towards a doorway halfway down the hall he entered the main room, only to find that the crowd scene, along with the music was all taped, and with the exception of the barman, and two bar girls who were hustling a couple of Russian sailors to buy them drinks, he was faced with an empty room.

The girls were employed by the establishment to boost the bar takings, as Greta had done only half an hour earlier, and may well have been offering the same special services that she had offered. Ray was glad that they were already busy, and although he very much wanted to leave he ordered a beer, as he was worried that he may never see his overcoat again if he didn't.

A few minutes later a man entered the bar, and although the barroom was almost empty, he chose to sit on a barstool beside Ray. He was short, middle aged, but although his hair was receding there was no sign of grey; in fact it was a rather unnatural auburn colour and Ray thought that it was probably dyed. The man's face looked crumpled like an unmade bed, while his waist line had expanded over the years from overeating, and too many nights spent in bars. He ordered a drink in fluent Dutch before speaking to Ray in perfect English.

"You are from England are you not?" he questioned.

"Yes I am," answered Ray, wondering how he could possibly have known.

"I am from Russia, my name is Vladimir."

"Ray," Ray answered and they shook hands.

"Do you work here in Holland, or are you here for your pleasure?" asked the Russian.

"I've been working in the south, but I'm in Amsterdam for pleasure until I return to England on Monday," answered Ray.

"What kind of work do you do?" asked Vladimir, apparently making small talk.

"I work in electronics, for a firm making components for televisions and radios," replied Ray, while wishing that the man would go away and pester someone else.

"Electronics is the future," Vladimir continued. "The Soviet Union needs comrades from the west with technological knowledge and new ideas."

Ray began to feel uncomfortable, the cold war was at its height, films and television were full of spy stories involving the Soviets, and calling him comrade sent a shiver up his spine.

"Why are you in Amsterdam?" Ray asked, but not really wanting to know.

Vladimir leaned forward and whispered as if it were of national importance, "I am the chief of security at a Soviet radio station here in Amsterdam," he answered. "I have been here for almost three years."

As he leaned forward, the jacket of his brown double breasted suit sagged open, and Ray caught a glimpse of a small calibre handgun in a polished brown leather holster beneath his armpit.

The sailors had left the bar and the bar girls descended on Ray and Vladimir like vultures. Ray was under the impression that he was obliged to buy the girls a drink in order to avoid trouble with the management, and so he chatted to her in a friendly way while she nuzzled into his neck and nibbled at his ear, Vladimir on the other hand had no such illusions, shouting angrily at them in what appeared to be Dutch. The girls left with their tails between their legs, going back to their original seats at the opposite end of the bar. Ray waited for the fallout from the bouncer, who had appeared in the doorway on hearing the commotion. He stared across in their direction, but after realising that it was the Russian who was doing the shouting he disappeared once again.

"We are having a nice talk," explained Vladimir in order to explain his outburst. "We do not want to be interrupted in our conversations by two silly girls."

Ray agreed with him out of politeness, although he had been enjoying the girls company far more than Vladimir's, which he found a little intimidating although he could not explain why.

"You must be aware that the Soviet Union will eventually annex the rest of Europe, including England," Vladimir continued as if nothing untoward had taken place.

"I think that the Americans might have something to say on that score," said Ray, feeling a little annoyed by the arrogance of Vladimir.

"When the technology of the Soviet Union becomes equal or superior to that of the Americans, and it will, they will not be interested in risking a nuclear war in order to protect Europe. You must realise, that they only pretend to be your friends so as to use Europe as a buffer zone between America and the Soviet Union."

Ray was feeling patriotic and more than a little angry. "The Germans thought that they could take over Europe during the last war but they came unstuck, perhaps the Soviet Union will not find it quite as easy as you seem to think."

"The Germans could easily have conquered Europe, if Hitler had not made the same mistake that Napoleon did over a century earlier," continued Vladimir knowledgably.

"What was the mistake?" asked Ray, walking straight into the propaganda trap.

"By attacking Russia of course," answered Vladimir, although he failed to explain that the terrible winter weather, and poor logistics on behalf of the French army had been the major factors in Napoleon's defeat, although the Russian army had been quick to take the credit.

"Most of Europe had already surrendered to the Fascists," he continued, "and your little island would not have been able to resist the might of the German Reich without our assistance."

"We weren't alone," continued Ray, bravely trying to fight his corner even though he was far from an expert on the politics of World War II. "We had the rest of the commonwealth and the Americans fighting alongside of us."

"And do you think that the Americans would have come to your aid, if the Japanese had not bombed Pearl Harbour? Churchill was very clever to declare war on Japan, otherwise America would never have declared war against Germany, and you would not have been able to maintain your independence without the assistance of Russia."

The debate wasn't going well for Ray, as his knowledge of things political, wasn't anything like good enough to challenge Vladimir's apparently superior knowledge on the subject.

"Most of your politicians are fools," continued Vladimir. "They fail to see the threat to their corrupt capitalist world, and they will not be ready to react when Western Europe is eventually annexed. Only Enoch Powell has the vision to see what is really happening, but after his Rivers of Blood speech he is discredited by your foolish government, branded a racist, and just like Winston Churchill when he warned of the danger to Europe from Hitler's Germany, no one will listen to him."

Ray was not aware of Enoch Powell's concerns about national security, although he did remember something of his Rivers of Blood speech.

Powell's constituents had been expressing concern at the number of Afro-Caribbean's, who had been settling in their area for over a decade. Kenya was forcibly removing its Asian population, and most, because they held British passports, were expected to settle in Britain.

Powell had speculated that at the current rate of immigration, Britain would have accepted seven million coloured immigrants by the year two thousand, plus the offspring of a generation, and that coloured ghettos would undoubtedly spring up, leaving the white population a minority in some area's, unless immigration was halted and repatriation begun. After his speech, he had been branded a racist by the newspapers and government politicians, while Edward Heath the leader of the opposition, had sacked him from his position as shadow defence minister.

Ray was at a loss as to Enoch Powell's involvement in cold war politics, perhaps he had also made a speech on Soviet expansionism, as shadow defence secretary it was quite possible, but if he had Ray was completely unaware of it. For whatever reason it was obvious that Vladimir considered Powell to be a visionary, concerned that if he became powerful within a future conservative government, perhaps even a future prime minister of Great Britain, it could be detrimental to the Soviet Union's expansionist plans, which were going full steam ahead with the invasion of Czechoslovakia in August, to depose the liberal regime of Alexander Dubcek.

Ray didn't like the tone of this conversation and wondered what all this political rhetoric was leading up to.

"We need operatives, friends who will work for us in the west."

"Are you talking about me?" asked Ray in surprise.

"Yes of course," answered Vladimir, as if it should have been obvious to Ray from the start.

"I work in a domestic electronics factory, making components for radios and television sets," protested Ray. "What possible use could I be to the Soviet Union?"

"You would be surprised how useful you could be," answered Vladimir, "What is more you would be well rewarded for your loyalty."

"I would never sell out my country," said Ray patriotically.

"If a third world war was to break out between the Americans and the Soviet Union, as it will inevitably do, Europe will be the battle ground and will be totally destroyed. Better a peaceful annexing of Western Europe than its destruction, don't you think? You would be helping to save the British people from certain annihilation not betraying them. Think carefully about what I have said, we will talk again soon."

This didn't make any sense, Ray hadn't told him his surname or where he lived, nor did he intend to do so, therefore he couldn't see how Vladimir could possibly contact him again, so he decided to humour him.

"I'll think about it," he said, even though he had no intention of doing any such thing.

The bar had filled while they had been talking, two Gypsy women in traditional peasant dress, who looked as if they could possibly be mother and daughter, were pedalling their wares. The older woman was selling roses and telling fortunes, while the younger one had a tray which was held by a leather strap around her neck. She was wearing a long black skirt which brushed the floor as she moved, and around her waist she wore a white apron which was tied with a large bow at the back. Above the skirt she wore a low cut white blouse with short puff sleeves, which was heavily embroidered around the neck with flowers, as was the hem of her skirt. She glanced at Vladimir and then turned her attentions to Ray.

"*Zijn jullie Russisch?*" she asked in Dutch.

"She would like to know if you are Russian," Vladimir translated.

"English," answered Ray, and then as an afterthought he translated into Dutch "*Engels*."

"You buy necklace for your sweetheart?" asked the girl in English, making his translation, which he had learned from the barman in Valkenswaard and of which he was rather proud, redundant.

She leant forward to display the necklace that she was wearing, lifting the pendant with her fingers and holding it close to his face. At first glance Ray thought that it was a flying swan in some kind of base metal, although on closer examination it turned out to be an erect penis and testicles with wings. It had taken him a considerable amount of time to concentrate on the pendant, as he could see down her blouse as she bent over to display it, and he found himself to be transfixed by her nipples, which were not pink but a very dark brown, even darker than her olive skin.

"I don't have a sweetheart," he protested regaining his composure.

"You buy one for yourself?" she insisted, unwilling to take no for an answer.

"No thanks." Ray insisted.

She glanced at Vladimir as if for approval, and when he showed no apparent interest in the transaction she continued with her sales pitch.

"Fucking scissors?" she announced, which took Ray aback.

She produced a pair of painted wooden scissors from the tray; they were about ten inches long, with a naked woman sporting huge breasts attached to one of the blades, while a naked man, with an enormous erect penis, almost as big as himself, was attached to the other. As she squeezed the handles, the two naked bodies came together, the huge penis disappearing and then partially reappearing as she operated the scissors. It would never have crossed his mind to take either of these offensive items home with him, so he declined the offer politely and she eventually moved on.

Ray looked at his watch; it was just after eleven o'clock.

"I think that I'll call it a night and go back to my hotel," he announced, still feeling uncomfortable in Vladimir's company.

"You don't really want to stay at a hotel?" said Vladimir, phrasing his comment like an instruction, but which Ray interpreted as a question, before adding, "so impersonal. Why don't you come home with me? I have a nice bed, big enough for the two of us, and I can cook us breakfast in the morning."

Suddenly the penny dropped, a man twice his age with dyed hair, who gets annoyed because his drinking buddy is receiving attention from a bar girl. He wasn't annoyed because she was hustling drinks at all; he was annoyed because she was flirting with Ray and he was jealous.

"I think that you've made a mistake," said Ray. "I'm only having a drink, not looking for a sleeping partner."

"I am very sorry if I have misread the signals," apologised Vladimir, "I hope that I have not offended you and that we can still be friends." He held out his hand to shake and Ray took it.

"You will accompany me to another bar where I know that I can find what I am looking for?" said Vladimir, ending with the word "Please" as an afterthought.

Ray wasn't sure if this statement was a request or an order, as Vladimir's requests all appeared to be orders, but he decided to go along with the plan so as to avoid any more unpleasantness.

Vladimir took him to a second bar; it was much larger than the bar that they had just left and much brighter. The bar-room was long and narrow, barely wide enough to walk around the enormous elliptical bar, which sat in the centre of the room like an island in a sea of chattering people. Loud music blared out almost drowning the noise of the chatter, which to Ray's uninitiated ear sounded more Bavarian then Dutch, rather like the music that he had heard played in the newsreels at Hitler rallies during the war years.

A couple behind the bar, who appeared to be mine hosts, were doing a polka from one end of the bar to the other and the atmosphere was electric. Ray was happy that he had been persuaded to come along, as for the first time since his arrival in Amsterdam he was actually enjoying himself.

They had two more drinks, Vladimir insisting that he paid for both of them as recompense for his earlier embarrassing mistake, before a skinny teenage boy with bleached blonde hair entered the room. He scanned the bar as if looking for someone in particular, until spotting Vladimir at the bar he approached, kissing him full on the lips in order to stake his claim in case Ray had any other idea's.

"This is my regular boy," Vladimir explained.

Ray was uncomfortable with the kissing and cuddling between this child and a late middle aged man, but then he had felt uncomfortable in Vladimir's company for most of the evening. Although he was enjoying the atmosphere in the bar and no longer wanted to leave, bidding them both good night he left.

CHAPTER SIX

At thirteen years of age Vladimir had become aware that he was different from most of the other children at his school, while his parents had come to the same realisation some years earlier. His father had regularly beaten him in a vain attempt to turn him into his version of a man, while his mother had walked around the small village with guilt written all over her face, ashamed for not having given her husband a real son.

At fourteen years of age, Vladimir had run away from home after a particularly vicious beating from his father, having stowed away on a freight train heading for Moscow. In the capital he had joined a group of street urchins, who prostituted themselves on the streets of Moscow in order to make a living. They were quite often to be found outside of the Lubyanka head quarters of the OGPU, or State Political Administration, on Lubyanka Square, while some members of the OGPU, later to be renamed the KGB, discreetly took advantage of what they had to offer.

Vladimir had quickly become the favourite of an elderly member of the OGPU, who took him into his home as a house guest, while finding him a job distributing the office mail at Lubyanka. From those early beginnings in 1933, he had become an operative of the OGPU, until its gradual metamorphosis into the KGB a decade later.

After his elevation from post boy to Soviet agent, and the demise of his partner and mentor, he himself began to use the services of the next generation of street urchins, in the house that had been bequeathed to him by the old man. When Khrushchev brought the KGB into existence in 1954 and his services were no longer required, he transferred to the GRU or Central Intelligence Office, a lesser known but much larger organisation than the KGB, the rivalry between the two, being even more intense than that between the CIA and the FBI.

The GRU was the name given to Soviet Military Intelligence, the existence of which was little known outside of the narrow confines of the intelligence community. Apart from the handling of Soviet military intelligence, it operated residencies all over the world, and in conjunction with signals intelligence; one of its main functions was to steal industrial, technological, and scientific secrets from other countries.

Although he could be ruthless, which was one of the qualities required of him by the Central Intelligence Office, Vladimir had never really been of the right stuff to progress beyond the lower ranks of that organisation. He had reached his zenith, as the head of a small team of operatives at a military radio signals station in the Netherlands, who in addition to their cover duties as station security, also assisted the Soviet Embassy and the Kremlin, with other more dubious tasks which did not officially appear on any job descriptions. Without his knowledge, Ray had become a part of one of those more dubious tasks.

■ ■ ■

He awoke on Sunday morning to the sound of church bells coming from the tower of *De Nieuwe Kerk,* which he could see over the roof tops not far away from his hotel. He was in possession of a thumping headache, and his mouth felt like the bottom of a birdcage. He looked at his watch, it was a quarter to ten, breakfast was served between seven o'clock and nine-thirty and he was already too late. He made himself a strong black coffee, which he drank while sitting in one of his armchairs wearing only his shorts. His eyes were puffy, almost closed, and the coffee tasted very bitter. Considering the coffee medicinal he forced himself to finish it, before going into the shower.

While he was in the shower there was a tap on the bedroom door, and a voice called out from the corridor, "*kamermeisje.*"

He didn't hear the chambermaid introducing herself because of the running water, but she took his lack of response to mean that he had gone down to breakfast, letting herself in with her pass key.

She was an attractive girl in her early twenties, dressed in the black and white uniform of a hotel maid, with a frilly little hat perched on the top of her head. After changing his bed linen, which he had only slept on for one night, she returned to the corridor, before opening the bathroom door with an armful of towels, just as Ray was stepping out of the shower.

"*Handdoek*," she said, offering Ray a hand towel with which to cover his modesty.

She was also carrying a large fluffy bath towel which would have been far more effective for the purpose, but she purposely withheld it. Showing no embarrassment at seeing Ray in the altogether, she busied herself by changing the remaining bathroom towels as if nothing out of the ordinary had just occurred, while Ray had to squeeze past her with the inadequate hand towel covering his private parts in order to access the bedroom.

By the time that she emerged from the bathroom carrying an armful of dirty towels Ray was already dressed. She walked past him without giving him a second glance, but as she reached the door she turned, crooked her little finger and cheekily waved it in his direction as she left.

He needed a walk in order to clear his head, and he was beginning to feel hungry despite his hangover. It was a sunny but frosty morning, and Ray found it quite pleasant as he was well insulated against the cold in his overcoat, Paisley patterned scarf, and leather gloves. As breakfast at the hotel was over, he strolled down the *Damrak* in the winter sunshine for a couple of blocks searching for somewhere to eat. Noticing a bar tucked away up a narrow alleyway advertising all day breakfasts, and displaying a large Union Jack and an equally huge Stars and Stripes on long diagonal poles, he decided that a good breakfast and the hair of the dog may be the remedy to his hangover.

He found himself a table beside the window. Being frosted, with leaded lights advertising the virtues of *Amstel Pilsner* in red and yellow glass, the window did not offer him much of a view, which in truth was far from picturesque anyway, but it did allow some welcome natural light to enter an otherwise very dark and dingy area, lit only by a number of dusty opaque globes hanging from the ceiling, and providing a very limited lumen intensity.

It was almost lunch time, as Ray could tell from the rumblings within his stomach, and he ordered a late breakfast of bacon, egg, sausage with mushrooms, baked beans, and fried tomatoes, along with a black coffee and a beer chaser. The bar quickly filled with native Dutchmen rather than the advertised for Brits and Americans, who were more profitable to the establishment because of their naivety.

Two couples entered the bar, and being very few seats available the two women sat directly across from Ray, while their male counterparts visited the bar in search of service. The women didn't acknowledge Ray's presence at all, not even to ask if the seats at his table were available, which Ray thought to be very rude. Presumably they had failed to notice the enormous flags outside in the alleyway, proclaiming that this was an Anglo American bar, as they began to have an extremely intimate English language conversation about their sex lives, which included measurements, frequency and duration, orifices, and battery operated devices, obviously assuming that he was a non English speaking Dutchman, which had they been in Amsterdam for any length of time they would have realised was a rarity.

Ray listened intently to their conversation, which opened his eyes to what women want from a sexual relationship, until the subjects of the conversation returned from the bar bearing drinks.

Downing the last remnants of his beer Ray stood up, and addressing the two young women he asked, "would you're friends like to sit here?"

He had thought that he would never see anyone who could blush redder than Godfrey, but he left behind him two very red faces indeed.

As he vacated the bar, a man in his early twenties with shoulder length blonde hair protruding from beneath a grey tweed cap, abandoned his half finished beer and followed Ray down the alleyway towards the street. He was wearing blue jeans, a black fabric bomber jacket, gloves, and a fluffy purple scarf, which was wound tightly around his neck so as to partly obscure his face.

Ray remembered seeing the man earlier lighting a cigarette as he had left the hotel. He probably wouldn't have noticed the man at all, except that the purple scarf, which now served as a disguise, had made an impression on Ray and now betrayed the wearer.

Ray headed off down the *Damrak* and the man followed at a discrete distance. Ray pretended to look at something in a tobacconist shop window, while the man followed suit, by examining children's clothing in another shop window a few hundred feet away. Going into the shop Ray purchased a guide book to Amsterdam, a quantity of pipe tobacco, and a large box of cigars, which he feared may exceed his tobacco allowance on his return journey. Ray wasn't a smoker, but it was expected that anyone travelling abroad for the company would take orders from the smoking fraternity, bringing back particular tobacco products which could not be readily purchased in England.

When he came out of the shop with his purchases in a large brown paper bag with string handles, he scanned the area for his shadow, before spotting him lurking in a doorway a safe distance away. Totally convinced that he was not being paranoid and was indeed being followed, he began to ponder the reasons why.

Was it Vladimir who was having him tailed? Perhaps he needed to be sure that Ray was in fact a tourist in Amsterdam as he claimed, and not a M16 agent trying to infiltrate his organisation. Another possibility could be that he was being followed by the Amsterdam police, because of his recent associations with Vladimir, or maybe the guy just intended to rob him because he looked affluent in his Crombie overcoat.

Reaching the bottom of the *Damrak* with his tail still firmly intact, he crossed the road towards *Amsterdam Centraal Station,* where he noticed a tourist barge ready to set sail. He had intended to walk the city, which was why he had purchased the guidebook, but gauging the distance between his shadow and himself, and realising that the barge would have sailed before purple scarf could reach it, he climbed aboard.

A short sail from the railway station they past *Sint Nicolaaskerk*, an imposing landmark in the *Oosterdok* or east dock area of the city, as opposed to the *Westerdok* which flanked the railway station at its opposite side, leaving it sitting on an island connected only by road and railway bridges. *Sint Nicolaaskerk* could not be described as pretty, but it was certainly imposing, with tall twin towers, a large dome, and a rose window made in the *Van Bossche* and *Crevels* workshop in 1886.

Purple scarf had followed the barge on foot thus far, but realising that he could not maintain the pace for very long, he gave up and returned to the advertising board where Ray had boarded the barge. He appeared to be checking the sailing and return times, and Ray presumed that he would be waiting for him when the barge returned.

At the end of the *Oosterdok* they took a right into the *Oudeschans Canal,* a particularly wide canal in the centre of Amsterdam. The tour guide was a woman in her mid thirties, who spoke first in Dutch, before translating into English and finally into German. She had a slow and dreamy voice, every letter S becoming a whistle, which Ray found amusing if a little distracting.

He photographed the *Montelbaanstoren* tower which dominated the waterside. According to the tour guide it was built in 1512, originally part of the protective wall of the city and once housed Amsterdam's city guard. A decorative spire and clock had been added in 1606, but the clock bells apparently rang at unusual times of the day, earning it the name of *Malle Jaap* or "Silly Jack."

They past the *Rembrandt* museum, sailing up tree line canals, with cars parked in every available space along the narrow roads which flanked the canals. He photographed some of the old neck gabled and step gabled houses and warehouses, which gave Amsterdam its unique character. Almost seven thousand buildings in the city centre, the tour guide announced, dated back to the sixteenth century. They sailed beneath humped back bridges, with cyclists aplenty passing over each and every bridge, while bicycles in huge numbers were leaning against the hand rails which flanked the bridges.

Returning to the *Oosterdok* by way of the *Voorburgwal Canal,* the guide pointed out *de Oude Kerk*, which she explained was the oldest church in Amsterdam, its original structure being built in 1306, and that they were currently in the red light district of the city. Anyone thinking of visiting the area's nightlife she explained, should visit in the early part of the evening, as it could become extremely rowdy later. Ray took notes and resolved to return that very evening so as to check it out.

He enjoyed the tour enormously, until the tour boat disembarked at the exact same spot where he had begun his tour an hour earlier. He scanned the area looking for Purple Scarf, who he was convinced must be in hiding somewhere nearby, but he could not be found. Perhaps the tail had changed since his cover had been broken, but although studying people to the point of paranoia, Ray didn't notice anyone else who might have been following him.

It was mid-afternoon and he was cold and thirsty, scouring the area he came across a coffee shop close to *de Oude Kerk*. While ordering a coffee, he noticed that everyone in the coffee shop appeared to be eating slices of cake. Thinking that it must be exceedingly good cake, he purchased a large slice and enjoyed it so much that he ordered himself a second helping.

Making his way back to the hotel he felt extremely relaxed, more relaxed in fact than he had ever felt before and somewhat euphoric, the last remnants of his headache having disappeared, he found that he was giggling to himself for no apparent reason, and then from somewhere deep in the recesses of his mind a memory formed. The Dutch he remembered had a passion for consuming cakes made with marijuana.

■ ■ ■

After dinner he returned once more to the red light district of the city. The streets were very busy by now, not just with men looking for sex as he had supposed, but with couples and even families taking in the atmosphere of the area. A Soviet naval vessel was in the harbour, and there was a strong contingent of sailors with red bobbles on their hats, and horizontally striped shirts of red and white beneath their uniform blues. The *politie* were also out in force patrolling the area. Ray never saw them alone in this part of the city, but always in pairs, with patrol cars within easy radio distance in case of trouble.

The girls were not all of European origin, some were black and some were from the Far East, in fact quite possibly every nationality in the world was represented in these windows. They were all very different but they all had two things in common, they were all attractive women, and they all sat beneath blue strip lighting wearing white underwear, which glowed under the light and made their skin look dark whatever the nationality.

Some of the girls wore only briefs and a bra, while others also wore white stockings and a suspender belt. Some wore French knickers, and some wore short underskirts, but they were all displayed to their best advantage like goods for sale in a shop window, which indeed they were.

Some of the windows were typical shop windows, while others were regular house windows, but all had a curtain behind the chair on which the girls sat so as to hide the room beyond. In some cases the curtains had not been properly closed, and a bed could be identified, where business would be transacted many times throughout the evening and long into the night.

Ray had stopped at one of the windows to study a particularly striking girl when he heard a female voice. The girl did not look directly at him, nor did she move her lips noticeably, but still he could hear the voice, which appeared to come from a circular adjustable air vent set into the window glass. He later discovered that the ventriloquist acts were necessary in order to deceive the police, as it was illegal for the girls to solicit for business, and the *politie* were watching for any signs of communication between the girls and the punters.

As the evening progressed, Ray observed that interested parties would enter the building and wait in a narrow hallway; the girl would then leave her seat in order to negotiate a deal.

Sometimes the punter would come out again and the girl would return to her seat, and other times she would disappear, leaving the window empty of its saleable goods for a short while until she returned, or until another girl took her place.

He walked around the red light area for a couple of hours in fascinated curiosity, but eventually the novelty of the experience began to wear off, and he decided to find a bar where it was warm and he could have a drink. He wasn't very far from the bar which he had frequented with Vladimir, and as it had been fun the night before, he decided to return.

When he arrived, he was surprised to find that the bar was almost empty, with a rather bored looking barman washing glasses. No music played to improve the atmosphere, while three customers all of which were men, were sitting equidistantly around the elliptical bar staring absentmindedly into space.

When he had first visited the bar it had been a Saturday, but now it was Sunday, which may have accounted for the lack of customers, but it was also much earlier in the evening than on his previous visit, so undeterred he positioned himself at the bar, leaving as much space between himself and the other customers as possible.

The barman, who happy to have something to do in order to relieve the boredom, wandered over and Ray ordered a beer. The golden beverage, which as usual consisted of half a glass of beer and the other half of froth, was delivered a few minutes later, although the barman refused to accept any payment. Pointing to a young man who was sitting facing Ray across the bar, he explained that the drink had already been paid for. Ray looked in the direction of the pointing finger and the young man smiled, while Ray nodded acknowledgement of the gift.

If Ray felt uncomfortable at that moment then things were only going to get worse. The barman returned a few minutes later with a second beer, pointing out a man of early middle age who waved to Ray as he looked across; when a few minutes later the barman returned with a third beer purchased by the final member of the trio, who had no intention of being left out, Ray began to feel panic. He was convinced, and rightly so, that these men were all after his body, but he couldn't understand why they should think that he was that way inclined.

While pondering his dilemma, he was approached by a woman who had silently crept up behind him unnoticed. She was in her mid twenties with a very pale complexion, indicating that she never went out into the sun; In fact she was so pale that perhaps she didn't venture out in the daylight hours at all. She had jet black bobbed hair with bright red lipstick, which made her face appear to be even paler if that was possible, and was wearing dark flared trousers, which looked as if she had been poured into them, and a very tight polo neck sweater which matched her lipstick, and seemed to magnify her otherwise underwhelming breasts. Although attractive in full face, in profile she had a rather pronounced bump on her nose which may have been genetic, or perhaps it had been broken sometime in the past.

"May I buy you a drink?" she asked in perfect English but with a pronounced French accent.

"Thank you," he answered, "but as you can see I have all the drinks that could possibly want."

"Do you mind if I sit here?" she asked, indicating the stool beside Ray.

"Not at all," replied Ray, glad of the distraction. "Perhaps I can buy you a drink," he offered.

She ordered a vodka and tonic, and he noticed that his three admirers seemed to have lost interest, having returned to staring absently into space after discovering his preferences. His problem appeared to have been resolved.

He wondered why an attractive female stranger should have approached him, while offering to buy him a drink as a man would when trying to pick up a woman. The only conclusion that he could come to was that she may be a prostitute looking to do business, but even if that were the case, he had never heard of prostitutes buying drinks for punters. If she was a prostitute then he wasn't looking for one, if he had been he would have used one of the window girls, but at least the situation that he now found himself in, was infinitely more preferable than having to deal with the advances of three raving queens.

He felt a light kiss on his cheek as he sipped his beer, and when he didn't object to her advances, she took his hand, and led him towards a small sofa which fitted perfectly into a secluded alcove. While kissing and cuddling on the sofa, they were suddenly interrupted by an angry voice.

"You swore to me that you were a strictly heterosexual man."

Vladimir stood in front of him with a look of betrayal on his face.

"I am," protested Ray indignantly, wondering what on earth Vladimir was so worked up about.

"Then why are you kissing this creature?" asked Vladimir with disdain.

The penny dropped, this was a homosexual bar, belatedly he noticed the narrow hips of his concubine and lack of waist, the Adams apple and the newly acquired breasts, which although real were only the beginnings of what was to be. Although he found it hard to believe, it now seemed that the previous evening's clientele had all been men.

Vladimir redirected his anger towards the French lady boy, and without making a comment, he or perhaps it was she, or more likely something in transit, flounced out of the bar in an exaggerated pantomime of anger.

"Will you join me at the bar?" Vladimir asked pleasantly, instantly reverting to a completely different self as he had done after his altercation with the bar girls.

Ray always felt nervous when he was around Vladimir, but only too pleased to have been rescued once again from a potentially difficult situation and duly obliged. To Ray's relief Vladimir kept away from the subject of cold war politics, instead they talked of Amsterdam and Ray's tour of the city earlier in the day.

At one point Ray tentatively broached the subject of his perceived tail, although Vladimir flatly denied having any knowledge of it, trying to persuade Ray that he had been mistaken in thinking that he was being followed. Ray however was not convinced by the argument, reasoning that Vladimir would have been very interested indeed had he not organised the tail himself.

Ray sidestepped questions about his home life, steering the discussion instead to the radio station where Vladimir worked, and was astonished to discover that rather than Russian folk songs and a little propaganda played to a Dutch audience, which had been his initial interpretation of a Soviet radio station, it was in fact a transmitting and receiving station for coded Soviet signals to Moscow and Soviet embassies around the world.

"We also intercept coded signals from western countries and attempt to decode them," explained Vladimir openly.

"Do the Dutch government know what kind of signals you are transmitting and receiving?" asked Ray in amazement.

"Of course," replied Vladimir. "We have to constantly change our codes as the west attempt to listen to everything that we transmit, while in turn they constantly change their codes as they know that we are listening to everything that they transmit.

"If your role is the transmitting and receiving of signals, what made you think that I could be of service?"

"Part of our function, is to appropriate industrial and technological advances which could be advantageous to the Soviet Union," Vladimir explained.

"You mean stealing and spying," said Ray.

"We need to be aware of what the west is developing as it may not be in our national interest," answered Vladimir.

"I work in a factory which makes thermionic valves, transistors, capacitors, and in the not too distant future delay lines for colour televisions," reminded Ray, hardly high tech or secret work; you can read about all of these things in the local library."

"You will be made aware of your importance in our plans," said Vladimir dismissively, "but until then let us not talk business but have some fun.

After a further tour of the red light districts bars with Vladimir as his guide, they returned to the Bavarian bar, which unlike earlier was packed with people once again. Soon Vladimir's rent boy appeared. Vladimir rose to leave; shaking hands with Ray in a very businesslike way.

"I hope that you have a pleasant journey home tomorrow, I will not say goodbye as I am sure that our paths will cross once again in the not too distant future," and with that he left the bar.

Ray wandered back to his hotel feeling very uneasy about what Vladimir had said; he went over it time and time again in his mind.

"I will not say goodbye as I am sure that our paths will cross once again in the not too distant future."

He tried to remember how much information he had given to Vladimir, although on reflection it appeared to be very little. He reasoned that Vladimir may have known that he was from the north of England because of his Lancashire accent. Vladimir definitely knew that he worked for an international electronics company with a sister factory at *Valkenswaard,* which could also narrow the search somewhat.

■ ■ ■

The following morning, he tipped the lift attendant for the final time, and left the *Rode Leeuw* in order to walk the half mile or so to the railway station. It didn't seem quite so far this time, as it was all downhill; while Amsterdam seemed to have shrunk considerably the more that he found his way around.

It was Monday morning and the *Damrak* was bustling with shoppers and business men. Every fifty yards or so there was a fairground organ, colourful and ornate with carvings of soldiers or dancers. Each organ was playing a different tune, but they had been carefully positioned so that each tune faded out just as another one came into earshot.

There were a number of stalls on the pavement, selling bags of salted raw fish, in much the same way that Ray purchased hot potatoes from a street vendor at his local bus station, which he always enjoyed and ate on the street with a knob of butter. Ray had always made a bee-line for the hot potato vender since early childhood and it had become a ritual, but he couldn't imagine himself holding up raw fish by the tail, and dropping them down his throat like feeding sea lions at the zoo.

He was too early to catch his airport bus, and so he spent his time exploring some of the large stores on his way to the railway station. Most were already trimmed up for Christmas with elaborate toy displays, decorated trees large and small, and with decorative garlands hanging from the ceilings.

Some of the non Christmas items would never have been tolerated by England's animal lovers. In one store a whole floor was devoted to animal skins, zebra, giraffe, cheetah, and even a lion and a tiger with the heads still on, intended to be used as wall hangings or rugs. Ray was appalled that this kind of trade was allowed to flourish in a civilised society, finding consolation in the thought that they may all be fakes and not real animal skins at all.

He caught a number ninety-two bus from outside of the railway station, which arrived at Schiphol Airport in plenty of time for his flight. He failed to notice a young man who was sitting at the rear of the bus; he also failed to notice the same young man while boarding the aeroplane. The tweed cap had gone, as had the purple scarf. His hair was now dark instead of fair and cut short rather than shoulder length. Instead of the bomber jacket and jeans he wore a striped business suite, dark overcoat with shiny shoes, and carried a tan leather brief case.

On this occasion Ray flew with the Dutch international airline KLM, who presented all of their passengers with a small plastic box, containing what appeared to be two small blue and white delft tiles as a souvenir of their trip to Holland. On further examination the first tile was indeed what it purported to be, with a picture of a Dutchman in national costume digging with a spade in front of a windmill. The second tile, which turned out to be a chocolate facsimile, was wrapped in blue and white paper and depicted a Dutch girl, once again in costume and holding a large bunch of tulips in her arms. He later used the real tile as a coaster for his coffee at work, although the chocolate facsimile never arrived in Manchester.

CHAPTER SEVEN

Everything had become routinely normal since Ray's return from Amsterdam, except that Elvis Presley had launched his comeback special, Oliver had been released in the United States, and the preparations for Christmas were now well under way. When he had first returned home, he had half expected Vladimir to knock on his front door any day. He knew that this was stupid, but something about the meeting in Amsterdam had worried him.

On his return home he had spoken to everyone that he knew about Enoch Powell. Although everyone remembered his Rivers of Blood speech, most agreeing that he had been harshly treated, for speaking his mind in a country supposedly proud of its tolerance to free speech; no one however seemed to have any recollection of him speaking out against the expansion of the Soviet Union, although being a Tory minister and at the opposite end of the political spectrum to the communists, it was quite possible that he had. After three weeks, he had come to the conclusion that Vladimir was just a crazy old queen, and he began to relax and think about Christmas.

On Christmas Eve the factory worked until noon, although in truth very little work was ever done. If a machine broke down, and many of them did, sabotaged by the machine operators so as not to have to work on Christmas Eve, the supervisor would have to shut down the machine until after Christmas, knowing full well that no electrician or fitter could be found to repair it.

The factory girls made repeated and unnecessary visits to the toilets carrying bunches of mistletoe, where the boy's would wait to receive Christmas kisses. Ray even stumbled upon an old classmate in the warehouse, lying with her legs akimbo on a pile of cardboard boxes that were waiting to be assembled. She spotted him just as he was about to make a discrete exit, and waved at him from her prostrate position, as if his appearance had broken the monotony of the service that she was performing.

■ ■ ■

At thirteen years of age she had been the owner of the largest pair of breasts in the school, making her a magnet for male curiosity. Ray had satisfied his personal curiosity at the age of fourteen, when after a game of cricket in the local park, she had taken his hand and led him into the rhododendron bushes, where she had encouraged him to remove her bra and to fondle her magnificently proportioned breasts. From that day to this, they were still the largest pair of breasts that he had ever been fortunate enough to handle.

■ ■ ■

Ray and Archie had heard on the grapevine, that some of the factory girls had planned to celebrate Christmas Eve at the Lord Nelson public house, when the factory closed at noon. It was an old Victorian pub which was due for demolition early in the New Year. It stood at the junction of two main roads where they merged into one, making the building a triangular shape, and giving it the nickname of the flat iron. The main entrance to the building was at the point of the triangle, with two additional doors accessed from each of the main roads which flanked it.

Ray had passed the Lord Nelson many times over the years. As a child he had always looked for the huge OBJ sign in neon letters, proclaiming the sentiment "Oh be joyful," which was the brewery slogan, and which travelled vertically from just below the roof line to just above the main entrance. The letter O of the sign bore a face which wore a top hat and a monocle. When lit one eye winked repeatedly, which appealed to Ray as a child, and it was always the highlight of a bus trip to and from the town centre with his parents. Even though Ray had drunk in almost every pub in the town, surprisingly he had never frequented the Lord Nelson, even though it was such a familiar landmark.

When Archie opened the front door it looked as though Ray never would see the inside of the Lord Nelson, as they were faced with a solid wall of people. One or two individuals fell out of the door as it was opened, because of the pressure emanating from within. After trying both of the side doors with similar results, there was nothing for it but brute force, and as Archie was by far the bigger of the two, he was nominated by Ray to lead the charge.

Accepting the challenge, Archie barged into the pub with drinks spilling all around, but he didn't get very far before being distracted by a pretty young girl with mistletoe in her hand. Ray was also quickly set upon, and being almost as popular as Archie, they both kissed their way across the room, with hardly time to draw breath, before being set upon by the next well wisher. They soon found themselves at the opposite door, and not wanting to leave they kissed their way back again.

The ceiling of the Lord Nelson was the only part of the room which had made any concessions to Christmas, being decorated with coloured paper chains, constructed using loops of gummed paper, exactly like the ones that Ray had made as a child at school in the run up to Christmas. The remainder of the Christmas decorations were marginally more sophisticated than the home made paper chains, being of the concertina type with cardboard ends, which when pulled revealed streamers of coloured tissue paper. The junctions of the streamers were punctuated with church bells and Bethlehem stars of paper and cardboard, which opened out in much the same way as the streamers into three dimensional objects, adding focal points to the decorations.

The room had been stripped of everything that could possibly have been damaged, including the Christmas tree; assuming that there had ever been a Christmas tree, while all of the chairs and tables had been removed from the room, so as to accommodate the maximum amount of people possible. Ray could imagine the sitting room of mine host on that particular Christmas

Eve afternoon, stacked to the brim with the cast iron Britannia tables and three legged stools, which usually furnished this type of traditional pub.

When they had kissed every female in the pub at least once, and some more than once, they fought their way to the bar. Finally and with great difficulty they managed to buy a drink, some of which was drunk quickly, with most adding to the growing pool of alcoholic beverage soaking into the carpet.

In the hopes of finding a quiet space to drink the remainder of their beer, they made their way towards a staircase with empty beer crates stacked beneath it. When they arrived however, they found that a young couple had already taken up residence in this particular space, and were risking arrest for indecent exposure by airing their differences under the staircase.

After spending the afternoon kissing girls, some who they knew and some who they didn't, they had large red patches of chapped skin and lipstick all around their mouths. At last the room began to thin out, as people made their way home.

Ray and Archie had arranged to meet Cookie and Goff at six-thirty in The Legs O' Man public house. Why they had arranged to meet so early was a mystery, even to them, but it had seemed to be a good idea to make an early start at the time. As the pub had called last orders and it was already well past three, they decided that it was time for them to go home and prepare for the evening's festivities.

Ray had left his motor bike at home in the expectation that he would be well over the drink driving limit by closing time. If kisses had been alcoholic he would have been legless by now, but as it had been extremely difficult to get served, and as he had been otherwise engaged for most of the afternoon he was actually quite sober. Having no personal transport therefore he reluctantly caught the bus home.

■ ■ ■

The bus queue was horrendous, with drinkers and last minute Christmas shoppers all trying to travel home at the same time. By the time that he reached The Legs O' Man it had already gone seven. Cookie and Goff were already there but Archie had still not arrived. He wandered in an hour later, having fallen asleep on the settee after first having had his evening meal.

"Thanks for coming," said Cookie sarcastically, which was the very same thing that he had said an hour before when Ray had arrived.

The Legs O' Man looked only marginally more festive than usual, with a little tinsel and some sprigs of holly along the top of a large mirror which proclaimed that "Bass Is Best." A small Christmas tree, not much in excess of a foot tall, with fairy lights like little houses with lights shining through the windows, stood in the corner of the room on a ledge, which ran along the back of the seating area. The corners of the room had been decorated with balloons, in the unfortunate combination of two circular balloons to one long central balloon. In some combinations the central balloon arched proudly upwards towards the ceiling of the room, as if pleased to see the revellers, while in others it drooped sadly towards the floor, looking a little shrivelled in a before and after scenario.

Ray having already drunk two pints of lager in the hour before Archie had arrived, coupled with the three that he had consumed in the afternoon, neglecting spillages, was already beginning to feel quite tipsy. Cookie and Goff who had worked all day had drunk just three before Archie arrived, while Archie along with Ray had drunk three in the afternoon, so that Ray was already two pints ahead of everyone else.

The evening was rather a let-down compared to the afternoon's action, and although there was some kissing going on the opportunities were relatively sparse, as many of the afternoon crowd were now out with husbands and boyfriends, or had gone to parties, or in any case had gone elsewhere. Ray's drinking had slowed to a crawl as he was feeling a little worse for wear; Goff had met up with one of his regular girlfriends and had disappeared at about eleven, while the remaining three friends ended up outside of the town hall at the stroke of midnight.

A group of carol singers dressed in Victorian costume and carrying lanterns were standing on the town hall steps.

They were singing carols to a large and continuously growing crowd of revellers which filled the pedestrian walkway. Among the crowd Ray spotted Chrissie and sidled over to wish her a Merry Christmas. Not having seen her since their first date, she informed him that her father had found her missing undergarment hung on the garden gate post, when he had gone out to buy his Sunday morning newspaper. He had returned to the house waving the garment while angrily shouting, "What kind of daughter removes her knickers and leaves them hanging on the gatepost."

She had strenuously denied ownership of the offending underwear, but her father had seen her underclothes too often on the washing line to be convinced that they belonged to anyone else.

Chrissie was accompanied by a friend who Ray had never set eyes on before; actually he couldn't see much of her now if he was to be honest, as Archie seemed to be trying to eat her face. Ray and Chrissie held hands, and as they listened to the carol singer's rendition of Silent Night, just like in the movies, snowflakes began to fall.

He walked her home, before consummating their meeting of a month ago, while standing against her father's coal shed in the falling snow. The snow flakes, which he had never in his life seen before on Christmas Eve, and which had seemed so romantic an hour ago, seemed less romantic when he failed to get a taxi home, and had to walk the five miles in the ever deepening snow, leaving large white water stains on his best shoes which never did come off.

■ ■ ■

When he awoke at eleven thirty on Christmas Day the house was empty. Although his parents were not particularly religious people, they eased their collective conscience by going to church on Christmas Day and Easter Sunday; the only other times being to attend weddings, christenings, and funerals.

Christmas was now a very different kettle of fish to the Christmas's when Ray was a child. In those distant days, he was far more likely to have woken while his parents were still entertaining the friends, who they had invited around for drinks on Christmas Eve. He would creep down the stairs in his pyjamas to ask if Father Christmas had been yet, while his mother would angrily march him back up the stairs saying, "No he hasn't; go back to sleep or he won't come at all."

On Christmas Eve the family would always go to see a pantomime at the Hippodrome theatre. It was strictly an amateur affair, but as a child Ray had always found it a magical experience; until the rainy January day, when he had witnessed Snow White getting onto a bus with her shopping bags while wearing a head scarf. The magic had been somewhat ruined after that.

Once when he was seven years old he had awoken at five o' clock in the morning. His mother always left a pillow case tied to the foot of his bed, and stuffed with Rupert bear, Dandy, and Beano annuals, some Dinky cars, and other stocking fillers including chocolates, so that he would not be hungry while they caught a few extra hours of precious sleep.

On this particular occasion after tiring of his annuals and colouring books, he had gone downstairs to see what else Santa had left for him. On entering the sitting room he had seen his main present which dominated the room. It was exactly what he had asked for in the letter which he had carefully written to Santa, using some of the crayons that he had received the previous Christmas. He had posted the letter in the up-draught of the chimney addressed to Santa Clause the North Pole, because as every seven year old knows, if Santa comes down the chimney with presents, then obviously the best way to contact him is by sending a message up the same chimney. There it had stood his best ever present, a two wheeled bicycle; not wrapped like the other presents, which he dared not open until his parents were awake, but standing upright on its stand in the centre of the sitting room waiting to be ridden.

The bicycle had been placed on a rear wheel stand so that the wheel made no contact with the ground. Sitting on the seat he had peddled furiously, with the rear wheel spinning harmlessly, until the moment when vibration had shaken the bicycle of the stand. The wheel had hit the floor at speed, propelling him into the sitting room wall, buckling the front wheel, and denting his pride.

His parents had always been generous at Christmas time, often spending money that they could ill afford. As he had gotten older his presents had changed from toys to clothing; chosen by his mother, they were usually things that a trendy young teenager would rather die than be seen wearing in public.

His mother had always refused to cook on Christmas Day, so rather than eating sandwiches they usually booked Christmas dinner at a local hostelry. It had always been four for dinner until his grandmother had died suddenly from a stroke, and now it was three. They always visited her grave after lunch in order to say Merry Christmas, and to leave a wreath of holly and mistletoe, which had been hanging on the front door of the house in the run up to Christmas.

After the churchyard it was off to visit his father's sister, where over a boiled ham salad tea with tinned peaches and Carnation milk, they would exchange presents, and discuss what other goodies Father Christmas had brought.

Ray didn't mind going to his aunts when he was younger, even though it was a wrench to leave his new toys behind. His uncle always made a kite in readiness for his visits. It was constructed from bamboo garden canes, strung together with twine and with a string tail, weighted with scrunched newspaper to help keep it upright while in flight.

In the summertime visits, the kite would have a skin of brown wrapping paper, fastened to the frame with gummed parcel tape. At Christmas time, his uncle always used Christmas wrapping paper, and sticky tape covered with holly and robins, in order to make it a more festive affair. They would fly the kite on the recreation ground for an hour or so until it went dark, then it would be up to his cousin Caroline's bedroom, where they would beat each other senseless with the pillows from her bed, until the year that a pillow burst and the room was filled with goose feathers. From that moment on that particular seasonal ritual was well and truly banned.

This year, as in previous years since Caroline's marriage at the tender age of seventeen, he was bored with playing card games and watching re-runs of The Queen's Christmas speech. This year The Queen had asked for racial tolerance in the wake of the Powell speech, and the influx of Asians from Kenya. The National Front had gained popularity as a result of the discontent in some areas of the country, having hijacked the Union Jack as their insignia, in an attempt to persuade people, that the British way and racial intolerance were one and the same thing, and should therefore fly under the same banner.

It had also been a year for racial intolerance in America, with the freedom marches of black Americans resulting in violence and police brutality. The violence culminating in the assassination of Doctor Martin Luther King, when he was shot and killed in Memphis Tennessee by James Earl Ray, while mediating a garbage workers strikes on the balcony of the Lorraine motel.

Racial hatred was not only a one way street, only two months after the death of Doctor King, Robert Kennedy, the brother of ex President John F Kennedy, was assassinated in Los Angeles by Sirhan-Sirhan, a Palestinian Arab claiming to be acting in the interests of his national identity.

He excused himself from the card game claiming to need some fresh air, and went for a walk in the slush left over from the previous night's snow. At twenty-five he preferred to be in the company of younger people, and with the absence of Caroline, there were other places that he would rather be and other people that he would rather be with, although he had to admit that it was so quiet in town on Christmas Day that it was hardly worth going out at all.

CHAPTER EIGHT

On Boxing Day he began to feel a burning sensation as he urinated. He noticed that he had a discharge and sought medical assistance from his friends. They told him horror stories of Gonorrhoea and Syphilis, about umbrella's which were inserted into the penis and then opened and dragged back out again. He was left in no doubt by Cookie in particular, who was enjoying his predicament enormously, that unless he sought urgent professional assistance, his wedding tackle would undoubtedly fall off in the not too distant future.

Ray found it embarrassing to have to speak to his family doctor about such matters, as he had been a patient at the practice ever since a child. Summoning up his courage he bit the bullet, and to his astonishment he found the doctor to be very understanding about his predicament. Although he could not make an immediate diagnosis, he arranged for Ray to attend the venereal disease clinic, telling him that he would receive an appointment in the post within a few days.

After returning from his appointment at the doctors, Ray switched on the television. Three astronauts, Frank Borman, James Lovell, and William Anders, who had successfully orbited the moon on Christmas Eve in Apollo 8, had splashed down and had been picked up by USS Yorktown somewhere in the Pacific Ocean.

■ ■ ■

Ray had always been interested in space travel, from the time when as a child he used to pay six pence of his pocket money, in order to watch Flash Gordon at the Saturday morning picture show. It was serialised each week with Flash heading for certain destruction at the end of each episode, only to escape the following week in a second cut, which bore little resemblance to his apparent demise of the previous Saturday.

His other space hero had always been Dan Dare. Ray had always looked forward to reading of his daring exploits with the evil Mekon, a green alien with a huge head, who inhabited the front page of his weekly Eagle comic.

There seemed to have been an obsession with space travel since the report in nineteen forty-eight, denied by the United States government, that aliens had crash landed at Roswell. All through the fifties it appeared that everyone was seeing flying saucers. The film industry had got onto this extremely lucrative band wagon, by making dozens of B movies about aliens landing on earth, while astronauts explored new worlds in space. Ray had probably seen them all, although his favourite had always been *"The Day The Earth Stood Still,"* where Michael Rennie as an alien in a shiny silver space suite and aided by a huge robot, had landed his flying saucer on what appeared to be the White House lawn.

■ ■ ■

Borman and Lovell had both flown previous missions together with Gemini V11. Their first mission had been to rendezvous in space, while Lovell had flown a further mission in Gemini X11, the last of the Gemini missions.

The Apollo missions were a new era of space exploration, with the ultimate aim of landing a man on the moon, Apollo 8 being the first successful moon orbit. As it was Christmas time, Ray had only managed to snatch a few glimpses of what had been taking place, luckily the report repeated all of the film clips that had been shown earlier. Ray was fascinated to see filmed pictures of another world, a world which up until now had only been visible as a light in the night sky.

The same report reminded viewers of the untimely death of Yuri Gagarin; the Russian cosmonaut had been the first man into space a decade earlier, and had died in a plane crash earlier in the year. Hearing about the Russian cosmonaut, reminded Ray for a moment of Vladimir and his talk of Soviet superiority. The Soviet Union had won round one of the space race when Yuri Gagarin became the first man into space. It now looked as though America had well and truly overtaken them, which would send out a powerful message of superiority to the rival super power.

■ ■ ■

He managed to get a hospital appointment on New Year's Eve and had to follow a yellow line to the Out Patient 2 department. He was convinced that everyone would know why he was following the yellow line, but when he entered the waiting room most of the patients were mothers with small children. There were three separate doctors on duty at the clinic, but only one of them appeared to be dealing with sexually transmitted diseases, and to Ray's relief this fact wasn't advertised. Another doctor seemed to be dealing with women's problems and infertility, while the third was probably a paediatrician, as she appeared to be seeing all of the mothers with babies, and weighing them on a basket scale in the waiting room.

He was pleased to discover that he did not have Syphilis or Gonorrhoea as his friends had so graphically diagnosed, but a Chlamydia infection diagnosed by the doctor as Non Specific Urethritis. This translated from medical speak meaning we don't know what it is exactly, but an antibiotic should cure it within a few days.

He was asked to identify any of his sexual partners who may have passed on the infection, and to bring them in for treatment. As the incubation period was between one and six weeks, he could not be sure who had been the source of his infection, and was therefore unable to make a positive identification. Chrissie was not a viable suspect, as he had discovered the discharge less than two days after their assignation. There had been other sexual partners during the past six weeks, one of which had been *Weis*, but he chose not to believe that she was the source of his current misery.

It was New Years Eve, he was told that he must refrain from unprotected sex as he was contagious, and from alcohol because he was taking an antibiotic. To make matters worse, Archie had gone to Scotland with his brother for Hogmanay and had splintered the group.

The two brothers could not have been more different. While Archie was tall, his brother was short, while Archie was slim; his brother Roger, nicknamed Podger, was chubby. They were also completely different in temperament and it was rare for the two brothers to be seen together.

When they were in each other's company, Podger's frustrations at having drawn the genetic short straw came to the fore. He took delight in attempting to humiliate Archie, but Archie being Archie, he never retaliated and always took it firmly on the chin.

Archie had invited Ray to accompany the brothers to Scotland, but Ray had declined as he was none too keen on Podger. When he was in Podger's company, which was mercifully rare, he always wanted to give him a very hard slap on Archie's behalf.

■ ■ ■

Ray, Goff, and Cookie, wandered into town as usual, but they had nothing special planned for the evening. On their usual pub crawl around town Ray bumped into an old school friend. In truth they hadn't really been friends at school at all, as Alfie had been a year behind Ray. All of the younger kids at school always knew and looked up to the older ones, the reverse however wasn't necessarily true, as it was deemed un-cool to recognise the lower orders.

Alfie was a loner and somewhat of an eccentric. His real name wasn't Alfie at all but Alan, which had been modified to Al by his classmates at school, before some bright spark had resorted to adding an extra letter for some inexplicable reason. Alf had then been his name for the remainder of his school days and it suited him, until in 1966 the Bill Naughton novel Alfie was made into a film starring Michael Cane. From that moment on he had become forever known as Alfie.

Alfie was a couple of inches smaller than Ray, of average build, and on this occasion he looked as if he had just stepped out of a Noel Coward play. He wore grey flannels and a blue blazer with brass buttons, highly polished black shoes, a pristine white shirt, and a yellow cravat with a bold red paisley pattern.

You never knew what you would get with Alfie. The last time that Ray had seen him, he had looked like a down and out, with scruffy clothes and unkempt hair, but now his hair was cut short, and even Goff had to admit that technically it was an extremely good haircut.

■ ■ ■

Ray had been totally unaware that Alfie's real name was Alan, when he had called at his house after renewing their acquaintance, some considerable time after leaving school. He had knocked on the door, not quite sure if he had found the right address, and asked his mother, who he had never met before, if Alfie was at home.

His mother had worked for many years, as a psychiatric nurse in the mental ward of the local hospital. Due in part to her long association with psychiatric patients, it was becoming increasingly difficult to tell the difference between one and the other, except for the uniform that she wore.

When she had answered the door, she had told Ray that there was no one named Alfie living at the address, before slamming the door in his face. As he had retreated down the drive, confused and trying to come to terms with what had just happened, Alfie had chased after him. After taking him back into the house his mother had remained unapologetic, defiantly sticking to her guns, that anyone who came to the house asking for Alfie would be told exactly same thing.

■ ■ ■

It transpired that Alfie had been in the Merchant Navy for the past two years, having arrived home just before Christmas for two months shore leave. Alfie didn't usually keep his jobs for very long as he was a bit of a Jonah, and Ray was surprised that he hadn't either sunk the ship, or been abandoned by the crew on a desert island.

■ ■ ■

For some reason which Ray could never fathom, Alfie always considered Ray to be his best friend, even though it was sometimes years between their reunions. On one particular occasion, Alfie had turned up at the Vallard factory asking for Ray in person at the security lodge. It was a very hot day in the summertime and he was wearing shorts with flip flops, and a short sleeved Hawaiian shirt covered with palm trees. He had a dog tied to a piece of cord, and had pleaded with Ray to help him to find employment at Vallard.

Alfie had served his apprenticeship as a mechanical fitter, although Ray could never understand how he had managed to complete his training, as his attention span rivalled that of a goldfish. Although Ray had been convinced that he wouldn't have a snowballs hope in hell of getting Alfie a job, he had spoken to the foreman fitter on Alfie's behalf, who to Ray's astonishment had employed him on the spot for a trial period. As usual Alfie had only lasted in the job for a matter of weeks, before being dismissed as unsuitable, after being asked to construct a small vibrating hopper, to supply metal transistor canisters to the production line. It had taken him the best part of three weeks, to do what for any other fitter would have been a three day job, and to make matters worse, on completion it had to be scrapped because it looked like a car crash.

The last time that Ray had seen Alfie must have been around the time that he had joined the Merchant Navy. Once again he had just been sacked, after a single day as a van driver delivering meat to local butcher's shops. Going up a steep hill, the back doors of the van, which had been left unfastened by Alfie, had flown open, and all of the carcasses of lamb, beef, and pork, which had been hung on a rail like clothes in a wardrobe, had fallen out of the van one by one, until he had arrived at his next delivery point with an empty van.

■ ■ ■

Alfie's mother and step father had gone away for the New Year holiday to see his step sister who lived in Nottingham, which meant that Alfie had the house all to himself for a couple of days.

"This calls for a welcome home party," suggested Cookie cheekily, as he had never met Alfie before in his life, but Alfie was already ahead of him.

"I've already got in some beers this afternoon," he said. "All we need now are girls."

They wandered around their usual haunts inviting people, mainly girls, to an all night party. They gave out Alfie's address, telling them to arrive around midnight after the pubs had closed.

As the evening wore on they bumped into Michelle and her friend Brenda. Michelle was tall, as tall as Ray and taller than either Goff or Alfie. She was a little overweight and although she was not what you would call beautiful, she was extremely striking, with long bleached blonde hair and large pouting lips covered in bright red lipstick.

Ray had bedded Michelle at all night parties before; but after informing Goff that if giving blow jobs ever became an Olympic sport, Michelle would be a gold medallist, before Ray could make his move Goff had invited Michelle to the party, and he was left to fight it out with Cookie and Alfie for the rather plainer looking Brenda.

Ray had never met Brenda before and he didn't find her particularly attractive. She had short mousy coloured hair and wore a loose fitting and rather ugly bottle green winter coat, which protected her from the sleet and the winter chill. She had never unfastened her coat while in the pub and Ray wasn't quite sure what lay beneath, but as she appeared to be quite plain in general, his expectations weren't very high.

They arrived at the party just before midnight and Ray steered Brenda into the first bedroom that he could find. When she removed her coat, it was as if a beautiful butterfly had just emerged from a very dull bottle green chrysalis. She wore a very tight pure silk mini dress which shimmered in colours of pink, mauve, and purple. It was very low cut revealing ample amounts of cleavage, with thin straps over her shoulders with which to hold it up. She had the most fantastic figure and it was obvious that she wasn't wearing a bra, as her nipples seemed to be trying to bore holes through the thin material of the dress. There was no panty line showing through the dress, and Ray suspected that the reason for this was that she wasn't wearing any.

Sitting on the edge of the bed she first removed her shoes and tights, before slipping the straps of her dress from her shoulders and allowing the dress to fall onto the floor, proving Ray's assessment of her underwear, or lack of it to be correct.

He undressed as quickly as he could and began fitting the condom, which he had borrowed from Goff as he never carried any himself. She was impatient and told him to forget about the condom as she was on the contraceptive pill, but pregnancy was not Ray's motivation for insisting on wearing the condom, in fact pregnancy hadn't even entered his mind.

It was now seven years since Enoch Powell the then Minister of Health, who seemed to be cropping up a lot lately, had announced that the oral contraceptive pill Conovid could be prescribed through the National Health Service, but this was the first time that Ray had ever met a single girl who openly admitted to using it.

The door burst open just as Big Ben was chiming midnight on a television set situated in the adjacent sitting room, while a raiding party lead by Cookie charged into the bedroom laughing and shouting, "Happy New Year." They tore the bed covers from the copulating couple and dragged a naked Ray from the double bed, leaving Brenda frantically trying to cover her nakedness from the prying eyes of the raiding party with a pillow, while Ray cursed Cookie aloud for being the ring leader and promised to get his revenge.

As Ray got to his feet naked, embarrassed, and angry, he noticed that Brenda was sitting on the edge of the bed; she was already fully clothed, if you can call a dress fully clothed, and was silently staring at the floor while in the process of replacing her tights and shoes. When she had finished dressing, she grabbed her coat from a bedside chair and without a word she left the room.

CHAPTER NINE

January was always the most miserable month of the year; the days were short and the weather was cold and damp. December was equally bad, but at least there was always Christmas and the New Year to look forward to. Easter, which was the next public holiday period and the harbinger of better weather to come, seemed to be a long way off.

Ray felt depressed; Archie had been staying home because he had spent all of his savings while in Scotland for Hogmanay. Goff lived in a flat over his shop and seemed to be hibernating, probably with his latest girlfriend, while Ray still hadn't forgiven Cookie for humiliating him on New Year's Eve.

While working in Holland, Ray had been living on his company expenses and had managed to save a full week's wages. This had helped him out over the Christmas holiday period, but now his money was all gone. Since New Year's Eve he had spent three boring weeks at home, watching television with his parents or listening to music alone in his bedroom.

At work everything was much the same. The delay line machines had still not arrived from Valkenswaard although they had been expected in December, while Godfrey was back to his obsession for collecting plastic coffee cups.

Ray was working the day shift. He worked a three shift system of six o'clock in the morning until two in the afternoon, two in the afternoon until ten in the evening, and regular days of eight until five with an hour for lunch. He shared these shifts with Rick Fordham, a six foot two inch twenty-one year old, who still had the face of a schoolboy, a girlfriend, and kept a well stocked tropical fish tank. He had even interested Ray in keeping fish, to the point where he now kept a small tropical fish tank in his bedroom, with a single black angelfish, two three spot blue gouramis and a small tiger barb, which took lumps out of the other three although it was only a fraction of their size.

His other workmate was Jack Garrett, who was ten years older than Ray and whose assets included a wife, a dog, and a fish and chip shop. He had a receding hairline and receding teeth to match, as he always had a pipe in his mouth which had worn his teeth down considerably at one side.

When he was working on days Ray always tried to lunch with Archie, who worked on permanent days for the Plant department installing machinery throughout the factory.

"One more week until pay day," he said, glancing at Archie between mouthful's of shepherd's pie.

"Yes thank goodness," replied Archie. "I owe my mother a fortune after my trip to Scotland."

"I told you that you couldn't afford to go," said Ray insightfully.

"I know but it was one of life's experiences," replied Archie without any sign of regret.

The bell rang to terminate their lunch break. Ray and Archie left the staff canteen and entered the main canteen on their way outside. A man who was sitting alone at a table close to the adjoining door, beckoned Ray over to his table. Although he was a familiar face, Ray didn't know his name never having spoken to him before, and he wondered what the man could possibly want.

He was small in stature, in his late twenties, with dark receding hair and a Mediterranean appearance. Although he wasn't a physically impressive looking man, it was impossible not to have noticed him, as he always wore cowboy boots, inset with rhinestones, and his trousers tucked inside of them.

He introduced himself as John, and when asked said that he was of Italian extraction.

"Please sit down for a minute," he said to Ray.

Ray sat down. "This will have to be quick, my lunch break is over and I have to get back to work."

"Vladimir has a message for you," he announced.

Ray's heart sank, it had been seven weeks since he had left Holland and he had almost forgotten about Vladimir altogether. He had hoped that all of the talk in Amsterdam had been just that, talk, but it now seemed that Vladimir had been serious about his offer of employment, as he had gone to the not inconsiderable trouble of finding him once again.

"How do you know about Vladimir?" Ray asked startled.

"I do his bidding when required," answered John.

"He told me that he worked for a Russian radio station in Amsterdam," protested Ray disbelievingly.

"He does, among other things," replied John.

"What other things?" probed Ray.

After an uncomfortable silence when John failed to answer his question Ray continued.

"What does he want from me?" asked Ray, getting right down to the nitty-gritty.

John leant forward in a secretive fashion and spoke in a whisper.

"This company have been developing a new machine in *Eindhoven*. It is designed to record pictures from a television set onto a magnetic tape, in much the same way that an audio cassette recorder records music from the radio or from a record player."

"Yes I know what a video recorder is," Ray snapped impatiently. "Ampex built one in America in the fifties. In fact in 1959, they used it at an exhibition to record a meeting between Richard Nixon and Nikita Khrushchev."

"You're right," agreed John, " but the Ampex model was a reel to reel recorder, similar to the old fashioned tape recorders, and it was huge, the size of a small car in fact and not nearly portable enough. The Vallard model will be a lot smaller and will use a cassette tape; it will be easily portable and could be hidden away in a drawer or a cupboard."

"And why would Vladimir be interested in what Vallard are developing?"

Weekend in Amsterdam

John didn't answer Ray's question but carried on with his well rehearsed speech.

"Eventually every home in Western Europe, the United States, and Japan will have one, in order to record their favourite television programs. Vallard are keeping it top secret for the moment, as the Japanese are also working on their own Betamax and VHS systems, and would love to beat Vallard onto the market place."

"Are we talking about industrial espionage here?" asked Ray.

"It is part of Vladimir's duties to acquire industrial and technological secrets for the Soviet Union," John informed him.

"And why would he want to acquire this particular secret; is Vladimir planning to sell the idea to the Japanese?" enquired Ray still puzzled.

"No you are missing the point," said John frustrated by Ray's failure to catch on.

"What if a hidden camera was to be connected to one of these video recording machines, what have we got?" asked John trying to make him think.

Ray thought for a moment and the penny started to drop.

"Surveillance equipment?" he speculated.

"By George he's got it," said John relieved. "If the Soviet Union or the Western Alliance has this kind of surveillance equipment and the other side does not, then the victor will have surveillance superiority for a number of years, until video recorders eventually become commonplace."

"And what is my part in all of this?" asked Ray, even though he didn't really want to know the answer.

"One of our operatives almost managed to steal a prototype of the N1500 at the Eindhoven factory, but he was disturbed and had to leave it behind in order to make his escape. We have already a number of infiltrators in the *Eindhoven* factory and the Dutch have become jumpy. They think that secretly transferring the development here will make it a more secure proposition."

"Where is the development section going to be?" asked Ray, although he thought that he could probably guess.

"In the moulding department that is being cleared out on E Z corridor," said John. "It will be a restricted area but you will have limited access to do essential maintenance work."

Ray now realised what Vladimir had meant when he had told him that he would be surprised how useful he could be.

"And Vladimir would like me to steal a prototype of this N1500," said Ray ironically.

John didn't appear to notice the irony of Ray's comment, or he chose to ignore it.

"That would be brilliant," he answered, "but photographs, diagrams or instruction manuals would all be useful, and perhaps easier to acquire."

"I would never get anything out of the door if security is going to be as tight as you say," Ray argued.

"I'm sure that opportunities will arise if you use your initiative. Try to be resourceful," said John, making light of the task. "And if all else fails sabotage is also an option."

"And what would be my personal motivation for all of this resourcefulness?" Ray asked out of interest.

"Five thousand pounds sterling if you get something that we find useful to us," replied John, "that's five years salary after tax."

Ray thought about it for a moment, he could certainly use the money, but he wasn't a thief, and the implications of giving the Soviets' surveillance superiority, or sabotaging his company's products could have serious implications.

"You can tell the old queer to go and screw himself," he said after his short contemplations, and with that he walked away.

Ray went back to his department where Rick Fordham was working the morning shift, but it was quiet and he had little to do. Ray didn't like the morning shifts as he had to be up by five in order to get into work by six. He hated getting up in the mornings at the very best of times and especially hated getting up at that ungodly hour.

When he worked the morning shift, he would arrive just before six and go directly to the cloakroom, where the first aiders kept a stretcher in order to transfer casualties to the medical department when necessary. He would then make a pillow from

Weekend in Amsterdam

his coat or an overall, and sleep on the stretcher underneath the hanging coats until Godfrey arrived at around eight.

The production supervisors needed his cooperation in order to keep their sections running smoothly, and as he normally gave them a good service they were happy to keep his little secret. If a machine broke down before eight, they knew where to find him and they would come to wake him up, but as he wasn't in the best of humours in the early morning, they only disturbed him if it was absolutely necessary.

Ray and Rick had very little in common so they usually spent any free time talking about tropical fish. Rick had kept tropical fish from childhood and was a bit of an anorak on the subject. His one topic conversations drove Jack to near lunacy, but Ray, having spent most of his childhood messing about in ponds and streams with a fishing net and a jam jar, showed more interest in the subject.

■ ■ ■

Ray's own experiences of fish keeping, apart from the sticklebacks, cadis' worms, water scorpions, and other strange pond life, which always inhabited a jam jar on his mother's kitchen window sill, was limited to caring for a goldfish, which he had won at the fair by throwing ping pong balls into empty goldfish bowls. It had lived in a bowl on the sideboard, with some gravel and a single bunch of oxygenating pond weed for almost eight years. Every week to his mother's annoyance, he would fill the bath and let it swim for half an hour, while he cleaned the bowl and changed the water.

He had also kept a cold water catfish in a sweet jar for a couple of years, until it grew too big for its surroundings and rather than buy a fish tank, his father had insisted that he release it into the Leeds-Liverpool Canal, where it either grew to be three feet long, froze to death, or was eaten by a passing pike.

■ ■ ■

At two o'clock Rick went home to his fish and Jack Garrett began his afternoon shift. Most people hated the late shift, but it was Ray's favourite. He could stay in bed for as long as he liked in the morning, as his parents would go to work without waking him. As he quite often didn't return home until five or six o'clock in the morning, it was often the only time that he got any meaningful sleep.

The day shift always left at five o' clock, so from five until ten he was on his own from a supervision point of view. If it was a quiet evening, he would watch his black and white portable television set in the maintenance workshop, or perhaps read the latest of the James Bond novels which were his passion.

On warm summer evenings he would take a walk around the factory grounds. Sometimes he would sit on the benches which were strategically placed amongst the rose beds and shrubberies. There he read his books, but was always sure to leave a message as to where he could be found.

Ray had a lot more in common with Jack than he had with Rick, even though Jack was a good deal older than Ray. Jack was a keen Manchester United fan, and although Ray supported the Rovers, he always played devil's advocate and pretended to support Manchester City, which was the surest way to wind Jack up. He would read all of the match reports for the United and City games, watching them on television as often as he could, so that he was knowledgeable enough to annoy Jack with any positive reports of City, or negative reports of United. Today though he wasn't in the mood for banter; he was preoccupied with his own current situation.

He began to think that perhaps the meeting between himself and Vladimir had not been accidental after all. Suppose that he had been selected for this task before he had even gone to Holland; suppose that Vladimir had arranged for their meeting in the bar to take place. It was surely no coincidence that Vladimir had a man on the inside at Vallard already. Perhaps someone had been tracing his movements for weeks, which could explain how Vladimir had found him, even though he had given him very little information about himself. What now would be the consequences of his refusal to cooperate? Maybe he shouldn't have been so rude about Vladimir's sexuality. Perhaps he should have declined the offer more politely, after all Vladimir appeared to demand respect in Amsterdam, and probably wasn't the kind of person to be messed with.

He wondered if he should report the incident to factory security, or to the police. If he did perhaps Vallard would have another change of plan and move the problem elsewhere. He gave the matter some serious thought but the story sounded quite fantastic, if no one believed him that may make his position with Vladimir even worse than it already was. He was scared of what might happen and he didn't know quite what to do. He wondered if Jack or Rick had also been approached, as they were in as good a position as he was to satisfy Vladimir's requirements.

When Jack returned from repairing his first machine of the day he decided to broach the subject.

"Have you heard what they are going to do with the Canary Shit room?"

The real name of the department was Mepalesco, where they injection moulded a hard protective case onto the flat foil capacitors, which were wound on machines in the main building. The process consisted of injecting a yellow powder into a mould, and compressing it under heat to produce the outer body. The whole place was covered in the yellow powder residue, which is how it earned the name.

"It seems to be very hush-hush," answered Jack. "Even God doesn't seem to have any idea."

"Have you been in there lately?" asked Ray, trying to appear nonchalant.

"While you were in Holland, I was in there almost every day disconnecting the machines that were being shipped out. It's empty now, and there's a specialist cleaning firm in to clean the place up and to re-decorate it." Jack answered.

Ray wondered if the outside contractors had also been infiltrated by Vladimir's people, if so they could be planting bugs or whatever they planted right now.

"Do you know the Italian chap who wanders around the factory wearing cowboy boots?" Ray asked quizzically.

"I've seen him knocking about but I've never met him, why do you ask?" replied Jack.

"Oh nothing I just wondered what he did," pondered Ray. "Have you seen him talking to anyone in particular?"

"I've seen him talking to a chap called Ivan who works in J block."

"Do you know this Ivan?" asked Ray hopefully.

"Not really," answered Jack, "but I've spoken to him once or twice, I think that he's Hungarian or Polish; some kind of Eastern European anyway."

Ray wondered if Ivan was also involved with Vladimir. Did John work for Ivan or did Ivan work for John, and how many more people in the factory worked for Vladimir?

■ ■ ■

During January Rupert Murdoch had purchased The News of the World, The Soviet Union had sent two probes, Venera's 5 and 6, towards Venus, and launched two manned spacecraft, Soyuz 4 and 5, which had rendezvoused in space, transferring two cosmonauts from Soyuz 5 to Soyuz 4 after a space walk. The USS Enterprise had suffered an explosion near to the island of Hawaii killing 27 and injuring 314, and Richard Nixon had succeeded Lyndon Baines Johnson as the 37th president of the United States of America.

Ray had been in hibernation in his bedroom and had hardly noticed, he hadn't left the house for the past three weeks except to go to work, and he needed a hair cut badly. His last trim had been in late November before going to Holland, and he had begun to look like an Old English sheepdog.

He rode the BSA over to Goff's place the following Sunday afternoon, even though he could barely afford to buy the petrol. When he entered the salon Alfie was in the chair having a trim. Ray was surprised to see him there, as he had been a stranger to Cookie and Goff until he himself had introduced them on New Year's Eve. Since that night, it appeared that they had all become friends.

"Hello stranger," said Cookie trying to break the ice.

"I'm not speaking to you; you're a prick," Ray answered angrily.

He poured himself a coffee before turning his attentions to Goff.

"You're not much better either, you jumped in quick with Michelle on New Year's Eve didn't you?"

"You were definitely right about her being world class," said Goff in response.

"This idiot didn't spoil your chances then," Ray said, gesturing towards Cookie.

"He never got the chance because she dragged me into the bathroom and we locked the door."

"Go on," said Ray intrigued.

"We decided to take a shower, and then she did her party piece, with the water running and people banging on the bathroom door wanting to use the loo."

"Have you seen her since?" asked Ray, expecting Goff to reply that it was just a one night stand.

"As a matter of fact she's been round to the flat about twice a week since New Year's Eve," Goff answered, obviously reliving the experiences as he spoke.

There was an awkward pause before he continued. "There's something else that I think you should know."

He glanced at Cookie as he said it and received a slight nod of approval.

"Cookie as been banging Brenda here at the flat."

"You rotten bastard," said Ray, turning his attention once again towards Cookie. "You spoiled my chances on New Year's Eve so that you could give her one yourself."

Cookie had always been jealous if Ray had a girlfriend and he didn't, which was pretty much all of the time. He had always tried to spoil Ray's chances of success, but he had never overstepped the mark like this before. Ray realised that on this occasion, he had not only been jealous because Ray had a girl in his bed and he didn't, but because Ray had the girl in his bed that Cookie wanted for himself.

Ray didn't really fancy Brenda even though she had a great body, and if Cookie hadn't ruined New Years Eve it would still have been only a one night stand for him. Besides he had no room to talk. Not only had he slept with Goff's wife, an action for which he was admittedly blameless by virtue of not having known Goff at the time, but he had also slept with Archie's wife.

Archie had been married for two years and separated for one. His wife was an attractive girl, with long auburn hair which fell almost to her waist. Although Ray had always found her physically attractive, he had never really liked her very much. He had thought from the very beginning, that Archie was making a serious mistake when he said that he was going to marry her, and he had said so. Archie hadn't appreciated his candour, but Ray had taken no delight when he had later been proved to be right.

Archie had asked his own brother Podger to be his best man, despite the animosity shown towards him, and Ray to be an usher. From the very beginning things had begun to go wrong. For a start she liked a drink, and to make matters worse she didn't know when it was time to stop. Even though she had become a married woman, she had continued to go out with friends, and had become something of a joke in the town for always being drunk.

■ ■ ■

Ray had stumbled across her in town soon after he had broken up with Goff's wife, and some six months after she and Archie had separated. She had been drunk as always, and had asked Ray if he would take her home, as she was struggling to stand. He had agreed out of regard for Archie to see her safely home, without any intentions of taking advantage of her, as even though they were separated she was still Archie's wife.

Although she had been legless when he had met her, it was still quite early, and they had caught the bus back to the Shadcroft Estate. She had been wearing a very short silky black mini dress, which showed an expansive amount of her cleavage at one end, while barely covering her rear at the other. When she insisted on climbing the stairs to the top deck of the bus Ray had tried to dissuade her, not only because he was afraid that she would fall, but also because he was sure that everyone getting onto the bus behind them, would be able to see her next week's washing. As it turned out he was incorrect in his assumption that she would flash her undies, for as she climbed the stairs he hadn't been able to resist a sly glance himself, and it soon became apparent that next week's washing basket would be very empty indeed.

Ray had walked her home from the bus stop, to the council flat on the Shadcroft Estate, which she had once shared with Archie. On their arrival at the first floor flat, she couldn't get her key into the keyhole no matter how hard she tried, falling into hysterical laughter on the doorstep, as Ray tried to unlock the door with one hand, while supporting her limp frame with the other. Finally he had managed to get her into the flat, but before he could close the door behind them, she had unzipped his trousers with rather more dexterity than she had shown when using the front door key.

A long hallway led past two bedrooms, a bathroom, and a kitchen, and by the time that they reached the sitting room, she had managed to unzip his trousers a number of times, even though she could barely stand as they staggered together down the hallway. Every time that she had unzipped them Ray had zipped them up, but finally being weak, as men quite often are in these situations, he had succumbed to her needs, not to mention his own, and they had lain down on the rug in front of the fireplace, both in too much hast to reach the bedroom.

He had felt guilty about Cheryl, as after all she had still been Archie's wife, but that didn't stop him from arranging to meet her again in mid-week, borrowing his father's car, so that they could travel to another town where they wouldn't be recognised. On this occasion they had both had a little too much to drink, and while driving back to her flat she once again unzipped his trousers. He had told her to stop as he was trying to drive, but she insisted that she was only checking to see if it was working. As it turned out it most definitely was working, and her head disappeared into his lap, causing him to lose control of both the car and himself.

Almost immediately, he noticed a police car in his rear view mirror with its large blue stop sign flashing. He was convinced that the policeman was trying to stop him because his driving had become erratic, which would hardly have been a surprise as he was well over the drink driving limit, and coupled with what was taking place in his lap, it was little short of a miracle that he was still driving on the road at all. He pretended that he hadn't noticed the police car until he could get her to stop what she was doing, but she was having fun and ignored his plea's.

The police car finally overtook him, and slowed down with the "STOP POLICE" sign flashing until he was forced to pull over. He had persuaded her to sit up by this time, but had great difficulty in getting his manhood back into his trousers, as it was still standing bravely to attention despite the panic that he was experiencing. He had only just managed to zip up his trousers, when the police constable appeared at the window and asked him if he wouldn't mind stepping out of the vehicle.

Ray, who had quite recently read a book called the Naked Ape, remembered the advice on how to deal with a policeman if stopped while driving a car. Doctor Morris the author, had informed in his narrative that you must vacate your car and meet you're adversary on neutral ground, because as an ape you are more likely to become aggressive when you are protecting your own territory, while the police are likely to be more aggressive while invading your territory. So acting on this advice Ray had stepped out of the car immediately, even though he still had a huge bulge in his trousers.

The policeman first asked if he was the owner of the vehicle, before escorting Ray to the rear of the car, where it was pointed out that Ray only had one rear light in operation. Ray apologised and assured the officer that he would inform his father of the problem. He was then asked why he had not stopped when signalled. Ray answered untruthfully, that due to his rear window being steamed up he had not realised that the car behind him was a police car. He was told in no uncertain terms that his window should not have been steamed up at all, before being asked if he had been drinking, which was a rather silly question, as his breath would have fuelled a central heating boiler for a week.

At that moment the policeman had received a message on his radio. Ray waited patiently, expecting to be asked to walk a straight line, or to stand on one leg and touch his nose with his eyes closed. After answering his radio however, the policeman turning back to Ray, had told him that he was a very lucky boy, before leaving in a hurry to respond to a more urgent call.

■ ■ ■

The following morning Ray awoke early, and had already dressed while Cheryl was still asleep. He decided, that he would have just enough time to return home and change his clothes before going into work, although in truth it was not unusual for him to go straight into work after an evening out, which is why he always kept a change of clothes in his work locker for just this kind of situation.

He had intended to tip-toe out without disturbing her, but as he was about to leave she awoke, jumping out of bed in an attempt persuade him not to go. Standing on tip-toe with her arms around his neck, he had spotted their image in a large mahogany swivel mirror which stood by the bedroom door. It had been a strange experience being a lover and a voyeur at the same time, as he watched a fully clothed man and a naked woman kissing. As his father went to work on the train and didn't need the car, he made the decision to delay his departure, and once again went to work dressed in his best suite.

Believing the old adage that you may as well be hung for a sheep as a lamb, he had begun to stay at her flat most nights of the week, while still going out with Archie and the others at the weekend.

One evening Archie had turned up at the flat while Ray was staying there. It felt a bit like *de javou,* as Archie had banged on the door and shouted angrily through the letter box, but Cheryl had refused to let him in. Surprisingly, even though Ray's motor bike was parked outside of the front door Archie never made the connection.

In November just before Ray had gone to Holland she had asked him to move in with her on a permanent basis. Ray had been correct in his thinking that she wasn't the right one for Archie. He also knew that although she was great fun and fantastic in bed, she was not the right one for him either and so he had refused. She had become unbelievably angry at his refusal, hitting him around the head and screaming. Although he had tried to restrain her, she had become hysterical and he had been forced to give her a slap in order to stop her tirade. The following day she had rung Archie and told him all about the affair.

Archie had been extremely hurt, not because of his wife's affair because there had been many of those. What had really hurt was the betrayal of trust by his friend. Archie and Ray remained friends as Archie was a forgiving person, but there would always be hurt on one side and guilt on the other, driving a wedge between them so that things would never be quite the same again.

■ ■ ■

Ray felt a similar kind of betrayal now. It wasn't because Cookie had stolen his girl. For a start Brenda wasn't his girl and he didn't want her to be, it was the way in which he had been deceived that rankled; now he had some idea of how Archie must have felt. To his credit Archie had not been angry nor had he sulked, surely he could be big enough to do the same as Brenda meant nothing to him.

Cookie stepped forward and held out his hand. "I won't see her again if you don't want me to," he said.

Ray took his hand. "You don't have to do that," he said.

"The three of us are going to the Astoria on Saturday to see Mike Berry and The Outlaws*," said Goff changing the subject. "If you want to come I'll lend you the money."

Mike Berry was an actor turned singer, who'd had two or three hit singles and was billed as the British Buddy Holly. Ray was a big Buddy Holly fan, and he also knew that where pop stars go, female fans were sure to follow.

"No need to," Ray said, "I get paid on Friday."

---

*Mike Berry & the Outlaws had three hit records during the nineteen-sixties, "A tribute to Buddy Holly," which reached No 24 in the UK charts, "Don't you think it's time," which reached No 6, and "My little baby," which reached No 34. Mike, real name Michael Hubert Bourne, had his fourth UK hit single in 1980 with "The Sunshine of Your Smile," but was probably better known for his portrayal of Mr Spooner in the British situation comedy "Are you being served."

CHAPTER TEN

It was the first day of the working week and Ray was working the morning shift. Instead of sleeping on the stretcher as he usually did, he decided to investigate E Z building, where the development of the video recorder was due to take place. The contract cleaners had left and with them all of the canary shit, leaving the building empty except for the scaffolding, which went all the way up to the ceiling awaiting the painter's arrival.

Ray climbed the scaffolding and examined the ceiling. He hadn't a clue what he was looking for, a bug maybe, but what did a bug look like? He searched for an hour but he found nothing unusual. The building had been stripped of all its electrical wiring, and Ray decided that if bugs or cameras were going to be planted, they would probably be concealed at the electrical installation phase.

He was wondering if the electrical work would be done by the Vallard Plant department or by outside contractors, when a security guard with a peaked cap pulled low over his face, and wearing the three stripes of a sergeant on his arm, entered the room.

The security guards wandered the factory every couple of hours recording their journey at various check points. Because the factory was so large, as soon as one security guard had returned from his patrol, another one set out to repeat the task.

This particular security guard, who answered to the name of Bernie, was a similar age to Ray, and they shared the distinction of having both started work at the factory on the very same day.

■ ■ ■

On one occasion Ray's father had run out of putty while re-glazing a window at his home, broken by children playing football on the street. As the tradesmen in the factory all swapped favours, Ray had volunteered to get him some more from the joinery and painting department. The painters, who kept a large tub of putty in the storeroom, had scooped out a generous amount, much more than he actually needed, and enough to re-glaze all of the windows in the house if he so desired. Although he had protested that it was far too much for his needs they were insistent, filling a plastic bag and informing him that putty never goes as far as you think it will.

The security guards stood at the main gate at the end of each shift, stopping people at random to be searched in the security lodge. Ray had been stopped once before by security when he was much younger. Having endured a full body and bag search, he had missed the last of the special buses which ferried workers from all around the area, and as the factory was not situated on a service bus route, he had been forced to walk to the nearest bus stop and arrived home an hour late.

His mother had panicked when he hadn't returned home at his normal time, and on finding out what had happened, she had written a strong letter of complaint to the managing director of Vallard, to which she had received an apology and an assurance that the matter would be investigated, although if an investigation ever did take place the findings were never ever disclosed to the Evans family.

Returning to the occasion of the putty, Bernie had stopped Ray on his way out of work and asked him what was in the bag. Ray didn't have a cat, but the first words that came out of his mouth were cat meat. Bernie must have been able to smell the putty, because the following day as Ray had entered the factory gate, Bernie had called to ask him if his windows had stuck in with the cat meat.

■ ■ ■

"Hi Ray what are you doing in here?" called Bernie.

"Just having a nosey around, do you know what they're going to do in here?" asked Ray.

Weekend in Amsterdam

"Not really," answered Bernie, "it's all a bit hush, hush, need to know basis only."

"And do you not need to know?" asked Ray surprised by his answer.

"From what I can gather they are bringing in their own security team to fit coded key pads. It appears that we'll have very little to do with it."

"I've heard that it is to be a development department from Holland," said Ray fishing for some answers.

"Who told you that?" said Bernie startled. "No one is supposed to know what this department will be."

"Oh you know what the grape vine is like," said Ray trying to make light of it, "somebody hears something and then adds two and two to make five."

He returned to E block having learned very little. When Jack came in at eight, he made some excuse for leaving the building, and went across to J block to search out the maintenance electrician there.

Each building had its own maintenance electrician, the electrician in J block being Mick Rogerson. He was old enough to be Ray's father and always wore a blue boiler suite and a flat cap.

■ ■ ■

When he had been an apprentice, as part of his training, Ray had worked for six months in every building in the factory, including six months in J block with Mick. Mick was a grumpy old so and so, but surprisingly all of the apprentices liked him as his bark was far worse than his bite.

None of the apprentices had ever seen Mick without his cap on his head, which lead to speculation that he was trying to hide the fact that he was bald. Even when he had been spotted out at the weekends in some pub or other, he still always wore the same battered flat cap that he always wore for work.

On one occasion one of the rooky apprentices was dared by the others, who knew better than to try it themselves, to snatch the cap from his head. Accepting the dare, the brave young fool had grabbed the peak of Mick's cap and whipped off his head gear. To every one's surprise he had a full head of hair which showed few signs of grey let alone hair recession. Even more surprisingly an arm had shot out like lightning, punching the young miscreant on the nose and leaving him bleeding profusely down the front of his overall. After that none of the apprentices had the nerve to extract the Michael out of Michael.

■ ■ ■

He found Mick sat at his workbench reading the Daily Mirror.

"Good morning Mick, how's things?" asked Ray politely, as Mick could be a prickly customer at the best of times.

"What do you want?" Mick replied without looking up.

"That's a nice welcome I must say, not good morning Ray, but what do you want."

"You wouldn't be here if you didn't want something," grumbled Mick.

"Do you know a chap called Ivan who works in here?" asked Ray.

"I know everyone who works in here," replied Mick with his head still firmly stuck in his newspaper.

"Can you point him out to me?" Ray asked.

"Yes," he replied, but continued reading his newspaper as if the question had never been asked.

Ray rephrased the question. "Would you mind pointing him out to me please Michael?"

"Over there on number eight wire drawing machine." Mick pointed to a tall well built handsome man of middle age with wiry greying hair.

"Does he ever leave the building during working hours?" asked Ray, trying to establish if he was allowed to wander the factory.

"You can't even go for a piss without permission in here, those machines are not allowed to stop and if they do I'm in deep shit until they are running again," answered Mick, insinuating that he was hard done by.

"What nationality is he; Polish?" speculated Ray.

"Ukrainian," Mick corrected with a smirk, as if it should have been obvious to anyone from looking at him.

"How long has he worked here?"

"What is this, twenty bloody questions?" Mick wanted to be left alone to read his newspaper in peace.

"I've only asked you five questions you bad tempered old sod," Ray responded.

"He's been here for about two years if you really must know," Mick snapped.

He folded his newspaper knowing that he would get little peace until he had answered all of Ray's questions.

"Has he any friends in the factory that you know of?" asked Ray, wondering if cowboy John may be one of them, although it appeared unlikely as their ages were very different.

"He seems to get on with everyone," answered Mick. "Likable sort of chap really for a foreigner.

"What I mean," said Ray, "is does anyone come to see him from outside of the building?"

"Only Italian John," said Mick. "Ivan is shagging his mother."

"What do you know about this Italian John?" Ray asked, sensing that he had started to make a breakthrough.

"I used to know his mother when she was young," Mick replied with a twinkle in his eye which spoke volumes.

"She got pregnant with an Italian prisoner of war in nineteen forty-three. After the war they went to live in Italy."

"How does she happen to be back in England?" pressed Ray.

"After the war the Fascists in Italy were hated by certain internal factions, and John's father became active in the Italian Communist Party. He became so involved with the party that the whole family left Italy and went to live in Russia. They lived there for a couple of years until the father was drowned. In rather mysterious circumstances actually."

He paused thoughtfully and then continued.

"After the father died John and his mother came back to England to be closer to her side of the family. When John was old enough he came to work at this factory."

"Thanks Mick."

"Is that it?" Mick was getting into his stride by now and wanted to carry on with his walk down memory lane.

"Just one more question," said Ray. "Does Ivan work on shifts?"

"Everybody works days in here, why do you want to know?"

Ray didn't answer his question, but he now knew when he needed to be concerned about Ivan and John, inside or outside of the factory. "Got to go, see you Mick."

As he left the building he literally bumped into April and almost sent her flying. She was eighteen now, having had a crush on Ray since she was first employed at the Vallard factory to deliver the internal mail. She was small in stature, with sandy coloured shoulder length hair and the tiniest little baby teeth that you could imagine; giving the impression on occasions that she may not have had any teeth at all.

■ ■ ■

Soon after they had met she began to unnerve him. He would arrive at work for the start of his shift and she would be waiting for him at his workbench. He would go home after a late shift and she would be sitting in his living room talking to his parents.

His mother became concerned, asking him why he was encouraging young girls to call at the house. He replied that he was not trying to encourage her at all, quite the opposite in fact, but she couldn't seem to take a hint and he was becoming increasingly concerned that she was stalking him. After their conversation his mother began to lie on his behalf whenever she telephoned, saying that he had gone to a friend's house or to the cinema. It made little difference, as she would arrive at his home within the hour in order to embarrass her in her dishonesty.

On one occasion when she was only seventeen years of age, she had invited Ray to an all night party at her house. Knowing that it was a mistake but not wanting to offend her he had foolishly attended, only to find that her parents were away for the weekend and that he was the only guest. She had bought him beer from the local off-licence, and had made a small buffet of sausage rolls, party pies, and sandwiches. Wanting to leave, but not wanting to hurt her feelings after the effort she had gone to he had stayed for a while. They had kissed a little on her instigation, but he had remained cool towards her advances, as he didn't want to encourage her any more than he already had. He didn't trust her either and thought that she may be out to trap him. She had a nice little figure, but he couldn't help but notice that she had developed a little round tummy of late, which had left him wondering if she was already pregnant and looking for a fall guy.

As it turned out, the proceedings came to an abrupt end by divine intervention when he suddenly became violently sick. He hadn't had very much to drink and his first thought was of food poisoning, but April had eaten everything that he himself had eaten and without any adverse effect. She turned out to be a proper little Florence Nightingale, staying awake throughout the night and wiping his brow with a damp cloth to lower his temperature, while he slept intermittently between bouts of sickness in her bathroom.

He had returned home the following day feeling only slightly better than he had twelve hours earlier, but otherwise feeling worse than he had ever felt in his life. His mother had taken one look at his yellow eyes and had called for the doctor, who instantly confirmed her own diagnosis of yellow jaundice.

■ ■ ■

Before this latest encounter Ray hadn't spoken to April for months. During the time that he had been seeing Cheryl he had not had any contact with her at all, as Cheryl had threatened her with physical violence if she went anywhere near him. Even though April was obsessed with Ray, Cheryl could be a very scary lady when roused, and April had no desire to find out if she was bluffing.

He helped her to pick up her mail from the pavement.

"Sorry April," he apologised.

"That's alright, it's nice bumping into you again," she said, laughing at her own pun.

"I believe that it's all over between you and Cheryl," she said in a self satisfied manner.

"Yes, it didn't work out," admitted Ray. "We finished it over two months ago."

"She wasn't right for you," she said, indicating that she may have always known who was.

"Yes I know," he answered wistfully.

He noticed that she still had the same little round tummy that had given him such cause for concern almost a year ago. Unless it was the longest pregnancy in the history of the world, it meant that he had probably been a bit paranoid about her motives on that memorable occasion.

"Are you seeing anyone at the moment?" he asked, instantly biting his tongue for bringing the matter up.

"Yes, as a matter of fact I have a boyfriend now." she answered smiling.

"Good for you," said Ray. "Is it the real thing?

"He's good to me, but I could never love him the way that I loved you.

He read the danger signs, and not wanting to pursue this line of conversation any further, he made his excuses and went back to E block.

The rest of the week was uneventful, except that the delay line machines finally arrived from Valkenswaard many weeks late. There were a few problems getting them to work satisfactorily, prompting Godfrey to arrange a return visit to Holland in order to extract more information from *Heir Wiener*.

"Have you a message for me to give to *Weis*?" he asked.

Ray hadn't thought about *Weis* since before Christmas, and as he had no plans to return to Holland in the near future, or even at all, there seemed to be little point in starting up the relationship all over again.

"No, I think that I would prefer to let sleeping dogs lie," he replied disinterestedly.

"Does that mean that something happened between you and *Weis* after I left?" asked Godfrey in surprise.

"You could say that," answered Ray.

"Come on then Casanova spill the beans," Godfrey was interested.

"A gentleman doesn't kiss and tell," Ray said, refusing to say another word on the subject, even though he was heavily pressed by Godfrey to break his vow of silence.

All through the week he had been expecting a visit from John with a further message from Vladimir, but John didn't appear. He checked out E Z building again on Friday to find that the painters had painted half of the room; it would be another week before the electricians could start with the re-wiring.

■ ■ ■

On Saturday evening Cookie arrived at Ray's house in his new car. It was a second hand Ford Zephyr but it was new to Cookie. It had red leather look seats and had recently been resprayed in two tones of grey, Goff and Alfie were already in the car and so he slipped into the back seat besides Alfie.

"Nice wheels," said Ray looking around the interior. "How much did this set you back?

"A hundred and fifty quid," answered Cookie proudly.

"A hundred and fifty quid; how can you afford a hundred and fifty quid?" spluttered Ray.

Cookie was a labourer on a much lower salary than Ray, but due to his lack of funds Ray had been forced to borrow his father's car for months, as he couldn't afford to have his own car repaired.

"My dad lent me fifty quid for the deposit, and I am paying the rest off at a fiver a week out of my wages," said Cookie defensively.

"That must be a quarter of your wage after tax," probed Ray.

"More," reflected Cookie.

"What litre is it," asked Ray with interest?

"Two point five," answered Cookie, not realising the significance of this statistic as it was his first car.

"It will probably only do about twenty miles to the gallon, pointed out Ray, have you any idea how much it will cost you to run this gas guzzler with petrol at six shillings and two pence a gallon? And then you have the road tax, and insurance will be high, not to mention the cost of repairs."

"I haven't really thought about it," answered Cookie sheepishly.

"Well you will have plenty of time to think about it, because you will be staying in a hell of a lot to pay for it."

Things went very quiet, Ray realised that he had been a bit of a wet blanket, taking the shine off what for Cookie had been a very special occasion. He hadn't been purposely trying to be a kill joy; he was just concerned that Cookie had bitten of more than he could chew.

"I suggest," he said in an attempt to make amends, "that when we go out in Cookie's car we have a collection to help pay for the petrol."

He was genuinely concerned about Cookie's finances, although he also had an ulterior motive. Since borrowing his father's car to take Chrissie to the cinema, his father had continued in allowing him to use the car, with a caveat that Ray would not drink while driving, which was why he now borrowed it very sparingly.

Another stipulation of the loan agreement, was that he contributed towards the running costs of the car on those occasions, but even though he always made a point of filling up with petrol while his friends were sitting in the car, they had never offered to contribute to the running costs, and he hoped that the new arrangement with Cookie would also set a precedent on those occasions.

They all reluctantly rooted around in their trouser pockets, something which they had never done before, contributing two shillings each, which would more than cover the petrol costs for the journey, which was little more than a twenty mile round trip.

It was the first time that they had ever been to the Astoria and it would definitely be the last. The room was filled with teenagers, some as young as fourteen or fifteen, while Ray and his friends looked to be the only ones who were over twenty. They circled the room a couple of times, while the girls dance around their handbags in a tight formation like a wagon train circled to repel the Indians. Ray felt like a granddad among these children and wanted to leave, but Goff, who was never one to give up easily, wasn't beaten yet. Ray and Cookie stood in front of the stage and watched Mike Berry, while Goff and Alf did a few more laps of the dance floor, searching to find dance partners who might conceivably have left school.

Whilst watching the show, Ray and Cookie failed to notice a group of teenage boys gathering to one side of them. They were between sixteen and seventeen years of age and their numbers were growing all of the time. By the time that they attacked they must have been at least twenty in number.

Cookie was the first one to be struck and he staggered backwards in surprise; Ray noticed what had happened from the corner of his eye, and floored the youngster who had attacked Cookie with a single punch. Immediately he was hit in the face by a second teenager, who was also quickly dispatched by Ray to join his colleague on the floor.

They were queuing up to throw punches at Ray now, and as he dispatched the third youngster he felt himself falling, as the three on the floor pulled at his legs and a fourth and fifth tried to bungle him over. He knew that once he hit the floor he would be in big trouble, and tried to stay on his feet for as long as he could, but it was impossible to stay upright as the sheer weight of numbers overpowered him.

Kicks rained in from all sides as everyone in the hall seemed to want a piece of him, as they swarmed around like a shark attack after the smell of blood. Ray tried to protect his head from the kicks but in doing so he felt one of his ribs crack. When his arms went to protect his damaged ribs, he was kicked in the head and his teeth came through his bottom lip. Eventually he passed into unconsciousness.

Roy A. Higgins

He regained consciousness momentarily as he was being carried out of the dance hall on a stretcher. The crowd on the pavement had parted, in order to let the stretcher pass through towards the waiting ambulance, and from his prone position, through swollen eyes, he thought for a moment that he caught a glimpse of Italian John in the crowd, a moon face grinning at him like the Cheshire cat from Alice in Wonderland, before he lost consciousness once again.

CHAPTER ELEVEN

Ray was in the hospital for five whole days suffering from a concussion, a cracked rib, eight stitches in his bottom lip, and a further two in his eyebrow. Cookie's situation was far worse, although on the surface he didn't look anything like as bad as Ray, a bang to the head had caused a haemorrhage inside of his skull, and he had endured an emergency operation in order to stop the bleeding.

On the day that Ray was due to leave the hospital, the Beatles gave their last public performance on the roof of Apple records and Cookie was released from intensive care, enabling Ray to see him for the first time.

"Thanks mate," said Cookie, believing that he had been the target of the attack and that Ray had only been injured by coming to his aid.

"Do you know why it kicked off?" asked Ray.

"Not a clue," replied Cookie. "I can only think that it was mistaken identity."

"They probably just thought that you were an ugly bastard," suggested Ray in jest.

Cookie tried to laugh but it obviously caused him considerable pain.

"They can't have liked your face very much either, because they've made a dam good job of remodelling it," he retaliated.

They talked for a further ten minutes and then the nurse interrupted them.

"Mr Cook will need his rest now," she announced, indicating that it was time for Ray to leave.

Ray promised to visit again in a couple of days, and left the ward so that he could telephone for a taxi to take him home.

Over the next week his wounds healed nicely, it was painful to eat but only his rib remained a real problem. He was scared to breathe in as the pain was so intense, while getting comfortable in bed was a near impossibility. To make matters worse, the elastic bandage that he was forced to wear around his torso, had begun to cause severe itching which was driving him mad.

He constructed a makeshift backscratcher from a planting device that he used for his fish tank. It had a razor blade on one end for cleaning algae from the glass, which he removed in the interest of safety. On the other end it had a forked plastic attachment for pushing plants into the gravel, which made an ideal back scratchier, but the more that he scratched the more itchy he became.

He went stir crazy watching daytime television day after day, but finally the bandage came off and at last he could have a long awaited bath. He enjoyed it so much, that he lay in the hot soapy water for almost an hour, until the water was almost cold and his skin had shrivelled up like that of a prune.

Godfrey had arranged for him to come back to work on the day shift for the first couple of weeks, in order to see how he would cope. He had returned from Holland armed with masses of documentation, but as he was not in the habit of performing physical tasks himself, he had left the machines standing idle for almost two weeks awaiting Ray's return, before starting with the setting up process.

It was the middle of February, and on the first Monday in March, a charge hand from Valkenswaard was due at the factory in order to train the operators. This left them with only two weeks to get all of the machines set up and running satisfactorily.

"You've certainly made a big impression on *Weis*," said Godfrey. "She tore into me for not bringing you back with me, and she told me to tell you that you promised to write."

"I'm useless at writing," Ray admitted. "In any case; I'm never going to see her again. It would all fizzle out in time."

"You never know," said Godfrey positively. "Maybe you'll have to return to Valkenswaard one day. If the opportunity arises I'll make sure that you get to go."

"Is E Z finished yet?" asked Ray, changing the subject.

"The painters are out and the electricians are almost finished," Godfrey informed him.

"Will the Plant department be doing the wiring?" Ray wanted to know.

"No, the job was too big for them to cope with," replied Godfrey. "G H Jones is doing it."

■ ■ ■

G H Jones was an electrical contractor based in Manchester with an office locally; they worked on the Vallard site almost continuously, as they did on many other sites throughout the region.

Ray had left Vallard's and gone to work for G H Jones as soon as his apprenticeship was completed. He had felt trapped always working in the one place and couldn't resist the pull of the open road.

He had been sent to work at the Leyland truck division, where he had stayed for ten months. Initially everything had gone well, until a disagreement about the safety of the scaffolding that they were expected to use, had resulted in a down-tools, for which Ray had been held largely responsible and shipped off the site. After that he had been branded as a trouble maker, and as the word got around he had been shunted from site to site, before being returned to of all places the Vallard factory.

Roland Martin was the electrical foreman in C block, and already had four shift electricians working under his control. When Ray had been a rooky apprentice, Roland had spent a lot of his free time re-wiring people's houses in the evenings and at weekends. He had seen the potential in Ray at a very early age, and always asked him to assist with his part time jobs rather than any of the other apprentices.

When he discovered that Ray had returned to Vallard's, he had approached him explaining that he was being put in charge of a second department in E block, and that he would require a further three shift electricians in that department. He also explained that he would eventually require a charge-hand electrician in E block, as C block already kept him very busy, and that he saw Ray as the ideal candidate for the job.

Ray had left Jones's on this flimsy promise of a future promotion, but what Roland wasn't aware of at the time was that his superiors viewed things very differently. Six months after Ray's appointment as maintenance electrician in E block, Roland had been permanently removed as foreman so that he could concentrate on his other department, Godfrey having been appointed in his place, which made the need for a charge-hand completely unnecessary.

■ ■ ■

As soon as he got the chance he wandered into E Z building, he knew most of the electricians who were working in there; in fact he had been extremely friendly with two of them while working at G H. Jones.

Thomas Wilkes had been his closest work college while working for Jones, though everyone knew him as Tommy Brush, primarily because he was as daft as a brush, a colloquial term derived from the erratic behaviour of the tile industry workers known as brushes, who a century earlier had been poisoned by spirits of mercury which they painted onto the tiles before firing.

Tommy's friend was Moe Mc Doughnut, his real name was Mc Dermott but he was known to his friends as Doughnut. These two were extremely good friends and frequented a local hostelry on the outskirts of the town. Although it was far from the bright lights of the city centre, it had a regular clientele both male and female, who had formed a into a tight little click, to talk, drink, play darts and snooker, in fact they did everything together, and didn't seem to need the company of outsiders to muddy the waters of their little world.

■ ■ ■

Weekend in Amsterdam

On short break holidays this little party always hired a coach to take them to a village in the Lake District. The village was so tiny, that it consisted of a single cul-de-sac street which culminated at a farm gate. There was a row of eight or nine stone built terraced cottages along one side of the street, the last of which being a post office and village shop. Five of the cottages were used as holiday lets by the local pub, and the party of friends usually hired two or three of them.

At the junction with the main road stood the village pub, its front garden faced the main road and was dotted with wooden picnic tables, while the white painted gable of the pub faced the cottages some way down the street. A long back garden, which the pub used as a tent site during the summer months, nestled behind a tall brick wall, and stretched all the way to the farmyard at the opposite end of the street. Beyond the pub gable and planted in a hole in the pavement, stood the largest cherry tree that Ray had ever seen in his life, which must have looked magnificent on the 1st of May, although Ray never managed to engineer a visit on that particular date in order to witness the glorious sight.

The pub landlord was a well known ex-climber who had married an Austrian woman, who he had presumably met during his climbing days. The dome of his head was completely bald, while what hair he had was long and tied in a ponytail. He also sported a long grey beard, which he parted in the middle, while tying the tips with ribbon so as to keep the two ends apart in a fork. After the official licensing law closing time, he would retire to his bed after a long day behind the bar, while his wife, who was more of a night owl, would lock the doors and keep the bar open for the regulars, and for those staying in the cottages or tents, until dawn if necessary.

Once all of the doors had been closed and her husband had gone to his bed, she would remove her clothes, which didn't take long, as she only wore a drab grey knitted woollen dress and flip flops on her bare feet. The spectre of Posey on one of these late night drinking sessions was not a pretty one. She was around thirty pounds overweight, in her late fifties or early sixties, and with long grey straggly hair and pendulous breasts, which dropped to what must once have been her waist.

She had a fancy for all of the young men who came into the bar, newcomers being initiated into the late night drinking sessions as the landlady sat on shaking knees, before burying frightened heads into her drooping breasts, which had to be physically lifted from around her midriff especially for the purpose.

Because of his notoriety in climbing circles, the pub was regularly visited by climbers and walkers who were keen to meet the landlord, while because of her notoriety as a stripper, it was always full after hours with temporary residents of the cottages, campers, and the local farm workers, who wanted to watch the floor show.

One Easter weekend, Ray and Archie had been persuaded by Doughnut and Tommy to go with them on one of their little jaunts. The group had already hired two of the rental cottages, one for the girls and the other one for the boys. Each cottage slept six, including the use of a bed settee downstairs, and as there were already six boys and five girls going on the trip, it seemed to Ray and Archie that the cottages would not accommodate all of them. When Ray had voiced his concerns however, Tommy had insisted that they need not ring to change the booking, as they would always be able to hire another cottage on arrival if they needed one.

On arrival however it was a very different story, as all of the cottages were fully booked being a bank holiday weekend. The landlord told them that there was no room at the proverbial inn, and as he didn't have a stable he offered to erect a two man ridge tent on the lawn, which in all probability had seen service in the Himalayas, perhaps even on Mount Everest itself.

One of the girls in the party, having heard stories of Ray's reputation from Tommy and Doughnut, had crawled into Ray's tent on the first afternoon of their arrival hoping to gain some first-hand experience. Ray had been more than willing to satisfy her curiosity, but quickly let out a cry of pain as his manhood withered and tried to hide deep inside his body.

He should probably have been circumcised as a child but he hadn't been, and now it looked as though he might just have performed a DIY job. She helped him in his efforts to staunch the flow of blood, and when the bleeding had finally stopped he had bravely insisted in continuing what they had started, if somewhat gingerly, convincing her of what a brave little soldier he was.

The other girls in the party all showed concern as word of his trauma got around. Either because of their maternal instincts or their morbid curiosity, they all wanted to view the damage and offer their medical experience. From that moment he was not allowed to sleep in the tent, and was moved from bed to bed by the girls like pass the parcel.

On the first evening of their arrival, Tommy Brush had lived up to his daft as a brush image, by jumping from the top step of the stairs while shouting Spiderman. On hitting the floor he had broken his leg but had refused to see a doctor or go to a hospital, spending the next three days in the bar, which never closed as long as someone wanted a drink, using alcohol as an anaesthetic to ease his pain.

On the following afternoon all of the boys, with the exception of the injured Tommy, had gone fishing at the tarn, which was a mile of a hike up a steep path onto the fell which ran behind the village. Archie had caught a ten inch brown trout, the first fish that he had ever caught in his life, which he had proudly taken back for the girls to cook. The girls had already agreed that they would do all of the cooking, provided that the boys agreed to do all of the peeling of vegetables and the washing up after. To compound his daft as a brush image, Tommy had stuffed the fish down his trousers and unzipped his fly so that the head poked through. There it had stayed, until three days later the fish had burst open with all of the roe and guts running down his legs.

■ ■ ■

"Hi Tommy, been to the lakes recently?" asked Ray.

"Not since August, but we're going again at Easter if you want to come."

"I'll ask Archie and let you know," replied Ray. "How's the job going?"

"Nearly finished," said Tommy. "We should be out of here by Friday."

Ray scanned the room; there was only one face that he didn't initially recognise.

"Who's the new guy?" he asked, "the one with the blonde hair up the ladder."

"Oh that's Stefan," replied Tommy.

Suddenly Ray could once again see the young man with the flat cap, bomber jacket, and purple scarf. His hair was shorter and seemed to be growing out from a darker colour, but Ray was convinced never the less that it was the same man.

"Unusual name for a Lancastrian," speculated Ray. "Is he foreign?"

"He's from East Germany; say's that he escaped over the Berlin wall," replied Tommy obviously impressed by his bravery."

"I thought that they shot people for trying to reach the west," said Ray, unable to hide his scepticism.

"They do, but he says that he was lucky; brave I call it."

"Perhaps he had a little help," whispered Ray, more to himself than for anyone else to hear.

"What do you mean?" asked Tommy overhearing his musings.

"Oh nothing," said Ray nonchalantly, "what's he like?"

"He seems okay, but it's not easy to hold a conversation with him because his English isn't very good."

"Neither is yours, but we still speak to you," Ray quipped.

"Piss off," said Tommy laughing.

"It must be difficult living in a foreign country without any friends," said Ray, fishing for information once again.

"He has a friend who works here in the factory; an Italian guy sometimes comes around to see him, always wears cowboy boots."

"Have you noticed anything unusual about him?" asked Ray his suspicions having been aroused.

"I think that the cowboy boots are pretty unusual, don't you?" Tommy answered.

Weekend in Amsterdam

"Not the Italian guy you moron, Stefan.

"What do you mean unusual?" Tommy wasn't following Ray's line of thought.

"You know," prompted Ray, "anything a bit cloak and dagger."

"What the hell are you talking about cloak and dagger?" asked Tommy, raising his voice in frustration.

"You know secretive," prompted Ray.

"Doughnut, come over here a minute," called Tommy.

Ray repeated the question.

"I did see him installing smoke detectors," answered Doughnut.

"Why did you think that it was unusual?" asked Ray.

"Because smoke rises, so you would have expected him to install them on the ceiling, and not on the wall. Not only that but I had already installed two of them on the ceiling and they were the only ones indicated on the diagram."

■ ■ ■

Ray met up with Archie for lunch as he usually did when working on the day shift.

"Glad to see you back at work mate," Archie greeted him.

"I'm glad to be back, said Ray, "I was going mad sitting at home."

"I believe that Cookie is going to be released from hospital today?" queried Archie.

"Yes I saw him on Friday, he was waiting to see the specialist but it will be a long time before he's back to normal."

"Why do you think that they picked on Cookie, had he been mouthing off again?

"He said not, he said that he'd never seen any of them before, but in any case I think that I might have been the target not Cookie."

"Why do you say that?" asked Archie in surprise. "They attacked Cookie first didn't they?"

"Maybe they wanted the big man out of the way so that they could concentrate on me," suggested Ray.

"Why do you think they might have been after you?" asked Archie still puzzled.

"Because as they carried me out on the stretcher I'm sure that I saw someone that I know, someone who I told to go and screw himself not very long ago."

"Was he one of those who attacked you?" asked Archie.

"No," admitted Ray. "I didn't recognise any of them, but I think that he might have arranged it."

As they left the canteen, Italian John was waiting for him at the same table just as before.

Ray turned to Archie. "See you later," he said, "I need to speak to someone."

He sat down at the table opposite to John.

"Vladimir was wondering if perhaps you might have had a change of heart," said John as Ray settled into his seat.

"Now why would he think that I may have changed my mind?" said Ray pretending to be puzzled. "Let me guess."

"He just thought that now that you have had time to review the situation you may feel more disposed to cooperate," said John coolly.

"I got your message," Ray said. "A further verbal one seems hardly necessary."

"What message?" John pretended to be puzzled.

Ray pointed to the scars on his face.

"You think that I had something to do with that?" asked John in mock surprise.

"I saw you watching as I was carried to the ambulance," insisted Ray. "Was Ivan or Stefan with you at the Astoria by any chance?"

"I think that you must have been hallucinating," replied John giving nothing away. "Besides Ivan is just a friend of my mothers, he has nothing at all to do with Vladimir and I don't know anyone named Stefan."

"It just seems strange to me that a paid up member of the Italian Communist Party and a Ukrainian national, who claims to have escaped from the brutal Communist regime, would both be living together under the same roof," pondered Ray. "I would have thought that your politics and his would be totally at odds, unless of course you were both secretly working for the same side."

"You have been doing your homework," said John impressed.

"Is that all?" said Ray rising from his seat.

John motioned for him to sit down again.

"Vladimir said that he would prefer to be referred to as the old queen rather than the old queer. He also asked me to inform you that he wishes he could screw himself as you suggested, as it would be a most memorable experience, but although he is extremely well endowed, that is a trick that even he has not yet managed to master."

"He has a sense of humour then," commented Ray.

"Most certainly, but remember his good humour is not inexhaustible," warned John.

"I bet it isn't," agreed Ray.

"Before you leave," said John," I must say that I am sorry to hear about your unfortunate beating. But look on the bright side; it could have been much worse."

"Is that a threat?" asked Ray.

John ignored him and carried on with his speech.

"I am sorry that you are still unwilling to help us, and Vladimir will be also. It might be wise to reconsider his offer as E Z is almost finished, and Vladimir would like to get the matter resolved as quickly as possible."

"Tell him that I have received his message loud and clear. I don't want any trouble so here is the deal, he forgets that he ever met me and I forget that I ever met him, and of course you."

"Is that your final word?" asked John disappointed with the answer that he had received.

"It is," replied Ray adamantly.

■ ■ ■

By Thursday evening all of the delay line machines were up and running. Ray expected to be put back onto maintenance duties the following day, but Godfrey called him into the office at four-thirty in the afternoon.

"There's a new armoured cable to be pulled into E Z building tomorrow, if you're feeling up to it I would like you on the tug of war team."

Whenever a new mains cable was to be installed it took every electrician in the factory, as a large diameter steel wire armoured cable is a very heavy piece of kit. When the cable is on the drum and only a small amount has been reeled off, it takes only a few men to handle it, but as more of it is reeled off it becomes heavier, and more men have to be recruited from their usual jobs in the factory in order to assist.

Ray was placed on the initial team along with Archie and two others, Ted Reeves and Bopper.

Ted was a fun guy and a little older than Ray, he was not tall but stocky and looked like a boxer with a flat nose, dark curly hair, and a permanent grin.

■ ■ ■

His boxing skills had been put to the test, when he had travelled out of town for a boy's night out, with Ray, Archie, and another Vallard electrician named Peter Black. Ted and Ray had picked up two local girls in one of the out of towns pubs, which was popular because of the live entertainment. As they were being taxied in Blackie's car and the girls lived a bus ride away, they were forced to settle for a walk to the bus stop and a kiss goodnight.

At the bus stop they had been approached by a group of local boy's, one of which had convinced himself that the girl sucking the face of Ted was his girlfriend. A fight had broken out and although it had been four against two, the fight hadn't been going at all badly for Ted and Ray, as both of them could handle themselves.

Superficially they were completely unmarked, although Ted's tie had been torn from his neck, and when the knot was later unfastened it separated into two pieces, causing great mirth among his friends. The damage to Ray's clothing had been a little more severe, his grazed knee peeping out through a gaping hole in his best suite trousers.

Their antagonists wore more visible scars of the conflict, and to make their plight even worse; Blackie and Archie had crossed the road, dodging between the moving traffic in order to enter the affray. Archie, who was already six foot four inches tall held his arms high into the air as he ran, which made him look even taller than he actually was and he was roaring like a wounded bear.

Archie was usually quite passive and never punched anyone, in fact Ray had never before seen him fight at all, but on this occasion he had grabbed two of the antagonists by the scruff of the neck, before physically throwing them one by one into a garden hedge, which formed a boundary between the householder's property, and the many drunken trouble makers who regularly waited at the bus stop. As the local boys ran off well and truly routed, all four sat on the garden wall and laughed until the tears ran down their cheeks, a mixture of relief and the exhilaration felt by the victors due to an adrenalin rush.

■ ■ ■

Bopper was married, a decade older than Ray and lived in a nineteen-fifties time warp. He still wore the Teddy boy uniform of the late nineteen-fifties, with drain pipe trousers, and knee length draped jackets of every hue with contrasting velvet collars. His hair which was died black and heavily greased, was combed into what in the fifties had been referred to as a D A, as it resembled a ducks arse at the back. He always wore a bootlace tie with a bovine head of silvered metal, and a coloured shirt with metal points on the collars. On his feet he wore crape soled beetle crusher shoes, with wedged heels and aluminous pink or lime green socks. Ray wondered if Mrs Bopper wore a pony tail, net underskirts, and bobby socks, but as he didn't know anyone who had ever seen Mrs Bopper, her appearance remained a mystery.

No one messed with Bopper. On one occasion a foolhardy electrician named Colin had managed to get on his wrong side. Bopper's response had been to stand the unlucky Colin onto a chair, before tying a window cord around his neck, and kicking away the chair to leave him dangling in mid-air. The windows of the building had metal frames hosting a number of small panes of glass. They opened by pivoting at a central point in the window frame, but as they were in H block, which was the chemical building, they were corroded and hadn't opened in years. As luck would have it, the weight of the writhing electrician on the end of the window cord, had caused the window catch to open for the first time in living memory, and the rusty old windows had slowly opened, lowering Colin safely, if a bit uncomfortably, to the ground before strangulation occurred.

■ ■ ■

Dan Rhymes always coordinated the cable pulling as everyone needed to pull at the same time. He was in his early fifties with receding fiery red hair and a moustache to match, having been the works convenor for the electrical trades union for many years. Dan was a thoroughly nice guy, and had been of assistance to Ray in his official capacity on a number of occasions.

Ray and Archie removed the first manhole cover. Under the factory floor was a labyrinth of tunnels which the electricians referred to as cable ducts. They were a meter high and a meter wide, and normally had a few centimetres of water covering the floor.

Beneath this particular manhole cover was a square shaft of about a meter deep, used to drop in a submersible pump in order to pump the water from the tunnels. Although on this occasion the drain hole was filled to the brim, with the excess water overflowing out into the tunnels, they decided not to waste any time by draining it as the water in the tunnels was very shallow.

Ray climbed down the hole first, being careful not to step into the deeper water. It was dark in the tunnel, and it took him a few moments for his eyes to adjust to the poor lighting conditions. He had been in the factory cable ducts on many occasions, but this time was different, as it appeared that the walls and the ceiling were moving, making him feel a little dizzy as his eyes couldn't reconcile to what they were seeing. He closed his eyes and re-opened them but the same situation remained.

"Archie, pass me a torch," he shouted back up the manhole.

Shining the torch into the tunnel he quickly discovered the source of his visual problems, a moving mass of cockroaches some five or six centimetre's thick, climbing all over each other on the walls and the ceiling. They took up another couple of manhole covers along the duct allowing light to enter the tunnel, and after a few minutes the cockroaches dispersed looking for darker and more favourable conditions.

The four man team began to pull in the cable, as they did so the water on the floor of the duct became rather muddy completely hiding the shaft. It became great fun, as more and more electricians were recruited to help, to forget to mention the shaft in the muddy water, waiting expectantly to see who would step into it. Most of the electricians did, before pulling back only after the water had filled their wellington boots.

Ben Ainsworth was the smallest electrician in the factory. He was nicknamed Maverick in deference to the western gambler from the television series, because of his winning ways at cards. He was particularly good at poker, probably doubling his weekly salary by taking money from the other seasoned card players at lunch time.

Instead of lowering himself carefully into the hole, as the most of the others had done, because his feet were so far from the floor of the tunnel, he had launched himself from a sitting position on the edge of the manhole, expecting to land on the floor of the tunnel a few inches below his feet. Instead to every ones amusement, he went straight down the shaft until he was standing chest deep in the dirty cold water.

In the final stages of the cable pull, Harry Harrison and Alvin Greenhalgh arrived. Alvin was laughing because he had grabbed the last pair of wellington boots in the stores, leaving Harry to wade around in the shallow water in his work boots. Taking off his brand new yellow leather work boots, he carefully placed them well away from the manhole so that they would not be splashed, before slipping on the wellingtons. He laughed even more as Harry splashed around in the shallow water of the tunnel, until he realised that Harry had removed his own boots before replacing them with Alvin's brand new ones.

Late in the afternoon after a hard days graft the cable was finally into position, ready to be connected by the jointers. All of the electricians began vacating the cable duct, and as Ray and Archie were the first in and therefore the farthest down the tunnel; they were also the last to leave. The cable was long, and so it took them some considerable time to make their way back to the nearest open manhole. Realising on their arrival that the manhole cover had already been replaced, they crawled to the next manhole only to find that the cover had also been replaced. Convinced that the wet feet brigade were getting their own back for the trick that they had played earlier, they crawled to the final manhole, which was still open as they approached, but closed just before they reached it trapping them inside.

They waited, expecting the cover to open again to reveal the perpetrators enjoying the joke. After a few minutes however, during which time nothing happened, they tried to move the heavy concrete filled manhole cover by themselves but it wouldn't budge. Even though it was very heavy the two of them together should have been able to dislodge it, but being unable to make an impression, they soon realised that it had been fastened down using the manhole cover keys. Surely if this was just a joke the perpetrators wouldn't have locked it.

Waiting for a little while longer they gathered their thoughts. Archie checked the time on his illuminated watch, it was five past five, the day shift would have gone home by now and the late shift would be at tea.

"Who's on the late shift?" asked Archie.

"Jack Garrett," answered Ray.

"Perhaps they have left a message with Jack to let us out after he has had his tea," suggested Archie hopefully.

After waiting until nearly six o' clock they realised that no one was going to come to let them out. The air in the tunnel was by now very stale and it was becoming increasingly difficult to breathe, realising that they were trapped in the tunnel until they suffocated, unless they could find another way out soon, they both began to feel panic.

Common sense told them that they would not be heard calling for help through six inches of concrete floor, but they called out anyway. Their voices echoed through the tunnels, bouncing from the walls until they were lost in the far distance. They continued calling for some time until they became hoarse, finally giving up after realising that calling was futile.

The tunnels were ventilated through grills under the loading bays, and they made the decision that they must try to find one. The longest tunnels ran under the corridors one on each side of the factory. These tunnels connected all of the buildings in the factory. They ran from A block at one end of the site near to the factory gate, all the way to E block where Ray himself worked, while on the other side of the factory they ran from the chemical H block to M block. Tunnels ran off the corridor tunnels into each building, while other shorter tunnels ran in the opposite direction into smaller buildings, suffixed Z buildings, which terminated at the loading bays.

Ray and Archie were in total darkness as Bopper had taken the torch with him. Remembering that there was a ventilation grill at the opposite end of the cable, they crawled back on hands and knees in the muddy water feeling for the cable as they went.

Occasionally they heard the squeaking of rats and felt them brush past in the darkness of the tunnel, one jumping onto Ray's shoulder and running down his back in order to pass, while another could be felt wriggling beneath his buttocks when he sat down to rest. Finally they reached the end of the cable, where it turned upwards before disappearing through a hole in the floor and into the electrical distribution board, waiting be connected up after the weekend.

"We must be under E Z building now," said Ray stating the obvious.

They tried calling for help through the hole in the floor, but the building was in darkness and they knew that it would be left unoccupied until Monday morning. Although it was dark outside, they could see the light from the loading bay coming through the ventilation grill some ten meters away. Making their way towards it, they breathed in the fresher air which was extremely welcome after the stale air of the tunnel.

On reaching the grill they pushed in unison but it wouldn't budge, they called for help through the grill but the loading bay was deserted. After working on the grill for a further ten minutes but to no avail, they realised that it was hopeless and resolved to find the next grill behind D Z building.

They took a few deep breaths of the cold February air before retracing their steps, following the cable until they were back at the original manhole cover, where the end of the cable had been left so that it could be jointed to an older cable, which snaked back to the substation a quarter of a mile away.

Following the old cable they could easily miss their turning, so once the new cable had run out they began to feel the walls instead, looking for the next opening on the right, as a left turn would take them under one of the main buildings, and they could very easily get lost in the maze of tunnels and not be found for years.

As they felt along the walls searching for the opening they could feel cockroaches moving beneath their fingers, some cracking as they leant against the walls for support. They couldn't help brushing against the ceiling as they crawled and cockroaches fell onto their hair and shoulders, some of them getting inside of their clothing and could be felt crawling down their backs.

When they finally reached an opening in the wall they turned right towards the loading bay, although when they arrived at the ventilation grill the area was once again deserted, except for one of a large number of feral cats, which lived among the discarded machinery on a grassy hill overlooking the loading bay. The cats survived by hunting rats, mice, and even cockroaches in the tunnels, with supplements of cat food put out for them by well meaning employees. It peered at them through the grill with large black eyes, its irises wide open to make the most of the available light.

■ ■ ■

Ray was reminded of the time when a directive had been issued that the cats were to be rounded up in order to be gassed, as they had become too numerous and very wild. A team of three strong men with more muscle than brain, were employed to move all of the heavy equipment within the factory. They were known by the Plant department as the heavy gang, and were given the job of rounding up all of the cats.

When they had caught a sack full, they had taken them to the boiler house with the intention of gassing them in the boiler. Unfortunately they had made the mistake of not only turning on the gas, but also firing up the boiler. After a while they had turned off the gas supply, and had opened the boiler expecting to find a sack full of dead cats. Instead what they found were very much alive but badly singed cats, which having taken the heavy gang by surprise had escaped from the sack to re-colonise the factory.

■ ■ ■

The cat soon became bored with the staring contest, and with a look of disdain it moved off to look for its supper elsewhere. They tried the grill but it wouldn't move, they called for help but no one heard them, so they took more gulps of fresh air before beginning the search for the next grill.

By the time that they reached C Z loading bay they were wet, cold, and exhausted, after pulling in a heavy cable all day, following which they had now been crawling around in the tunnel for a further two hours. This ventilation grill wouldn't move either, and Ray cursed the builders for doing such a good job when fitting them.

"I wonder How long can we live without food?" asked Archie, worried that they might starve to death before Monday morning.

"A couple of weeks," Ray speculated.

"That's good because we have water, even if it is dirty," said Archie relieved. "If the worst comes to the worst, someone will hear us on Monday morning if we call for help."

"The temperature out there is already below freezing you idiot," Ray told him. "It could fall as low as minus four Celsius tonight, we're already sitting in wet clothes, and it's a cast iron certainty that we'll die from hypothermia long before Monday morning, so drinking water is not the problem."

Archie began to panic, he screamed and shouted and while lying on his back in the water, he began kicking wildly with the soles of his boots at the grill. He must have summoned up super human strength in his anger and panic, because to Ray's surprise the grill started to give way, a little at first but with perseverance it began to move more and more. It took a further twenty minutes with both of them trying in turn, but finally they were free and out onto the cold February night.

CHAPTER TWELVE

Ray usually went out for a drink or two on Friday evenings, but he'd had enough excitement for one day. He told his mother that he'd been working late, locking himself in the bathroom to have a long soak in the bath, before going to bed early and sleeping until noon the following day.

Archie had to work on Saturdays; in fact he had to work every day of the week. Production ceased in most departments over the weekend, giving the installation staff an opportunity to disconnect some of the machines and transfer them to different areas of the factory, which seemed to be a favourite pastime of the production department managers.

■ ■ ■

Ray had worked for seven days a week just like Archie when he had worked in the Plant department, which was one of the reasons why he had become a maintenance electrician instead of working on plant installation. The downside of a transfer to a maintenance job was working on shifts, but at least it was a five day week, and what you lost in overtime you gained in shift allowance.

Archie's boss was one Phil Whitehead. Cost meant nothing to Phil, but he was a stickler for perfection. If any part of the installation was not to his personal satisfaction, he would have the whole job stripped out regardless of the cost, before making the offending electrician begin all over again even if it took him an extra week.

Ray had always got on well with Phil, as he was a good worker and a bit of a perfectionist himself. Unfortunately their relationship had soured after six years of working every hour that God sends, sometimes until midnight on Sunday, or even into the early hours of Monday morning, to ensure that no production would be lost at the start of the production week.

He had once asked Phil for a Saturday afternoon off; as he had been asked to officiate at a friend's wedding. Phil had not taken the request kindly. On Sundays they were paid double time, but only time and a half on Saturdays. Phil had an unwritten rule, "no Saturday, no Sunday," as many of the men tried to get out of working on Saturday afternoons so as to watch the Rovers play. He had insisted that Ray decline the wedding invitation and the honour which went with it, but Ray had refused, and instead declined to work the weekend at all if he couldn't have the afternoon off. Phil had taken offence at his refusal to work, and didn't speak to him on a personal level for over a month, refusing to offer him any weekend work at all, and finding him all of the worst jobs in the factory which were usually reserved for Archie, until Ray had handed in his notice and gone to work for G H Jones.

■ ■ ■

At break time Archie sought out Ted and Bopper, he found them sitting on a workbench in the Plant department eating egg and bacon tea cakes, which they had purchased from the works canteen, while drinking mugs of tea bearing threatening slogans like, "Keep off, this is mine" and "Touch this mug and your dead."

"Which of you idiots put the manhole covers back yesterday?" shouted Archie angrily.

"What the hell are you talking about?" snapped Bopper indignantly.

"Somebody put the manhole covers back while we were still in the ducts," Archie informed them.

"Well it wasn't us," said Ted.

"You must have been the last ones out of the ducts," insisted Archie, turning his attention to Ted, as Bopper was obviously in no mood for his unfounded accusations.

"We were," agreed Ted," but we didn't put the manhole covers back."

"When we got out," interrupted Bopper, "Dan Rhymes asked if we were the last ones out. We told him that you and Ray were right behind us, so he told us to leave the covers off, expecting you and Ray to replace them when you got out."

"Did Dan leave with you?"

"Yes, it was almost five; we all went to clock out together," said Bopper.

"Then who did replace the manhole covers," asked Archie.

"Search me," said Ted.

Archie was puzzled, but Ray had no doubt in his mind who had replaced the manhole covers, what's more, he intended to kick the crap out of the Italian cowboy the very next time that he saw him.

It seemed obvious that Vladimir had not taken his suggestion of a truce very well. The beating had been intended to make him co-operate, but this on the other hand had been an attempt to silence him for good.

John checked the air vents under the loading bay for the second time in two days, having also checked them the previous day to be sure that they were secure. Having joined the Communist Party after his father's death, he had been recruited to work for the cause. He had been happy to follow in his father's footsteps and join the party, as it would be a fitting memorial to the father who he missed and loved. He was sure that his father would have been very proud of him.

When he had accepted his commission, his expectations were that he would have to pass on information, maybe even steal secrets for the cause, but in his wildest dreams he had never envisaged having to murder anyone. This was his first active service. He had been a sleeper ever since Vladimir had recruited him, almost forgetting in the intervening years that he worked for the GRU at all. At first he had found it exciting, passing on threatening messages from Vladimir to Ray, while paying the gang of teenagers at the Astoria in order to soften Ray up. All of a sudden he wasn't sure that he liked what he was being asked to do, but he knew that he dared not refuse or he himself might become the recipient of Vladimir's wrath.

■ ■ ■

John had met Vladimir while in Moscow as a child, as his father also worked for the GRU. At the time he had no idea of his father's occupation, only knowing that his father and Vladimir were friends and work colleagues. Over time he had begun to refer to Vladimir as Uncle Vladimir, who always brought him treats and toys, grooming him for the day when as a young adolescent, he would try to cajole him into having homosexual sex and when that failed violently rape him. John had been frightened and upset after the incident, but he had never told a soul. Apart from the fact that Vladimir scared him, he had also been very well paid by his adopted uncle for his silence.

John was totally unaware that his father knew about the rape, but he had in fact come to an untimely end because of it. After a confrontation with Vladimir on the banks of the Moska River, a fight had ensued in which Vladimir had drowned John's father in shallow water, before weighting his body with rocks and pushing his body out into deeper water. His father had meant everything to John, and in his ignorance of the facts surrounding his father's death, he had felt that by working for Vladimir he was somehow honouring his father's memory. Had he known the truth, he would surely not have been trying to kill Ray now on Uncle Vladimir's orders.

■ ■ ■

He walked down the loading bay checking all of the ventilation grills in turn, until he came to an ornate cast iron grill, which was lying on the ground and revealing a gaping black hole into the duct.

"Damn," he muttered under his breath.

Vladimir had made it quite clear that Ray's death must appear to be an accident, as he didn't want attention drawn to the mission. John knew that his failure would not be well received in Amsterdam, and so he resolved to make a second attempt to dispose of Ray before Vladimir discovered the truth of his failure.

CHAPTER THIRTEEN

On alternate Saturday afternoons, Ray would usually go with Cookie to watch the Rovers when they were playing at home. This Saturday they didn't have a game, as they were due to play Manchester City in the FA cup fifth round the following Monday, besides it would be quite a while before Cookie was fit enough to go and watch the Rovers play again.

His father was sitting in his favourite chair, reading the Daily Express and laughing at the Giles cartoon. Before Ray's grandmother had passed away, Ray had regularly teased her that she looked like the grandmother in the Giles cartoons. Having a great sense of humour she always laughed, while agreeing that she did. His father had always been a big fan of Giles, and at Christmas time, Ray had bought him an annual containing the year's cartoons, which had kept him amused until the middle of January.

Ray and his father had little in common anymore. When he was young they had both supported Accrington Stanley, attending every home game together. If the away ground was accessible they would also attend away games, if not they would go with a handful of die-hards to watch the reserves play.

They had once travelled to Halifax Town with Stanley, but not having been to the Shay ground before, they had parked the car and followed the crowds, realising far too late that they were on the rugby ground by mistake. They even went to Anfield when Stanley played Liverpool in the FA cup, where standing on the kop, Ray was swept up and down the terraces by the motion of the crowd, his feet barely touching the ground, until at half time someone had urinated down his leg through a rolled up newspaper. When Stanley had gone into liquidation in the early nineteen-sixties, his father had lost interest in watching live football altogether and they had drifted apart ever since.

Superficially he resembled his father in appearance, except that where Ray's hair was fair like his mothers, his father's hair was dark, heavily Brylcreemed and swept back with a centre parting. They had the same dark eyes and facial features, but Ray was an inch or two taller than his father and more athletically built.

Conscious that they had drifted apart, Ray had many times invited his father to accompany him to watch the Rovers, or to go across to the local pub for a drink, but his father being neither a drinker nor a conversationalist, preferred to stay within his own comfort zone and always refused.

Ray was not a big newspaper reader like his father, who was hardly ever seen without a newspaper covering his face. Apart from the Giles cartoons, a rare shared interest, he only ever read the final scores on Saturday evening, and the football match reports in the Sunday newspapers.

"This might be of interest to you Raymond," said his father, instigated a rare conversation with his son, while reading aloud from his newspaper.

"On the ninth of February, a proto-type Boeing 747-100 called the City of Everett made its maiden flight. The new Boeing is twice the size of the Boeing 707, and because of its super size it has been nicknamed the Jumbo Jet."

Ray had always been interested in aeroplanes since a child, lately his interest had been re-kindled by his visit to Amsterdam.

"Just imagine," said his father, "Four hundred seats."

"Where do they put them all?" asked Ray, interested for once in something that his father had to say.

"It seems that it has two decks," explained his father. "Apparently they intend to strip out most of the seats when supersonic flight takes over, and use the main body of the plane for cargo, just leaving the smaller top deck for passengers, which will initially be for first class passengers only.

"Can you remember the first time that you flew?" said his father reminiscing.

"I remember us flying to the Isle of Man when I was eleven."

"No, I mean well before that," said his father. "When you were five or six, you saw an aeroplane doing sightseeing trips around Blackpool Tower. You pestered me for weeks to go up in it; eventually for a little peace and quiet I said that we would. We took off from Squires Gate Airport in an eight seat bi-plane made from plywood and canvas. It was the first time that either of us had ever flown, I have never been so scared in all of my life, but you loved every minute of it."

"I do remember, do you know I had totally forgotten," said Ray, travelling with his father down memory lane."

"It say's hear," continued his father reading once again from the newspaper, "That Pan American have placed an order with Boeing for twenty five of the aeroplanes. It also appears that an Anglo-French supersonic aeroplane called the Concorde is in its completion stages."

"That means that it travels faster than the speed of sound, doesn't it?" interjected Ray.

"I can't believe," said his father, "that it's only twenty years since we flew around Blackpool Tower on an eight seat bi-plane made of canvas and wood, and now they're building supersonic aircraft."

He removed his reading glasses, folded his newspaper and placed it onto the coffee table.

"You're mother has gone into town shopping and I have no idea when she will be back," he said. "Should we go to the Royal Oak for a pie and a pint?"

■ ■ ■

On Saturday evenings they always met up in The Legs O' Man public house. It was a dingy place on the fringes of the red light district of the town. Being a free house, it sold strange concoctions like Old Peculiar, Guards Ale and Dragons Blood.

The Legs O' Man was the final building left standing, of what had once been a row of early nineteenth century cottage shops adjoining the cathedral grounds. The shops obscured the entrance to the cathedral, so that when a careless property developer had tried to rebuild the frontage of one of the shops without planning permission, the council had seen their opportunity, and grasping it with both hands had forced him to demolish the building. This had made the rest of the row unstable, which had been an excellent excuse for the council to compulsory purchase the remaining shops, and ultimately demolish them one and all. The Legs O' Man was deemed to be safe by an independent surveyor, and as the council had no reasonable excuse for revoking the drinking license, it was left standing at least for the time being, a carbuncle on the clerical landscape.

The décor inside The Legs O' Man consisted of gloss painted walls and ceiling of undetermined colour, with a generous coating of nicotine on top, which had begun a gradual transition from dirty yellow towards the browner end of the spectrum.

The pub was frequented by elderly ex-prostitutes, now acting as enthusiastic amateurs in return for free drinks from the male clientele, which consisted of ageing petty thieves and semi retired house breakers.

Goff and Alfie were already halfway through their first pint of Flowers bitter when he arrived.

"Where's this new place that we are going to tonight?" asked Ray, as he sat down with a bottle of Guards Ale, the only one that he would be allowed to drink all night, as Goff had suggested that they visit a pub on the outskirts of town, which was under new management and quickly gaining a reputation as the in-place to be.

"If you want to have a drink tonight I'll drive," suggested Alfie, who hardly ever finished a drink anyway and wouldn't miss it.

"Over my dead body," responded Ray. "Besides numb nuts, I'll still have to drive home after dropping all of you free loaders off."

■ ■ ■

Ray had the dubious honour of being Alfie's first driving instructor. Alfie had bought himself a car, a ten year old Vauxhall Wyvern in immaculate condition. True to form he had turned up out of the blue, asking Ray if he would take him out for a driving lesson. As the Rovers were playing away and he had nothing else to do on that particular Saturday, he had foolishly agreed.

They spent the afternoon driving around an empty car park outside of the football ground, and although Alfie had a very short concentration span, at the end of three hours he seemed to be getting the hang of it. Alfie had asked Ray if he would take him out that very evening in his new car. As Archie's marriage was still intact at the time, Cookie had been away visiting relatives in Yorkshire and he hadn't yet met Goff, he had said that he would.

When Ray picked him up, his mother had made it clear that Alfie was not under any circumstances to drive the car on the road, so after another quick lesson on the car park, they went off for a night out with Ray behind the wheel.

They arrived at a country pub a few miles out of town, which was packed with young people enjoying themselves, but Alfie's short attention span had soon got the better of him, and before he had even finished his first pint of beer he wanted to leave. As they returned to the car Alfie had insisted that he was going to drive. As it was his car and he couldn't be persuaded otherwise, Ray had reluctantly given in to his demands.

Alfie had positioned himself behind the wheel of the car, checked his rear view mirror, put the car into reverse gear, and reversed out of the parking space just as they had rehearsed during their afternoons practice. Unfortunately he had turned the steering wheel a little too early and clipped the rear wing of the car parked alongside.

Although his actions had resulted in only superficial damage, he had completely lost his head and in consequence control of the car. Shooting backwards before Ray could stop him, he reversed into a car parked across the exit lane. He then slammed the car into forward gear, and in his haste to escape the consequences of his actions, he had bounced of one car after another as if he were a ball bearing inside of a pin ball machine, before shooting off down the road, with his rear bumper dragging on the road and throwing up a shower of sparks as he made his escape in tears.

■ ■ ■

When Archie arrived, late as usual, he pulled Ray to one side as his topic of conversation didn't concern the others.

"I asked Ted and Bopper who put the covers back on the manholes, but they said that it wasn't them, and that they had no idea who could have done it as they were the last to leave with Dan. Who on earth do you think could have done it?" he asked with a puzzled look on his face.

"Search me," said Ray disinterestedly, and the subject was never mentioned again.

They arrived at their target destination, an old coaching house which had recently been extended and modernised by the brewery. It sat in total isolation on the dark and lonely moor, overlooking the much brighter lights of the town below. The car park was full, which was always a good sign when you were out on the pull, making it necessary to park on the narrow country lane which passed by the hostelry, and had once served as a coaching road for the stage coaches travelling between the hill towns and hamlets. Unfortunately for the boys, being some distance from any town or hamlet and not being on a recognised bus route, all of the girls in the pub were in cars driven by dates or boyfriends, so after just one drink they decided that it was time to move elsewhere.

On returning to the car Ray noticed that he appeared to have a flat tyre.

"Bastards," he said, as he reviewed a slash in his tyre wall, which had been deliberately inflicted using a knife blade.

They set about changing the wheel in the darkness, Ray doing most of the work while the others stood around watching, while chipping in now and then with comments of unconstructive criticism.

One of the cars which had been parked up the road, suddenly switched on his headlights as the engine roared into life. As half of the road was blocked by parked vehicles, and there being only a muddy grass verge on each side of the road, terminating in a ditch for run-off water, it was necessary for the friends to be changing the wheel in the middle of the road in the darkness.

Paying no attention to their predicament the vehicle began to move forward, slowly at first as if stalking them, before rapidly picking up speed unexpectedly. Temporarily blinded by the headlights of the oncoming vehicle, they realised too late, that the car was driving not only towards them, but directly at them and at breakneck speed.

They scattered in every direction, while attempting to dodge the worst that this guided missile had to offer. Archie was closest one to the oncoming vehicle, and was struck on the elbow by the car's wing mirror as he attempted to squeeze between two parked cars for safety, while Alfie narrowly avoided being struck as he threw himself aside at the very last moment, ending up wet and muddy and lying in the run-off ditch.

It soon became obvious that Ray was the intended target of the attack. As he was unable to squeeze between the parked cars for safety as Archie and Goff had done, he decided to run for the grass verge on the opposite side of the road, where Alfie already lay wet and uncomfortable in the safety of the ditch.

The car veered from side to side in Ray's direction whichever way he tried to run, and for a moment he appeared to be trapped like a rabbit in the headlights, unable to decide on his best course of action. He realised that he would have to put some considerable distance between himself and the approaching car if he were to have any chance of crossing the road to the grass verge on the other side. Ray had always been an excellent sprinter, and his school record for the hundred metres still stood eleven years after leaving school. Sprinting diagonally across the road he almost reached the other side, before he was catapulting into the ditch as the car struck him on the hip as he dived for safety.

Had any one of them taken a direct hit they would most certainly have been killed, tossed onto the bonnet of the car to strike the window screen, or run down and crushed beneath the wheels of the car as it drove over him. Goff was the only one who managed to escape scot-free, although more by good luck than by good management, and he rushed to the aid of Ray and Alfie who were lying in the ditch, while Archie cursed and swore while dancing around holding his damaged elbow.

Lying in the mud, with an incredible pain in his hip which ran down the whole of his leg until it reached his ankle; Ray watched the tail lights of the offending vehicle, as it sped off at breakneck speed down the dark narrow country lane.

CHAPTER FOURTEEN

On Sunday afternoon Ray and his friends all met in The Legs O' Man to give Alfie a good send off. His leave was almost over and it was time for him to return to his ship that very evening. Archie had his arm in a make shift sling to ease the pain from the heavy bruising to his arm, while Ray's leg had stiffened up to the point where he could hardly walk, but they could both be thankful that nothing was broken or worse.

Cookie wasn't able to come at all, his hair was growing back after his operation and he was improving slowly, although he still had a long way to go, spending most of his time with Brenda, who had been visiting him throughout his convalescence.

"Strange what happened last night," said Archie.

"You mean the puncture?" asked Ray innocently.

"I mean the car that tried to run us over. Why would he do that?"

"I haven't got a clue," said Ray, as if it was no big deal.

"Well I think that you have," contradicted Archie. "There's something going on here that you are not telling us."

"Oh leave him alone," said Goff. "He obviously doesn't want to talk about it."

"To hell with that," said Archie angrily. "Cookie's had to have a brain operation because he was beaten up, I nearly died of exposure down a fucking hole," he glanced towards Ray venomously, "and then we were all nearly killed by a hit and run driver. I think that we deserve some kind of an explanation before we all end up in the morgue."

"He's right," said Ray, "but you won't believe me if I tell you."

"Try us," said Archie.

"Remember the day that we were coming out of the canteen, and I had to leave you because someone called me over."

"You mean the little Italian guy?"

"That's the fellow," confirmed Ray, "he told me that Vallard were developing a video recorder."

"What's that?" asked Goff, who didn't have the engineering background of the others.

"Well it's like a tape recorder, but it records pictures as well as sound."

"And?" said Archie impatiently.

"And they're planning to complete its development in E Z building."

"And why would Italian Joe be interested in that," prodded Archie.

"John," Ray corrected.

"Whatever."

"Because he is working for the Soviet Union," Ray continued, "and he wanted me to steal or sabotage anything related to the video recorders before they come onto the market.

"Why are the Russians so interested in video recorders?" asked Archie.

"Soviets," corrected Ray.

"Same thing," said Archie belligerently.

"They see the video recorder as a surveillance tool, to record people's actions and conversations; if they could gain access to one years before they come onto the market, they would have an information gathering advantage over western governments, and if that is not possible, they would rather see the development destroyed rather than see the west get their hands on one first."

"It all sounds a bit cloak and dagger to me," said Goff.

"I told you that you wouldn't believe it."

"And what did you tell this Italian geezer when he asked you to work for the Soviets?" asked Archie.

"I told him to go forth and multiply," answered Ray.

"Good for you," said Archie, proud of his friend's integrity.

"But that's when the trouble started," continued Ray. "First we were attacked at the Astoria to soften me up, and poor Cookie got the worst of it."

"How many Soviets are involved?" queried Archie, wondering if half of the dance hall was working for the Soviets.

"There are at least three of them, including Stefan."

"Who's Stefan?" asked Goff.

"He's the guy who planted the bugs in E Z," replied Ray.

"Bugs, bloody hell this is unbelievable," chipped in Goff.

"And who are the other two?" asked Archie, taking the matter a little more seriously.

"One's a chap called Ivan who works in J block with Mick Rogerson, but I'm not sure yet if he's involved."

"I think I know him," said Archie. "Polish isn't he?"

"He's Ukrainian, according to Mick Rogerson."

"Where's Ukrainia?" asked Alfie.

"You're the bloody sailor, you tell me," responded Ray short temperedly.

"And who's the other one?" Archie prompted.

"The other one is a Russian called Vladimir, who thinks that he recruited me to work on his espionage team while I was in Amsterdam."

"Have you told the police?" asked Alfie.

"Tell them what," asked Ray. "That I got beaten up in a dance hall by the KGB, or that I was trapped under the floor at work by the KGB, or perhaps I should tell them that the KGB slashed my tyres before trying to run me down outside of the pub.

"Your right they wouldn't believe you," said Goff.

"What are you going to do?" asked Archie.

"I'm going to have a word with Italian John on Monday."

"Well it had better be a serious word, because if I see him first I'll break his bloody neck," said Archie angrily.

All of this talk had put a bit of a damper on Alfie's farewell party.

Weekend in Amsterdam

"Come on this is supposed to be a party not a wake," said Ray. "Let's get rat arsed."

■ ■ ■

On Monday morning the jointers were connecting the main cable between the substation and E Z building; Ray wandered in to inspect the smoke alarms which Doughnut had mentioned to him.

As he expected, there were two fitted onto the ceiling which had been installed by Doughnut himself. Stefan it appeared had installed a further four, one on each wall at around head height, and connected to the electrical trunking which ran around the room using short pieces of metal conduit. Ray agreed with Doughnut's observation that smoke alarms would work much better if mounted onto the ceiling, which aroused his suspicions.

The smoke alarms appeared at first glance to be the normal Vallard issue, bee hive shaped metal fire proof cases, connected to the mains supply to continually charge the batteries while not in use, so that the device would work if the electrical supply was cut off.

Ray was not an expert on these devices, as smoke detectors were a relatively new acquisition to the factory, having been invented by accident in the late 1930's, when the Swiss physicist Walter Jaeger, who while trying to build a gas detector without much success, had lit a cigarette and realised that he had inadvertently invented the smoke detector. Thirty years on with the advent of solid state components, they were now being manufactured commercially, but were so expensive that only business premises and wealthy householders could afford to fit them.

He removed the lid from the first smoke alarm, and even with his limited knowledge of the devices, he realised instantly that the alarm speaker had been replaced by a microphone of similar size, although it was the electrical circuit board, which may have appeared normal to the untrained eye, that immediately set alarm bells ringing in Ray's head. Although it fitted perfectly into the space provided, it was not the original manufacturer's circuit board, but a handmade replacement supporting a carbon rod wound with varnished copper wire, which to Ray meant just one thing, a radio aerial. Removing the bogus alarms from their cases, he dumped them unceremoniously into the waste bin after first crushing them beneath his heal.

Having made the decision that avoiding involvement in Vladimir's activities was not going to be an option, he went looking for John. He questioned John's work colleagues as to his whereabouts, following every lead, although John failed to be in any of the places that had been suggested to him; eventually he gave up the search and returned to his work place.

The reason that the Italian cowboy was nowhere to be found, was that he was keeping watch outside of the electrical drawing office, while Stefan searched through a large stock of cable diagrams trying to find the right one. If caught John would have found it difficult to explain his presence in the drawing office, a place where his normal duties had no reason to take him, which was why Stefan was searching for the diagram.

Stefan had been in the drawing office a number of times before in order to collect wiring diagrams, and if caught he could easily pretend to need something further. He also knew from past experience, that the draughtsmen were always occupied in a staff meeting for the first hour of every Monday morning, which meant that he would have unfettered access to the master drawings for some time to come.

■ ■ ■

In the afternoon Dan Rhymes arrived to commission the new cable.

"I'm so sorry about what happened on Friday with the duct covers," he said, obviously distressed by the guilt that he felt.

"It wasn't your fault," said Ray, trying to make him feel a little better.

"Oh but it was," replied Dan. "I was the one responsible for the job, and I shouldn't have left until I was sure that everyone was safely out."

"No harm done," Ray reassured him.

"But there could have been," insisted Dan, still trying to punish himself. "I've been thinking about the possible consequences, ever since Archie told me what had happened on Saturday morning. If you hadn't managed to get out," he sighed. "It doesn't bear thinking about."

He checked the jointers work and metered the fuse board, before they walked the quarter of a mile up to the substation.

The substation sat on the top of a bank, set apart from the rest of the factory and built into the factory perimeter wall. It had an access door from inside of the factory grounds to the first floor where the switchgear was housed, while another door on the second floor, situated at the top of a flight of concrete steps, led onto the road outside of the factory.

■ ■ ■

Every electrician in the factory was in possession of a substation key, which on numerous occasions, had encouraged Ray and Archie to sneak out of the factory through the substation, after first parking Ray's motor bike on the road in order to make a quick getaway, and clocking in after lunch for the afternoon shift.

They usually played snooker for a couple of hours at the local snooker hall, where Alex Higgins and Dennis Taylor** were almost always in residence, practising to be future world champions, and hustling overconfident idiots like Ray and Archie, who thought unwisely that they had some chance of winning.

On a number of occasions during the summer time, they had recruited Ted Reeves as an accomplice in their deception. Ted would for a small donation, clock them in at lunch time, while they travelled to Blackpool for the whole day out. Often

---

**Alex Higgins later won the world snooker championship twice, beating John Spencer in the final in 1972, and Ray Reardon a decade later in 1982, while Dennis Taylor defeated Steve Davis in the final of 1985.

on these occasions they would work for free on the dodgem cars on the Golden Mile, jumping from car to car collecting the money, while chatting up all of the girls who were on holiday in the resort.

■ ■ ■

It was a beautiful early spring day and unnaturally warm for the time of year. As they climbed the bank to the substation, the first of the year's daffodils had already bent their heads in readiness to burst open, while all around them a carpet of crocuses in whites, yellows, and purples had already started to bloom.

In the substation were six 11 kilovolt switches, they were eight feet tall, free standing in the centre of the room and made from cast iron. At the front of each switch was a horizontal toothed track, which allowed the switch contacts to be wound in and out. Four of the switches were already in use, with the two centre switches wound out along the tracks, indicating that they were not.

"Which one is it?" asked Dan, more to himself than to anyone else, as he consulted the diagram newly collected from the drawing office.

"The fourth cable is a spare, so it isn't that one," he said, still thinking aloud.

Unused cables were normally connected to earth, as if it came into close proximity to a magnetic field from another cable in use, a current could be inducted into the spare cable making it live.

"Number three is the cable supplying E Z building," Dan pronounced confidently after some thought.

Ray started to wind in the third switch, but it was very stiff as it hadn't been used for many years, he got it half way along the track and then stopped, panting.

"This track needs oiling," he said. "I'm knackered."

"Let me have a go," offered Dan.

Dan continued to wind in the switch, while Ray wandered out of the substation to sit on the grass in the early spring sunshine, as he was out of breath and his arms ached from winding in the switch. Suddenly there was an almighty explosion and flames shot out through the open door of the substation. They were so fierce, that Ray who was sitting ten feet from the door had his hair and eyebrows singed, while his face and hands reddened as though he had been in the sun for too long.

The flames died away almost instantly, although thick black smoke continued to plume high into the sky from the doorway. At first Ray was unable to enter the substation because of the choking fumes, but eventually he ventured through the thinning smoke with a handkerchief over his mouth. The main switch was unrecognisable, looking more like an eight foot candle than a metal switch, with molten metal running down its sides and dripping onto the floor, forming pools of liquid metal which were so hot that they refused to solidify for some considerable time.

The lights had gone out in the substation, as they had all over the factory, even so, with the aid of the light from the doorway, he could just make out the charred and blackened remains of a body lying smoking on the floor. There was nothing that he could do, and he returned in shock to sit on the bank of daffodils and crocuses and cried. A short while before, the daffodils and crocuses had been a cheerful harbinger of spring and new life to come. Now they held a more sinister connotation.

The police, fire brigade, and two ambulances arrived within minutes, one ambulance to take Ray to the hospital for the treatment of minor burns and shock, the other to take the remains of Daniel Rhymes to the hospital morgue.

After treatment, Ray was released into police custody for questioning. He explained to the sergeant that Dan must have wound in the wrong switch, but that he had been extremely careful to check with the drawings before he had begun.

"You will have to give evidence at the inquest," said the officer, before taking Ray's name and address and arranging for him to be driven home.

His mother insisted that he take a few days off work in order to get over the shock, but despite her best efforts he stubbornly insisted on going to work the following day, as his motor bike was still parked in the car park. Secretly, he also wanted to know if the blast had been an accident or if somehow John had been involved.

■ ■ ■

There was an air of gloom and doom around the factory the following day, and he soon tired of answering peoples questions. Having spent over a year working in the drawing office as an apprentice, Ray knew the entire complement of draughtsmen very well. He approached Colin Fielding, once his mentor in the Plant department, although after his altercation with Bopper and the window cord, he had accepted a position in the drawing office as a safer alternative.

"I heard the news about Dan; shocking," he said, before blushing with embarrassment at his unintended pun. "Are you okay?"

"I'm fine?" responded Ray, even though he felt far from fine, "but I need to see the master drawing for the switch arrangement in the substation."

Colin guessed instantly why he wanted to see it.

"Do you think that there might have been a mistake?" he asked.

"Maybe," responded Ray.

Colin produced the acetate master diagram from which all of the paper copies were produced, including the one which Dan had received the previous day. It was a very old three elevation diagram, similar to the drawings that Ray himself had produced in technical drawing classes whilst at school, and later in this very same drawing office as an apprentice. Probably drawn in the 1930's when the factory was newly built, it showed a front elevation, a side elevation, and a plan, with a legend in the top right hand corner numbered from one to six, showing the location within the factory supplied by each switch alongside the relevant number.

The diagram had remained largely unchanged since its conception, as the switches had remained constant throughout the years, although the legend had been changed a number of times using Tipp-Ex, which was the usual way to make alterations or correct mistakes, as the Tipp-Ex never showed up on the photocopy.

All of the Tipp-Ex alterations appeared to be old ones, with the exception of the most recent change, which clearly showed that the third switch was now the new switch supplying EZ building.

"Pass me a scalpel will you Col?"

Ray scratched away the Tipp-Ex carefully so as not to destroy what lay beneath, eventually revealing that switch three was in fact labelled spare, while switch four had been previously labelled E Z building.

He went in search of Italian John in the late morning, but was told that he hadn't reported for work that day, nor had he sent in a message to say that he was sick. Failing to find John, he went instead in search of Stefan. Tommy Brush and Doughnut were sitting in the site cabin drinking mugs of tea.

"I heard about the blast in the substation," said Tommy as he entered. "What the hell happened?"

Ray had answered this question many times throughout the morning, but he patiently did so once again.

"I'm actually here looking for Stefan," he said, "do either of you know where he is working?"

"Too late mate," answered Doughnut. "He gave in his notice yesterday after the blast, said that he was returning home to Holland."

■ ■ ■

As chief technician at the Soviet signals station in Amsterdam, Stefan had been despatched by Vladimir on Ray's flight from Amsterdam, for the dual purpose of keeping tabs on Ray, and to gain employment at the Vallard factory in order to support John and to manufacture and plant the bugs. He had also been instrumental in the substation blast at John's request.

John had failed twice to dispose of Ray, and had approached Stefan on the Monday morning in a panic. Vladimir would have to be told of his failure and he didn't want to have to face the consequences.

Having discovered that Ray and Dan Rhymes were scheduled to commission the cable during the afternoon, Stefan, who had previously been made aware of the policy of earthing unused cables, had came up with what appeared to be a brilliant idea.

■ ■ ■

When Jack reported for work at two o'clock, he brought with him an early edition of the Lancashire Evening Telegraph. As he changed into his overalls, Ray was once again required to discuss the accident. While doing so, he idly picked up Jack's newspaper and to his astonishment the headlines read,

"LOCAL MAN FOUND DEAD."

There was an extremely unflattering full face picture of John, which may have been taken from his passport or from an arrest photograph with the number cut from the bottom. The narrative said that a local man identified as John Ponte, had been dragged from the Leeds-Liverpool Canal early this morning, the police having refused to rule out foul play. His mother, named as Mavis Ponte, was said to be distraught and being comforted by friends and relatives. The narrative went on to say that Mrs Ponte and her son, had lived in England since by sheer coincidence his father had also been drowned a decade earlier. Ray wondered if this was the price of failure for John.

■ ■ ■

Ivan was the main comforter of Mrs Ponte; in fact he had been comforting her for a number of years, sometimes twice a night since her husband had died. In those bygone days he had also worked for the OGPU, and later the GRU along with Luca Ponte and Vladimir.

He had started out in much the same way as Vladimir, by running away from his home in the Ukraine and begging on the streets of Moscow. He had never been blessed with the ruthlessness or the ambition of Vladimir, and although he was senior to Vladimir in years, he was still firmly stuck on the bottom rung of the ladder, while Vladimir had climbed several rungs to head his security, transmission, and espionage team.

When John and his bereaved mother had left Russia after the death of Luca, Ivan had requested permission from his Soviet masters to follow them to England. As a condition of his re-deployment, he had agreed to become a sleeper under the control of Vladimir, who had happily evacuated him to England, perchance he made the connection that the murderer of Luca Ponte was no other than Vladimir himself.

Ivan had been surprised when John had been activated for service, as he himself was by far the more experienced operative. Although he had been aware of John's actions throughout, he had not received an official wakeup call and had therefore only offered advice to the inexperienced John. He had hoped that he could sleep both metaphorically and literally with Mavis Ponte for the rest of his life, but he knew that with the absence of Stefan, he would have to break his silence and inform Vladimir about John's death himself.

■ ■ ■

In the evening whilst watching the television programme Z cars with his parents, a real life police Z car stopped outside of his parent's house. Two uniformed officers walked up the drive, and knocking on the door asked him to accompany them to the police station.

His mother was distraught, "Oh the shame," she wailed, as the net curtains in the road began to twitch. "No one in this family has ever been in trouble with the police; you bring shame on us all."

If the old black and white photographs in the attic were to be believed, his mother had been a pretty child and a very attractive woman in her younger days, although Ray had always thought that she looked a little too skinny on most of them.

She had gained quite a few too many pounds over the years, while middle age had lined her face more than it should have done, due in part to the skin damage received during her childhood in the South African sun, smoking for many years until the birth of Ray, when she had been advised to quit to protect her unborn child, and running her own retail business for two decades with all of its associated problems, but also due to the worry that Ray had brought to her door over the years.

She was still however an attractive lady, always smartly dressed, with bleached blonde hair which had once been a more natural blonde, and after viewing the same stock of old black and white photographs of his father as a young man, Ray quite often wondered how she had ever been attracted to his father.

The officers wouldn't say why Ray was to be questioned, and his father insisted on following to the police station in order to protect his son's best interests.

"Don't you worry son. I'll get you a lawyer," he shouted as they bungled Ray unceremoniously into the back of the police car.

At the police station he was lead into a very stark room. The walls were covered with chipped and cracked white tiles, while a double row of glass bricks, close to the ceiling and just above street level, allowed the only light into the room by day, while a single harsh fluorescent tube lit the room by night.

Two men sat on tubular steel framed chairs with plywood seats and backs, in front of a table of similar construction with a melamine top, all of which looked as though they had been commandeered from the police canteen. Ray was ordered to sit on an identical chair facing his two antagonists, by one of the uniformed officers who had earlier manhandled him into the car.

"For the tape Detective Inspector Briggs and Sergeant White in interview with; state your name sir," said the sergeant glancing disinterestedly at Ray.

"Raymond Evans," Ray responded to the prompt.

Briggs had made inspector when he was in his mid thirties, there were younger inspectors on the force but most had been fast tracked straight from university. Briggs was proud of the fact that he had risen from the rank of uniformed constable within fifteen years of joining the force, having been promoted

Weekend in Amsterdam

from detective sergeant when his predecessor had been forced to take early retirement due to ill health.

Five years had passed since his last promotion and further promotions seemed unlikely, but as he had never expected to rise above the rank of sergeant when he had joined the force, he was more than happy with his lot.

He was now a family man approaching forty, with the comfortable look of a settled man. His hair was dark, greying slightly at the temples, and parted close to the centre, his nose was long and his lips were thin. He wore reading glasses perched on the end of his nose, in order to decipher the documents laid out before him on the table, smoked a pipe, which had turned his teeth yellow, and looked very much like the accepted image of Sherlock Holmes but without the deerstalker.

Sergeant White was tall and well built, with wild dark hair which stuck up in tufts when it was cut too short, as it was now. He had a repaired hair lip, a flattened nose as if he had once boxed and sounded adenoidal when he talked. He had been promoted to sergeant in the same reshuffle as Briggs when he was barely thirty, and although he was dressed in plain clothes, because of his demeanour he had copper written all over him and could never have worked undercover.

"Mr. Evans. Do you know a Miss April Rayne?" began the inspector.

"I know an April, but I don't know if her surname is Rayne."

Ray wondered if her parents had realised the significance of calling their daughter April when their surname was Rayne, or perhaps they had chosen it deliberately. It sounded like something that members of a flower power cult might call their child, but April must have been born in the early fifties, when flour power meant McDougall's self raising.

"Did you know her boyfriend John Ponte?" asked Briggs. Ray was stunned.

"I knew John Ponte, but I had no idea that he was her boyfriend."

"How did you know Mr. Ponte?" asked the inspector.

Ray decided that it was probably time to come clean and fully involve the police. He told of the plot hatched in Holland by Vladimir. He told of the recruitment attempt, by what he thought in his ignorance was a member of the KGB as he had never heard of the GRU. He told about the new video recorders soon to be manufactured at the Vallard plant. He told of his meetings with Italian John, and of the beating that he and Cookie had received at the Astoria when he had refused to cooperate. He went on to say that he was convinced that John had tried to murder him on three separate occasions, finally killing Daniel Rhymes during one of his botched assassination attempts.

The inspector wasn't expecting anything like this; he already had a prisoner and a confession. This interview was only meant to tie up loose ends, and to establish if Raymond Evans was in anyway involved in the death of John Ponte. A whole new can of worms had suddenly been opened up, which he found difficult to get his head around, and although he may have superficially resembled Sherlock Holmes in appearance, he didn't have anything like his intellect and was frankly out of his depth.

"I find all of this very difficult to believe Mr Evans," said Briggs. "Are you sure that you would really like to make a formal statement to that effect?"

"I think that I should speak to a solicitor before making any formal statement," replied Ray. "My father is probably waiting for me in reception with one as we speak."

"That won't be necessary Mr. Evans, you are not under arrest and we are already holding Miss Rayne for the killing of Mr Ponte."

Ray wrote out his statement and signed it, before asking if it was possible to speak with April. The detective inspector and the sergeant both left the room and the uniformed officer stepped back inside. Before long White reappeared with April, who broke free from his grasp, darting across the room towards Ray and throwing her arms around his neck. She was instantly apprehended by the hitherto static and silent constable, who forced her to sit on one of the chairs opposite to Ray, before he returned to his statue like position by the door.

"They say that you killed John Ponte and that he was your boyfriend, I didn't even know that you knew him." Ray was puzzled.

"I did it for you," said April, who was by now in tears.

"For me, why would you want to kill Ponte for me?" asked Ray in surprise.

"Last Friday," she began between sobs. "I saw John helping one of the electrical contractors to replace the manhole covers in the corridor behind E block. I didn't know at the time that anyone was down the hole, but I thought that it was strange that John was replacing manhole covers. I just figured that the electrician had seen him passing and asked him for help. Then on Monday I bumped into Archie at work and he told me that you had both been trapped underground for hours; he also said that someone had tried to run you down in a car on Saturday night. John didn't meet me on Saturday night; instead he told me that he had something very important to do. Putting two and two together, I went onto the car park to check his car, and guess what?"

"There was a dent on his driver's side wing," speculated Ray with obvious success.

"Then there was the explosion on Monday afternoon and you were involved once again," continued April, who had by now ceased crying.

"I was convinced by this time that he was jealous of our past relationship and wanted you out of the way, so I arranged to see him on Monday evening and we took a walk along the canal towpath to try to sort things out. I lied to him by telling him that I didn't love you anymore, and asked him to promise that he wouldn't hurt you, but he appeared to have no idea that we had once had a relationship. I challenged him with my accusations that he wanted you dead and he didn't deny it, but told me that it was none of my business, and that it would wiser for me to forget all about it if I didn't want to get caught in the crossfire. I told him that I would not be threatened, and said that I would go to the police if he didn't promise to stop what he was doing. With that he grabbed me around the neck and began to choke me."

She leant forward and unfastened the top button of her blouse to show him the finger mark bruises on her neck.

"I was scared that he was going to kill me and I knew that I had to act. I had a pair of scissors in my handbag and I managed to reach them, even though I was beginning to feel faint, and stabbed him in the neck. I must have hit an artery because blood shot out like a fountain before he collapsed onto the ground. Not wanting him to be found, I rolled him into the water thinking that he would sink to the bottom or float away, but he hadn't travelled very far from where I killed him before he was discovered and I was arrested."

"Good God April what have you done?"

Ray was breathless after what he had just heard, and he sat quietly for a few moments in order to gather his thoughts. He wasn't sorry that John Ponte was dead, but he was sorry that April had been arrested and accused of killing him; he wished that he had somehow acted sooner, before she had become involved in this mess.

As he left the police station with his father, he wondered if he was still in danger, or if the death of John Ponte would signal the end of his personal nightmare.

PART TWO

CHAPTER FIFTEEN

In the weeks that followed things began to return to normal for Ray. Ivan had been questioned and released without charge, there being no evidence to suggest that he had been involved in any way.

The inquest into the death of Dan Rhymes recorded a verdict of accidental death. Despite Ray giving evidence that the diagram had been tampered with, the coroner could find no evidence to suggest that it was anything other than an honest mistake, on the part of some unknown member of the drawing office staff. The funeral was a sombre affair, with Mrs Rhymes and her adult daughter crying continually throughout the day.

Ray felt guilty that Dan was dead while he was still alive, and found it hard to speak to Mrs Rhymes, although she had no idea whatsoever as to why he felt so guilty, and graciously accepted his condolences.

The day after the funeral Ray returned to the graveside. He had purchased a bowl of crocuses from his local florist, in yellow, white, and purple, and had placed them on the grave. He would never again see a crocus, without remembering the charred and smoking body of Dan Rhymes.

After the inquest, to Ray's relief, Vallard closed E Z building down and moved the development of the video recorder to an undisclosed site.

April was held on remand awaiting trial for the unlawful killing of John Ponte. Although the judge had granted her bail, her family was not in a position to act as bondsman and she continued to be held in custody awaiting her trial, which was scheduled more than six months away. Ray was hopeful that because of the bruising evidence around her neck the verdict would be self defence, but that was by no means certain.

Concorde, the first supersonic aeroplane ever to be built flew for the first time at Toulouse in France. Sirhan-Sirhan admitted to killing the presidential candidate Robert Kennedy, while James Earl Ray pleaded guilty to the murder of Martin Luther King. Golda Meir became the first female prime minister of Israel, and the former United States wartime general and president Dwight D Eisenhower died in Washington.

Archie had returned to his wife for a trial reconciliation, which was a surprise to all concerned, Cookie was a lot better, although he and Brenda were by now inseparable, while Goff was spending more and more time with her friend Michelle, and as Alfie was back at sea, Ray was on his own for the very first time in his life.

He went into town as usual on Good Friday evening, although he bypassed The Legs O' Man, as he knew that no one that he deemed to be of any consequence would be there. He looked for familiar faces in the crowds, and although the venues were the same, everything was different, as he didn't recognise anyone that he knew. The change must have been taking place for quite some time, but as he had failed to notice the door closing on his past, the realisation came to him as quite a shock.

For the past seven or eight years this had been his turf, his happy hunting ground, he had known everyone and everyone had known him. Now it seemed that this hallowed ground suddenly belonged to others, he was the stranger here, he had lost his privileged position as one of the alpha males, and the good times it seemed were well and truly over.

In those not so distant days when he was top dog, the girls had flocked around him like bees around honey, but he was now almost twenty-six years old and the girls around him were much younger, seventeen or eighteen years of age and of a different generation it seemed. They had been infants during the rock and roll years, and school children throughout the swinging sixties. They annoyed him with their infantile giggling, and if they noticed him at all, it was to view him as an aging intruder who had stumbled accidentally into their world.

He realised that the girls who he had been dating in recent years had all been a number of years his junior, a fact that had never really struck him before. Now even they had all found permanent partners and disappeared forever from the scene. It seemed that he had been having such a good time that life had simply passed him by, and he hadn't noticed it happening.

He did the rounds of all the usual haunts, hoping to come across someone from his past, and finally just before closing time he encountered Buddy, with his two rather unsavoury looking friends in tow.

Buddy had worked with Ray and Archie at the Vallard factory during his apprenticeship years, having spent the last year of his life in prison with his two surly companions. Buddy was small in stature and slightly built, with long dark straggly hair, which looked to be badly in need of a good washing. His front teeth sloped backwards in an unusual way and were always visible as he never stopped grinning.

His two claims to fame were that he was the biggest Buddy Holly fan in the western world, which is how he acquired his nickname, and he was also notorious for his frequent farts, which could clear a room in seconds. It caused him great mirth to let one go in a crowded room, while watching people running for cover as if a nuclear device had just been exploded.

His two companions although of a similar height to Buddy, couldn't have been more different in all other respects. They were both stocky and so alike that they could have been twins, but were in fact merely first cousins. Both had adopted the uniform of the skin head culture, with shaved heads, shortened jeans supported by red braces, and bovver boots, which were steel toe capped work boots, worn in order to inflict injury on others.

■ ■ ■

A year ago almost to the very day, Buddy had organised a coach trip to the nearby town of Oldham. Ray had booked to go along, until on the evening of the trip he had suddenly become violently sick, so that Buddy and the Tow-rags, along with the rest of the coach party had gone without him.

In Oldham a fight had broken out in one of the pubs. The place had been trashed, and the landlord had been badly hurt after being slashed with a broken bottle, while everyone in the pub had been arrested and charged with violent disorder.

At the magistrate's court, most of those who had pleaded guilty to the affray had been sentenced to six months at her majesties pleasure, with the exception of a minority of the coach party, including Buddy's two wayward friends, who being found to have the landlords blood on their clothes, had been sentenced to a year inside without parole.

Buddy, who had been smooching with some girl in the corner of the room at the time that the fighting had broken out, had along with a small number of other innocent parties pleaded not guilty. The courts however appeared to take exception to a not guilty plea, and for having the audacity to plead innocent even though he was, he had been sent to the Crown Court, where he was sentenced to the longer term of two years, despite the fact that not a single witnesses had identified him as one of the miscreants, or that any physical evidence of his involvement was ever produced.

■ ■ ■

"When did they let you out?" asked Ray.

"Yesterday," replied Buddy, "Tony and Brian had to serve their full sentences," he added, indicating the Tow-rags, "but I got out a year early for good behaviour."

"You wouldn't know good behaviour if it bit you on the arse," said Ray teasing.

Ray acknowledged Buddy's friends with a nod, they had been Buddy's friends since schooldays but Ray didn't like either of them. Wherever they went trouble was sure to follow, and it was a racing certainty that this pair had started the fight in Oldham.

■ ■ ■

Weekend in Amsterdam

The first time that he had come in contact with the Tow-rags, was on a summer bank holiday weekend, when along with Cookie and Buddy they had decided to go to Blackpool for a couple of days away. Out of the blue, Buddy had turned up with Tony and Brian; they had just been released from prison, where they had spent most of their teenage years and early twenties.

Ray, Cookie, and Buddy, had very little money saved for the weekend, but the Tow-rags had arrived without any money at all, the inference being that they didn't intended to contribute anything towards the cost of renting a room, or anything else for that matter.

After tramping the streets of Blackpool until their feet hurt, they had consistently failed to find accommodation, each establishment telling them that they had no vacancies, even though the sign in the window clearly said otherwise. Finally after many hours of searching, they managed to rent a scruffy attic apartment close to the Pleasure Beach.

Bare floor boards on the last flight of stairs led up to their attic room, which was obviously intended to sleep only three; with a double bed and a single, both with rather unsavoury looking bedding. The room also housed a small two ring electric cooker which was thick with grease, and a dirty cream enamelled sink, with the dual purpose of washing and washing up. The shabby bathroom with a filthy shower curtain was situated on the floor below. It was pointed out that they must share it with the occupants of two adjacent bedrooms on that floor, one of which as it turned out was occupied by three rather attractive girls from a nearby Lancashire town.

The Tow-rags, who were not officially staying in the room at all, quickly introduced themselves to the girls in the room below, while borrowing a single tea bag which they used to make numerous cups of tea over the next three days, before on the day of their departure, drying the tea bag on the cooker, removing the tea, and wrapping it in toilet paper in order to smoke it.

At breakfast time each morning the Tow-rags went out door-stepping, returning with bottles of milk, eggs, and sometimes if they were lucky with bacon wrapped in tissue paper, which they had picked up from doorsteps after the milk man had just delivered.

Ray and Cookie had given this unsavoury pair a wide berth throughout the weekend, going off alone each day while leaving Buddy with his troublesome charges, until every night the Tow-rags would return to the attic room to sleep on the floor, with spurious items of stolen property, which they had acquired but failed to sell around the pubs of Blackpool.

Ray as usual had wasted very little time in getting to know the girls in the room below, and by the second night of their holiday was sharing a bed with one of girls, who turned out to be a police officer. Although attractive with a boyish hair-style and fair complexion, she was considerably taller than Ray, which would normally have embarrassed him to the point of not wanting to be seen with her, but as their relationship didn't involve standing up very much, on this occasion it didn't seem to matter.

The Tow-rags, who had been drinking heavily for most of the evening and without this vital piece of vocational information, had gate crashed the girl's bedroom in the early hours of the morning, and while Ray and his law enforcement companion lay naked in bed, they had tried to sell her a very old fashioned women's coat, which they had removed from a coat stand in a hotel foyer.

All three of them, including Buddy, had been to see a tattooist, Buddy agreeing under peer pressure to have his very first tattoo; a snake wrapped around a sword having been tattooed on his left arm, had gone to bed in great pain swearing never to do it again. The Tow-rags, who were already covered from head to toe with tattoos, had used all of their ill gotten gains to have a dotted line and the words "Cut here" tattooed across their throats, and when Ray had asked in amazement why they would possibly want to do that, he had been told that you have to draw a line somewhere.

■ ■ ■

"How's Cookie?" asked Buddy.
"He's courting," Ray informed him.

"Cookie's got a girl, you must be joking," Buddy looked surprised. "What's she like?"

"Not much in the looks department, but she has a cracking body," said Ray, with a mental picture of New Years Eve still in his head.

"Have you given her one yet?" asked Buddy.

"I've given her half of one before she started seeing Cookie." He told Buddy all about Cookie's bedroom raid at the party.

"And how's Archie?" Buddy asked.

"He's having a trial reconciliation with Cheryl," answered Ray.

"I bet that you've been there too, haven't you?" speculated Buddy.

"Only when I thought that their marriage was over," answered Ray defensively.

"You're all heart," mocked Buddy. "Remind me never to introduce you to any of my girlfriends."

"You'll never have a girlfriend your too ugly," teased Ray," and even if you did, I'm hardly likely to fancy her if she fancies you am I?"

A broad smile came across Buddy's face; Ray had seen that smile many times before and knew what it meant. Soon there was a stampede of people trying to get out of the building, as Buddy stood alone in the middle of the room grinning.

"Were going to the Cat's Whiskers, are you coming?" asked Buddy once every one was outside on the street.

The Cat's Whiskers was an underworld dive masquerading as a nightclub; not the kind of place that Ray would normally consider patronising, but exactly the kind of place that Ray would have expected the Tow-rags to frequent.

"Ok," he said reluctantly, having nothing better to do and nowhere better to go.

He had never been to the Cat's Whiskers before, but it was exactly as he had expected that it would be, a dark and dingy room, with no entertainment and a bar for late night drinking. He recognised a handful of the drinkers, not because they were friends or even acquaintances of his, but because they were infamous in the town and well known to the police. What he hadn't expected to see was Doreen, an ex girlfriend who was drinking vodka and tonic with Mo Halsey, one of the most infamous ruffians of them all.

Ray acknowledged her presence while Mo wasn't looking, before paying a visit to the men's room. After washing his hands in cold water, which came from either tap irrespective of which colour adorned the top, and drying them on his handkerchief, as the roller towel which had come to the end of the roll was soaking wet, filthy, and trailing on the floor as if it hadn't been changed for days, he tried to leave but Mo Halsey blocked his path.

Mo was a man mountain, with unruly black hair and a three day beard, his hands were like shovels, and he weighed in at least five stone heavier than Ray.

"I believe that you know my sister?" he said in an aggressive tone.

"I don't think so," answered Ray shakily, his mind racing and his heart pounding.

"Yes you fucking do; Doreen Halsey." he reminded Ray forcefully.

"Oh Dore's your sister, I didn't know," apologised Ray in appeasement.

It transpired that Maurice and Doreen had been fostered separately when Doreen was only two years of age and Maurice was eight. They hadn't been in contact for over twenty years, until recently discovering that they were in fact brother and sister.

Apart from the fact that they both had dark hair, they could not have been less alike. Her hair was beautifully styled, while his was wild and unkempt. She was immaculately dressed, while he was scruffy, and she was trim and pretty, while he was a hulk of a man, with all the looks, charm, and charisma of an all in wrestler.

"She says that she fancies you, but I can't imagine why," Mo remarked, looking Ray up and down as if he was something that he had recently scraped off his shoe.

"You look like a Nancy-boy to me, but then there's no accounting for taste is there?"

When Ray didn't answer he continued with his recitation. "She wants you to take her home tonight."

"Are you're okay with that Mo?" Ray asked, trying hard not to offend.

"It's what she wants not what I want, and if there's any funny business I'll break your fucking legs," said Mo, trying not to make the deal appear too attractive.

"Message received loud and clear," said Ray, not wanting to get on the wrong side of hard man Mo Halsey.

"Good, now go over and talk to her, and remember I'm fucking watching you."

Doreen was relieved to see him and wanted to leave immediately. "Isn't it awful in here?" she said. "Normally I wouldn't be seen dead in a place like this, but Mo wanted to take me out for a drink so that we could get to know each other and he likes it here."

"I didn't know that Mo was your brother," said Ray, still shaken by the news.

"Neither did I until a couple of weeks ago, I believe that he's a bit of a hard case."

"You can say that again," agreed Ray. "He's definitely one to avoid if you can."

"He didn't force you to take me home did he?" she asked, mortified that he may not be taking her home of his own free will.

"No I wanted to," replied Ray honestly, "but as a parting shot he did say that if I touched you he'd break my f***ing leg's."

"We'd better not tell him then," she said smiling cheekily.

He went to tell Buddy that they were leaving.

"Are you mad?" screamed Buddy, "Mo will kill you."

"It's okay; he's given me permission to take her home, just so long as I don't touch her in an inappropriate way."

"And you're going to comply with that requirement?" said Buddy mockingly.

"She says that if I do get a little fruity, she won't tell him."

"Be it on your own head," warned Buddy.

■ ■ ■

Ray had first got to know Doreen in Caernarfon, North Wales, after he had split with Goff's wife the previous summer. Ray and Cookie had been broke as usual as the holidays approached, but they had been told that it was possible to walk along the beach at Pthwelli, and enter the Butlin's holiday camp without paying. If this were true, they could spend all day in the camp, and if they were lucky find two gorgeous girls who would allow them share their chalet for the rest of the holidays.

This was a nice little fantasy, but as Ray was contagious with crab lice from his liaison with Goff's wife, and Cookie was not much of a ladies' man at the best of times, as a contingency plan they had taken along Norman Hassam, an acquaintance who they had encountered at the Mecca ballroom on the eve of their trip. Norman had an English mother and an Arab father, who was no longer in evidence at the family home, but most important of all he had a two man ridge tent.

On hearing about Ray's infestation problem, Norman, who was something of an expert on the subject, had advised Ray to shave his pubic area, so that the little buggers, as he put it, had nowhere to hide. The following morning he brought along with him a noxious smelling substance in a medicine bottle, which he himself had procured for the very same complaint some weeks earlier.

At the time Ray had owned a nine year old Austin Westminster motor car, a huge three litre gas guzzler, in two-tone grey and pale green, with pale green leather seats, a real classy number.

Unknown to Ray it had been involved in a serious motor accident, but having been re sprayed, it looked magnificent with its new chrome grill, headlights and bumpers, but beneath the new paintwork, the bodywork was rotting and it misfired badly, pouring out clouds of thick black smoke every time that he revved the engine.

Miraculously they had managed to reach the holiday camp, even though the car had jumped, jerked, backfired and stalled, for quite a large proportion of the journey. Following instructions given to them before their departure, they had driven backwards and forwards in a cloud of smoke, searching for a narrow lane which would take them under the railway line, which fed the camp with holiday makers, and onto the beach where they had pitched their tent.

For the next seven days, they had entered the camp in the morning by walking along the beach, returning after midnight by the same route.

On the day that he had encountered Doreen, they had gone for a day trip to see Caernarfon Castle. She was not completely unknown to him, as she had been engaged to be married to a casual friend on the fringe of his circle, so that when he saw her, he had been confident enough to cross the road and say hello.

She had asked him if he was thinking of returning home any time soon, as she and her friend had run out of money and had no way of getting back. Ray had responded that they hadn't intended to return home for a few days, but if she and her friend would like to return with them to the tent, he would give them a lift home as soon as they decided that the time was right for them to leave.

Doreen had slept in the car with Ray that night, while her friend had taken Ray's place and bunked down with the boys in the tent. Doreen had explained that she had called off her engagement, and that she now considered her ex boyfriend to be a pig for cheating on her.

That night they had kissed, and when he made no further move other than touching her breasts, she had tried to move things along by unzipping his trousers and reaching inside. Embarrassed about his parasite condition, he had stopped her on her expedition, much to her surprise, and she was left puzzling as to why he had refused to look a gift horse in the mouth.

On the third day after the girl's arrival, a group of Gypsies had appeared on the beach, using a truck to tow a caravan, which they parked next to Ray's car. Ray had been fiddling with the car's twin carburettors as they arrived, even though he had no idea what he was doing, so that when they had offered to help, he had been grateful if a little distrusting, as he had a stereotypical image of Gypsies being inherently dishonest.

In no time at all the Gypsies had the car running like a dream, which was something that the garage had failed to do, even though the car had been in their possession for a full four days prior to the holiday. To show his gratitude, Ray had given the Gypsies a fiver that he could ill afford, as his meagre resources had begun running low, especially as he had been subsidising the girls, who had completely run out of money.

One pleasant summer evening, a couple of days after the arrival of the Gypsies, they had all dressed in their finery and walked along the beach and into the camp as usual. On returning some time after midnight however, they had discovered that the Gypsies had gone, as had the ridge tent and everyone's luggage. That night all five of them had slept in the car, squashed together like sardines, and when the morning came after a long and uncomfortable night, they admitted defeat and returned home.

■ ■ ■

Ray had not seen Doreen from that day to this, although he had heard from Cookie that she had reconciled once again with her boyfriend. Now however it appeared that the engagement was off for the second time, and she was fair game once more.

Ray had been smitten the previous summer, wishing on numerous occasions that the circumstances of their encounter could have been different. It would do her a disservice to call her attractive, she was more than attractive she was beautiful. She had a very slim but shapely figure, while unusually for one so slim, she had an impressive frontage. Obviously aware of her assets, she always wore low cut dresses and tops. On this occasion she wore a very tight fitting black dress, which was extremely low cut both at the front and at the back, with arguably more of her breasts on display than were still hidden within the dress.

They walked arm in arm towards the multi story car park where Ray had parked his car. He had been banned from borrowing his father's car once more after the tyre incident, but at least his father had been prompted to loan him the money to get his own car repaired and back on the road.

"What happened to your other car, the big comfortable one?" she asked, looking at the Triumph Spitfire in dismay.

The Austin Westminster had the advantage of two comfortable bucket seats in the front, and another even more comfortable bench seat in the back. The Spitfire on the other hand had not been bought with romance in mind, but to satisfy Ray's passion for speed in a way that only his motor bike had previously done, consequently it had two separate and rather uncomfortable bucket seats typical of a sports car of the time, with both a gear leaver and a hand brake sitting unhelpfully between them.

"Oh it was clapped out, so last year after the holiday I part exchanged it for this one," Ray answered.

"It doesn't look very practical," she said unenthusiastically.

"It gets me about," said Ray a little deflated, as he loved it almost as much as he loved his motor bike.

"I don't mean practical for getting about, I mean practical for parking up," she explained.

"Think yourself lucky," he answered, "Until a couple of weeks ago I only had a motor bike.

"I thought that you bought this car last summer?" she asked, puzzled by the inconsistency in his story.

"I did," he answered, "I was taking a friend for a day out to the Lake District."

"A girl friend?" she enquired, interrupting his explanation with just a hint of jealousy in her tone.

"Yes a girl friend," he admitted, irritated that she had interrupted the story. "We were approaching the Forton service station just touching one hundred miles an hour."

"You were showing off for that girl," she interrupted again, spitting out the words as if they left a bad taste in her mouth.

"It was the first time that I had taken it onto the motorway, I was just seeing how fast it could go," he said defensively. "Anyway the big ends went and I just managed to limp onto the services. We had to catch two buses' back.

"Are you still seeing her?"

He had expected her to ask what the big ends were but she had other things on her mind.

"No not anymore," he answered, hoping that he had answered the final question on that particular subject, but the interrogation continued.

"Did you make love to her in this car?" she pressed.

"No, I haven't made love to anyone in this car, I'm not even sure if it's possible."

Doreen was renting a bedroom above the hairdresser's shop where she worked, but as the proprietor forbade male guests in her room, she instructed him to drive to a nearby country park.

"Don't stop here," she said, as he drove through the gates and onto the car park. "Carry on up the drive."

The park had once been the grounds of a very expensive Victorian house in the nineteenth century, a mill owner's mansion, but it had burned down in the nineteen-thirties and was now little more than a ruin. After the fire the family had decided not to rebuild the house and had donated the grounds to the town, which was now designated as a country park.

There were no lights in this part of the park and the lights from the town were blocked from view by trees, so that when he turned off the headlights they were in almost complete darkness.

"I need to take a leak," said Ray getting out of the car.

He walked for a few yards up a narrow track, and found a convenient tree trunk. He found it eerie alone in the darkness, every rustle in the bushes or hoot of an owl startling him so that he jumped and almost wet his trousers. He was about to zip up when he felt a presence behind him, two arms slid around his waist and two hands began to gently caress his chest. He could feel warm breath on the back of his neck, and lips began to nibble at his ear. The hands began to slowly travel south while the lips ceased nibbling just long enough to whisper into his ear, "Got yah."

CHAPTER SIXTEEN

For the next month Ray and Doreen were inseparable, with the exception of Friday nights which was still reserved for boy's night out. On Saturday evenings they went to the cinema, to a pub with entertainment, or to a cabaret lounge, but for the rest of the week she came to his parent's house, where they watched television with his mother and father, and explored each other's bodies when he took her home in the car.

His mother was pleased that he had found a nice girl, feeling that it was high time that he settled down and produced some beautiful grandchildren for her to spoil. She was pleased with his choice, so much so, that she even began to travel to the hairdressers where Doreen worked in order to have her hair done, even though she had to catch two buses in order to get there.

■ ■ ■

On May Day, Ray decided to take Doreen for a day out in the car. They travelled to the coast by way of the country route through the magnificent Trough of Bowland, both to avoid the bank holiday motorway traffic and also to enjoy the scenic route.

Stopping at an ice cream kiosk at a very popular picnic spot, they bought two large ice cream cones, which they ate with the top down on the car as it was such a lovely day. Everyone seemed to be eating ice cream, hot dogs, or sandwiches brought from home, and the lay-by was full of chaffinches, the males with their pink plumage and blue grey caps, and the females plainer but with white wing bars, strutting from car to car to beg morsels of bread or wafer biscuit.

"I enjoyed the wedding last Saturday," said Dore, while eating a raspberry ripple.

Ray had been best man at the wedding of Bill Bailey on the previous Saturday. Bill's real name wasn't Bill at all, but with the surname of Bailey, it was inevitable that he would always be called Bill by his workmates at the Vallard factory.

Ray had been surprised when Bill had asked him to be his best man, as he hadn't realised before that they were such close friends. Bill had been half of a couple for as long as Ray had known him, meeting his future wife within weeks of his coming to work at the factory as an apprentice. Although he had been out with Ray, Archie, and some of the other electricians at work on a number of occasions, Ray had been amazed that he didn't have closer friends from somewhere in his past who he could have asked, but obviously he didn't.

"Yes it was good once I got my speech out of the way," agreed Ray.

"Speeches aren't my strong point at the best of times, and as I barely know Bill or his wife, it was difficult to find anything to say about them."

"Wasn't the brides dress lovely?" she commented. "Just like the one that I would like, and the bridesmaids, I think that I'll have peach for my bridesmaids."

Ray wondered who she was thinking of marrying, as he had only been seeing her for a month and the thought of marriage had never even crossed his mind. He changed the subject to pheasants as they continued over the moor. He had to keep slowing down for dozens of the beautiful but silly creatures, as they insisted on running down the centre of the road rather than moving off to the side for safety.

They had a few problems with the bank holiday traffic going through the city of Lancaster, but once at the coast they parked easily, had some lunch, and walked along the beach hand in hand, finally reaching the dolphin arena, which was built in the bay and accessed by a stone jetty near to the art deco Midland Hotel.

After walking through the aquarium and looking at the fish, which interested Ray but not so much Doreen, they watched the sea lions, balancing balls and standing on one flipper in an annex to the main arena, before the stars of the show the dolphins were let out into the main pool.

Ray had never been to a dolphin performance before; in fact he had never seen a live dolphin before.

"Where lucky, there are seats right at the front," said Ray, making a bee line for the front row seats before they were all snapped up.

In the first minute of the performance they discovered why the front row seats of the arena weren't taken, as the dolphins leaped high into the air, hitting the water with a huge splash and leaving them soaked to the skin. People in the rows behind sniggered at the stupid couple at the front, who were gasping for breath from the shock of the wall of cold water which had just enveloped them, but after their first soaking, to wet to care, they just sat and laughed, getting wetter and wetter.

It was a warm day, and as they walked back along the beach they soon began to dry off in the sun.

"Did you see that little page boy in his satin suite, didn't he look cute?" she was off again. "And the flowers weren't they beautiful? I still have the bouquet that I caught on my bedside table, traditionally that means that I will be next," she informed him.

Ray wore a gold ring on his little finger with a single large diamond. It had belonged to his favourite uncle, who had died suddenly from a heart attack as he stepped from the bus on his way home from work. His aunt had passed on the ring to Ray after his uncle's death, along with another more mundane gold signet ring with a plain square top, which he had paid to have engraved, and which unlike the diamond ring he wore every day of the week.

They held hands as they walked along the beach, and feeling the diamond ring on his finger she asked if she could try it on. Being a man's little finger ring it fitted her engagement finger perfectly, the stone looking huge on her tiny hand as it sparkled in the sun.

I'm afraid that this ring is never going to come off," she said, pretending that the ring was stuck.

"There's only one thing for it."

"What's that?" he asked, believing that the ring really was stuck and thinking in terms of hot soapy water.

"You will have to ask me to marry you," she informed him, which was a radically different solution to soapy water.

He wasn't sure what came over him at that moment, perhaps it was because all of his friends had wives and girlfriends, perhaps he was scared of being left on the shelf, or perhaps he just loved her and wanted to spend the rest of his life with her, but in a moment of madness he got down on one knee in the sand, and still holding her hand he looked up into her face.

"Doreen Halsey, will you marry me?" he asked.

They hurried home as Doreen couldn't wait to tell his mother that they were engaged to be married. His mother was pleased; he had been a worry to her for a number of years with his drinking and staying out all night; she would be glad to see him settled and off her hands.

That evening he tried to retrieve his uncle's ring, explaining that it wasn't her actual engagement ring, and that he would buy her a more appropriate one at the weekend, but she was having none of it.

"I don't want another ring," she insisted. "I love this one, it's the one that you gave to me when you proposed, and another ring would just not have the same meaning."

The fact that he hadn't given it to her at all, seemed to have slipped her mind, but she had accepted his proposal and even though she had manoeuvred him into proposing, she had no intention of relinquishing the ring.

He told Archie about the engagement at work the following day, but he had to wait until Friday to inform the others. They met in The Legs O' Man as they usually did, but only Archie and Cookie turned up. Privately Ray felt that Archie and Cheryl should not be going out separately on Fridays, but he didn't say so. Cookie was still seeing Brenda, but for the first time in months had resumed going out with his mates, if only on Fridays and to the football match.

"Where's Goff?" asked Ray, when it was obvious that he wasn't going to make an appearance.

"He's gone to the Mecca with Michelle," explained Cookie.

"Not again," Ray complained. "It's boy's night out and he saw her last Friday."

"I know," said Archie," he seems to be getting very serious about her."

"Speaking about getting serious, I've got engaged to Dore," he told Cookie.

Cookie looked sheepish, "Look mate I didn't want to have to tell you this, but last Friday Goff and Michelle saw Dore at the Mecca with another bloke; I believe that she sees him every Friday."

"Who is he?" asked Ray in shock.

"I don't know, replied Cookie, "but Goff says that they were all over each other like a rash."

"I've got to go," said Ray jumping up.

"Don't do anything silly," shouted Archie as Ray went out of the door, but he knew full well that he would.

When Ray arrived at the Mecca ballroom he gave the dance floor a quick once over, but as he couldn't see her dancing, he headed upstairs to the bar, which was situated behind the stage, on a balcony which ran all the way around the room.

As he entered the bar, he immediately noticed Doreen, who was standing with her back towards him facing the bar counter. She had her arm around the waist of some bloke, who was admiring himself in the mirror which stretched all the way along the back of the bar counter. He fiddled with his hair and then admired himself some more, while his arm casually slipped from around her waist until it was situated on her bottom. He gave it a squeeze, causing her to giggle at his familiarity and she slapped him playfully on the arm.

Ray felt sick inside, as an uncontrollable anger rose within him, Doreen saw him for the first time as he grabbed her molester by the shoulder, spinning him around, and hitting him twice in quick succession before the groper realised what was happening to him. Groper's legs buckled as he went down, his face crashing into a stack of empty glasses which were standing on the bar counter waiting to be washed, sending them flying in all directions as he slid to the floor in a heap of broken glass.

Ray caught a glimpse of Goff and Michelle staring at him in horror, as he was grabbed by two burly bouncers, who twisted his arms so far up his back, that he was forced to walk on tip toe as they escorted him to the exit, where they unceremoniously threw him out onto the street.

■ ■ ■

He awoke the following morning feeling terrible, as he had entered the pub directly across from the ballroom on his extrication, and had got extremely drunk. His right hand was swollen and he had the imprint of two front teeth between his second and third fingers, which began to bleed again as he moved his hand.

A letter was awaiting him on the coffee table, as he consumed a breakfast of black coffee and little else around noon. The envelope, which contained only his Christian name in cut out letters, did not contain a stamp, indicating that it must have been delivered by hand, although his parents had not witnessed the act. He opened the envelope, to reveal a plain white sheet of paper of the writing pad variety, and on it, in letters again cut from a newspaper or magazine were the words,

"IT'S NOT OVER."

He wondered what wasn't over, could this note have come from Doreen, but if so, why was it so curt, and why was it not signed. Why also would she cut out letters from a magazine instead of writing it, before catching a bus to his house when she could have posted it, and if she had come to his house, why did she not ring the door bell and talk to him to his face? It didn't make any sense, and in any case as far as he was concerned their relationship definitely was over.

Perhaps this was a threat from her boyfriend of the previous evening, that he would get his revenge for Ray's attack, but cut out letters, that didn't make any sense either, when a ring on the doorbell and a punch in the face would have been far more effective. His head was pounding and he felt sick, while his brain rebelled at the forced labour of working on the conundrum. He threw the note into his bedside drawer, promising himself that he would give it more serious consideration later.

The football season was over. Rovers had finished a terrible season by losing 2-1 away to Huddersfield the previous week, although he met Cookie in the pub as usual.

"I heard what happened last night," said Cookie.

"Did Goff call you?" Ray asked, although he already knew the answer to his question.

"He did," replied Cookie.

"What does she see in him?" asked Ray, although he didn't expect an answer from Cookie. "He must be at least thirty-five, he may even be older."

Cookie dropped a bombshell. "The guy that you clobbered wasn't the one that she's been seeing."

"Who the hell was it then?" asked an astonished Ray.

"That my friend was Vic the Vain," announced Cookie, as if he were some kind of celebrity.

"And who the hell is Vic the Vain?" asked Ray, still puzzled.

"He's only the most infamous fence and shady dealer in town, and good friend of your one time future brother in law and local heavy Mo Halsey."

"Shit!" Ray exclaimed. "So why was he feeling her arse?"

"The girls hang around him because he spends money on gin and tonics and champagne, in return he feels arses and few of them complain," Cookie explained.

"So she wasn't seeing him at all?" Ray needed to get things straight.

"No," Cookie reaffirmed.

"So why wasn't she with the other guy; the guy that she's been seeing?" He was still confused.

"She told Goff after your involuntary exit, that she'd dumped him on Friday night because she'd got engaged to you."

"I'm in the shit now aren't I?" speculated Ray.

"You're most probably in the shit with both Dore and Vic the Vain," answered Cookie. "I'd keep a low profile for a while if I were you."

In the evening he went into town alone, heading for Yates Wine Lodge in the hope of bumping into Buddy once again. While standing at the bar and ordering a drink, he heard a familiar voice behind him.

"Well if it isn't Cassius," said the voice, comparing him to the heavy weight champion of the world Cassius Clay.

The crowd had backed away to leave him facing his antagonist like two gunslingers in a western movie. He tried to appear calm, but just like a swan swimming on a lake, although everything on the surface looked serene, underneath he was paddling frantically in order to stay afloat.

"Hi Mo," he said, trying to appear nonchalant.

"I believe that you gave Vic a hiding last night," said Mo.

"News travels fast," he answered.

The crowd in the bar were standing in total silence, watching the confrontation unfold as if they were watching a film.

"I'm impressed Cassius, I didn't know that you had it in you," said Mo, with a reluctant hint of respect in his tone.

"Have you seen him since last night?" asked Ray.

"Yes," answered Mo, "he wants me to give you a fucking good hiding."

"Is that what you intend to do Mo?" asked Ray, pretending to be unconcerned.

"It could be worth a few drinks," said Mo, relishing the occasion.

"Did he tell you that he was feeling her arse when I hit him?" asked Ray, trying desperately to gain some kind of advantage which would rescue him from the hole that he currently found himself in.

"He was feeling whose arse?" snapped Mo, even though he already knew the answer to his own question.

"Doreen's arse, who do you think?" replied Ray, re-enforcing his earlier announcement.

"No he fucking didn't," replied Mo angrily.

"How's Vic?" asked Ray, eager to know how effective his attack had been on the groper.

"He's lost both of his front teeth, his eyes are both closed and he has a dozen stitches in his face, in fact you made a hell of a good job of it." Mo began to laugh and Ray joined in.

"I'm just getting myself a pint, do you want one?" asked Ray, as a way of reinforcing Mo's lightening of mood.

"I'll get them," said Mo, "you won't pay for another drink tonight Cassius."

The tension in the crowd started to ease as the crisis appeared to be averted, although some of the onlookers seemed to be disappointed.

"Am I likely to be in trouble with anyone else besides you Mo?" asked Ray with trepidation.

"Stick with me tonight Cassius and I'll sort it," Mo assured him.

They went around the red light district of the town, known locally as the Barbary Coast. In most of the pubs, Ray's feet stuck to the carpet because of the spilt beer and discarded chewing gum. Mo advised him not to drink from the glasses, but to order bottled beer and to drink straight from the neck of the bottle after first wiping it.

Sam's Vaults was by far the worst pub that they entered all evening. There were brass spittoons on the floor around the bar, while the bare flag floor had been covered in sawdust to soak up the spit and spillage. The walls were covered in nicotine from tobacco smoke, while high on a tiny homemade stage built into an alcove was an old man playing an upright piano very badly. For his pains, he was regularly pelted with cigarette packets or any other litter or debris available to his audience, which he dodged expertly while his piano playing never faltered in its awfulness.

In every pub Mo introduced Ray to the town's lowlife, who stared at him sullenly as Mo made it plain that Ray was under his personal protection. They ended up at the Cats Whiskers and as Mo went to get the drinks, Ray went to have a word with Buddy who he had spotted at the other end of the bar.

"What the hell are you doing with Mo Halsey?" asked Buddy. "I thought that he would have beaten you to a pulp after last night."

"You've heard then," said Ray, who wouldn't have been surprised if it had been announced on the local radio.

"Heard; "shrieked Buddy, "you're the talk of the town, nobody messes with Vic the Vain."

"I'm out with Mo so that he can warn people off," explained Ray.

"You really are a jammy bastard; said Buddy in admiration, "I don't know how you get away with it."

■ ■ ■

Ray hadn't told his mother that the engagement was over. She asked him why Doreen hadn't been around for a few days, but to buy some time until he could speak to Dore personally, he had assured her that everything between the two of them was fine, and that she was just very busy at the salon.

Nothing had been resolved by the time that his mother went to have her hair done the following Wednesday, in fact he had never even seen her and she had refused to come to the phone. Doreen had told his mother the whole story, or at least her version of it. It seemed that as far as Doreen was concerned the engagement definitely was over. She accused Ray of being a coward for attacking Vic without any provocation, and for hitting him without giving him a chance to defend himself. The fact that he was feeling her arse at the time, or that she had been seeing someone else behind Ray's back hadn't been mentioned, but at least she had returned his uncles ring and he replaced it on his little finger where he felt that it belonged.

CHAPTER SEVENTEEN

It was lunch time the following day before he awoke nursing the usual hangover; there was another hand posted letter awaiting him on the coffee table, it bore the same cut out printing as the first one, and when he opened it, it simply read,
"NOW IT'S PERSONAL."
Mo Halsey had assured him that Vic would not be retaliating for the beating that he had received. Dore had made it clear that she never wanted to see him again, so it was hardly likely that she would have written either letter, besides this letter was an anonymous threat. Who could have sent him the letters and why?

■ ■ ■

Ivan was living in a flat in the low rent area of the town. Since John's death Mrs Ponte had become inconsolable and even worse unreasonable, although Ivan had done all that he could to make her happy since the death of her son, their relationship had finally broken down and he had sadly, at her insistence, moved out of her home.
When he had contacted Amsterdam with the news of John's murder Vladimir had been furious, blaming Ivan unfairly for not protecting him. A few days later after he had become a little more rational, he had contacted Ivan again, placing him on active service along with the relevant pay, which was welcome news for Ivan as he was now without a job, Vallard after considering his position, having decided that there could be no smoke without fire after Ray's allegations. In case he was under police

surveillance, Vladimir had ordered him to lay low for a while before issuing him with any orders.

The waiting had finally come to an end, along with his long term relationship with Mrs Ponte, and things had become very personal for Ivan. He blamed Ray, not only for the loss of his job and the break-up of his relationship, but also for John's death, and the fact that he was now living in a shabby bed sit in the worst part of town.

■ ■ ■

Tom Farnsworth was a decade older than Ray, and had been one of his mentors when Ray had been serving his apprenticeship. Tom was not Scottish, but as he played a drum in the local Scottish pipe band, his workmates called him Tam Mac Farnsworth.

As a child Ray had watched the pipe band at carnivals and at church walking days, fascinated by the spectacle of the pipers in their kilts and sporrans, with jewel handled dirks tucked inside of tartan stockings. He liked to hear the drummers beating out a marching beat while the pipers took a rest, and to watch the drum major twirling his baton and throwing it high into the air, where it spun and twisted before being expertly caught, without missing a marching beat, as it fell.

When Ray bumped into Tam on that Monday morning, it was Tam's first day back at work after surgery for testicular cancer, while to make matters worse for the poor man, his wife, who had been having an affair with her employer for a number of years, had chosen this rather insensitive time to move in with her lover, taking the family car and leaving Tam to catch the bus into work.

"I can give you a lift home after work if you like," offered Ray on hearing of Tam's plight.

"I'd be grateful if it's not too much trouble," responded Tam.

"No trouble at all," said Ray, only too pleased to be of service, as Tam had always been a good friend to him.

The white Spitfire came with a red leatherette soft top, and a matching tanoak cover which zipped across the middle. When the roof was down, the driver could sit at the wheel while the passenger seat remained protected against inclement weather, and when parked, the zip would ensure that both seats would be protected, making it unnecessary to sit on a wet seat.

Ray liked to drive with the top down whenever possible, but the Lancashire weather had been so erratic this year, one day warm and the next day cold, one day sunny the next day wet. On this cold and wet day, he had taken the trouble to remove the tanoak cover and replaced it with the soft top, even though it was always a bit of a fiddle.

Tam was a big man, and with the roof on the car he found it difficult to settle into the passenger seat, having to duck in order to squeeze himself in.

"Bloody hell Ray," said Tam. "Why don't you buy a proper car instead of a bloody Dinky toy?"

"It's designed to make beautiful people look good, not for big ugly sods like you," Ray responded.

Tam wasn't conventionally handsome but he certainly wasn't ugly. He was quite good looking in a strange sort of way, tall, dark and handsome some might say, while others might disagree, as he had quite a large and slightly twisted nose, which looked as if it could have been knocked out of kilter in some past disagreement.

On the way home Ray tried to avoid the taboo subjects of Tam's wife and his testicles. Instead, he reminisced about old times when the two of them used to work together in the Plant department.

"Do you remember before they converted the boiler house to gas?" Ray asked, "I got Alvin Greenhalgh to look at his reflection in a barrel of fuel oil, and then you threw a brick into it."

"Yes I remember," smiled Tam, "he came out looking like the tar baby from the Uncle Remus stories. I thought that it was funny at the time, but 'I'm not very proud of myself for doing it now."

"And what about the time when you made a fire blower out of sheet metal, and tried to sneak it out of the factory inside of your newspaper. It was so windy that people were struggling to stay on their feet, while you walked through the gates nonchalantly reading a stiff newspaper."

"Until the wind caught it like a sail and dragged me into the arms of security," added Tam laughing.

They talked of this and that, and laughed a lot until the moment that they approached the Old Mother Redcap public house, which was situated in a short stretch of countryside between two neighbouring towns. Ray had just increased his speed as he left the speed restricted area, while a petrol tanker coming in the opposite direction was reducing his speed as he approached the same restriction zone.

As the tanker drew level with Ray's Spitfire, a large white van quite suddenly appeared from behind the tanker, where it had been completely hidden from Ray's view. The road was wide and Ray pulled the Spitfire over to let the van go through the gap, but although there was plenty of room for the van to pass comfortably, it appeared instead to be steering straight towards him. In a last ditch effort to avoid a collision Ray mounted the pavement but too late, the van collided with the Spitfire pushing it into a farm yard wall, before spinning out of control until it overturned some two hundred meters down the road, sliding along its side in a shower of sparks until friction brought it to a halt in the middle of the road.

Ray watched in amazement as the driver of the van opened his driver door, which now faced upwards towards the sky, and he began to climb out. He appeared to be unhurt as his movements were easy, and he was wearing black motor cycle leathers and a crash helmet. A moment later a motor cycle screeched out of a side road, stopping briefly to pick up the driver of the van, before speeding off through a red light, narrowly missing a bus and then they were gone.

The van had struck the front wing of Ray's car just in front of the driver's door, the front end had completely collapsed and the car appeared to be totalled. The driver's door had crumpled form the impact of the collision, and the dashboard appeared to be much closer than usual, but had the van hit the door rather than the wing, it would most probably have been curtains for

Ray. He turned to look at Tam. Ray had been able to brace himself against the collision because he was holding onto the steering wheel, and although his arms had turned to jelly with the strain, he appeared to have survived the impact intact.

Tam on the other hand had not been quite so lucky, his head had hit the window screen with such force that he had cracked the glass, and blood was streaming down into his eyes from a horrendous gash on his forehead. Against the farm wall stood a wooden telegraph pole, and the impact of the crash had pushed the Spitfire into the pole so forcibly, that the car had wrapped itself around the pole, crushing the side of the car and trapping Tam against the dash board.

Ray wasn't sure if Tam was dead or alive as he reached to feel the pulse on Tams neck, thankfully it was still there, but only for a moment, before he removed his hand he felt it stop. Frantically he searched, trying to find the pulse again, before realising that the blood had stopped pumping from the gash on Tam's forehead.

He tried to get out of the car, but the crumpled door refused to open. People began arriving at the scene in an attempt to help, and then he saw the smoke appearing from under the damaged bonnet. This was quickly followed by flames and he tried desperately to open the car door, break a window, or tear off the roof before the car became an inferno.

People began to back away from the car fearing that there may be an explosion at any moment, wanting to help but fearful for their own safety. He was trapped and surprisingly he suddenly became very calm, resigned to his fate as the flames began to grow under the bonnet of his car and lick out around the sides.

He must have had a guardian angel, or alternatively the nine lives of a cat, as once again luck was to be on his side. One of the drivers who had stopped to help, raced back to his car on seeing the flames, and returned with a small portable fire extinguisher, bought from his local car accessory shop, which very quickly had the flames under control.

As the last of the flames died away, Ray heard the approach of a cacophony of sirens. First a police panda car arrived, a Morris

Minor in pale green with white doors, which had been patrolling nearby, followed almost immediately by the fire brigade, all flashing lights and bells, and soon after that by the first of two ambulances' and then a second police car. The cavalry had arrived.

The police wasted no time in setting out cones and directing the traffic, which had already backed up for a couple of miles in both directions. Ray had been driving with the window slightly down before the accident, but now it refused to wind either up or down, and a fireman who approached the car spoke to Ray through the small gap in the window.

"Can you tell me your name son?" he asked.

"Ray," answered Ray through the window gap.

"Ok Ray, my name is Andy, don't worry we'll soon have you out of there."

"Are you injured Ray?"

"No I'm fine," answered Ray, although he didn't feel fine, far from it.

"Good, what's your friend's name Ray?"

"Tom, but everyone calls him Tam," answered Ray.

"Tam can you hear me?" Andy called through the gap in the window.

"He can't hear you he's dead," said Ray sadly.

Andy didn't show any reaction at all to this piece of dramatic news.

"Ok Ray, how does this top come off?"

"There are two wing nuts on the top of the windscreen here inside, and press studs on the outside around the boot."

"Can you undo the fastenings on the windscreen Ray?"

"Yes," answered Ray, undoing the first one before leaning across Tam's body in order to reach the far one.

Before he had managed to release the windscreen screws, the fire crew had unbuttoned the studs around the boot and the roof was quickly off.

"Turn your face away Ray, I'm going to break your window now," said Andy.

"Can't you chaps do anything without breaking things?" quipped Ray, without mirth.

Andy laughed.

Ray turned his face towards Tam, something that he had been trying very hard not to do. He felt some kind of sheet being draped over his head and everything went black, then he heard a crash and felt the shattered glass shower all over his back. Two firemen were kneeling on the boot of the car; one removed his glove and felt Tam's neck for a pulse, looked towards the waiting ambulance men he shook his head. They gripped Ray beneath his arms.

"Were going to lift you now," said Andy. "Are you ready? One, two, three, lift."

They dragged him backwards and upwards at the same time, after first checking with Ray that he still had feeling in his legs. His legs came out from under the dashboard easily, even though the well had been partly crushed, before Andy grabbed them and lifted them over the broken side window.

While sitting in the ambulance a policeman arrived to speak to him.

"I'm PC Lofthouse; I'll be accompanying you to the hospital."

"I don't need to go to hospital," said Ray, "I'm not hurt. Apart from aching arms from bracing against the collision," he added.

"I think you should go anyway," insisted the constable. "I'll follow you up there."

The constable stepped back out of the ambulance and just before they closed the doors he asked.

"Would you like us to inform anyone for you?"

Ray gave his parents address to the policeman, and as he didn't ask about Tam, Ray assumed that they must have got Tam's details from inside his wallet.

At the hospital he was given a priority examination and pronounced fit.

"Can I go home now?" asked Ray.

"No, were going to keep you in overnight for observation," said a very efficient but rather bossy staff nurse.

"There's nothing to observe," Ray argued, but was treated as delusional and made to get into bed by the nurse, who pulled a screen around him, and gave him a hospital gown to wear which only partly fastened down the back. She left him to his own devices for a few minutes, and on her return she gave him the once over.

"You can take those off," she said, pointing at Ray's boxer shorts, which he had stubbornly left on underneath the gown. Although he protested strongly, the bossy nurse insisted that he remove them, and when she could finally see his bare arse, she happily tied his gown for him and got him into bed.

Soon after the nurse had left his parents arrived, his father immediately began chastising him for being a menace on the road, while his mother just cried.

"I hope that you're not going to go around blaming me for this accident," Ray scolded his father.

"For a start this was in no way my fault, and as a man as died, I wouldn't want the police to think otherwise."

His mother had brought with her a pair of pyjamas for him to wear. Ray was not in the habit of wearing pyjamas, having last worn this particular pair while having his tonsils removed in this very same hospital half of his lifetime ago.

He was sure that they couldn't possibly still fit; after all it was thirteen years since he had last worn them. His mother pulled around the curtain for a second time, giving him no option but to try them on. He was surprised to discover, that due to her habit of always buying his clothes a couple of sizes too large when he was a child, insisting that he would grow into them, they fitted him perfectly, and for once he was happy to wear them if it meant dispensing with the hospital gown.

When the curtain opened once again PC Lofthouse was waiting there.

"Do you feel up to making a statement?" he asked.

"Got to do it sometime," said Ray resignedly.

PC Lofthouse was not at all what you would expect of a police officer. For a start he didn't look tall enough to meet the minimum height requirement for the police force. His helmet looked far too big for his head, and only the fact that he had ears like jug handles stopped it from slipping down and covering his face entirely. He was slightly built, spotty faced, and wore metal-rimmed spectacles, which made him look more like a librarian than a policeman.

"In your own words Mr Evans, can you tell me what happened," he began.

"Look no offence," said Ray, "but I'd like to speak to Detective Inspector Briggs."

"DI Briggs doesn't deal with road traffic accidents sir," answered the constable patiently.

"But that's the point, this wasn't a road traffic accident," argued Ray.

"Oh I'm sure that it was sir," replied PC Lofthouse smugly.

"Look," said Ray forcibly, "the driver of the van deliberately drove into me and tried to kill me."

"What speed were you doing at the time of the accident?" continued PC Lofthouse, ignoring Ray's argument of attempted murder completely.

"Wooden top," muttered Ray under his breath.

"I beg your pardon sir," asked the constable, unsure if he had heard correctly, even though he had ears like an African elephant.

"I said that he wouldn't stop," Ray lied to cover his insult.

Ray decided to humour him, telling him his version of the collision without the conspiracy theory, so as to get rid of him as quickly as possible.

"Have you traced the other driver yet?" asked Ray after giving his statement.

"No, it seems that the van may have been reported stolen this morning, answered the constable.

Ray wondered what where the criteria for selecting police constables these days. In PC Lofthouse's case it didn't seem to be either brawn or brain, or even the ability to look good in the uniform.

After Lofthouse had left, he told his parents what had happened, but let them think that it was just another road traffic accident caused by the reckless driver of a stolen van.

Until this point his mind had been kept occupied by questions from the police, the fire brigade, and the hospital doctors.

He had remained strong, but after his parents had left he began to cry, not only for Tam but also for April and Daniel Rhymes.

■ ■ ■

He was released from hospital the following morning, after a terrible night where he had hardly slept a wink, due to the continual noise of people snoring, and shouting for the nurse to assist them with toilet duties. He decided to ring the police station to see if he could talk to DI Briggs, but the inspector was out and so he left a message.

After tea, as he was settling down to watch television, the telephone rang, it was Briggs.

"I received a message that you would like to talk to me Mr. Evans," he said.

"Yes Inspector," replied Ray.

Ray told him about the accident of the previous day, about the stolen van, and the helmeted driver who was spirited away by an accomplice on a motor cycle.

"So you think that this was another attempt on your life?" asked the inspector.

"Don't you?" asked Ray, a little surprised that Briggs didn't appear to see things in quite the same way that he did.

"But the last time that we spoke you were sure that John Ponte was your assailant and now he's dead," pointed out Briggs.

"I know, but Ponte was working for Vladimir and he had other accomplices in this country.

"You mean that fellow Ivan Borkovsky?" asked the inspector.

"And don't forget Stefan," added Ray.

"Oh yes, the chap that you say you caught planting the transmitters that were never found," said Briggs condescendingly.

"They were never found because I destroyed them before you became involved," Ray pointed out, a little disgruntled at the insinuation that they had never actually existed.

"And you think that one of these two associates of Vladimir was the driver of the car, while the other drove the motor cycle."

"That's about the size of it," said Ray, breathing out heavily after finally making his point.

"Have you any other evidence to prove that this wasn't just another road accident?" asked Briggs.

"I've had a couple of threatening letters," said Ray, mentally chastising himself that he hadn't reacted to them since they had first arrived.

"Have you still got them?" asked Briggs.

"Yes, there on my bedside cabinet," answered Ray.

"I'll send someone around to pick them up," volunteered Briggs, "will you have them ready for my courier?"

After Briggs had rung off, he went upstairs to get the notes from his bedroom, but even though he searched he couldn't find them anywhere.

"Have you seen the letters which were on my bedside cabinet?" he asked his mother.

"No dear," she answered, although he knew very well that she had, although without ever registering the event.

His mother was a very house proud woman, but because house cleaning is not the most exciting of occupations, she tended to do all of her housework in a dream like state and things had a habit of disappearing.

For a start, Ray had a drawer full of odd socks sadly awaiting the return of their missing partners, which for some unknown reason never ever reappeared. He had even begun to buy nothing but black socks, so that all of the odd socks in his drawer could be re-matched into new pairs.

There was also always a shortage of tea spoons in the house, even though his mother replaced them with new ones on a regular basis. Many times he had rescued a wayward teaspoon from the kitchen waste bin, thrown away with a used tea bag while making a cup of tea, and finding the milk had begun to be a game of hide and seek, which usually resulted in the milk bottle being found inside the cooker instead of in the fridge.

From his past experiences of missing items, he accepted that the notes had disappeared as mysteriously has his socks, never to be seen again. He called Briggs once again to relay the bad news. Briggs was not impressed that another piece of vital evidence had been lost and he said so.

As soon as he had put the phone down Archie called. "How are you doing mate?"

"I'm okay under the circumstances," Ray replied.

"What the hell happened?" asked Archie.

Ray told him about the accident, but he didn't mention his theory that it wasn't an accident at all.

"Have you heard when the funeral is Archie?"

"Yes it's on Friday at Holy Trinity church, a lot of the chaps from work will be there. Vallard's have agreed to give all staff who knew him time off so that they can go."

"What time is it booked for?" asked Ray.

"Eleven," answered Archie.

"I'll see you there," said Ray, wishing that this funeral wasn't happening at all, especially so close to that of Dan Rhymes.

■ ■ ■

The funeral passed off well enough, or as well as funerals can be expected to pass off. Tam's wife showed up, but thankfully without her boyfriend. She even managed to shed a tear for the man who had shared so many years of her life.

"Look mate," said Archie seriously. "I have something I need to tell you."

"What is it?" asked Ray apprehensively.

"It's Cheryl," he said, "we've split up again."

"Oh not again Archie, I thought that you were getting on well this time."

"So did I, but it seems that she's met someone else at the golf club."

"I didn't know that she played golf," said Ray surprised.

"She doesn't, she wouldn't know one end of a golf club from the other, but she spends a lot of time at the nineteenth hole."

"Have you moved out of the flat again?" asked Ray.

"No, she's moved in with him. He has a house near to the golf club, but I'm leaving the flat anyway, I've joined the Merchant Navy, Blue Funnel Line."

"Isn't that the company who owned the Titanic?" asked Ray, remembering that a colour was somehow involved.

"No that was White Star Line you ignoramus," corrected Archie.

"Thank God for that," said Ray with relief. "Have you told them at work that you're leaving?"

"Yes I'm on a month's notice starting from last Monday. Listen Ray, before Cheryl and I split up I booked a coach holiday to Italy, now I need someone to go with me or I'll have to cancel and lose all of my money."

"Are you asking me to go with you?" asked Ray.

"It's all paid for, it wouldn't cost you anything except for spending money, but you would have to travel as Mrs Brough," explained Archie.

"You know that everyone will think that we're queers," Ray informed him.

"We'll have to show them that were not then," said Archie defiantly.

"Ok you're on, said Ray. "When is it?"

"A week tomorrow, you'll have to ask for your annual leave on Monday."

■■■◆

Archie was already in The Legs O' Man when Ray arrived that evening, which surprised him as Archie was usually late. He was sorry that Archie's marriage had failed once again, and even sorrier that he was leaving to join the Merchant Navy. He was going to miss him badly.

"I wish that you weren't leaving Archie, it won't be the same when you've gone," said Ray sadly.

"Why don't you come with me," suggested Archie, "You have nothing to keep you here."

"I'd like to mate, but you know what a terrible sailor I am. I couldn't even sail to the Isle of Man for the TT without being sick."

"That's true," said Archie reminiscing. "Do you remember the year that we sailed from Liverpool on Mona's Isle, and it was listing at about seventy five degree's to port all of the way to Douglas? The waves were coming over the bow, streaming down the deck and running off at the stern."

"Do I?" said Ray. "It makes me feel sick just thinking about it. I was up on the deck, hanging on to a mast and soaking wet from the spray, while all of you unsympathetic bastards were in the bar drinking."

Archie laughed.

"What started me off, "continued Ray, "was going into the toilets to find them flooded, with people standing ankle deep in water, piss, and puke. I felt queasy at the sight of it and so I decided to go up onto the deck to get some fresh air. As I passed the engine room door, an old stoker was cooking bacon and eggs on a hot shovel and that was it. The smell of the bacon and eggs, mixed with the diesel fumes and the memory of the puke filled toilets started me off. I spent two miserable hours soaking wet with water running into my shoes, spray blowing into my face, and I could still smell the engine room and the blasted bacon and eggs until we docked in Douglas."

"Bad idea, sorry I mentioned it," Archie apologised.

"They spent the evening travelling down memory lane, never leaving The Legs O' Man until it was almost closing time.

The bar staff where calling last orders as they entered the Little White Bull, and they fought their way to the bar to get a drink. Everyone in the Bull seemed to be very young. It didn't surprise Ray anymore as he had become accustomed to the changed situation, but Archie was as devastated as Ray had been to realise that they had outgrown the place.

Ray spotted a woman sitting alone at the bar. She was a throwback from Ray's generation and obviously feeling every bit as out of place as he and Archie did. She looked familiar, and after a little memory searching Ray recognised her as Katy Day, a girl who he had met a number of years ago while working in M block, a department at Vallard of predominantly women workers. Turning she gave him a smile, obviously glad to see a familiar face in a sea of strangers. Ray didn't need any further encouragement and went over to speak to her.

"Katy isn't it?" he asked.

"I'm surprised that you remembered," she answered.

"I never forget a pretty face," he said, laying on the charm with a trowel. "I always fancied you when you worked at Vallard, but never plucked up the courage to ask you out."

"I wish that you had," she answered, "because I always fancied you, but thought that you hadn't even noticed me."

"I noticed," he said, making her feel good with his complementary comment.

There were so many other girls in the department," she continued, "and every one of them fancied you like crazy. The girls who you dated told us stories; I envied every one of them and wanted to find out what you were like personally."

"Well now's your chance," offered Ray. "I can't promise to live up to any fanciful reputation that you may think that I have, but I am willing to give it my best shot."

"Have you got a car?" she asked.

"Sorry," he replied. "I crashed it last Monday, but on the plus side my parents are on holiday, so I have the house to myself, and I do have the taxi fare."

"Let's go." she said, slipping her arm into his.

He went to tell Archie that they were leaving, and they all walked to the taxi rank together; Archie let them take the first taxi that arrived, promising to speak to Ray about the holiday on Monday at work.

After arriving home, he led her into his own bedroom, as he was afraid to use his parent's double bed in case he left clues as to his nocturnal shenanigans. The more that he looked at Katy, the more beautiful she seemed to become. She was small and slightly built, with the bluest of blue eyes which almost rivalled those of *Weis*. She had a little turned up nose and long natural fair hair, and he thought how young she looked, child like almost, and he had to remind himself that she was in fact very close to his own age.

He undressed quickly and lay on the bed, watching with interest as she herself undressed without embarrassment. Once naked she sat astride him as he lay on his back, with her long hair tumbling down over her small but beautifully shaped breasts. Ray was reminded of Lady Godiva, as she rode her horse naked through the streets of Coventry, while in imitation of the aforementioned lady, she herself rode naked; slowly rocking backwards and forwards and from side to side, with her large blue eyes tightly closed and her head rolling around on her shoulders, until finally her steed came to the end of his journey, incapable of continuing.

■ ■ ■

Ray awoke the following morning and made breakfast. He had been up for an hour by the time that she awoke, and during that time he had decided that he would like to see more of her.

After they had breakfasted, he took her to her mother's house on the back of his motor bike and asked if he could see her again.

"I'd like to see you again," she said, "honestly I would, I wish that we had got together years ago, but I live and work in London now. I've only come home for the weekend to visit my mother. I have to return this afternoon."

"Couldn't you leave London and come home for good?" he asked hopefully.

"I'm sorry I should have told you," she apologised, "I'm not free. I'm married to an Iranian man called Ali. He came here to Blakewater to study textiles at the local college, and after his three year course we moved to London when the cotton mills began closing. I've been marred for five years now and I have a four year old son called Ahmed."

CHAPTER EIGHTEEN

He brooded throughout Sunday while continually watching the clock. At one o'clock she would be getting onto the train at Blakewater station. At two she would be changing trains at Preston, and at four she would probably be somewhere in the Midlands.

■ ■ ■

On Monday Archie informed him that their holiday commenced at a travel agents on London's Tottenham Court Road. At one-thirty a coach would pick them up there and take them to Luton Airport. Archie had decided that they would catch the midnight bus from Blakewater on Friday, which would get them into London at approximately five am on the day of their flight.

Ray had started to feel apprehensive; Ivan would have reported to Vladimir that the latest attempt on his life had failed by now. Vladimir would probably have given orders for a further attempt to be made on his life. He was going to spend the rest of the week looking over his shoulder, the sooner that they left the country the better he would like it. Hopefully by the time that they returned from their holiday Ivan and Stefan would both have been apprehended?

He decided to ring DI Briggs to see if they had made any progress with the case. Briggs was out but DS White answered the phone.

"Have you any news?" asked Ray. "I'm living on the edge here."

"We have made some progress Mr. Evans," answered the sergeant. We've tracked down the bus driver, who confirms your story that a motor cycle with a pillion passenger ran a red light and almost collided with his bus. He was so incensed that he managed to get a partial index number and reported the incident to us.

"Have you traced the bike sergeant?" Ray asked.

"It's taken a while because we only had a partial index, but it belongs to a local man, and was reported stolen some days before it was used for the getaway. It was found on the market car park two days ago, the parking attendant reported that it had been there since late Monday.

"Have you got any more leads?" asked Ray hopefully.

"An old lady, who lives near to the scene, reported that a young man on a motor cycle sat outside of her house for over half an hour on Monday afternoon. He was talking to someone on what she described as a "walkie-talkie," and at about the time of the accident he sped off.

"Do you agree with me now that it wasn't just a road accident?" asked Ray, desperate to be believed.

"Well it does appear that you could be right," replied the sergeant.

"You certainly are a master of understatement," commented Ray.

"We have to be very careful what we say," replied White.

■ ■ ■

Ray was working on the morning shift and so he finished work at two o'clock on the eve of the holiday. He had plenty of time to pack and to have a nap, as they were going to be travelling throughout the night and for all of the following day. Before he went to bed he rang the police station once again.

This time DI Briggs himself came to the phone.

"Good afternoon Mr. Evans," he said cheerily. "We have more news."

"Have you caught them?" asked Ray hopefully.

"Not exactly," replied Briggs cautiously. "We have been in contact with our counterparts in the Netherlands, and Vladimir, they have confirmed, is known to them. He is on their files as a low ranking Soviet agent, who uses the cover of chief of security at a Soviet owned transmission station."

"I knew that already," said a frustrated Ray. "In fact I told you at our very first meeting."

"And the Dutch have now confirmed your story Mr. Evans," said Briggs condescendingly.

"Have you any information that I don't know?" asked a frustrated Ray.

"It seems," began Briggs, "that they transmit communist propaganda to the west, while as a side line they uncover and pass on secrets of Dutch national security to the Soviet Union, with a little industrial espionage thrown in for good measure. Because Vladimir works for the Soviet government he has diplomatic immunity, but even so the Dutch keep a very close eye on him. Stefan has also been confirmed as one of his team. Officially he is a radio technician, but he is most probably used to plant surveillance devices and to send and intercept messages. It would appear that he was sent to Blakewater primarily to plant devices at the Vallard factory, but it is also probable that he helped John Ponte to plan the explosion in the substation, as it would have taken some considerable electrical knowledge, which I doubt that Ponte possessed. After the explosion he returned to Amsterdam, and then three weeks ago he re-entered the country, probably to assist Ivan."

"Where is Stefan now?" prompted Ray.

"We believe that he's returned to Amsterdam once again," Briggs told him.

"What do the Dutch know about Ivan?" asked Ray, knowing that he was the one who he needed to be concerned about at the moment.

"Ivan and John Ponte are unknown to the Dutch authorities or to MI5," explained the inspector. "They were probably both part of a sleeper cell, planted here many years ago and living perfectly normal lives, until being awakened for duty only recently. Probably the fact that they were inexperienced, having never been active before, coupled with their orders to make your demise look like an accident, has been the reason why they have bungled your assassination on so many occasions."

"Have you any news of Ivan's whereabouts?" questioned Ray.

"We found the apartment which he had been sharing with Stefan. They paid their rent for a month in advance, vacating it on the day of the most recent incident. It's as clean as a whistle and we have no idea where he is now. He has definitely not left the country with Stefan, so he may have remained in order to make another attempt on your life. This time there will be little point in him trying to make it look like an accident.

"Thanks I needed that," said Ray ironically.

"I'm sorry, but you need to be made aware of the position," said Briggs solemnly. "Look on the bright side. Now that you have told the police everything that you know, Vladimir has no further reason to want you out of the way."

"Except that the notes that I received said "it's not over, now it's personal," Ray reminded him.

"You never told me what it said in the notes;" said Briggs, surprised that Ray had known the contents of the notes all along without telling him, "but maybe now that the police are involved, Vladimir will decide that you're demise is not going to be worth the trouble it could cause."

Ray hoped that he was right, but somehow he doubted it. He caught a few hours sleep before it was time to meet with Archie. His father drove him to the railway station, amidst complaints that he had been forced to stay up until midnight, when he was usually hard and fast asleep by ten-thirty.

Ray waited at the appointed meeting place for about twenty minutes, while Archie arrived at the last moment, just as the bus was pulling into the bus station. Ray had expected to be travelling by coach, and was surprised to find that their holiday transport was a double-decker service bus. They loaded their suitcases, and headed for the next pickup points at Bolton and Manchester before hitting the motorway.

When Archie had informed Ray that they were catching the twelve o'clock bus, Ray had complained that he would not be able to sleep on a bus. The next thing that he remembered was waking up in the centre of Birmingham at two in the morning, even though he had already slept for five hours before leaving home. They left the bus to stretch their legs, as it was scheduled for a thirty minute stop in Birmingham. Some passengers got off the bus and others got on, while Ray and Archie looked for a toilet in the bus station.

Before returning to the bus they found a dark and dingy bus station café, with buffet room written in old fashioned faded gold letters on the glass door panel. Inside, the buffet room had made few concessions towards the twentieth century. The gas lights had been replaced by electric lighting some thirty years earlier. Other than that and a large chrome plated cappuccino machine on the counter, it looked like a Victorian museum.

Ray could imagine the passengers of horse drawn buses and stage coaches using this self same buffet room in the nineteenth century, ladies with long dresses and men with bowler hats, accompanying children in sailor suites and small boys dressed like little girls in dresses.

There was no one serving behind the counter, even though all of the lights were on in the buffet room and the doors were wide open letting in the early morning chill. The only person present was a very large West Indian lady, who appeared to be lost in her thoughts while lazily mopping the floor with dirty water.

"Can we get a cup of coffee?" asked Archie.

The woman didn't answer, but pointed to a further concession to the twentieth century which they had failed to notice on their initial perusal, namely a coffee vending machine in the corner of the room hidden behind the open doors, which was standing next to a snack vending machine, dispensing chocolate bars and crisps. They bought two coffee's, white with sugar, along with two Mars bars, before returning to their seats on the bus, where they consumed their prizes as people continued to get onto the bus for the final leg of their journey.

At two-thirty on the dot with an almost full bus, they set out for London, and with only one comfort break at a motorway service station, they arrived exactly on time at Victoria bus station.

Even though it was five o'clock in the morning, the black cabs were already lined up on the taxi rank and Ray and Archie hailed the lead cab.

"Tottenham Court Road please," said Archie, and the cab sped off through the early morning traffic.

They travelled down Victoria Street, passing the end of Buckingham Gate, the driver pointed out that they could see Buckingham Palace if they looked to their left, before travelling on to Parliament Square, past the Houses of Parliament and up Whitehall towards Trafalgar Square. They drove around Nelsons Column, past the National Portrait Gallery, into Charing Cross Road and onto Tottenham Court Road.

They found the travel agents close to the Grafton Hotel, which just as the brochure had promised was opened at six o'clock in the morning, so that they could leave their luggage until their pickup later in the day. They waited for fifteen minutes until it opened, before finding an early morning greasy spoon café close to Euston station, where they ravenously consumed a full English breakfast of bacon and eggs, sausage, baked beans, mushrooms, fried bread and toast; with a large pot of dark bitter coffee, which tasted to Ray like the stuff that came in liquid form from a bottle, and didn't much resemble real coffee at all.

"What the hell are we going to do for six hours?" asked Ray. "We've already seen Buckingham Palace, the Houses of Parliament, Nelsons Column and had some breakfast, and it's still only seven o'clock."

"I've always wanted to see the Tower of London," said Archie; "why don't we go there?"

They caught the tube at Euston Square, getting off again at Tower Hill. Ray found the underground claustrophobic. Even before the train arrived at Euston Square he had trouble breathing the recycled air in the tunnels, and when the train did arrive it was even worse. They found themselves in the middle of the morning rush, and even though it was the weekend, the train was full to the point were not only were there no seats available, but very little standing room either. Ray wondered how people could put up with this way of life on a daily basis, while thanking his lucky stars that he at least didn't have to.

When they reached Tower Hill station, they got off the train and walked down to the Tower of London. Ray couldn't believe that building work had begun on the tower by the order of William the Conqueror nine hundred years earlier. He was amazed that what he had thought of as a primitive society in 1066 could have built something so impressive. Something that although already nine hundred years old, would undoubtedly outlast the multi story flats which had been springing up everywhere throughout the sixties.

Being a little too early for the opening of the Tower, they strolled down to the Thames and watched the boats sailing passed on the river. Ray had been to London once before with a school party when he was much younger. They had visited the Science Museum and the Natural History Museum, before having a sail on the Thames. They had sailed past the Tower of London by which they now stood, and under Tower Bridge, which was currently opening to allow for the mast of a large yacht, which was sailing steadily up the river but not under sail.

Ray and Archie watched as the Victorian bridge opened and closed, both being engineers they argued about the unseen mechanism required to produce this awesome sight. Archie was convinced that that it would be opened by electric motors and cables, while Ray was convinced that it would be opened by a hydraulic mechanism using water from the river.

"How could it possibly open with electric motors?" argued Ray, "Mains electricity wasn't available when this bridge was built."

"It could have been converted later," insisted Archie, stubbornly sticking to his guns although he secretly felt that he was losing the argument.

On his previous visit to London, Ray had been more impressed with the dinosaur room at the Natural History Museum rather than with Tower Bridge. He remembered in particular the full skeletal remains of the largest dinosaur of them all Diplodocus, and a large Blue Whale which dwarfed all of the dinosaurs and hung from the ceiling, although he would have been devastated had he known that they were both in fact replica's.

He had also been impressed by all of the stuffed animals at the museum, imagining himself as a white hunter in Africa, where his mother had been born at the advent of World War I. In his mind he had hunted wild animals with his grandfather, who had only recently passed away in Africa, and who he had never actually met; although he did until his grandfather's demise, receive postcards, photographs, and greetings cards from Africa for his birthday and at Christmas.

In truth his grandfather had never been a white hunter at all, but a piano tuner, travelling between all of the big cities of South Africa, while bringing tuneful music to the suburbs of Johannesburg, Pretoria, Cape Town, and Durban, which was his home.

Ray could imagine all of these animal trophies on the walls of his home, lion, cheetah, leopard, and springbok heads mounted on the walls, zebra rugs, with reptiles and birds in glass cases on the sideboard, but in truth he loved all animals and wouldn't hurt a fly.

After his visit to London, he had bought a stuffed razorbill in a glass case from a school friend for half a crown. It had been a whole week's spending money at the time, but having taken it home with the intention of keeping it in his bedroom, his mother had refused to have it in the house, saying that it would harbour fleas. She had later relented after many arguments and tears, providing that he kept the offending creature in the attic, where he visited it from time to time.

A queue had begun to form outside of the tower gates. Ray and Archie stood behind a large party of Japanese visitors, who continually smiled and bowed, photographing everything that moved and everything that didn't. Two Yeomen of the Guard, or Beefeaters, one clothed in the red dress uniform trimmed with black and the other a negative of the first, stood by the gate to keep the queue in order. Taking turns to walk down the line, chatting to the crowd and telling interesting and fantastic stories of the tower.

Once inside the walls, they joined a party of school children in the courtyard, who were standing on the very spot where the execution of Henry the eighths wife's, Ann Boleyn and Katherine Howard had taken place, while another Beefeater told the story in graphic detail of the execution of Sir Walter Raleigh on this very spot in 1618.

After the talk they headed for the White Tower expecting to find the Crown Jewels. Instead they found themselves in the armoury looking at suites of armour, which with the exception of the armour worn by Henry the eighth were extremely small. There they stood like a Lilliputian army, with Ray feeling like Gulliver as he towered over them. Henry's armour was huge in comparison to the others, with a cod piece big enough to house a bull's wedding tackle let alone that of a king, while a second suite of Henry's armour sat on the replica of a shire horse, which was also in armour, and Ray thought what an awesome sight the King must have been to the little people of Tudor-land.

When they came out of the armoury, they asked a Beefeater where the Crown Jewels were kept and he pointed them in the direction of Waterloo Barracks. As they walked across the court yard towards the barracks, the ravens which according to legend would cause the downfall of England should they ever leave the tower, strutted around proudly as if they owned the place. Treated like royalty for fear of the terrible prophecy coming true.

Having been very close to the front of the queue when entering the tower, they would have been first in line to see the Crown Jewels had they gone straight away to Waterloo Barracks. Now the queue snaked backwards and forwards around metal barriers, with signs saying half an hour, one hour, and one and a half hours. They had spent so long in the White Tower and the Royal Fusiliers Museum, that they didn't have the time to wait for half an hour, let alone an hour and a half, and so were reluctantly forced to admit defeat. The only thing left to do was to visit the chapel of St Peter ad Vincula, which contained the crypts of some of the notables who were executed in the tower grounds.

After three hours of history and culture, they were overdosed on that particular topic and caught the tube back to Euston Square. They lunched at the same greasy spoon cafe, which had been the source of Ray's indigestion throughout the morning, before boarding the coach for Luton Airport.

The airport bore little resemblance to the recent grandeur of Manchester Airport. Although being a modern single story building, it seemed to Ray to be more like an upmarket bus station than an airport, housing a small café, toilets and rows of coloured plastic seats, although not nearly enough for the volume of passengers awaiting their flights.

When their flight was announced, they had to walk to the aeroplane carrying their suitcases, leaving them on the tarmac in order to be loaded, while they boarded the aeroplane. The aeroplane itself was nothing like the BEA Trident 2, on which Ray had recently flown to Amsterdam. It was an old Vickers Viscount four engine propeller aircraft from the 1940's, which rattled down the runway with its wings flapping like an old goose trying to take off. They flapped so much that Ray was worried that they might fall off before they had even taken to the air.

It had been a beautiful day whilst still on the ground, but once in the air they flew into a storm. Being a propeller aircraft, they were unable to rise above the inclement weather, and for most of the journey the plane was in darkness from the angry clouds which surrounded it, as rain lashed against the windows and blue lightening danced along the wings and the fuselage.

Ray thought about all of the dangers that he had encountered in recent months, and he put this experience right up there along side of them. What Vladimir's team had failed to achieve, it now seemed that nature most certainly would. Just as he was beginning to lose all hope that they would ever arrive safely, they quite suddenly came out of the storm. Ten minutes later the Viscount touched down at Maastricht Airport, taxiing down the runway with its wings still flapping. The goose had landed.

The plane taxied to a standstill outside of the small single story terminal building, while all of the passengers were invited

Weekend in Amsterdam

to disembark and make their way on foot to the main terminal building, where their suite cases would follow.

"What country are we in?" asked Ray, who had not seen the travel documents for the holiday and didn't know where on earth Maastricht was.

"It's on the Dutch, German border," said Archie with some authority, as he had been studying the details of their forthcoming journey for weeks.

"Are we in Germany or Holland?" Ray wanted to know.

"Holland you ignoramus," answered Archie, "where did you think that Maastricht was?"

"Well for a start I didn't know that we were flying to Maastricht," protested Ray, " and in any case it sounds more German than Dutch to me."

Holland was the last place in the world that Ray wanted to be. He was sure that Vladimir would be unaware that he was back in Holland, but it still felt a bit like entering the lion's den and it made him nervous. The sooner that they crossed the border into Germany the better Ray would like it.

They stood in the terminal building watching the baggage handlers unloading the aeroplane, and stacking the luggage onto a train of small trucks which was pulled by a tractor. There was no carousel at the airport, passengers being expected to identify their luggage as it was unloaded from the trucks at the terminal building.

Ray noticed that the sky had begun to darken once again. Suddenly the heavens opened with hailstones the size of golf balls raining down onto the runway. The baggage handlers ducked under the aeroplane for shelter, while the suite cases stood out in the open taking all that the weather could throw at them. In a matter of minutes the airfield resembled a scene from a Christmas card.

"Bloody hell," said Archie. "I've never seen hailstones like that in winter, never mind in May."

They stared dumbstruck at the suite cases, which were now little more than a mound in a sea of white. While Archie didn't appear to realise the significance of the scene, Ray could imagine unpacking a case of wet and smelly clothes the following evening when they arrived in Italy.

After ten minutes the storm had passed just as quickly has it had arrived, allowing them to collect their damp suite cases and load them onto the waiting coach ready for the thirty hour trip to Rimini.

They boarded the coach, which looked like a Darby and Joan Club outing. Elderly and late middle aged couples suffering from arthritis and angina struggled to climb the steps, while singleton's who had managed to wear out their overworked husbands many years earlier, enjoyed the fruits of their widows pensions and life insurance payouts.

Ray and Archie headed for the back of the coach, as the elderly fought for the front seats close to the exit. When they reached the long back seat, it was already occupied by what appeared to be a married couple in their late thirties or early forties, and three teenage girls.

Ray and Archie sat on the second seat from the back in front of the girls and introduced themselves. The girls responded with the names Kathleen, Irene, and Helen.

"Are you here with your parents?" ventured Archie, casting a glance at the couple sitting beside them, who were reading a newspaper and magazine respectively, and taking little interest in the chatting up procedure that was taking place.

"Certainly not," said Irene indignantly, when in fact it was the first time that they had ever been allowed to go on holiday without parental supervision.

Ray thought that they were a little on the young side, but Helen in particular had taken his fancy. She was dark haired with a skin that tanned easily to a very dark mahogany colour, and had already done so even though it was still only May, while Ray and Archie were still as white as milk bottles, from the lack of appreciable sunshine at their home in the frozen north.

It transpired that the girls came from Somerset, which conjured up images of men in smocks with scarecrow hats and straws in their mouths, and when Helen informed them that her surname was Coates, the jingle from a television advert for cider began to play on a loop system inside of Ray's head, "Coates comes up from Somerset where the cider apples grow," which continued to drive him mad as he didn't seem to be able to remove it no matter how hard he tried.

The girls were keen to learn what Ray and Archie thought of Adge Cutler and the Wurzels. They had apparently been to see them on a number of occasions, and were disappointed to find that Ray and Archie had never even heard of them.

"What do they sing?" asked Ray, as a West Country accent continued to sing "Coates comes up from Somerset" inside of his head.

"They rhymed off songs about drinking cider, tractors, worsels, and other country yokel matters.

"What's a wurzel?" asked Ray.

Have you never heard of Wurzel Gummage?" asked Helen.

"Yes, he's some kind of scarecrow from a children's story," said Ray knowledgably, even though he had never owned or read any of the Barbara Euphan Todd stories.

"Well what is his head made from?" she prompted.

Ray ventured a guess, "A turnip?"

"It's a kind of turnip fed to the livestock," she said, pleased with her success in attracting a suitable answer.

"Everyone is so old on this trip," said Irene changing the subject. "I was hoping that there would be some handsome boys on the coach."

"And what may I ask is wrong with us?" asked Archie indignantly, cut to the quick by the remark, as he had obviously got his eye on Irene.

She was blonde and pretty, and at five foot two they would have looked like a mop and bucket standing together, but then Archie's wife was also of a similar height and that had never seemed to bother either of them.

"You're not young," answered Kathleen peevishly, as the four of them seemed to be getting along so well and leaving her on the periphery of the conversation.

Although not so pretty as the others, she was not unattractive, although quite skinny with frizzy blonde hair, and at five foot ten she would have been a much better physical match for Archie.

"You must be as old as my parents," she went on unashamedly.

"You cheeky young madam," said Archie. "I'll have you know that I'm only twenty-seven."

"Well that's old," she answered, "and in any case you look much older."

Archie turned away feeling hurt, as the courier picked up his microphone and the coach set off.

Ray had hoped that they could get on well with the girls, while spending a large part of the holiday together, but that now looked extremely unlikely.

"My name is Alex," said the courier in a rather girly Scottish accent, "and your driver is Henry," which he pronounced *Honree* in his best French accent. "*Honree* is from Belgium and unfortunately does not speak very much English."

"Neither do you," called a voice from half way down the coach, and a few people around the heckler laughed.

Alex was in his late twenties with bleached curly hair. He was smartly if effeminately dressed in the blue blazer of the tour operator, with the company logo and his name badge prominently displayed. He wore grey flannel trousers with white shoes, while wearing an open neck shirt and sporting a blue polka dot cravat.

Henry, who was in his mid to late fifties with dark thinning hair which was greying at the temples, wore a grubby collarless shirt with rolled up sleeves, shiny black trousers, due to the excessive wear caused by sitting for too many hours, and an equally disgusting black waistcoat with old food stains down the front. He sported a dark bushy moustache which was also greying and hid the whole of his mouth, and a two day growth of whiskers.

Alex, who seemed to be overly embarrassed by the heckling, quickly ended his welcome speech and sat down.

They soon crossed the border into Germany, and everyone had to show their passports to a German border guard who came onto the coach. He showed little interest in the contents of the passports just so long as every hand was waving one, getting off the coach after only wandering about a quarter of the way up the aisle.

Henry soon found the Autobahn after the passport checks had been completed, and settled into a steady hundred and fifty kilometre per hour, passing everything on the Autobahn until they stopped at the services for a welcome meal.

Ray and Archie were starving as they hadn't eaten since the early afternoon. It was now seven in the evening by Ray's watch, which he had failed to put forward by an hour, so that it was in fact eight o' clock German time.

They entered the cafeteria expecting to see customers sitting at the tables, and counters with people busily serving food as in the English motorway service stations. Instead they were faced with a spotless but empty room, except for an old man who was washing the tables and emptying ash-trays. In place of the counter was a wall of small chrome plated doors, with glass panels to view the meals which were on shelves behind the glass. When Ray looked through one of the glass panes it was a very different story. The kitchen behind the glass pane was buzzing with staff; they were cooking and stacking the shelves behind the doors with *wiener schnitzel, sauerkraut,* and *apfel strudel,* ready for the next coach party to arrive. He put a *Deutsche Mark* into the coin slot, and selected something covered in breadcrumbs with chips and the ubiquitous *sauerkraut*.

Back on the coach and tired after a very long day he instantly fell into a deep sleep. Consequently as the coach rejoined the Autobahn, he failed to notice the motor cyclist who had pulled out of the shadows in order to follow the coach.

He slept for a full eight hours and awoke to the sound of gunfire. In his dreams he was being chased through a dense forest of pine trees by men in Eastern European uniforms, gunfire was all around, and bullets whistled over his head as he ran and thumped heavily into tree trunks, or threw up soil from the path both in front of him and behind.

He awoke in a panic, and looking out of the window he was relieved to see that the gunfire came not from Soviet assassins, but from a number of tanks in a field to his right. They were travelling in the same direction as the coach and firing at a target somewhere in the far distance. He checked his watch, which he had finally put forward by an hour on Archie's advice; it was five in the morning. It was a strange sight but quite exciting to watch the manoeuvres, until the coach which was travelling much faster, left the tanks behind in its wake.

Henry had been driving for almost twelve hours without a break. He was still travelling at one hundred and fifty kilometres an hour, when suddenly the Belgian driver decided to leave his seat. He shook Alex who was sleeping on the passenger seat. Alex, who was still half asleep and more than a little shocked, took the wheel, as Henry calmly took his place on the passenger seat, as if it was the most normal thing in the world to do; almost instantly he went to sleep. Ray's heart was beating like a train and he realised that they were in the hands of a madman.

After leaving the Autobahn, they stopped at a small family run hotel on the outskirts of Nuremburg. There they breakfasted on cheese and ham, served with a rather bitter coffee and some very hard bread rolls, which were causing havoc with the dentures of some of the more senior members of the coach party.

Unknown to the breakfast diners, a motor cyclist who was passing by the hotel and carrying a hunting rifle slung diagonally across his shoulder, was taking a more than passing interest in the coach.

■ ■ ■

Stefan wasn't happy with the task that he had been given, never having been asked to murder anyone before. He had been born into poverty in East Berlin at the end of World War II, in which his father had been killed fighting for the Third Reich. His mother had become a drunk on hearing the news that she had been widowed, later turning to prostitution in order to pay for her newly acquired alcohol addiction, and the survival of her son during hard times.

Stefan had been heavily influenced by the communist propaganda that had surrounded him for all of his young life, hating capitalism with a vengeance. He was prepared to do all in his power to fight against the corrupt western way of life, but this wasn't a mission sanctioned by Moscow and that worried him.

Vladimir had made a huge error of judgment when he had tried to recruit Ray in Amsterdam. He had made an even bigger error of judgement, when he had confidently instructed John Ponte to contact Ray with his first assignment. This had resulted in the destruction of the Vallard fledgling cell and the loss of one of his men. For this miscalculation he had come in for a good deal of criticism from his Soviet masters in Moscow. His future was now hanging in the balance, and as he blamed Ray for his misfortune, he was determined to extract his revenge, but without the knowledge or sanction of Moscow, so that using a trained assassin was out of the question.

Vladimir had recruited Stefan for sexual favours while serving at the Soviet embassy in East Berlin, in much the same way that he himself had been recruited in Moscow some twenty years earlier. They had formed a bond over the years, as Vladimir had rescued Stefan from a life of neglect, and although they rarely slept together anymore, as Vladimir preferred younger boys, Stefan still loved him as a son would love a father and was totally loyal, not only to the communist cause, but to Vladimir on a personal level.

He had been dispatched to Maastricht as soon as the news of Ray's travel arrangements had been relayed to Amsterdam. He had been equipped with a false West German passport, a hunting rifle, and a booking reservation for a fake hunting lodge somewhere in Austria.

Ivan, who had been keeping a low profile since the botched assassination attempt, had been watching unseen as Ray and Archie had caught the London bound bus. He had radioed a message to Vladimir, who although in bed with one of his rent boys, was instantly on the telephone to the Soviet Embassy in London in order to call in a favour. By the time that Ray and

Archie were getting into the taxi at Victoria bus station, a black cab used by the Soviet Embassy was pulling out into traffic in order to follow them. Once Ray and Archie had left their suitcases at the travel agents, the embassy man had given the duty representative a choice between a fist and a five pound note for information about the trip. The rep had chosen the latter.

■ ■ ■

After breakfast the coach made its way through Bavaria and into the Austrian Tyrol. Henry had slept for three hours and was once again behind the wheel, as they sped through cuckoo clock villages with flowered balconies, startling the locals and on one occasion scattering a group of hens who were pecking around on the roadside. Ray was unaware that hens could fly, with their heavy bodies and short wings, but he definitely saw two or three flash past the coach window at head height as he looked out.

The *Europabrucke* overlooking the historic and picturesque city of Innsbruck was a wonderful sight. It was the tallest bridge in Europe at a height of 180 meters and straddled the Sill River. It had been completed in 1963 to reduce the frequent bottle necks to the Brenner Pass, therefore saving travellers a great deal of time, although at a price, for at the western end of the bridge stood a chapel to commemorate the workmen who had died during its construction.

The coach had stopped in a lay by to allow passengers to enjoy the views from the bridge. Ray and Archie were inspecting the valley below when the first shot rang out. It struck Ray at the top of his arm, and he felt a burning sensation and the warm blood soaking into his tee shirt. Archie who's eye had been attracted by the sun glinting from the telescopic sight of the rifle, had seen the flash of gunfire and had already begun to pull Ray to the ground; otherwise the shot may have been more deadly. People screamed and scattered in all directions as the second shot rang out. The bullet hit Ray in the lower leg as he tried to crawl beneath the coach for protection. Luckily it passed through his calf and out of the other side, nicking his tibia in the process, but missing any vital arteries, so that the bleeding was limited.

Weekend in Amsterdam

The Austrian police arrived within fifteen minutes of the shooting. The gunman was more than ten miles away by then and disposing of the hunting rifle, after first wiping it clean of any fingerprints.

Stefan was not a marksman, although he had done some fire arms training. With the aid of the telescopic sight he was sure that he had hit Ray at least once, although he knew that he hadn't killed him as he had seen him scramble beneath the coach after the second shot. He didn't want to be caught with the rifle in his possession, as the police would soon have ballistic evidence. If he needed to try again he always had the hand gun, which fitted neatly into a foam filled compartment under the seat of his motor cycle.

Ray was taken by ambulance to the University Hospital in Innsbruck, along with two old ladies who had been standing beside him when he had been shot, and were now being treated for shock. No serious damage appeared to have been done, his wounds were soon dressed and he was pronounced fit to leave, although he was advised to stay in the hospital overnight for observation. Ray had no intensions of staying behind after the coach had left, although the old ladies chose to remain in hospital and to return home the following day.

While in the hospital, he was interviewed by a police officer who informed him that he was probably a random target. He explained that the *Bolzano-bozen* province of the Tyrol was until 1919 part of Austria, with 93% of the inhabitants speaking German. The region was given to Italy, as part of the price asked for entering the First World War on the side of the allies. When the Fascists took control of Italy in the nineteen-thirties, the German speaking people were forbidden to wear traditional costumes, to be christened with German names, or to be members of nationalist groups. This caused animosity and underground Austrian and German factions arose. They targeted Italians living in the Italian Tyrol, which resulting in reprisals being taken by Italians against Austrian families.

He went on to explain that most of the skirmishes occurred in *Bolzano-bozen* province at the opposite end of the Brenner

Pass. Although he was unaware of previous shootings in this particular area, skirmishes including gunfire had spasmodically broken out in the region for many years. He speculated that perhaps this was a new development, intended to damage the Austrian tourist industry and embarrass the Austrian Federal Government. After the history lesson Ray was convinced that he had just been the unlucky target of a random shooter, so as soon as he was pronounced fit to travel, he re-joined the coach party for the journey into Italy.

CHAPTER NINETEEN

His leg hurt like hell even though he had received a pain killing injection. Looking on the bright side, his arm felt reasonably comfortable once it had been dressed, as it amounted to little more than a graze, although it had bled far more than his leg. The hospital had also provided him with a quantity of strong pain killing tablets to take with him, and judging by the current level of pain in his leg he was obviously going to need them. To ease the pressure from his leg as he walked, they had provided him with an old walking stick, left behind by someone, who for whatever reason, had no further use of it.

As he entered the coach a huge cheer went up from his fellow travellers. It was partly initiated because he wasn't seriously hurt, but mostly because they could now leave Austria and get on with their holiday. Ray was happy that the coach had waited for him, but it wasn't really a matter of choice. Henry was extremely agitated that the *polizei* had held up the trip until every passenger had been interviewed, as he had to reach Bologna in time to meet an Italian coach, which was returning with holiday makers on their way back home to England.

At Bologna all of the passengers were expected to change coaches, Ray's group travelling to Rimini with the Italian coach, while Henry's brief was to return to Maastricht with the homeward bound group. Henry didn't really care if the returning holiday makers missed their return flight to England; his main concern was that he had only twenty four hours turn around at Maastricht, before his next trip to Bologna, and it was important to him to return home to Brussels to see his family.

Stefan waited by the border control, he wasn't sure if Ray would still be on the coach, but if he wasn't he could always return to Innsbruck, it may even be easier to dispose of him in the hospital. He knew in which seat Ray had been sitting, and as the coach approached, he would have been tempted to take another shot had he still been in possession of the hunting rifle, but he had panicked, deposing of it quickly in case he was stopped by the *polizei*. Having discarded it prematurely, he would need to get a lot closer to his target in order to use the handgun.

On the Austrian side of the border everything was done with military precision, the border guards were smart in their uniforms, while on the Italian side the contrast couldn't have been more apparent. One border guard came onto the coach and spoke to Alex, but didn't bother to check their passports. The other three who looked sloppy in ill fitting uniforms with ties undone, scanned the windows until they spotted the girls. This was the trigger for a lot of simulated masturbation and thrusting activity, which caused the girls to giggle, while the more mature members of the coach party looked on in disgust.

After a drastically shortened late lunch, they made just one more stop before the Bologna rendezvous, at an Italian vineyard in the Dolomites, where they were treated to the local white wine and a slice of melon, while sitting in the welcome shade of a grape vine covered pergola.

Ray had never drunk wine before, except for the odd sherry at Christmas time and a very unpleasant oily substance which was marketed as Australian white wine in his local Yates Wine Lodge. He had never in his life eaten melon either, and was surprised to find that eaten with a glass of chilled white wine, it was a very compatible combination, an experience which he had every intention of repeating at every available opportunity.

The coach transfer at Bologna, which coincidentally was the birthplace of Luca Ponte, the father of cowboy John, was made some forty minutes late, despite Henry's best efforts to make up the lost time. The Italian driver, who was the exact opposite of Henry, drove at a snail's pace, and by the time that they reached the hotel an hour and fifteen minutes behind schedule, Ray was already beginning to lose the will to live.

After checking in at the reception desk, they were finally shown to their room just after midnight, some forty eight hours after leaving Blakewater bus station. Without a proper wash during all of that time Ray was feeling particularly grubby, so as Archie unpacked his suitcase Ray hobbled into the bathroom, unsure as to how he would shower with his bandaged leg, only to find that barely a drip of water came from the shower rose. He tried the washbasin taps with the same result. When he rang the reception desk to complain about the lack of water in his room, he was told that the water pressure was always too low to reach above the second floor at this time of the year, due to the high water consumption of the holiday makers, but that he need not worry about it, as everyone smells in Rimini.

When he came off the telephone Archie was hanging his wet and smelly clothes over the balcony rail, his suite case appearing to have taken the brunt of the unseasonable weather experienced at Maastricht Airport. Ray opened his own suite case expecting the worst, but was relieved to find that his things, in contrast to Archie's, were perfectly dry.

They both flopped onto their beds exhausted, and by the time that they awoke the following morning, they had missed breakfast by a good two hours. There was still no water in the taps, so Ray hobbled to the nearest provisions shop and bought bottled water in order to clean his teeth.

While he was out, he noticed that each hotel had its own stretch of beach, with sun beds and umbrella's, and most important of all a cold shower, in order to wash off the salt and sand when bathers came out of the sea. He quickly cleaned his teeth, and returned to the beach carrying soap and a towel to wash off the stench of two days of travel.

They had booked a ten day holiday, but because of the travelling times they were only in the resort for six of them. For the first four days Ray couldn't walk very far, so his holiday consisted mainly of lying on the beach and sunbathing. He spent a lot of his time reading his book on the beach, and drinking

Italian beer in the hotel bar, but he did manage to spend some time in the sea, as his leg was easier when it was supported by the water, and the salt appeared to be helping with the healing process.

Archie wasn't much of a sunbather; in fact he went the colour of a lobster if he spent more than ten minutes exposed to daylight. He was much more alive after dark; consequently he spent most of the morning in bed, and all of the afternoon in one of the circular thatched beach bars, which were to be found at regular intervals along the beach.

There were no young people in the hotel, or anywhere in the vicinity of the hotel for that matter. The town of Rimini was a very long walk along the seafront, and the buses were so crowded that they made the London Underground look like the wide open spaces. Ray couldn't face being pushed, jostled, and kicked on the buses, and the walking distance to either Rimini in one direction or Cattolica in the other was currently impossible for him, making them virtual prisoners in the hotel. By the fifth day his leg felt much better, he happily dispensed with the old walking stick, and they caught the bus into Rimini town.

The bus trip was even worse than he had expected it to be, as all of the seats were taken and even standing room was at a premium. People were expected to get on at the rear of the bus and alight at the front, but because of the volume of passengers, Ray and Archie were forced to get off two stops earlier than they had intended, as they were literally pushed from the bus by the pressure of the passengers getting on behind.

Rimini consisted of an historic old town, which had once been the capital of the Adriatic in Roman times, some buildings dating back two thousand years, like the Arch of Augustus built in 27 BC, which once formed part of the city walls, and the Tiberius bridge, or *Ponte di Tiberio,* begun by the emperor Augustus in 14 AD and completed by the emperor Tiberius in 21 AD, it's five arches built in order to cross the river *Marecchia* and still connecting the city centre of Rimini to Borgo San Giuliano, along with the 2nd century Roman amphitheatre every one of which appeared to be peppered with bullet holes from the fighting in World War II.

In contrast the Adriatic coast of Rimini consisted of mid twentieth century hotels and bars, which stretched for miles all of the way from Rimini to Cattolica. There was a long jetty at the mouth of the Porto Canal, where they watched Octopus being caught by local fishermen, while nearby, to Archie's delight, was an English themed pub named the Coach and Horses.

The bar area wasn't particularly spacious, but it did open, by way of French windows, onto the promenade behind, which had been fenced off with portable steel barriers, of the kind used by the police for crowd control. A rock band had set up their equipment inside of the bar, facing outside towards the makeshift arena.

The band struck up and the bar began to fill. Most of the audience were British, but a few Italian stallions started to gather on the promenade beyond the barrier rails. They had little interest in the music, nor did they have any money to spend on drinks, they were only interested in the British girls. Best of all from the Italian perspective, the silly creatures believing that the Italians were actually in love with them, were prepared to become a meal ticket throughout their holiday.

■ ■ ■

The nineteen-sixties were a time of free love in Britain, but in Italy girls were still chaperoned by relatives if they wanted to see a boy. Ray and Archie had been naive enough to think that they could find themselves a Latin lover when they had embarked on the Italian holiday, Ray having had that privilege once before when he had gone to Torquay with Cookie.

They had met two Italian girls on the seafront late one afternoon, and although the girls had been on holiday with chaperones, chaperoning in earnest didn't begin until the evening, as they were deemed to be safe from temptation during the daytime hours. Ray and Cookie had invited the girls out for a drink that very evening, but although the girls had shown an interest in coming along, they had declined, as they were not allowed to go out alone in the evening.

The girls, who had been keen to talk about British history, had expressed an interest to see Plymouth Hoe, where Drake, who they had constantly referred to as a pirate, had played bowls while the Armada had sailed up the channel heading for the Isle of Wight. Ray had become quite irritated about this slight on a British national hero, although on reflection, he had to admit that they were probably correct in their analysis, as Drake robbed the Spanish fleet at every opportunity.

They met the girls the following day for the trip to Plymouth. Cookie's partner for the day was petite, with short dark hair, olive skin, and horned rimmed glasses, which made her, look intellectual. She wore dowdy knitted clothes in shades of grey and air force blue, her only concession to colour being a rather gaudy red and yellow silk scarf, which she wore around her neck even though the weather was hot.

Ray's first impression was that of a rather plain and politically motivated individual, who liked to debate every point, and was very opinionated on everything that you could care to name. She spoke extremely good English and argued her points well, and as time went by Ray began to like her more and more. She even began to look more attractive to him, as he began to see the person beyond the spectacles and the dowdy clothes.

In stark contrast, Ray's partner for the day looked like a younger version of Sophia Loren, beautiful, with an hour glass figure and large breasts. She was wearing a cheerful white flower printed summer dress with large pink roses on it, which was low cut at the neck, revealing a large amount of her ample bosom whenever she bent forward, which she seemed to delight in doing at every opportunity. Ray had found his eyes being drawn to that part of her anatomy whenever she moved, and although he saw a lot of flesh, on no occasion did he notice any sign of an undergarment.

She was unable to speak even a single word of English, making courtship a little difficult, all of their conversations having to be translated by her friend Eva. Although her real name turned out to be Maria, Ray insisted on calling her Sophia.

The analogy seemed to please her and she happily answered to Sophia throughout the day.

Ray had enjoyed their day on Plymouth Hoe, holding hands with Sophia and chatting via their opinionated interpreter, who was more interested in the activities of Francis Drake than translating small talk between attracted opposites.

They checked out the shops and cafés, and visited the naval dockyard at the insistence of Eva. Ray could never have envisaged such a venue for a date and would never have dreamed of suggesting it, but Eva loved it, while Sophia seemed happy just as long as they were holding hands.

They walked among the destroyers and cruisers in various shades of grey, so similar in colour to the clothing of Eva, that Ray was afraid that they might lose sight of her altogether due to the camouflage effect. Sophia received many wolf whistles from the sailors who were working on the ships decks, she enjoyed the attention enormously and waived back enthusiastically after every whistle or shout.

On their return journey to Torquay, Ray had pulled the car off the road at the entrance to a wheat field. Ray and Sophia had headed into the field holding hands, while Cookie and Eva had stayed in the car arguing; this time as to whether Italian women or English women put on the most weight in middle age.

At the time Ray had a stereotypical image of homely Italian mothers, who cooked and ate copious amounts of pasta and cheese, but after visiting Italy and seeing the beautifully slim, middle aged Italian women, wearing smart clothes and jewellery, and carrying designer shopping bags, he would retrospectively have had to agree with Eva.

The wheat had been well over waist high, as they picked their way across the field, choosing a spot far from the road where they would have some privacy, and dropped to their knees in the long grass, although Cookie and Eva were far too preoccupied with their argument to notice what they were doing, even if they had been doing it in the back seat of the car.

As they kissed, Ray had unzipped her dress, sliding the straps from her shoulders and letting the dress fall to the ground to reveal her half naked body kneeling before him. She had initially demonstrated her vulnerability by covering her breasts with folded arms, while staring fixedly at the ground. Ray had gently removed her arms from across her chest and placed them down by her sides. She didn't try to fight him or try to replace her arms, but she did remain staring at the ground, unable to look him in the face. He had lifted her chin so that she had no option but to look at him, and kissed her gently on the lips once their eyes had met. Throwing her arms around his neck she had pulled him towards her, pressing her naked body against his, while kissing him hard on the mouth. Thinking that the situation had changed, he had tried touching her breasts, causing her to pull away abruptly, the word *"no"* so sharply delivered, that he felt the need to check to see if he was bleeding.

Ray found it difficult to believe, that someone who had been unable to utter a single word of English until that very moment, could have learned to speak just one word, the one that he least wanted to hear, although unknown to Ray, *"no"* meant exactly the same thing in Italian as it did in English. Ray would never be able to understand her mixed signals, but in the wheat field on that sunny afternoon, Sophia had been barely fifteen years of age, on a school trip, and still a virgin.

■ ■ ■

With Sophia the chaperone system hadn't worked very well, but here in Italy it was working only too well. The only Italian girls out without chaperones in the evening wore the uniforms of waitresses, barmaids, and hotel receptionists, while the streets were full of Italian boys looking for romance.

The British girls on holiday were also looking for romance, unfortunately they were not interested in the home grown variety, but in the groups of Italians, who pursued them along the promenade with their well rehearsed chat up lines of *"mi scusi bella ragazza come si chiama,"* whilst pinching or patting a passing bottom at every opportunity. If the chosen group of girls ignored their advances, they would follow a few paces behind until another group of girls came in the opposite direction, instantly their affections would change to the new group, with the same protestations of love.

The band covered many of the hits of the sixties in their first spot, while the Italian boys called to the girls to come out to from behind the safety of the barriers, which were jealously guarded by the Brits. From time to time it became too much for the British lads to bear, and they charged the barriers, while the Italians scattered along the promenade, only to regroup when the British had once again returned to their seats.

Ray had been hoping to see Helen and her friends at the Coach and Horses public house. He hadn't seen her since the day that they had arrived, as they weren't staying at the same hotel. In fact nobody of their age was staying at their hotel. It seemed that all of the singletons were booked into a different hotel closer to Rimini town, so as not to upset the older holiday makers on the trip with their late night activities. Although Archie and Ray came under the category of singletons, Archie had booked the holiday as Mr and Mrs Brough; consequently they had been separated from the girls on their arrival.

After their conversation with the girls on the coach, the fact that they were in separate hotels may have seemed to be of little significance, except that Ray had caught Helen glancing at him many times during the coach journey, looking quickly away whenever he caught her eye.

He had recognised the look as he had seen it many times before; in fact he had come to rely upon the look as a signal to come and get me. To further substantiate his suspicions that she liked him, she had refused to get involved in the castration process on the coach, when her friends had rubbished Ray and Archie as being older than God. Sadly Helen didn't show up, and after the band had finished their second spot, Ray and Archie headed into the old town.

People were making their way to the nightclubs, and while Ray and Archie were keen to follow their example, they decided that if they wanted to have a few drinks, it was probably going to be much cheaper to drink in the bars and go to the clubs later. They discovered a bar situated in a small square, where they drank a number of local beers, while watching the people promenading, and heading for the late night dance clubs.

They stayed in the bar for around an hour, until the square began to clear as people went back to their hotels or to a nightclub. Ray suggested that it was time for them to leave also, but Archie would have none of it, as he was having such a good time.

After a few drinks he liked to sing rugby songs, and to draw strangers into the singing. His choir of eight was in full flow when the Italian police arrived in the square. Ray tried to warn Archie of the impending conflict, by waving his arms around and pointing in the direction of the constabulary.

"*Police,*" he hissed ; "he's behind you," rather like a child at a pantomime, unsuccessfully trying to warn Widow Twanky of the danger hiding in the wings, and although everyone else had stopped singing, Archie carried on regardless with his rendering of "*Oh she has a lovely bottom set of teeth.*"

The two policemen, carrying hand guns in polished leather holsters on polished leather belts, came up behind Archie who was still singing his solo, totally oblivious to the fact that everyone else in the choir had stopped singing. Archie was head and shoulders taller than either of the policemen, but the long arm of the law came into action, when one of them tapped him on the top of his head with a coloured disc on a stick, which could only be described as a lollipop. As Archie turned, the policeman put his finger to his lips and whispered, "*Silencio.*"

After that the choir quickly disbanded. Ray and Archie were finishing their drinks, as a motor cyclist wearing black leather, and a matching black full face helmet stepped from the shadows. A shot rang out and Ray was struck on the top of his head, creasing his skull and rendered him unconscious on the floor, with blood streaming down his face, while Archie hit the ground and scrambled beneath the tables, crawling towards the entrance to the bar for comparative safety.

The gunman came forward stealthily, holding the handgun at arm's length, with one hand on the other wrist in order to steady his aim. He edged around the tables in order to get a better view of his quarry, which was lying on the floor amongst the overturned tables. He lifted his weapon, pointing it threateningly at bystanders who were trying to get a better view of the proceedings, forcing them to back away out of range. He edged closer and closer, inch by inch; this time he had to be quite sure that Ray was dead. The second shot was fired from somewhere in the darkness across the square, it struck the gunman in the chest and he was dead before he hit the ground.

CHAPTER TWENTY

Antonio Vicelli had been a police officer for over eight years. He had used his lollipop on numerous occasions, every day in fact, but this was the first time that he had ever been asked to use his fire arm. His aim however had been true. He peered through the blackened windows of the ambulance with glazed eyes, in a state of shock at what had just taken place, on what in every other respect had been just another ordinary day. Occasionally he glanced at the young man who lay unconscious on the bed before him, blood still trickling down his face. Surely he had done the right thing. If he hadn't fired when he did, he told himself, this young man would now be a corpse on its way to the morgue.

His colleague had stayed behind with the body of Stefan, until a higher ranking officer could arrive to take control of the situation. In the interim, he began collecting the names and hotel addresses of the witnesses, asking them to kindly wait in order to be interviewed. Presently a high ranking plain clothes officer appeared at the scene, followed soon after by a police doctor, who to no one's surprise pronounced that Stefan was dead.

A forensic team were on the scene shortly afterwards, taking photographs of the deceased from every angle, measuring distances and checked for powder residue and shell cases. Finally a chalk line was drawn around the body and then the assassin's helmet and visor were removed. Archie was asked if he could identify the body, but never having seen Stefan before he could not.

Once Archie had been interviewed, he was taken at his own request to the hospital in order to visit Ray. They had wasted little time in shaving some of the hair from just above Ray's forehead and stitching him up; although he was still unconscious after being sedated he looked comfortable.

The nurse told the detective who had accompanied Archie to the hospital that he was suffering from a concussion, but would probably be able to make a statement by the following morning. She informed Archie that there was little point in him staying, as Ray would probably sleep throughout the night, but to return the following day in order to see his friend.

Archie was dropped off in Rimini town centre by the police car. He looked at his watch, it was almost three, and it would take him the best part of an hour to walk back to the hotel. As the hotel closed its doors at 2 am, and he was unable to get into his room until six, when the hotel reception re-opened for early morning incoming flights and coach parties to check in, he would have to wait for two hours outside of the hotel for it to re-open. He decided that the best course of action was to hit the bars on his way back to the hotel, as they didn't close until six, and even then for only long enough to clean up before reopening at around eight.

By the time that he reached the hotel, after being ejected from the very last bar at six in the morning it was broad daylight, people were buying morning newspapers and walking their dogs along the beach. It was a new day, he was very drunk, and had almost forgotten about the shooting incident altogether.

They were due to leave the hotel in twelve hours time, and had to vacate their room by ten that very morning. He collapsed on top of the bed, and slept for four hours without undressing, until he was awakened by the hotel manager banging on his door.

"Mr Brough, please open the door, you must vacate the room so that the cleaners can get in to prepare the room for the next guests."

For the very first time since their arrival there was water on the third floor and he showered quickly, even though he had a terrible hangover. He packed both suitcases, left them in a spare bedroom designated for the storage of suitcases destined for home, drank a black coffee and then caught the bus into Rimini, where he hailed a taxi to take him to the hospital.

Ray was awake when he arrived and nursing a very sore head, as was Archie but for completely different reasons. Ray had already given the police his statement an hour earlier. In it he had told the police that he knew who was behind the attempt on his life. They had checked his story with the Lancashire Constabulary and with the Innsbruck *polizei,* before making arrangements to return before he was discharged, so that he could identify the body of his attacker.

Archie went with him to offer moral support. He stayed outside of the mortuary, as Ray identified Stefan as an associate of Vladimir, and a Soviet specialist in electronic surveillance rather than an assassin, which probably accounted for the fact that he was such a poor shot, having failed to eliminate his target on two separate occasions. He was then allowed to leave, after first leaving his contact address in England.

The holiday had turned out to be something of a disaster from beginning to end, Ray having been shot three times on two separate occasions, being immobile for much of the holiday, and without having had a decent night out. Ray found a telephone and phoned home. The first shooting had only made the Austrian newspapers, as shootings in the area were relatively commonplace. He was convinced that this time the English papers would get a hold of the story, as it was front page news in all of the first edition Italian newspapers. He could visualise tomorrows headline in the Daily Express on his parent's breakfast table.

"ENGLISH HOLIDAYMAKER SHOT AND WOUNDED IN ITALY."

He phoned to say that he was fine and on his way home, before boarding the coach which picked them up at six in the evening, after first calling at the girl's hotel in Rimini town. Helen was concerned when she saw the bandage on his head, and her friends teased her mercilessly as she fussed around him.

"What on earth happened to you?" she asked.

"I got shot again," answered Ray, as if it were a daily occurrence, which currently it almost was.

"We heard that someone had been shot in the old town," said Irene excitedly.

"That was me," said Ray, pointing to his bandage as proof, if proof were needed.

"Have they caught the gunman?" asked Irene.

"Shot dead on the spot," chipped in Archie, as he was the only actual observer of the incident, Ray being unconscious at the time.

"Do you think that it was the same man who shot you in Austria?" asked Helen.

"I'm sure of it." said Ray. "The police in Austria convinced me that I had been caught up in a local feud, but now I'm sure that it was personal."

"Did you know him then?" asked Kathleen, joining in the conversation for the first time since she had upset Archie on the trip down.

"Sort of," answered Ray, as although he knew who Stefan was, he did not actually know him at all.

"Why did he want to kill you?" asked Helen, feeling that her initiative was being eroded by her friends.

"It's a long story," he answered, not really wanting to have to tell it.

"It's a long way home," she insisted.

He told the girls everything that had happened over the past few months, but tried to keep it as brief as possible.

"So you're a spy," said Helen excitedly when he had finished.

"Hardly," answered Ray, "I just got involved with some really bad people."

After a couple of hours on the road they met the Belgian coach at Bologna, with Henry still behind the wheel and Alex riding shotgun.

"What's the matter?" asked Archie.

"This bloody driver," answered Ray. "He's more dangerous than a loaded gun, and I should know."

"Welcome back," said Alex. "Have you all had a nice holiday?"

The whole coach, with the exception of Ray and Archie, chorused back in unison, "Yes."

"Well your holiday is not over yet. On our way back as you probably already know, we will be having an overnight stop. The itinerary said that we would be staying in Wurzburg, but that has now changed to Kitzingen, an historic town in the beautiful Franconian wine growing country. I am sure that you will not be disappointed, and we will still be making our scheduled evening visit to *Das Schloss,* as advertised in your brochure."

He studied his audience; languages were obviously not their forte, and seeing the blank faces he translated.

"For those of you who's German is not very good," and that as it turned out was everyone on the coach, "The Castle."

After the welcome back speech Ray decided to get some sleep, Archie, who had slept no more than four hours in the last thirty-six, had already beaten him to it and was snoring loudly, which made the girls giggle. When he awoke in the early hours of the morning it was still dark. Henry was as usual driving far too fast on the precarious mountain roads, and using both carriageways to get the coach around the tight mountain bends. One minute he was almost scraping the rock face on one side of the road, the next minute he was on the edge of a precipice on the other.

Ray stood up in his seat to look over the heads of the passengers in front. Through the front window he could see an endless stream of truck headlights coming up the mountain side. The trucks were articulated in the middle, so as to be able to negotiate the tight mountain passes. They disappeared and reappeared behind the rock face, winding their way up the mountain side.

Henry made no concessions at all to the heavy traffic, poor road conditions, and total darkness, as he continued to use both sides of the road, anticipating where the next truck would be as he rounded each bend. On a number of occasions he had to make rapid adjustments, by breaking hard, or leaving the tarmac road and throwing up gravel from the edge of a sheer drop into oblivion. When they finally reached the valley floor Ray's nerves were in tatters, he opened his eyes and looked around the coach, everyone else was sleeping like babies and totally unaware of the drama that he only had just witnessed.

They breakfasted in Austria and arrived at their hotel in Bavaria in ample time for lunch. After unpacking, they decided to explore the town of Kitzingen. Wandering aimlessly they stumbled upon the major tourist attraction of the town, the Leaning Tower, which dates back to the beginning of the thirteenth century.

Legend has it that the tower was built during a draught, necessitating the use of wine to make the mortar rather than water, which apparently accounts for its crooked roof. The tower, a simple circular stone structure with a ring of porthole windows beneath a twisted conical roof, was topped by a golden ball, which the locals believe to contain the heart of Vlad Dracula of Romania, and which casts a shadow towards one particular grave in the old cemetery across the street, a grave known as the grave of Dracula.

Returning to the hotel after finding little else to do on a quiet Sunday afternoon, they discovered an open air swimming pool, and collecting their swimming costumes they returned for a swim.

There was a bar adjacent to the pool, and after a short swim, they sat and watched the other swimmers as they drank a welcome cold beer.

Two men, who appeared to be in their early twenties and also wearing swimming attire, loitered beside their table. They both carried a bottle of beer which they were drinking straight from the neck of the bottle. One was short but powerfully built, with fair hair which was barely in evidence as it was cropped so short, He was handsome to a point and appeared to be a regular visitor to the gym, as his muscle definition would have won prizes in most amateur body building competitions.

His friend was quite the opposite in appearance. He was tall and gangly, with round shoulders and a stoop, the only similarity to his friend being his cropped hair, which was little more than a dark shadow on the top of his head. He seemed to be of Mediterranean or Middle Eastern extraction, with a large pointed nose which resembled a beak and dominated his face, and coupled with a long neck and his aforementioned stoop, gave the perfect impression of a vulture hovering over his much shorter friend.

"Do you guy's speak American?" asked the shorter one.

"We speak English," corrected Archie, obviously irritated by the high-jacking by a foreign power of the English language.

"That's sort of like American ain't it?" asked Shorty.

"Sort of," answered Ray, pre-empting Archie, as he appeared to be about to blow a fuse.

"Are you guys from England then?" asked Beaky.

"Where do you think that the English come from," answered Archie, who was obviously being rubbed up the wrong way by the Americans ignorance of England and the English language.

"Hey hold on there big guy," said Shorty, "we're just trying to be friendly here, I'll axe you nicely to have a beer with us?"

"Thank you," said Ray politely, while even Archie became more reasonable when he heard the magic word of beer.

Shorty returned from the bar with four bottles of beer, which he placed on the table.

"I never met a Limey before," he said on his return. "What are you guys doing here in Germany?"

"We're on our way home from Italy," answered Ray, "we're just staying overnight in Kitzingen.

"Why are a couple of Yanks in Kitzingen?" asked Archie, trying to be a little friendlier now that he had been treated to a beer.

"We're part of the 2nd brigade 3rd infantry battalion stationed here," explained Beaky.

"You're GI's" said Archie, unable to hide his surprise in spite of the giveaway haircuts. "I didn't know there was an American base nearby?"

"There are two answered Shorty, Larson Barracks and Harvey Barracks. Almost everyone here this afternoon is from one or the other, which is why we wanted to check you out."

"Why are the Americans here at all," asked Ray, although he could easily have guessed why.

"Kitzingen is a staging area for the United States European Command Air Defences," he replied proudly. "We're not far from the Czechoslovakian border here, which as you probably know is part of the Soviet Union. This is the front line in the

Cold War my friends, we're here to save you're arses against a possible air or nuclear attack."

He lifted his bottle and downed the contents without stopping. This was obviously going to be a drinking contest and Archie took up the challenge with gusto. Beaky drank his beer down in one and they all turned to look at Ray, who was sipping from the glass in which he had poured his.

"Leave me out," said Ray, who was only a social drinker in comparison to Archie, and knew that he would be the first to be flat on his back in any kind of contest.

The contest went on for most of the afternoon, although they did slow down somewhat after the first couple of beers. A crowd had begun to gather around the table, in order to watch the contest between their local hero and the tall Limey, as Beaky had by now fallen behind and ceased to be a competitor.

A group of four black GI's, who had joined the crowd and were attempting to watch the proceedings, were immediately told in a string of four letter word expletives to go away. Ray was sickened at the hatred that he witnessed from the white GI's towards their brothers in arms, especially from the ones with a southern drawl in their voices.

■ ■ ■

Ethnic minorities were relatively rare in nineteen-sixties Lancashire, although some migrant cotton workers from Pakistan, India, and Bangladesh, had begun to settle in the area. In the main they were single men and had not yet formed into family groups. Africans and Afro Caribbean's were as rare as hen's teeth in Lancashire, but for a few months Ray had been friendly with Francis White, who being a bit of character, and the only black man for miles around, was well known to everyone, if only by sight.

His real name wasn't White at all, but Francis saw it as an irony to call himself white, as he was the blackest black man that you were ever likely to see anywhere in the world. He always joked about his colour, most probably as a defence mechanism against racially inspired comments, although during the time that they were friends, Ray only ever once witnessed one racial incident involving Francis.

On that singular occasion, as they queued on the staircase to a second floor Chinese restaurant in Blakewater town centre, a drunken queue jumper had pushed past the people below them in order to get to the head of the queue. No one had dared to challenge the interloper, as he was a rough looking character and in no mood to be messed with.

When Francis had barred his way, he had stared at him with hatred in his eyes and said, "Get out of the way nigger."

Without a moment's hesitation, Francis head butted him in the nose, sending him arse over tit back down the stairs from whence he came.

The only other racist comments that Ray ever heard had come from the mouth of Francis himself.

On Francis's instigation they would swap racial insults, but never uttered in a vindictive way. When they were in a darkened nightclub, Ray would tell Francis to smile as he couldn't see him, while Francis would call Ray "White Boy," and turn up wearing his sunglasses, because he said that he was dazzled by the colour of Ray's skin.

On another occasion, Ray had gotten into an argument on the dance floor of the Cavendish Club, because he was dancing with some girl that he had only just met. A short but stocky skin head had claimed ownership of Ray's dance partner in a very aggressive manner, and looked well capable of overpowering Ray. Francis, who was well over six feet tall, had intervened when he had seen the trouble brewing. Standing so close to the skin head that he was not so much in his face as looking down on the top of his head, he uttered the immortal words, "You can't do nothing to me man; I got a flat nose and two black eyes already."

■ ■ ■

The kind of racism that Ray and Archie witnessed at the swimming pool; was the same vicious kind of racism that Ray had witnessed at the Chinese restaurant, and he didn't like it. The GI's had been very friendly towards Ray and Archie because they were white, although the treatment dished out to the black GI's had sickened Ray and he was ready to leave. It seemed that Archie may have felt the same way, having conceded the drinking contest to the good old US of A, which was very unlike him as he was normally a very competitive person, especially where drinking contests were concerned.

Apart from the fact that he was not a quitter, he was also not a fan of America or the war in Vietnam, and had attended many anti-war demonstrations and ban the bomb marches throughout the sixties. He was not a fan of Richard Nixon either. Even though it had been Lyndon B Johnson who had taken the Americans into Vietnam and not Nixon, Archie always chose to blame the current US president for all of the ills of the world, his politics being more akin to the thoughts of Mau Tsi Tung and his little red book than to a republican president.

The winning contestant was over the moon with his success. Although he was very drunk, he ascended the steps of the diving board and with whoops of victory; he dived from the very top board in celebration. With cheers of congratulations from his unit ringing in their ears, Ray and Archie quietly left the swimming pool.

After the lack of water in Italy, they had a very welcome hot shower at the hotel, and left on the coach for the short trip to *Das Schloss*. A meal had been organised for the coach party and for once it wasn't swimming in olive oil. Ray hated the stuff and had spent a week squeezing out lettuce leaves on his side plate, so as to make it marginally more edible, while the Italians added more olive oil from a bottle on the table, which on the first night of the holiday Ray had mistaken for vinegar and had poured onto his chips.

After dinner they entered the adjacent ballroom where dancing was already underway. Archie went straight to the bar and asked for, "Zwei *gross pilsners*," a smattering of German which he had learned from the American soldiers at the swimming pool.

He had expected to see the huge tankards that he imagined that the Germans always drank from, blue and white stoneware mugs with characters and scenes and with flip top metal lids, but instead the barman produced two half litre barrel glasses, similar to the pint glasses that he usually drank from at home.

"*Gross*," repeated Archie rather loudly, reinforcing his argument by pointing at a small quantity of one litre glasses positioned on a high shelf above the bar. The barman gave him a disdainful look, and produced a short step ladder with which to reach a handful of very dusty glasses, from an equally dusty top shelf. He washed the glasses for what appeared to be the first time in many years, before passing them full of foaming beer to a very happy Archie. Seeing the satisfied look on Archie's face, he spoke for the first time in very good English.

"You may keep the glasses as a souvenir."

Archie was overjoyed and joined Ray at a table with his prizes. He looked around the room to discover that all of the Germans seemed to be drinking from quarter litre glasses, not even the half litre ones that Archie had just rejected as of inadequate dimensions. He turned to a group of young Germans sitting at the next table and raising his glass into the air, he pointed at his drink, and remembering a word that he had seen written on the toilet door accompanying a silhouette wearing a dress.

"*Damen*," he said, and pointed to the Germans as he repeated, "*Deutsche damen*."

Ray waited for a reaction to Archie's taunts, but it wasn't a violent one as he had at first feared. Instead after a short discussion, the Germans went to the bar where the barman was once again forced to climb the stepladders, in order to reach six more of the dusty one litre glasses. It seemed that Archie's second drinking contest of the day was about to begin.

After two hours of heavy drinking with the Germans, with new songs being learned on both sides, Ray was feeling rather tipsy, and knew that he would not be able to compete for much longer without embarrassing himself. He was wondering how he could withdraw from the contest without losing too much face, when he noticed Helen hovering nearby, having enough Dutch courage by this time, he grabbed her by the hand and whisked her onto the dance floor; problem solved.

At the stroke of midnight, just like Cinderella, the coach arrived to return the party to their hotel. The bar was still open for residents, and Archie who was very drunk already, suggested that they might have a nightcap before going up to bed.

"You have a nightcap," Ray whispered into Archie's ear, "but give me an hour before you come up to bed."

Archie stuck up his thumb and gave him a pronounced knowing wink, nearly falling from his stool in the process.

Helen was an inexperienced lover, but definitely not a virgin. She was however a willing learner, and by the time that they fell asleep in the single bed, she was a whole lot more experienced than she had been an hour earlier.

Neither of them awoke as Archie came to bed, although he made enough noise to awaken the dead. He had taken his prized beer glass into the hotel bar, and had insisted on drinking from it until the bar had closed. It was now sitting between the two single beds on the bedside table, along with a bedside lamp and Ray's watch, as Archie was still wearing his, along with all of his clothes.

Ray was the first to awake in the morning. The first thing that he noticed was the smell. He opened his eyes and staring him in the face, no more than a foot away from the end of his nose, was Archie's litre glass, filled to the brim and overflowing with vomit. He emptied the glass of its revolting contents, washed it out, and opened the window to let in some fresh air, before stepping into the shower in an attempt to wash away his hangover of the night before. With the hot water running, he failed to hear the footsteps entering the bathroom. Feeling the draught as the shower curtain was pulled back, he turned to see a naked Helen stepping into the shower.

The previous day he had regarded her as little more than a child, barely sixteen and only just legal, still wearing the puppy fat of her formative years, while talking the rubbish of a child and dressing as provocatively as a prostitute. This morning everything appeared to be different. It was as though she had left her childhood far behind her and had become a woman overnight. The puppy fat seemed to have melted away, and instead of a silly girl full of inane chatter, a beautiful woman stood before him, expertly washing his body with the soapy sponge. Whether she had actually changed, or whether it was his perception of her that had changed he wasn't sure; but the transformation of the last few hours seemed to have been positively staggering.

They made love in the shower, which was a new experience for both of them, and once dressed Ray walked her back to her own room. Archie continued to snore, unaware of the erotic performance which had been taking place both in the bathroom and around his unconscious body as he slept.

Once on the coach, Helen insisted that Archie exchanged seats with her. She held Ray's hand and kissed him frequently for most of the way back to Maastricht, while Archie tried to sleep off his hangover with two silly young girls chattering constantly into his ears.

They flew into a thunderstorm once again whilst crossing the channel, and Ray was relieved when they finally arrived at Luton Airport, although he wouldn't admit it to Helen, who held him so closely with every lightning flash that she was almost inside of his skin.

They parted company at the travel agents on Tottenham Court Road and exchanged addresses at Helen's request. Helen promised to write first and she did. The first letter was sent about a week after the holiday to which she never received a reply. The second one was sent about six weeks later, telling him that she still loved him and was carrying his child. He never received either letter as he had given her a false address.

CHAPTER TWENTY ONE

When Ray arrived back at work, Rick Fordham was on his way out and Jack Garret was working on the day shift. They were both pleased to see him as they had been a man down for the past week. Jack had been forced to work Ray's morning shift, which meant that he and Rick had only crossed paths momentarily at the shift changeover.

"How was the holiday?" asked Jack.

"It was a disaster," answered Ray, "I got shot in Austria on the way there, and spent all of the holiday using a walking stick."

He pulled up his trouser leg to show Jack the scar.

"And what happened to your head?" asked Jack, pointing to the shaved patch and huge plaster which he still wore.

"I got shot again in Italy," he replied, as if everyone got shot twice when they went on holiday.

"Who shot you?" Jack asked in disbelief.

"Some deranged idiot with a hunting rifle," replied Ray, and even though Jack pressed him for more information as to what had happened, he refused to elaborate.

It had been almost a month since Manchester City had won the FA Cup, but Ray wasn't one to miss a golden opportunity. He started to chant "City: City: City:" under his breath, Jack as usual was visibly annoyed and bit hard onto his pipe.

"I've got some news that'll wipe that smirk from your face," he said. "Two of the delay line machines have been off-line for almost a week. The production manager is tearing out his hair, and God has been working on them around the clock without any success. Welcome back."

This was the moment that Ray had been dreading ever since the machines had arrived from Holland. Until this moment they had run flawlessly, but now, not one but two of them had unexpectedly stopped working at the same time. As Ray was the acknowledged expert on this particular type of machine, they were regarded as his personal responsibility and shunned by the other maintenance electricians. Feeling that he had learned very little about the machines while in Valkenswaard, the prospect of an evening shift spent trying to repair them, while other machines were also breaking down and requiring attention was not one that he relished.

When he arrived at the first machine Godfrey was in attendance, he had every available manual and diagram spread out on the floor and there were tools and test meters everywhere.

"Thank goodness your back the PM is having kittens; with only two machines on line he has had to put all of the operators on two shifts to keep up with production. If we don't get them up and running soon there will be hell to pay," whined Godfrey, with which he disappeared into his office to his coffee cup collection.

"Welcome back," said Ray, talking to no one in particular. "Did you enjoy your holiday? Not really but thank you for asking."

He stared at the mess in despair, but as it turned out both of the faults were identical in nature, meaning that only one diagnosis was necessary to repair both machines. He had obviously learned more in Holland than he had given himself credit for, because within an hour he had both machines up and running. He had also tidied up Godfrey's mess and was drinking coffee, white with sugar, back at his workbench.

Archie was working the final week of his notice before going into the Merchant Navy. He came over late in the afternoon, in order to tell Ray that he was having a farewell day out at the races the following Saturday.

"Most of the electricians from the Plant department are going, and I've booked a coach to Wetherby races," he announced. "I'm going to phone Cookie and Goff when I get home tonight, and I thought that I might ask Buddy if he would like to go."

"If you do ask Buddy, tell him not to bring the Tow-rags," Ray suggested helpfully.

"Who the hell are the Tow-rags?" asked Archie.

"Those tattooed idiots with shaved heads that he always has in tow, believe me they're trouble with a capital T."

"I'm sure that they'll be alright," said Archie in his ignorance of the facts.

"Well don't say that I didn't warn you," Ray told him.

When Ray arrived home after his shift, there were two messages awaiting him. The first one was a letter from his insurance company. It contained a check in full and final settlement for the Triumph Spitfire, which would help to pay for his day out at the races. The other was a message written by his mother on the back of the same envelope, asking him to ring DI Briggs during office hours.

When he awoke around mid morning the following day, he rang the police station.

"Could I speak to DI Briggs please?"

"Who should I say is calling?" said a rather sexy female voice at the other end of the line.

"Raymond Evans."

There was a long pause, presumably while she asked Briggs if he wished to take a call from a Raymond Evans.

"Just one moment Mr. Evans, I'm transferring you now," she announced in her sexy voice.

Ray wondered if her appearance matched her voice, but decided that although it was a possibility, she could just as easily have been fat and forty.

"Briggs," a voice from the other end of the line announced rather abruptly.

"Ray Evans, you wanted me to call."

"Ah Mr. Evans, thank you for calling; the reason that I wanted to speak to you, is because we have had reports from both the Italian and Austrian police about your holiday experiences. It appears that you have had quite an exciting holiday."

"A bit too exciting for comfort actually," responded Ray.

"Look I need you to come in to the station and add your statement to the continental police versions of events for our files."

"I can call in this afternoon on my way to work. About one okay?" he asked.

"That will be fine Mr. Evans; by the way, we spotted Ivan at the bus station on the night that you left for your holiday, it seems that he was following you."

"And so were you by the sounds of things," answered Ray.

"For your own safety Mr. Evans," replied the detective, "for your own safety."

"It's nice to know that you care inspector," said Ray ironically.

"It's all in a day's work Mr. Evans," answered Briggs equally ironically.

"Am I still being followed?" asked Ray.

"Let's just say, better not to drink and drive," said Briggs laughing.

"And what happened to Ivan?" Ray wanted to know.

"I'm afraid that he made his escape," answered Briggs, "he hasn't been on the radar ever since."

"So I'm still the tethered goat?" bleated Ray.

"I'm afraid so Mr. Evans."

Ray hung up the telephone before making some lunch, using a couple of grilled pork chops, some frozen peas, and packet mashed potatoes as advertised on television by some rather hysterical metal aliens.

■ ■ ■

After a busy week at work, Saturday came along very quickly. It was an early start by Ray's standards, the coach leaving the town centre at ten in the morning. The weather was miserable, fine misty rain, which while it didn't appear to be of much consequence, soaked him to the skin before he even reached the pickup point.

Unlike the modern air conditioned coach which had taken Ray and Archie to Italy, this one was old, unsophisticated, and from a completely different era. It was painted cream in colour, with a green flashes down its sides, and green mudguards on either side of a protruding bonnet. Sitting on stalks on each side of the bonnet and looking rather like spectacles sitting on the tip of a nose, it wore its headlights. The widow-screen of two flat panes of glass joined in the centre, pre-dated bevelled glass, and the seats, which were covered in what appeared to be more of a carpet material than a seat cover, were hard and probably stuffed with horse hair. Ray couldn't help thinking that they were in for a very uncomfortable ride.

The coach chugged along for more than two hours over the Pennines and into Yorkshire, belching out thick black smoke as it went, sometimes travelling as slow as fifteen miles per hour on the hills, with huge traffic queues gathering behind them on the narrow and winding roads. By the time that they arrived in Wetherby Ray was feeling rather queasy, due he said to the bumpy ride and the smell of the diesel fumes, as he refused to attach any of the blame to the large quantity of beer with which Archie had stocked the coach.

■ ■ ■

Even on a fine day, racing was not Ray's idea of a day out. He avoided gambling because he was probably the unluckiest gambler in the universe. If ten raffle tickets were sold and Ray had bought nine, he would still be certain to lose. Because of his poor relationship with Lady Luck, he never bought raffle tickets voluntarily, or put his money into fruit machines as some of his friends often did. He never played cards for money or bet on the horses, except on Grand National Day, and only then in order to be one of the lads. He knew nothing of form, and the only two jockeys whose names were familiar to him, were Sir Gordon Richards, because he was the only jockey ever knighted in 1953, and Lester Piggott because he shared a surname with his mothers cousin Frank.

■ ■ ■

On the one and only occasion that he had ever won anything, he had dreamt on the eve of the 1965 Epsom Derby, that he had been standing adjacent to a pigeon loft on the roof of a very tall building. In his hand he had been holding a stop watch, as he scanned the horizon for the first sign of a returning bird. When the first bird arrived, it turned out not to be a pigeon at all, but a seagull, which flew a lap of honour around the pigeon loft before alighting on its roof.

Studying the racing form in the newspaper the following day, he had hoped to find a horse called seagull in the running. As there didn't appear to be one, the obvious choice seemed to be a chestnut stallion bred in France and ridden by Pat Glennon called Sea Bird II. The dream had been so vivid that he had felt obligated to put on it everything that he could easily afford, especially as it was the favourite at short odds, and just like in his dream it came home an easy two lengths ahead of Meadow Court at 7/4.

■ ■ ■

The going was heavy because of the rain, and they at first made the mistake of standing far too close to the barrier, where great clods of earth and turf were thrown at them from the horses hoof's as they thundered by. Having had no dreams of seagull's, or winners of any kind on the eve of this trip, his luck ran true to its usual form, and by the end of the day along with Archie, Cookie, and Goff, whose tips he had readily accepted and now wished that he hadn't, had lost a significant part of a week's wages.

Ted Reeves, Bopper, Galley, and the Tow-rags had also lost heavily, while members of the card-school, who bet on the horses daily and studied form avidly, had won well, and teased them by waving wads of notes in their faces.

Wet, bedraggled, and almost completely broke at the end of the day, they climbed back onto the coach. Archie's plan of action was to stop on the way home for a fish and chip supper, before painting the town red on their return to Blakewater.

Near to the race course, they found a fish and chip café used by coach parties, which had a huge car park at the front to accommodate the passing trade. The card-school, which consisted mainly of the older members of the trip, with their daily winnings, went into the café for a slap up tea of fish and chips with mushy peas, bread and butter, and a mug of tea. While the losers of the day stood in the rain with a take away, as they had been told by the coach driver that he did not want any food taken onto the coach. Faced with a drenching or a tongue lashing, they chose to accept the tongue lashing by violating their orders and getting onto the coach with their fish and chips.

Soon the Tow-rags were up to their usual mischief, one of them sat in the driver's seat, and finding that the key had been foolishly left in the ignition, he started the engine.

"Let's pretend to leave the smug bastards behind," he said, while driving the coach twice around the car park and honking the horn, before taking it onto the open road having once attracted their attention.

In fairness, it had been his intention to return to the coach park after giving them a scare, but what he had not foreseen, was how difficult it would be to find a place to turn the coach around. Soon they were a couple of miles away from the café coach park and still heading in the wrong direction.

"This is stupid," said Archie beginning to panic; "We have to go back."

"I will as soon as I can find a place to turn around," said the Tow-rag, just as he glimpsed the flashing blue light of a police car in his rear view mirror.

■ ■ ■

"You stupid prick," said Archie an hour later, as he was bustled into a police cell with Ted Reeves and the Tow-rag who had driven the coach. The recipient of Archie's abuse had been charged with taking a vehicle without consent, driving without a Public Service Vehicle licence, or any other licence for that matter, while his conspirators had been charged with aiding and abetting the offence.

Ray was sharing a single cell with Cookie and Goff. They spent an uncomfortable night sharing a thin mattress which was laid on top of a cold tiled plinth, with only one threadbare blanket to cover all three of them.

At the very same moment that they were being ushered into the cells, the cream 1939 Bedford OB with green flashes and mudguards, was crossing the Pennines somewhere between Harrogate and Bolton Abbey. Although the twenty-seven seat coach had set out from Blakewater with fifteen passengers; on its return journey it only carried the six members of the card-school. On a drizzly evening as it crossed the moor, the coach suddenly and without warning exploded.

■ ■ ■

Ivan had been avidly watching the news on the small black and white television set in his dingy rented flat. When the explosion was reported on the ten o' clock news, with speculation that there had been no survivors, he had mixed feelings about what he had done.

He consoled himself with the thought that Ray had finally got what he deserved. Wasn't it Ray's fault that he was on the run and living in this awful place, wasn't it also Ray's fault that John Ponte was dead, and that his relationship with John's mother, and consequently his comfortable existence, was over.

On the other hand he was sorry that it had been necessary to kill a coach load of people. He had known some of the victims rather well from his time at Vallard, particularly Mick Rogerson who had been a work colleague for a number of years, and who Ivan also regarded as a friend.

Ivan had previously decided that a small bomb in Ray's car was the answer to his problem, but as Ray had not replaced his car since Tam's death, or been allowed to borrow his father's car, he had not been given the opportunity to use the device supplied to him by Stefan. For days he had observed Ray travelling to and from work on his motor cycle, but as the bomb was a little bulky, he had not been able to hide it anywhere on the bike.

On the morning of the trip, he had been watching Ray's house as he quite often did. Having followed Ray to the rendezvous point, he had observed from a distance as Ray had boarded the coach. Spotting Mick Rogerson arriving for a day out at the races, he had probed him in a casual way for information about the trip, and armed with this information he had returned to his flat to pick up the bomb.

It had been a long trip to Wetherby in order to plant the bomb, but on the plus side, the police there were not looking for him. His job would be much easier without having to be constantly looking over his shoulder. It had been an easy matter on his arrival at Wetherby, to locate the very distinctive coach at the race course. Twenty years earlier the Bedford OB would have been a common sight on the coach park, now however it was quite a rarity, and stood out among all of the newer coaches like a sore thumb. He had made a point of noticing exactly where Ray had been sitting on the coach, attaching the limpet bomb to the underside of the coach directly beneath Ray's seat, even though it would make little difference, as the bomb was large enough to destroy every seat on the coach and then some.

Having taken two hours to travel to Wetherby, he had calculated that it was at least a two hour drive back on the coach. Convinced that they would stop for a meal, he had set the timing device to go off two hours after the race meeting ended, speculating that the bomb would go off when they were about half way home. Even if they didn't stop for a meal he reasoned, they should still be on the coach two hours after the meeting was over. Apart from the arrest of Ray and the others, which he could not possibly have foreseen, his calculations had proved to be absolutely correct.

He telephoned Mavis Ponte as soon as the report of the explosion had been televised. Once she knew that he had avenged the death of her son, he thought; she would be able to put her grief behind her, and would be so grateful that things would quickly return to normal between the two of them. Unfortunately for Ivan he did not receive the accolades that he had been expecting. She was horrified at what he had done, and after she had slammed down the telephone receiver in anger, she immediately picked it up again and called the police.

■ ■ ■

After a very uncomfortable night in the cells, the miscreants were awakened in the early morning by a constable with a mug of tea, and a little light breakfast of toast and jam.

"You will all be interviewed individually when you have eaten," he announced, before leaving the cell and slamming the door behind him. The noise reverberated around the cell block, as he took a last look through the metal door flap before closing it with a bang. They were all ravenous and the small breakfast quickly disappeared.

It wasn't Ray's custom to be awake at this hour on a Sunday morning, unless he was on his way home from a night out on the tiles, and this wasn't an experience that he wanted to repeat. They had all been allowed just one telephone call the previous evening, his parents therefore knew that he was safe, but they were less than pleased that he was once again in trouble with the police, and locked in a cell overnight. Because of the hysterical reaction of his mother at the other end of the telephone line, he had been relieved when the constable had told him, in a voice loud enough for his mother to hear, "keep the call short, other people need to use the telephone."

After breakfast they were taken one by one into the interview room. Ted Reeves was the first to be interviewed by a detective chief inspector named Swan, which surprised Ted as he had expected to be interviewed by a more junior rank in uniform. He was even more surprised, to find that the interview was not regarding the taking away and driving of the coach as he had expected, but of the deaths of his workmates. Ted was stunned, but could shed no light on the bombing. He was completely in the dark as to the attempts on Ray's life, as was Bopper who was the next to be interviewed. When Archie was interviewed however, he was able to shed a little more light on what he thought may have happened, and suggested that they speak to Ray.

Detective Chief Inspector Swan was coming towards the end of a successful if not spectacular career. He was fast approaching retirement age, which showed in the colour of what remained of his hair, as it did in the lines on his face, all of which told a chapter in his life. He wore glasses in order to read, and was rarely seen around the police station without them perched precariously on the end of his nose.

Being a thorough man, he was not inclined to take Ray's story at face value as it sounded to be quite fantastic, but he agreed to telephone the Lancashire police for confirmation. DI Briggs was not on duty when the call came through, but he did get back to Swan within the hour. He had seen the report of the explosion on television, but had understandably made no connection to his own case.

The duty sergeant who had taken the call from Mavis Ponte, had forgotten to pass on the message after a busy night with the town's drunks and violent offenders, and Briggs was furious when he found out.

The miscreants were released by lunch time. As the owner/driver of the coach was not in any position to press charges, or to give evidence at a hearing, the charges were dropped and they were released with only a police caution.

They caught a train from Wetherby to Leeds, having pooled their meagre resources in order to raise enough money for the fares home, and a curled up sandwich at the railway station buffet room. They were in sombre mood, and even the fact that they had been released without charges could not lift the gloom.

Ray in particular was distraught, blaming himself for the tragedy. He thought about the victims of the explosion, Rick Mackay who had once broken the Queen's washbasin, Ben Ainsworth the one that they called Maverick, who had jumped into a hole full of dirty water only a few short months ago. There was Frank Massey, he had been Ray's first mentor after leaving the training school, and had made Ray's life a misery by sending him to the stores for a long stand, a tin of striped paint or a sky hook.

■ ■ ■

On more than one occasion, he had sent Ray up a ladder and onto the service pipes just before lunchtime. He had then taken away the ladder, which left him sitting on a hot steam pipe throughout his lunch break. On another occasion he had

Roy A. Higgins

locked Ray in the telephone exchange just before it was time to go home. It had taken a rather naïve fifteen year old over an hour, to realise that he could telephone the security lodge from the telephone exchange in order to be released.

It was also Frank Massey who had first called him Shirley Temple because of the length of his hair. He was also guilty of cutting Ray's hair and beard, along with two more of the victims of the explosion, Colin Fielding who Bopper had hung with a window cord, and Harry Harrison who had paddled in the ducts while wearing Alvin's brand new boots.

■ ■ ■

His mind went back to the time when as an apprentice he and Colin had helped on the filming of "A Kind of Loving," a feature film starring Alan Bates and June Ritchie, which won a Golden Bear Award at the 1962 Berlin Film Festival. Most of the filming he seemed to remember had been in the Preston, Bolton and Manchester areas, but the factory scenes had all been shot at the Vallard factory. Because the film crew were not allowed to touch the factory fuse boards under union rules, Ray and Colin had followed the filming, in order to connect and disconnect the cameras and lights for the film crew.

Many of the factory workers were used as extras in the filming, and because of their excellent work in assisting the film crew, the director John Schlesinger*** had agreed through an intermediary, to give Colin and Ray prime positions in a canteen scene to be filmed on a Sunday morning.

They were seated at a table adjacent to Alan Bates as he spoke his lines, each being expected to light a cigarette from a lighter which was to be held by Colin. Being a non smoker, by the eighth take Ray's head was spinning like a top, and unfortunately he missed the final take while being sick in the gentlemen's toilets.

■ ■ ■

*** *"A kind of loving" was John Schlesinger's first major film in 1962. He later went on to direct "Billy Liar: Darling: Far from the Madding Crowd: and Midnight Cowboy," during the nineteen-sixties, followed by, "Sunday Bloody Sunday: The Day of the Locust: Marathon Man: and Yanks," in the nineteen-seventies.*

The final victims of the bombing were grumpy old Mick Rogerson with his flat cap, who had unwittingly caused the deaths of all of the other passengers on the coach, when he had given Ivan information about the trip. There was also of course the cantankerous driver, who only a few hours ago had brought charges against them for driving away his coach, and had literally saved their lives by insisting that they be held in police custody.

Not all of the victims however had been on the coach at the time of the explosion. He thought about Dan Rhymes, the union man who had always supported him in his frequent disputes with Vallard's management, and of Tam Farnsworth who had taught him so much that he needed to know in his early working life. So many people had died in the last few months in a senseless compulsion to end his life, including the two would be assassins John Ponte and Stefan. Incredibly he had survived all attempts to end his life, but for how long.

With hindsight he wished that he had complied with Vladimir's request for him to work for the Soviets, surely it could not have caused anything like as much heartache as his refusal had done. After all how much damage could have been done to western security by allowing the Soviets to film a few secret meetings? On reflection he thought probably quite a lot, but would eleven men have had to die if he had come to a different decision.

On the train home he shed a tear for them all, including little April, who had sacrificed her freedom in order to protect him from the assassination attempts of John Ponte. She was now having to suffer goodness knows what kind of treatment from the system and her fellow inmates. He felt guilty about April, as he had hardly given her a moment of thought during the last few weeks; he resolved to apply for a prison visitors permit the very next day.

CHAPTER TWENTY TWO

Ray had left home for work, in time for his early morning shift. He was nervous about venturing outside, scanning the street carefully as he left. If he was indeed being shadowed by either the police or by Ivan, they were extremely adept, for the street looked completely disserted. The gloom that had engulfed him the previous day still hadn't lifted, and his thoughts were with the victims of the explosion every waking moment.

To further complicate his life, Cookie and Goff had cancelled Friday nights out for the foreseeable future, on the grounds that they lacked the necessary funds after their losses at the races. Cookie may well have been temporarily financially embarrassed, but Goff was never short of funds. Ray knew that what they were really doing was distancing themselves from the danger, and who could blame them.

Archie had for a number of years been Ray's best friend, and under normal circumstances would have stuck by him through hell and high water. Unfortunately, on this occasion he had sailed at midnight on the high tide from Liverpool, to Shanghai, Hong Kong, and Peking, leaving Ray feeling very vulnerable and alone.

■ ■ ■

An hour later Ivan was buying a newspaper at his local newsagents, he knew that he would have to leave the country as soon as possible, as his actions had made national headlines. Every policeman in Britain would now be looking for him, rather than just a skeleton staff at the local police station, which would make it increasingly difficult to remain anonymous for long.

He read the newspaper report of the explosion, and was dismayed to find that only six of the fifteen travellers who had gone to Wetherby, were actually on the coach at the time of the explosion. The report went on to say that the names of the dead could not currently be released, until the relatives of the deceased had been informed. He needed to know for certain if Ray was on the fatality list before he left the country, as Vladimir would be furious if he did not complete his task. Ivan knew from experience that when Vladimir was unhappy people had a tendency to disappear, if he wanted to disappear on his own terms, he would have to sit tight until he had more information.

DCI Swan was in the office of DI Briggs early on Monday morning, and he was less than pleased by how the operation had so far been handled.

"You mean to tell me that you have never searched for this man Ivan?" he shouted at Briggs.

"I don't have the staff for a house to house search," wined Briggs. "I have only been allocated one man to work on this investigation, because the superintendent isn't convinced that the death of Thomas Farnsworth wasn't just another tragic road accident."

"And who was supposed to be watching Evans on Saturday?" asked Swan.

"The last time that we watched Mr. Evans was over two weeks ago on the evening that he left for his holiday to Italy, since then I haven't had the staff to put a tail on him."

"You mean to tell me that Evans is going about his daily business believing that he has police protection, and all the while he is exposed to danger?" screamed Swan.

"I am afraid so," admitted Briggs.

"This is my investigation now," shrieked Swan. "I want a photograph of this chap Ivan circulated to every police station in the country. I want his picture in all of the national newspapers and on television, someone must have seen this man and I want to know where he is."

"We have received a tip from his ex-lady friend, that he is renting a flat in the Mill Hill area of the town," ventured Briggs nervously.

"And when may I ask did you receive this tip off?" asked Swan sarcastically.

"At about ten thirty on Saturday evening sir; but I wasn't informed until Sunday morning," answered Briggs apologetically.

"Have you acted upon it?" snapped Swan.

"I interviewed Mrs. Ponte yesterday, but like I said I don't have the staff to search for him."

"You do now," said Swan. "Get the local police on to door to door enquiries at all the known rental flats in the area. He must have neighbours and he must be paying rent to someone, so trace all of the registered landlords, and in the meantime I want Mr. Evans watched for twenty four hours a day. Understood?"

■ ■ ■

The following day at five thirty in the morning Sergeant White was dozing in his car outside of Ray's front door; Ray walked across and tapped on the car window.

"Is it a little early for you sergeant?" he asked, alluding to the fact that he seemed unable to stay awake.

"Actually it's a little late Mr. Evans. While you have been sleeping soundly in your bed, I have been sitting here watching your house throughout the night. I'm just going to follow you to your place of work and then its home to bed for me."

"I didn't notice anyone outside of the house yesterday?" queried Ray.

"No," said White, thinking on his feet. "Yesterday Ivan thought that you were dead so surveillance wasn't deemed necessary, by now he will have realised that you may not be dead after all and he will need to find out for sure."

Ivan opened his morning newspaper, to see a large photograph of himself taken when he had first been questioned by the police some weeks ago. This was accompanied by a tale of Russian spies and assassinations, which had been grossly exaggerated in order to sensationalise the story.

Knowing that he would soon be recognised from his photograph in the newspaper, he went into the bathroom and shaved his head. Using the fallen hair he formed a moustache by laying the hair neatly onto sticky tape. He trimmed the false moustache into shape using scissors, before adhering it to his upper lip using super glue. Knocking out the lenses from his sunglasses and wearing just the empty frames, he checked his appearance in the mirror. The moustache looked surprisingly realistic if not examined too closely, and he was happy that his own mother would not recognise him in his new disguise.

Although his appearance was now completely different, he had been seen by a number of his neighbours prior to donning his new disguise. Knowing that someone would soon recognise his photograph and report his whereabouts to the police; he quickly packed a holdall and left the apartment.

The police were at his apartment within a matter of minutes of his leaving. He had seen the police cars with their sirens blaring and lights flashing, as they had passed him heading towards his rented accommodation. Swan and Briggs were on the scene within half an hour of his departure, but apart from a little hair in the washbasin plug hole, and a few fingerprints to show that he had indeed been staying there, he had left no clues as to his current whereabouts.

■ ■ ■

On the 20th of July 1969, the commander of Apollo Eleven Neil Armstrong became the first man to first set foot on the moon, with the immortal words, "One small step for man, one giant leap for mankind." He was followed into history by Buzz Aldrin who had piloted the lunar module down to the surface, while the command module pilot Michael Collins orbited the moon awaiting their return.

Ivan had not been seen or heard of in almost a month. During that time Georges Pompidou had been elected President of France, Judy Garland had died from a drug overdose at her London home, Charles Windsor had been invested with the title of Prince of Wales at Caernarfon Castle, a title reserved for the heir to the throne of Great Britain, and Richard Nixon had begun the first troop withdrawals from Vietnam. Swan had returned to Yorkshire convinced that Ivan had left the country, and the man hunt had been drastically scaled down. Ray had hardly left the house during this period, except to go to work with a police tail and he was beginning to feel stir crazy.

On the very same day that Neil Armstrong had set foot on the Moon, a motor cyclist riding a 500 cc BSA motor cycle and wearing a World War II flying jacket, a yellow and black striped helmet with World War II flying goggles, was leaving the Vallard factory. He rode passed the Redcap public house where Tam had died only a few short weeks ago, accelerating as he left the speed restricted area. He crouched low to reduce the wind resistance and wound up the bike with a flick of his right wrist, enjoying the sudden rush of adrenaline which always came with speed. A few minutes later he was entering the speed limit once again, and he eased up on the throttle as he passed the thirty mile per hour sign doing forty.

There were three pairs of pre-war semi-detached houses to his left hand side, with pretty front gardens, before a turning which lead onto the local golf course. To his right stood a dairy and bottling plant, with a number of electric milk floats parked at the front after the day's deliveries had been completed.

The road in front of him was completely clear, until a green Morris Minor suddenly pulled out from the golf club and stopped in the road directly in his path. Without time to swerve or brake, the motor cyclist hit the Morris Minor and was catapulted onto the bonnet of the car. He caught a glimpse of the driver through the window screen of the car, amidst scenes of blue sky followed by tar macadam and then blue sky again, as he somersaulted for some distance before lying stationary in the road. He saw the car drivers face once again briefly, aware of him checking the pulse in his neck, before everything went black.

People were streaming out of the dairy to see if they could help. Once Ivan was sure that the motor cyclist was dead, he carefully folded the pocket knife, which he had intended to use as a backup weapon had he needed one, and replaced it unused into his jacket pocket. He walked back to his car as the dairy workers thronged around the body, calling excitedly for someone to ring for an ambulance, while a first aid representative from the dairy attempted artificial respiration without any success.

As Ivan reached his car, a second motor cyclist wearing a black leather jacket and matching trousers, riding boots, and donning a full faced silver helmet with smoked glass visor, parked his silver Norton Dominator and walked towards the driver. Ivan reached for the door handle but he never made it, he was grabbed by the lapels of his jacket, kneed in the groin and head butted twice in the face by the helmeted rider, before he was allowed to fall unconscious onto the ground with his nose badly broken.

The rider stood guard over the limp body, until the unmarked police car of Sergeant White arrived to take Ivan into custody. Ray removed the silver helmet, which he had recently purchased along with the new riding leathers and the Norton Dominator, from the insurance money paid out for the Triumph Spitfire, having sold his old bike, jacket, and helmet. The ambulance arrived soon after, with sirens blaring and lights flashing, to take the body of Ted Reeves to the mortuary.

Ray was devastated that another of his work colleagues had died. Watching the ambulance drive away he found little joy in the fact that he had captured Ivan under such circumstances. He wondered if Vladimir would now end the matter, or would he send a further assassin to complete the job that John, Stefan and Ivan had all failed to do. He would be looking over his shoulder for a very long time.

■ ■ ■

In Valkenswaard, *Weis* was on bar duty in the hotel Cordial. It was another quiet afternoon, except for the usual table of old men playing cards. They were on a limited budget and therefore drank very little; consequently she had little to do. She sat alone at one of the tables, having first selected one of the Dutch daily newspapers which were slotted into a rack for the customers and residents to read. A black and white photograph of a middle aged man stared back at her from the one of the pages, but his hair looked unnaturally dark for a man of his age. He had a slightly comic appearance she thought, but she was also instantly aware of a cruelty which seemed to lurk behind the staring eyes.

The newspaper reported that a man had been pulled from the *Herengracht Canal* in Amsterdam. He had been bound, gagged, and weighted down, killed with a single gunshot to the back of the head. He had been dead for more than a week and had only surfaced due to becoming entangled in the propeller of a passing barge. The body although not recognisable, was believed to be that of Vladimir Vostock, a Russian security manager at the Soviet People's Radio Station of Amsterdam, who had been reported missing by colleagues, when he had failed to turn up for work two weeks earlier. *Weis* shuddered and turned the page.

Lightning Source UK Ltd.
Milton Keynes UK
174405UK00001B/283/P